ROSALIND LAKER

Set in North America and England, Rosalind Laker's new novel spans thirty-five years of a woman's life. Lisa Shaw, one of the "Home" children shipped from orphanages in England at the turn of the century to new homes in a new land, has a chance meeting at the Liverpool docks with a fellow emigrant, a young Norwegian, Peter Hagen. Their paths divide, but her love for him sustains her through cruel exploitation and her struggle to attain the freedom that had been promised her. His search to find her again is unceasing, taking him across plains and prairies, to raw cities in the West and pioneer settlements. Events take an unexpected twist when he traces her to a rough logging site on the Pacific coast. Although fate allows them a brief and passionate interlude, her life has become linked with that of another man, Alan Fernley, who is involved in

(continued on back flap)

Books by Rosalind Laker

THE SMUGGLER'S BRIDE
RIDE THE BLUE RIBAND
WARWYCK'S WOMAN
CLAUDINE'S DAUGHTER
WARWYCK'S CHOICE
BANNERS OF SILK
GILDED SPLENDOUR
JEWELLED PATH
WHAT THE HEART KEEPS

What the Heart Keeps

Rosalind Laker

DOUBLEDAY & COMPANY, INC.
GARDEN CITY, NEW YORK
1984

My grateful acknowledgements for help in my research to Jessie Lucas, sister of the late Agnes Twidle; Jeanette Taylor and Sue Donaldson of the Campbell River and District Museum; Peter and Andrea Paup of Seattle; and Ronald and Betty Watson of Raymond, Alberta.

R.L.

Library of Congress Cataloging in Publication Data

Laker, Rosalind.
What the heart keeps.

I. Title.
PR6065.E9W5 1984 823'.914
ISBN: 0-385-18718-1
Library of Congress Catalog Card Number 83–11559

PRINTED IN THE UNITED STATES OF AMERICA
FIRST EDITION

To Betty and Ron

WHAT THE HEART KEEPS

One

She sometimes thought the colour of love must be gold. Not the hue of the precious metal but of the sun. Warm and rich and, between a man and a woman, holding a brilliance beyond measure. Standing in the dark-panelled hall of the orphanage, waiting in line with several other fourteen-year-old pauper girls, Lisa Shaw's romantic train of thought had been stimulated by the porcelain plate propped on a shelf above the door of the superintendent's study.

Its pattern of yellow and gold and garnet-red never failed to draw her gaze magnetically. Drably clad in institutional clothing, she had grown from childhood into adolescence within a grey environment broken only by the plate's radiance. Today, as always, it dazzled her. In her heart she coveted it. From the start it had stirred a latent yearning within her for some beauty in her life.

She was slightly above average height for her age, which made visitors to the orphanage suppose her to be older. Her face was oval and her chin had a little tilt to it, which in itself was indicative of a strong will, but also had the seductive effect of making it appear that the weight of her long plait of fair, silky hair was the cause of its angle. The sharpness of bone through an ivory skin bore witness to meagre diet, accentuating the large hazel eyes with greenish flecks under fly-away brows. Yet she suffered no lack of energy, though thin stews and poor gruel and dripping-spread bread made up most of the meals on the bare boards of the long tables.

Unlike her companions, some of whom were burdened with an unhealthy plumpness from the greasy food, she had a wiry resistance to infection and lassitude, for which she was grateful. Her mind was alert and eager, ever occupied. Musing over the porcelain plate, she was naturally composed in her stature, her stillness setting her apart from the agitation of those with her, every one of whom associated trouble with the summons to appear before the head of the orphanage at half-past four that afternoon.

Suddenly Lisa received a thump in the spine.

"Stop gaping at nothing, Lisa. Why d'you think old Mother Bradlaw wants to see us?"

Lisa shrugged, not wanting to be drawn into talk just now. Her dread of any confrontation with Mrs. Dorothy Bradlaw was no less than anybody else's, but she was perceptive enough to conclude that it was something more lenient than accusation and punishment that awaited all of them that day. And there was little she did not know about disciplinary situations. One of the most severe chastisements she had ever received had been caused by the sun-like porcelain plate. Her memory of the incident was as vivid now in this March of 1903 as when it had happened.

Only six years old at the time, a recent arrival at the orphanage, she had managed to lift a stool onto a side table and clamber up to reach out her hand just to touch the plate. Her fingertips had barely brushed the gilded rim when the stool had toppled, throwing her backwards. Miraculously, she had suffered no broken bones. Yet her head ached for several weeks afterwards from its impact with the floor, and the bruises had been aggravated by the whipping across the legs she had received. Only fear that a further attempt to touch the plate would result in its removal, had prevented her from trying again for a few magical seconds of closer scrutiny. She was not easily deterred from any aim she set herself. It was the cause of many such skirmishes she had had with those in authority over the years.

There came another sharp prod in the back. "You must have some idea, Lisa. There ain't much you don't know about what goes on in this place."

Lisa did not reply that it was simply a matter of using eyes, ears, and intelligence. Rosie, who had spoken to her, was showing every sign of being thoroughly afraid. "Don't look so worried, Rosie. We wouldn't have been told to put on a clean dress and apron in midweek for a ticking off. My guess is that we'll find a visitor in the study with old Mother Bradlaw." She was echoing the nickname for the superintendent that had been in current use among the inmates long before she or any of the other girls in the hall had been committed to the orphanage's care. "I heard a carriage arrive when I was with the babies."

"You still smell of 'em." Pointedly Rosie held her nose in a taunting manner.

Lisa refused to be needled. "I expect I do. I went straight to them when we came in from school, and I didn't know I had to come here until it was too late to do anything except put on a fresh apron."

It was the superintendent's policy that the inmates of the orphanage should take part in the running of the establishment. Thus costs were kept down and the girls were trained in every branch of domestic work at the same time. Lisa's duties were to keep an eye on the younger children and help in the nursery where the infants were mostly abandoned doorstep babies, or had been sent along from the local workhouse, which had no room for any more. Like every other section of the orphanage, the nursery was grossly overcrowded, often two or three babies to a cot.

"You'll catch it if old Mother Bradlaw sees you ain't changed your garb as ordered," Rosie stated with malicious satisfaction. Then, when her jibe was ignored, she pondered again on her own problems. Who was the visitor? What sort of carriage had arrived? Suppose it was the Law that had turned up in a Black Maria! A shiver went through her. Her trepidation echoed in her voice as she addressed Lisa again. "Ask Teresa up in front whether she can 'ear a man's voice or a woman's in the study?"

Teresa's reply came back that it was a female visitor. Lisa drew a further conclusion for Rosie's benefit. "It's either a charitable person wanting to see some of us before donating money to the orphanage, or a prospective employer about to give any one of us our first chance to take the domestic work she'll offer."

Rosie glowered. Lisa's book reading enabled her to reel off high-falutin words that nobody else could manage. Half she said didn't make sense at times to normal ears. "Then you're real sure we've not been called 'ere about nothing that's been snitched?"

Lisa gave her a sharp glance, able to tell she was seeking reassurance. Thieving was rife in the orphanage. To some it was a way of life. To the pauper victims the loss of even the humblest possession was a major tragedy. Equally as devastating was the theft for sale of the rag rugs that all the inmates from the youngest upwards, had to make in their spare time. Rosie was notoriously light-fingered. Lisa delivered the truth to her forcefully. "If that were the case, you'd be waiting here on your own today, Rosie Taylor!"

There was no chance of any foul-mouthed retaliation. Teresa, at the head of the line, had tapped on the study door as the clock on the wall struck the half-hour. Mrs. Bradlaw's voice bade them enter and all fifteen girls filed in to stand in two rows in front of her desk. All eyes went to the visitor who sat elegantly in a wing chair at one side of the room as though detaching herself, for the time being, from any proceedings. She wore a well-cut brown serge costume with a swirl of Russian squirrel around the collar, a plumed toque crowning her waved reddish hair. Her name, as they were to discover, was Miss Drayton of the Herbert Drayton Memorial Society. At the superintendent's nod, the girls introduced themselves to her in turn.

Mrs. Bradlaw watched them, her hands folded before her on the desk's blotter. She by no means deserved the derisive nickname that was no secret to her. At fifty, there was little grey in her dark hair; her complexion was smooth and her chin line firm. Had her expression been less stern and her mouth less severe, she might still have retained something of the good looks of her youth. But life had hardened her. Widowed by the Zulu War in South Africa, she had applied for the post of superintendent of the orphanage in her home town of Leeds and been accepted. Therein had commenced a battle that she sometimes thought was every bit as violent in its own way as any encounter with the enemy endured by her late husband and his regiment. Believing firmly in the adage that to spare the rod was to spoil the child, reinforced by the conviction that the devil found work for idle hands, she ruled the orphanage with an iron discipline while, at the same time, she fought unceasingly on the children's behalf against ignorance, immorality, poverty, and disease. She did not waste time on pity or compassion. To be sentimental was to be weak. She fought the pious governors who had appointed her with as much ferocity as she showed towards all else. It had taken the staid and stolid gentlemen of the board a long time to adjust to her outspokenness, her exceptional frankness in subjects normally veiled in more genteel terms, not to mention her tenaciousness towards any course of progress she held to be right for the orphanage. Always she refused to accept defeat. Clashes were most stormy when she harassed them for more money when funds were sinking too low to feed the orphans at a subsistence level, or the overcrowding had reached alarming proportions, necessitating a flow into paid foster homes. She was an advocate of fostering, believing that every child had a natural right to be absorbed into decent family life. Sadly, there were far too many unwanted children, as well as too much social stigma attached to bastardy, and never enough money for an idyllic solution to housing the young and helpless. Any spare time she had went towards campaigning for new laws for the greater protection of children, and at least in this venture she had the board's wholehearted support.

Nobody suspected the bouts of depression that sometimes sapped her seemingly indomitable strength. She felt it today in the presence of Emily Drayton, to whom she had taken an instant and irrational dislike at their first meeting in the presence of the governors a few weeks ago. Womanly intuition was a phrase that she would normally have tossed aside with contempt, but the feeling nagged at her that the Herbert Drayton Memorial Society, in spite of its impeccable testimonials, was not exactly what it should be. It angered her logical mind that doubt should persist without a shred of evidence to sustain it. *A Family Home for Every Homeless Child* was the society's slogan. How then could she quarrel with it when, as the governors succinctly pointed out to her after she had voiced her reserve, it endorsed everything she wanted for the children in her care.

She knew every one of the girls standing before her far better than any one of them realised. Teresa, the practical. Rosie, the dishonest. Nellie, the impulsive. Elsie, the indolent. Adelaide, the lonely. Myrtle, the optimist. Beatrice, the kindly. Lisa, the warmhearted. Her piercing dark eyes travelled on from face to face along the two lines. She was well aware of striking awe into them all. Some even quailed visibly as her glance reached them. Little did they suspect her deep concern for them. It was a tragic fact that conditions for lower-class working women were so bad, their wages so poor, and their prospects so bleak on the overcrowded labour market that a percentage of this youthful group was destined to end up on the streets. Why then did she distrust the Herbert Drayton Memorial Society which was to lift them from that dreadful future, and give each one a sound chance in life? Strain must be playing tricks with her mind. She would put all nonsensical notions from her completely and break the news she had to tell without further delay.

"Girls. You have had the honour of presenting yourselves to our distinguished visitor, Miss Drayton. She is here on a special mission, one that is going to change the whole course of your lives. Now you may, or you may not, have heard of many charitable schemes operating in this country to give secure work and good homes to orphaned and destitute children overseas. The good Dr. Barnado, whose work I admire most sincerely, is a leading light in this movement. Australia, New Zealand, and South Africa have all taken large numbers of children and absorbed them into these thriving corners of our great British Empire." She was speaking at a slightly slower pace than usual, wanting everything to sink in. "British North America has not lagged behind. You have learned about Canada in your geography lessons. Only last week, at my special request, you were given an extra lesson at school on that country's history and development. The Herbert Drayton Memorial Society, of which Miss Drayton is the trustee and administrator, was formed to take suitable young emigrants and settle them in domestic work there. All fifteen of you have been selected for this wonderful opportunity. With you will go ten of the younger ones who will be adopted into families." She proceeded to read out the names of those in the whole party from a list on her desk. Then she put it aside, looking at the girls again. "Every one of you will receive a welcome in your new land."

She paused to watch the effect of everything she had said to them. A stunned silence reigned. Some of the girls actually gaped, their mouths dropping open. Lisa's face had turned ashen, the cheeks drawn in, her pupils dilating with shock. It would be prudent, Mrs. Bradlaw decided quickly, to follow up at once with some reassuring details. Probably the girl was imagining the scheme to be an offshoot of the sentence of transportation meted out to young criminals in decades long gone by. Only Lisa, with her avidity for reading, would know enough history to make a comparison with what was happening in these more enlightened times.

"Your journey, in Miss Drayton's personal charge, will be by ship from Liverpool and by train from Halifax, Nova Scotia, to a very fine residence in Toronto. I have a picture of it here that Miss Drayton kindly brought with her for you to see." She held up from her desk a large photograph of a tall brick house of grand proportions with a pillared entrance in a setting of lawns and flower-beds.

"Lumme!" The exclamation came involuntarily from the back line.

"Yes, Myrtle?" Mrs. Bradlaw prompted, seeing that the reaction had been highly favourable. Since the fate of the girls was sealed into emigration, she must hasten all goodwill towards it.

Blushes and embarrassment. "It's posh, ain't it? Would we live there?"

"Until the right domestic employment is found for you. The

house is the society's Distribution Home, and you would always be able to return there for advice or help if any unexpected difficulties should arise."

Mrs. Bradlaw went on to explain how the Canadian residents put their names down on a waiting list to take a young immigrant. Good English servants were always in demand. She gave information about how interviews would take place, what hours of work and payment could be expected, and listed the social activities in which the girls would be permitted to join. In order to widen the whole picture for them, she spoke of boys in their own city of Leeds who, in the company of others from London and elsewhere, were going out in a steady stream to learn farming in Manitoba and Saskatchewan, either with a farmer and his family or at special farming schools.

From the chair where she sat, Miss Drayton listened and observed, an elbow resting on the mahogany arm, cream-gloved fingers supporting her chin. A benevolent expression softened temporarily the sharpness of her features, a gracious smile etched slightly on the thin-lipped mouth. She always found it best for the information to be given out by someone whom the chosen candidates for emigration knew and trusted. Or feared, as the case might be. It eradicated all preliminary uncertainties.

A sudden commotion among the listening girls gave her quite a start. One of them—was her name Lisa?—had pushed forward to the desk, looking as frantic as a foal about to bolt.

"I've made my own plans for the future, Mrs. Bradlaw! I've always known what I wanted to do with my life! I won't be sent away from England!"

Lisa's pent-up outburst had interrupted the superintendent in midsentence. Miss Drayton stiffened ominously in the chair, the feather on her toque set aquiver into peacock shades. She was no longer benign. Her expression had hardened into one of intense hostility at the showing of such blatant ingratitude towards the society's generosity. Fanatically reverent towards her late father's memory, she took the girl's rejection as a deadly insult to him. Had she been given a free hand, she would have struck the defiant girl to the floor.

Mrs. Bradlaw's face remained impassive. One dissentient was enough to upset everything. The situation must be handled mercilessly for the sake of the others. "Well, Lisa," she commented in freezing tones, "what position have you secured for yourself that makes you dare to interrupt while I am speaking?"

"Nothing as yet." In her distraught state Lisa gripped the edge of the desk, her face desperate. "But there's soon to be a vacancy for an under-nursemaid at the Grange in Mountfield Avenue. I heard about it when one of the men-servants brought a basket of cast-off baby clothing for our infants from the lady of the house. It's the sort of work I've always wanted. And a chance to better myself."

Miss Drayton was taking every word to heart. "Such impudence!" she exploded. "I've never heard anything like it in my life."

Mrs. Bradlaw held up a hand briefly, letting the visitor know that this was her province and an outsider was not to intrude. Inadvertently, she added to Miss Drayton's sense of grievance. Quite unaware of this development, the superintendent addressed Lisa again with the same cold sternness as before. "Have you applied in writing for the post?"

"I have the letter written. I was going to ask you for a character reference later today."

At any other time and in other circumstances, Mrs. Bradlaw would have given the reference. The girl had the intelligence and initiative that would enable her to adapt easily to the routine of a well-to-do household, but the request, even if it had been mannerly presented, had come too late. Three weeks too late to be exact, for it was then that the final list of names had been drawn up with the necessary papers and received the governors' signatures and approval. None of the other emigrants had Lisa's sense of responsibility. She had been earmarked from the start as the most useful aide to put in charge of the younger children on the journey.

"You will bring that letter to me, Lisa," Mrs. Bradlaw ordered stonily, "and tear it up in my study. The governors have decreed in your best interests that you shall go to Canada, and I support their decision. You may hope for a post of a nursemaid there." Ignoring Lisa's stricken stare, she gave one of her quick nods to encompass the whole group before her. "Dismiss."

A quarter of an hour later Lisa returned with the letter as instructed. Obediently she dropped the pieces into the wastepaper basket. By that time the two women were talking over tea at the lace-clothed table, a lamp lit cosily against the wet dusk outside. Over the teacup, Miss Drayton watched Lisa closely, able to define defiance lingering in the pressure of lips and tilt of chin. When the girl had left, the woman raised her eyebrows slightly.

"Refresh my memory about that girl," she requested in her excessively refined tones. "I read so many dossiers in the course of my work. Born illegitimate, was she not?"

"That is correct," Mrs. Bradlaw replied. "Her mother was a linen maid turned out of her employment when it became known she was pregnant."

Miss Drayton shuddered delicately. "I prefer to say *in the family way.*"

The reply was sharp. "I never use euphemisms. The young woman gave birth in a barn. A farmer's wife took pity on her and kept the baby until the mother found work in a clothing factory here in Leeds and was able to send for the child. Where the two of them lived I have never heard. Most probably in a back-street hovel. Eventually, as frequently happens, ill health brought the young woman lower and lower until finally she took Lisa to the workhouse with her and died a few days later." The superintendent frowned meditatively. "I have never heard a child scream so much at being taken from a parent."

"Who was the father?"

"Unknown, as far as records are concerned." Mrs. Bradlaw had her own theory about the fathering of Lisa, but since it was only a supposition she did not voice it. Servant girls were all too often seduced and taken advantage of by gentlemen in a household. Lisa had inherited an intellect from a source other than the illiterate creature who had died in a workhouse bed.

Miss Drayton accepted another cup of tea and mulled over what she had been told. She had seen right away that there was exceptionally bad blood in Lisa. Since the girl had been conceived in wantonness, as so many were, what else could be expected of a lustful union? It was all very well for her to be recommended as honest, hard-working, and conscientious. None of that held true when such girls became involved with men, for it was then that any sense they had flew out of their heads like a bird released from a cage. Lisa would have to be watched closely for her own protection as well as to guard the good name of the society. Miss Drayton prided herself on her own chasteness. In forty-three years no man's touch had ever defiled *her*.

"You do keep track of the children who pass through your Distribution Home, do you not?" Mrs. Bradlaw was saying.

Miss Drayton eyed the superintendent coolly. She could always locate mistrust, often when the persons themselves believed it suppressed. "My late father would not have it otherwise. I follow his precedent in all things to the best of my humble ability."

She kept a special, saintly voice in which to speak of her father. It came naturally to her, for she had maintained an illusion of their relationship for so long she had come to believe implicitly that he had been devoted to her and she to him. The truth was the reverse. At first he had adored his only child, born late in life by a second marriage. Made a widower again before she was a week old, he had indulged her extravagantly. It came as a great shock to him when he realised she had grown into a spoilt and selfish adult whom he thoroughly disliked. Out of his disappointment, he turned in his retirement from her insatiable greed, to concentrate his hard-earned fortune on children in real need, dealing with individual cases that came to his notice and giving generously to hostels catering for them. Although he tried to keep his good works out of the public eye, it was inevitable that his name should become widely known and esteemed. He refused no case of appeal that was genuine. His wealth drained away. When he died, Emily Drayton found herself practically penniless, with everyone looking to her to take her father's place.

Her pride caused her to flinch from admitting to penury. For a few weeks she did not know what to do or which way to turn.

Then she hit upon the idea of the Herbert Drayton Memorial Society and saw it linked to the homeless. After all, she was homeless herself, having had to sell her childhood home and everything in it in order to exist. From the moment she launched the society, donations flowed in and had never ceased. If the figures ebbed a little, a fund-raising appeal conducted in a ladylike and gracious manner soon adjusted matters. She had been transporting parties of children to Canada for several years and her organisation could not be bettered.

"I am well aware of your ideals," Mrs. Bradlaw was saying rather irritably. "You mentioned them several times to the governors in my hearing. It is just that my own experience has taught me how difficult it is to follow up young people who leave our care. You are dealing with vast areas and poor communications, yet you seem quite unbeset by any problems ensuring the children's welfare." Mrs. Bradlaw's frankness came through unadulterated. "I would have been more impressed if you had admitted that things go wrong sometimes."

Miss Drayton's poise was unassailed, although her sly grey eyes narrowed. "Canada is not England, Mrs. Bradlaw. There is no teeming population to swallow the children up without a trace. Outlying districts are visited at least once a year to see that all is well." Her voice took on a crisp edge. "On a point closer home, I may tell you that if I were in charge of this orphanage, I should keep immediate track of Lisa Shaw. She looked more than ready to flout your authority, in my opinion."

"Nonsense!" The superintendent reared her head. "That matter is completely settled." The dislike that each woman felt for the other spiked the air between them, even though somehow conventionalities were maintained. "Why not try the plum-cake, Miss Drayton?"

"Most kind." Miss Drayton took a slice, smiling maliciously to herself. No doubt Mrs. Bradlaw hoped it would choke her, but that would not stop her enjoying it. She was fond of good food, as she was of all the luxuries of life. Since the founding of the Herbert Drayton Memorial Society, she had never gone short of anything she wanted.

Mrs. Bradlaw was relieved when her visitor departed. There

would be no further meeting until Miss Drayton came to collect the emigrants and take them to Canada. She paced the floor slowly, barely noticing the two young inmates clearing the tea away in answer to her bell. To send for Lisa was tantamount to admitting that the odious benefactress knew more about those in her care than she did. Unfortunately, it could not be denied that Lisa had been a rebel once and might well revert under the pressure of disappointment and upheaval to the same state again. Twisting around on her heel, she addressed the child carrying the tea-tray from the room.

"Wait, Joan! When you have deposited those things in the kitchen, find Lisa Shaw and send her to me. At once."

She was still pacing the floor when the messenger returned, scared at having been unable to carry out the command. Lisa was nowhere to be found. Mrs. Bradlaw went upstairs immediately to inspect the dormitory cupboard where the older girls shared shelves. Lisa's few clothes and possessions had gone.

It was a long time since the orphanage had had a runaway. Mrs. Bradlaw found herself consumed with such rage against Lisa that when she returned to her study it was to close the door and lean against it, shaking from head to foot. How dare the girl humiliate her by making Emily Drayton's taunt prove true! It was particularly galling to realise that had she taken heed of the woman's warning when it was given, she would have been in time to stop Lisa making her escape. Worst of all, what credibility would she have with the board when it was learned that the inmate she had most trusted in the emigration party had let her down? She saw all her years of effort and struggle coming to naught, everything she had hoped for in the future baulked by those of the governors never in sympathy with her who, ever afterwards, would have her failure with Lisa to fling in her face.

With a muttered exclamation of fury, she swung across to the wall telephone and lifted the receiver, intending to notify the police and the governors in turn of Lisa's disappearance. Then she stopped abruptly in the whirling of the handle to alert the operator and quickly replaced the receiver. Not yet. She would let no one know yet. Even her staff must be kept in ignorance for as long as possible. It was a calculated risk, but she must take it. Clasping and unclasping her hands, she sank down into the chair at her desk, suddenly wearied. Had she been prone to tears, she would have wept with frustration.

Lisa had made a getaway through a downstairs window at the rear of the building. Outdoor clothes for the pauper children were always hand-me-downs donated by charitable people, and she had no fear of being detected on that score as she ran as fast as she could away from the orphanage. It was raining quite heavily, which was in her favour, for it made the March evening darker than it would otherwise have been. Gas lamps threw her shadow before and after her as she pounded along, clutching the small bundle of her possessions. Keeping to the back streets, she passed the clothing factories and the shirt-making sweatshops, an area where she had once lived with her mother and still, in places, familiar from those days. Often entrusted with errands by the superintendent, she knew Leeds well and had a particular destination in mind.

She was breathless by the time she reached it, the cobbled yard of a brewery that sent its ale far afield. The gates were still open, the men's long day's work not yet at an end, and she waited in the shadows as she watched wagons being loaded up with barrels and tarpaulins being tied down. When her chance came, she shot across, unseen to the nearest wagon, clambered up by way of a wheel, and slithered under the tarpaulin into the ale-smelling darkness.

There was little room, but she made herself as comfortable as possible. Her fast pulse came as much from the indignation that burned within her as from all the running. How dare it be decided for her that she should leave the land of her birth! She saw it as a personal affront to her spirit of independence, as abusive curtailment of her inherent right as an individual to decide her own future within the realms of possibility. A choice. That was what she and the others old enough to make their own decisions should have been offered. A simple, blinking *choice.* Not much to ask. She almost ground her teeth at the injustice and at what it had cost her. Being made to tear up her letter had been the last straw.

Her long cherished dream had been to become a nursemaid in a large household and work herself up through the hierarchy of the nursery world. It stemmed from the horrific day when she had been separated from her mother, whom she had never seen again. All warmth and security and happiness had seemed centred in a glimpse she had had of a kind-faced nanny pushing a perambulator in a park while a rosy-cheeked child in frilly clothes had skipped trustingly alongside, at the time she was being dragged, kicking and screaming into the orphanage. To this day she could not bear the sound of a door being slammed shut behind her.

The night was long. The rain did not ease its drumming on the tarpaulin until shortly before dawn. Yet in spite of her being wet and cold, her elation between dozes did not diminish. Somehow and somewhere she would get honest work and prove her worth. Not securing the nursemaid's post in Leeds was only a setback. One day she would be pushing the babies of the well-to-do through an English park on sunny mornings. On this vow to herself, she dozed again, waking when shouting resounded in the yard.

"Whoa back! Steady there!"

The dray-horses were being backed into the shafts of the loaded wagons, hooves clattering heavily on the cobbles. Her wagon creaked and swayed before it moved forward on a thunder of wheels out into the streets and before long into the waking countryside. She raised a flap of the tarpaulin to watch for a signpost to see in which direction she was travelling.

Southwards. Then she would make for London. There would be plenty of work there. Yet her spirits were not quite so high as they had been. She found herself thinking of the young ones whom she normally looked after in the early morning at the orphanage. How would they react when they found her gone? The toddlers were always desperate for affection, wanting her to kiss and cuddle them. Today they would be shouted at and probably cuffed by whoever was taking her place. Then there were the five- and six-year-olds. Little Sarah could never manage to button her own boots. Amy would weep. Cora, who always vomited if made to eat up a full plateful of gruel, would be given a standard portion instead of the small amount she could digest. As for eight-year-old Minnie, who pined for her mother, and a few others of the same age who, a few weeks ago, were starving and abandoned on the streets, they would run wild without proper supervision and end up being whipped by one of old Mother Bradlaw's assistants. Lisa groaned inwardly. The young ones had all known that before long she would be leaving the orphanage, for she had prepared them, but every child she had cared for personally would be bewildered and upset by the suddenness of her departure as well as her failure to say goodbye.

She would write to them. That was what she would do. Just as soon as it was possible. A London postmark could not give away her whereabouts in that vast city. To distract her mind from those she had left behind, she ate some of the loaf she had had the foresight to snatch from the kitchen before her flight.

Twice the wagon came to a halt during the morning. Both times Lisa feared discovery, but once it was for the horses to be watered and the second time was when the drayman alighted to relieve himself in some wayside bushes. She decided to leave her transport at the first opportunity, for the sooner she severed the last connecting link with Leeds the safer she would be.

When the wagon slowed almost to a standstill on an uphill pull, she slipped over the back of it to take cover at the side of the road. The drayman did not so much as turn his head and before long was out of sight. She began to walk.

She spent the night in a derelict cottage. Fortune appeared to be favouring her, for she found a couple of matches that had probably dropped from a tramp's matchbox and was able to light a fire on the hearth to keep her warm. Only thoughts of the children at the orphanage disturbed her rest.

In a village the next day, a gentleman on horseback tossed her a penny for darting forward to open a gate for him. It enabled her to replenish her food supply at the local store with a piece of cheese and half a stale loaf. She no longer feared pursuit and kept at an easy pace as she continued on again. It seemed as if fate were walking with her.

It was nearly dusk when she met a disordered flock of sheep

streaming along the road. Waving her arms and darting to and fro, she helped the hefty, ruddy-faced youth in charge to get them back into the pen from which they had escaped. He thanked her, wiping his sweaty brow and neck with a rag from his pocket. It turned out he was the farmer's son, and he took her with him to the farmhouse. There his mother gave her a hot meal to eat on the back doorstep. The food was good and she ate every morsel, but it was lonely to be shut outside while talk rumbled in the glow of the lamplight indoors.

Yet how much more lonely Amy and Minnie and Cora and the rest she had befriended would be without her presence in the unfamiliar surroundings of a ship and then in a new land. Dejectedly she pressed her head back against the door jamb by which she sat, all too able to picture their misery. If she believed Miss Drayton to be a kind woman, maybe she would have felt less plagued by leaving them; unfortunately, although the woman had smiled in the beginning, her eyes had been hard. Like glass beads. Then, when annoyed, she had looked quite vicious. There would be no mercy there.

After a while Lisa sighed resignedly to herself. Her conscience about the children was never going to let her get as far as London, so she might as well cut short her journeying now. She could not begin to consider the extent of the punishment that would have to be faced upon her return to the orphanage. Whatever it should prove to be, she would live through it somehow.

Her tap on the farmhouse door to hand in the emptied plate went unacknowledged. She left it on the doorstep and went off into the darkness. When she saw the farmer's barn looming against the first stars, she knew she had found a warm place for the night. Clambering into the hay, she flung herself down and was at sleep at once, fully at peace with herself now that her decision had been made.

She stirred when light penetrated her lids, thinking it must be morning. Then the hay rustled beside her. She opened her eyes wide and sat bolt upright in fright, blinking into a lantern.

"I thought you might be 'ere," the farmer's son said in a thick whisper, sitting back on his heels to hang the lantern on a nail and flick it shut. In the blackness he reached for her, even as in terror she began to scramble away, and threw her down again into the hay. His heavy hands pushed up under her skirt to fasten on her thighs and wrench them apart. She screamed, struggling wildly, but he made no attempt to silence her, the barn being out of earshot of the house. There was a terrible thoroughness about his actions. His weight and strength defeated all her panic-stricken attempts to free herself. He handled her breasts as if they were hard apples and his entry was brutal and bloody. Her agonised scream filled every corner of the vast barn.

She did not know if her shrieking continued as at last she was able to get away from him. Her mind and hearing were blank from shock as she dashed from the barn into the night. How fast and how far she ran she did not know. Having lost all sense of direction, she had no guide to safety except to keep the horizon ahead clear of buildings. She was far into a wood before she realised that it was the thickness of ferns and other undergrowth that was slowing her pace. Slumping against a tree, she heard her own sobs and rasped breathing for the first time. Her legs gave way and she slid down into a carpet of leaves where she remained throughout the rest of the night.

At first light she found a clear brook and bathed the abused parts of her body; purification in the iciness of the water. The state of her torn underclothing nauseated her and she buried it before leaving the wood to try and get her bearings. It proved impossible for her to recognise a single landmark from the previous day, whichever way she looked. Talking a lead from the rising sun, she simply turned northwards.

She was never quite sure how many days it took her to get back to the orphanage. She had left what food she had with her bundle of possessions in the barn and had nothing to sustain her except turnips from a field, a cabbage from a kitchen garden, and some crusts she managed to beg. She wore the soles of her old buttoned boots through until they flapped on her feet and had to be discarded. For a while her black stockings, wrapped around like bandages, gave some protection until they in turn fell into ribbons. She tramped the rest of the way barefoot. She was a sorry sight, dirty and dishevelled, when she arrived in the superintendent's study.

"I've come back," she said in a croaked voice.

"So I see," Mrs. Bradlaw replied drily. She did not add that she had banked on it, everything staked on Lisa's basic qualities. It was satisfactory beyond measure, quite apart from an overwhelming relief, to have been proved right about the girl. Unfortunately it was a triumph that could not be shared.

"Have you anything you wish to say in excuse to me?"

Lisa shook her head quickly. "No, ma'am."

"When did you last eat?"

"I can't remember. Yesterday, I think."

"Go to the bathhouse and get rid of the marks of travel. You shall have some clean clothes brought to you and some salve for your feet. Afterwards there will be a bowl of broth in the dining room. Do not gulp it or you will vomit it up. Take some rest for a few hours and then resume your allotted duties as usual. Dismiss."

In a daze, Lisa left the study. No punishment. No storm of recrimination. If it had not been a completely ludicrous supposition, she would have thought that briefly she and Mrs. Bradlaw had shared a mutual respect for each other.

Five weeks later, Miss Drayton arrived at the orphanage to take her emigration party in tow. Lisa still suffered from nightmares that had followed her ordeal in the barn, although a particular private worry as to its possible outcome had been put at rest. There had been some sad farewells to those being left behind. It was some comfort that a few of the better-natured girls had promised to look after the toddlers as she had done.

In the vestibule, Mrs. Bradlaw watched the party assemble, the older members helping the younger ones to attach the labels that each must wear, bearing their names and that of the society as well as their destination in Canada. She would have liked to see them depart in new clothes, but the governors were always parsimonious in matters of clothing, believing that donated garments were perfectly adequate. It riled her to see Miss Drayton's disparaging lift of the eyebrows when she saw how they were dressed. The woman herself was in a handsomely tailored travelling costume in a biscuit colour, which hardly seemed a practical shade in which to accompany children.

Mrs. Bradlaw began the process of shaking hands with each departing emigrant. When Lisa stood before her she thought, not for the first time, how changed the girl was since her few days of liberty. Yet her spirit was not crushed by whatever hardships she had endured. Whether Lisa realised it or not, she had been strengthened by her conscious decision to give up freedom in order to return to her duties. No adversity would ever break her if she continued to live by her principles, but life would go hard with her for doing it.

"Goodbye, Lisa. God bless you." The same words that had been spoken to each one.

"Goodbye, Mrs. Bradlaw."

Lisa took Amy by one hand and Cora by the other to go down the steps of the orphanage. Minnie, always nervous of upheaval and change, grabbed onto her skirt to keep close.

Together they joined everyone else getting into the waiting hackney cabs that were to take them to catch the train.

When they were being driven past the park, which was bright with daffodils and children playing and shining perambulators, Lisa thought of her own special dream. Maybe dreams were not meant to come true. Maybe they existed only to spur the dreamer on to whatever might lie ahead. She turned her gaze away from the park and looked resolutely in the direction of the railway station.

Two

At Liverpool the ship that would take them to Canada was being coaled up. Lisa and her companions had a glimpse of it as they left the train to follow Miss Drayton into the dockside buildings where she presented their documents, which were duly stamped. The woman made sure that her cabin trunk was wheeled off by a porter while her party had to continue to carry their own bundles. Briskly she led the way into the large and draughty embarkation shed where they were to await a signal to go on board.

Lisa was astonished to see how many people were gathering there. Not only individual passengers but young parties like their own, travelling under the sponsorship of a public-spirited organisation. The most nervous in her charge immediately gathered closer at seeing such a milling throng.

"Come on," she encouraged, shepherding them along. "We'll find a bit of space to ourselves."

She was unaware of being observed by a young man in whose direction she was guiding them. Tall, straight-backed, and strongly built, he was in the section divided off for those sailing with a sister ship to New York, his arms resting leisurely on the top rail of the intervening barrier. His ticket was steerage class, which meant he would be carrying his own luggage aboard. His travelling box was set on the ground beside him. Fashioned of

Norwegian pine with a domed lid and iron hinges, it bore his name on the side within a decorative panel: PETER HAGEN.

He had been trying to estimate the number of children that were Canada-bound. The way in which they were dressed was a guide to their collective identity, just as much as the colour of the labels worn attached by cord to a collar or button. Whole parties were stoutly clad in coarse tweed or thick serge or durable flannel, giving a clear indication of the amount of funds that had been available for rigging them out for the journey. Some, less fortunate, were attired in motley clothes that, in several cases, must have had two or three previous owners. Among the latter was a small cluster of young children who appeared to have detached themselves from the main party in the charge of an older girl. Still not noticing his riveted attention, Lisa brought them to a standstill close by.

"This'll do. We can join up with Miss Drayton and the others when it's time to go on board."

He studied her as she ranged them in a semblance of order. Her clothes were extraordinarily ill-fitting, and her silky hair, pale as if she had been born in his own northern land, slipped from under a crocheted tam-o'-shanter of discordant colours. Yet there was an air about her that overcame the disadvantage of her attire. It was related to something vital and alive in her, a warm femininity that imbued her voice with soft cadences as she continued to address her charges, all of whom were agitated, two or three decidedly truculent, and one noisily tearful.

"Stop crying now, Amy," she coaxed, patting the child who still clung limpetlike to her. "There's nothing to be afraid of when I'm with you. Think how nice it's going to be in Canada. You'll be in a real home with a proper family to call your own instead of being stuck in the old orphanage. What did you say?" She bent her head to catch the muffled words. "No, you won't be away from me on the ship. I've promised to keep you near me." Abruptly her note became stricter, although not unkind, as she tapped another child on the shoulder. "Don't scuff the toes of your boots, Minnie. You don't want to arrive in Halifax with your feet sticking out. I know what that feels like," she added crisply, more to herself than anybody else. Then with a practised turn of speed she dragged apart three who had begun to pinch each other spitefully. "Quit that, Lily and Bridget and May! Do you three always have to squabble? Stand still now. What would happen if the Captain saw you? He would never allow you on board."

The warning took effect. Nobody wanted to be left behind. Peace was momentarily restored. Lisa found time to look around properly at last while keeping a comforting hand cupped about the head of Amy, whose tears had diminished into a few shuddering sighs. What a busy scene! What a chatter! Her head turned as she looked towards the neighbouring section of the shed.

Abruptly her scanning gaze was snapped to a halt, held by the penetrating, dark blue stare of the stranger within touching distance at the rail. Some trick of reflected light in that vast cavern of concrete and steel and grimy glass held him in its reflected rays. It gilded his tow-coloured hair, burnished the well-cut bones of his squarish face, and cast indented shadows into the corners of his firm mouth as it widened into a slow smile at her. To her dismay, she felt a deep and terrible blush soar into her cheeks. Worse, she wanted to shy away and run. Run, run, run.

"May I ask if these children with you are solely in your charge?" he inquired with interest. An unmistakably foreign accent tilted his words and, in spite of her sudden confusion, intrigued her ear.

"They have been allotted to me for the journey." At least her initial reaction was subsiding. It was a distressing fact that her nerve ends still played tricks with her at times when she was caught unaware by any unexpected turn of events, however slight.

"All the way to Halifax?"

"Further than that." She stooped to rescue a dropped hat and thrust it back onto its owner's head. Then automatically she pulled another potential trouble-maker safely to her side. She thought sometimes that her arms moved as rapidly as if she was pulling out organ-stops when keeping control of her present band. "We're going to Toronto."

"You vil be kept busy."

She glanced at him swiftly. He had said *vil* instead of *will.* It had sounded funny. And pleasing, too. "I'll manage them," she said phlegmatically, no trace of the smile she felt inside.

Briefly he took his eyes from her to glance around at the groups of children interspersed with adults keeping order. He knew something of what it was like to have an uprooted childhood. The travelling box that he had with him now had been specially made for the occasion of his first leaving home. In his country of Norway, where times had been hard for centuries, it was not uncommon for a couple with a large number of children to let one or more be brought up by childless relatives. It would even have been considered a trifle selfish not to share such a God-given bounty in a land where children were cherished as the very meaning of life. Since the arrangement was kept within the family circle, contact with the parents was maintained and much benefit resulted. Nevertheless, he himself he found it a traumatic experience at the age of five to leave the farm and valley, where he knew everyone, to travel many miles up the coast to a new home. On the point of departure, when he would have flung himself back into his mother's arms, weighed down by a sick feeling in his stomach at leaving all that was dear and familiar, she had taken him by the hand deliberately. Never one to show emotion, she had given him over to his uncle, who had lifted him up into the seat of the waiting carriole. He had understood that she expected him to show the same courage as she was sustaining. He obeyed her. It had been a hard lesson in partings. He had learnt it well.

He wondered how many children in the embarkation shed were leaving parents behind. In their case it would be through having been abandoned for one reason or another. Soon the severing would be completed by the sheer breadth of the Atlantic Ocean lying in between.

"Is every group going to the same place in Canada?" he queried, a faint note of incredulity in his voice at the prospect.

"No, there are different reception centres. I've heard there is one at Ottawa and another at Niagara-on-the-Lake. I believe Winnipeg is the distribution point for boys going out to learn farming. We're twenty-five in our party from Leeds and we're being sponsored by the Herbert Drayton Memorial Society. The younger ones will be adopted and we older girls are to be skivvies." When she saw that the slang phrase puzzled him, she explained more fully. "We're to be housemaids and scullery maids."

He nodded quickly in comprehension. Like most people fluent in another language, he was annoyed with himself at being caught out by a word he had not known. To cover his lapse, he held out a hand quickly across the rail to introduce himself. "I'm Peter Hagen."

She put her fingers into his. "My name is Lisa Shaw."

He shook her hand firmly, ducking his head in a formal bow. "How do you do, Miss Shaw."

"Nicely, thank you," she replied. Until he had straightened up from leaning on the rail, she had not realised how tall he was, and she became fully aware of his fine physical appearance for the first time. Curiosity was overcoming all earlier qualms. "Where are you from, Mr. Hagen?"

"From Norway. I was born not far from a town called Molde on the fjord of that name, but I was brought up by an aunt and uncle far north of there at Namsos."

Although her education had been sparse at the local elementary school, she had filled in many gaps for herself by reading every dog-eared book that came her way. Norway. Land of mountains and fjords and the midnight sun. Over a thousand miles long as the crow flies. Twenty-two thousand miles of indented coastline. Peopled by only three and a half million, one of whom was facing her across a wooden barrier. Having started to question him, she could not stop now.

"How long have you been in England, then?"

"Three days. I arrived in Newcastle from Bergen and came by train to Liverpool." It had cost him fifteen shillings in hard-earned money to cross the North Sea, and a further nine pounds was to cover his fare to the New World. The spirit of adventure was so high in him, his ambition so strong, that he would have travelled the long distance if it had taken the last coin in his possession and he had had to survive on mouldy bread to reach

America. He liked what he had seen of England. It struck him as a quiet land with an inner sense of peace, much like Norway. He had been fascinated by his first sight of the great shire horses working the fields and pulling everything from buses to brewers' drays in the streets. The first thing he had done upon his arrival in Liverpool was to go into a pub. Knowing how his own countrymen could drink when liquor came their way, he had expected to find raucous brawling and wild drunkenness. Instead, it had been as still as a church with a few men talking quietly and a respectable young woman knitting a sock behind the bar. She had served his order with a pleasant word and returned to the clicking of her needles while he had seated himself at one of the tables to drink his first glass of English beer. It had tasted extremely good. He had seen drunkenness since in the dock-area pubs, but he would never forget his surprise at discovering that, on the whole, these establishments were orderly, and in the evenings, jolly places, each ruled over by a muscular landlord ready to throw out any real disruptors of other people's enjoyment.

"Why come to England to take ship?" Lisa asked him.

"If there had been a direct line from Norway to the United States, I would have taken it. As it was, I had to follow the same route as many of my fellow countrymen before me."

"But your English," she persisted. "You haven't learnt to speak the language in three days?"

He shook his head vigorously, much amused. "My father's sister, who brought me up, was a teacher before she married a farmer in North Norway, and she grounded me in the language from my first days there. It was useful, you see. When the English gentry arrived there in the summertime for the salmon-fishing, she took some in as guests in the farmhouse. My uncle was always too busy to spare them any time, and as soon as I was old enough I rowed boats for them on the river Namsen, loaded their guns when they went after elk or ptarmigan, and acted as their guide. I always had to do a full day's work, however it was fitted in, with the haymaking and harvesting, which was much more enjoyable as far as I was concerned. I have never liked to be at anybody's beck and call."

"I can understand that," she interjected with feeling.

He smiled, giving a ruminative shake of the head. "Do you know, however long their sojourn, those gentlemen never tried to learn one word of Norwegian! However, it was lucky for me, because it meant my knowledge of their language increased steadily every summer. Now that I'm emigrating to start a new life in the United States, my being able to speak English should stand me in good stead."

Lisa listened intently. She thought him fortunate to have been taught in the main, albeit inadvertently, by those who were masters of the English tongue. She loved the flow of orderly speech unadulterated by bad grammar or ugly obscenities. On that basis she had tried to improve her own vocabulary for a better understanding of all she read and to express herself articulately.

"Why are you leaving home?" she asked him. It would be interesting to know what had prompted his willing departure, which was entirely different to her own.

He pondered how he should answer her without giving away personal reasons. In a nutshell, he could say he had fallen victim to the emigration fever that had been sweeping Norway over the past decade. Many of those leaving home intended only to make their fortune and return again to buy businesses and land that they could never afford otherwise. On the strength of this notion, a number of men became betrothed or married to the girl of their choice before departure, fearful of losing her to someone else in their absence. Or, on a more mercenary level, they wanted to ensure that their interests at home were being watched over on their behalf.

His eldest brother, Jon, was one of these. After marrying Ingrid, a childhood sweetheart, he had impregnated her on their wedding night and left for America the next day. Jon was presently working as a logger in the state of Oregon, saving money towards the day when he had accumulated enough to return home and take over the farm from his father to run it on more profitable lines. Ingrid had moved in to keep house for her widowed father-in-law, as well as her bachelor brothers-in-law when they were home from the sea. Near her time, depressed at having received only one letter from Jon since his departure, she had looked worn and weary when Peter had gone home to his place of birth to say goodbye. It had been distressing when his father had broken down at the moment of farewell, despairing that a faraway land which had swallowed up his eldest son was now about to consume his youngest, with whom he had always shared a special bond of affection. At least Jon had promised to return within three or four years, but Peter had made it clear he intended to become a citizen there—a Norwegian-American, like so many others, gone from their homeland never to see it again.

None of this was anything to be divulged to someone barely met in an embarkation shed. Yet Lisa Shaw should receive a straightforward reply. "I could see no future for myself in Norway."

That was the stark truth of it. He had always known that the Namsos farm was entailed to the next in line on his uncle's side of the family, and he did not intend to remain a farmhand to the end of his days. His uncle was disgruntled at his going, but his aunt approved his decision, having always hoped for him to have a chance in life. She wanted to pay his passage out of her own savings, but he would not let her. Instead, he did a hard season with his fishermen brothers in the Arctic seas, which provided him at the age of eighteen with his fare to America and just enough to keep him from starvation until he was settled in work of one kind or another.

"What do you plan to do in America?"

"First and foremost, I aim to become my own master," he answered cheerfully. "That will take a little time, I daresay. Meanwhile, I'll work at anything and everything, whatever comes my way. I'll travel around, too. I want to see as much as I can of that big country. How else will I know which is the best place when the time comes for me to strike roots there?"

Unexpectedly, Lisa found herself greatly touched by his words and did not know why. It could be that he had unwittingly given her a measure of encouragement towards her own future, for his optimism shone out of him, melting away some chill from her heart. For the first time her serious, rather concentrated expression relaxed and she gave him a full smile. Nobody had ever told her that she had a singularly beautiful mouth, and when she was smiling her whole face took on its radiance.

"I wish you luck, Mr. Hagen."

A look had come over his face, half pleasure, half surprise. "I thank you. I trust all will go well for you, too."

There was a sudden interruption from a few yards away. "Lisa Shaw!" screeched an unpleasantly familiar voice. "What *are* you doing? Come away from that barrier at once!"

Lisa had turned with a start of humiliation. Miss Drayton was bearing down on her, thrusting aside viciously the children of other parties to get through to her. Her approach acted like a signal for pandemonium among Lisa's charges. Amy began to cry again, while the rest, the instinct of their origins being to scatter at the first sign of trouble, dived in all directions into the crowd.

"Come back! Gertie! Minnie! Cora! Hold fast there, Bridget! Lily, do you hear me?" She managed to grab one child and the unbuttoned coat came away from the fugitive into her hand, an old trick of the back streets. Her exasperation increased, more with the society's organiser than the children themselves. It would take time and patience to calm them down again. The woman should have known better! Admittedly one of the society's rules was that there should be no flirting with the opposite sex. Not that a plain conversation across a dividing barrier amounted to dallying. It should have been obvious enough that nothing was amiss.

Two runaways were ensnared. Miss Drayton, further outraged by the children's flight, made no attempt to help with the rounding up. She simply grabbed them in turn as Lisa brought each one to her, threatening a severe whipping if any one of them dared to move an inch away from her.

Finally only Minnie was missing. Lisa's searching became desperate. Uniformed officials in peaked caps at the entrance door and the exit onto the dockside assured her that no child had run past them. Then, when it seemed to her that Minnie must have vanished into thin air, she saw Peter signalling to her.

"Over here! I've found her."

He was holding the wriggling, kicking Minnie by the arm. She had squeezed through the rails of the barrier and he had spotted her taking refuge in a corner. Picking her up, he handed her back into Lisa's care. She clutched the child tight in her embrace, her relief as genuine as her desire to quieten a nigh-hysterical fright.

"It's all right, Minnie. Nobody is going to punish you. Your Lisa knows why you ran off and you're safe now." Her soft tones eventually took effect. Disengaging Minnie's clutching arms from about her neck, she set her down on her feet again. Stooping herself, she tidied the child's appearance, still talking all the time until she could be sure there would be no more darting away. Rising up again, she took the child by the hand and moved close to the barrier with a smile, eager to thank Peter for his help. But she was given no chance. She was whirled around by the shoulder and shaken furiously.

"You brazen creature!" Miss Drayton's drawn-back lips were tight in her temper-ridden face. "Men, men, men! That is all your sort thinks about. The opportunity to make a decent life for yourself is wasted on a gutter girl like you. Get back to the rest of the party!" To give further impact to her words, she gave Lisa a violent push to send her on her way.

Lisa stumbled. If she had not had a tight hold on Minnie she would have fallen. She was burning with shame at being publicly disgraced; heads everywhere turned in her direction and all within the hearing of the Norwegian friend she had made. Unable to look back and meet his eyes, she took Minnie quickly away to join with the others as ordered. It did not matter that she and Peter Hagen had shared the briefest of encounters and would never meet again. She would have liked to part from him in amiable circumstances and not in her degraded state, for the woman's vile abuse had recontaminated her in her own eyes with the physical defilement she had suffered with such pain and anguish in the barn. Her teeth bit deep into her lower lip, which was trembling uncontrollably. It would never do to let the little children see her weep. In any case, Amy, who had rushed forward to meet her, was shedding enough tears for both of them.

It was not long afterwards that the signal came to start going aboard. Lisa had hoped to keep away from the dividing barrier, but the press of the crowd brought the Herbert Drayton group alongside it. Yet she need not have worried. The space had been vacated, everyone there having already gone out to join the other ship. By now Peter Hagen would be safely out of range and she was spared any look he might have given her, curious or otherwise.

At a slow pace, Lisa and the rest shuffled forward. Soon the warm April sunshine, which had only penetrated the shed through skylights, fell full on her face. The ship loomed high before them. S.S. *Victoria.* She felt her pulse quicken. The feeling of encouragement she had received from Peter Hagen had not ebbed, in spite of what had happened in between.

If her gaze had not been set on the gangway that she was soon to ascend, she would have seen he had retraced his steps. As he had hoped, the ill-tempered organiser was at the head of the party while Lisa was more to the rear. Leaving his travelling box where he had set it down on the cobbles, he ran to her. As he plucked at her sleeve to draw her attention, her eyes widened and she looked as if she might faint at seeing him there.

"Miss Shaw! Lisa! Forgive me for being the cause of some trouble for you."

"It wasn't your fault!" She was frantic, fearful that at any second Miss Drayton would glance back and spot him keeping pace with her as she moved along with the rest.

"I want to make amends. Please accept this token." He thrust a sizeable paper cone at her. "There's a pedlar selling these caramels on the dockside. I thought they would help you to keep the children happy. Farewell!"

He dashed off before she had a chance to thank him. The sun flashed across the surface of the travelling box as he hoisted it up onto his broad shoulder. Holding it secure, he hastened away in the opposite direction towards his own waiting ship. All her good wishes went silently with him as well as something more than gratitude. It was a strange feeling, poignant and tender. She did not recognise it for what it was. To her it was simply as if her heart were destined to retain its own special memory of him, linked forever to this day of endings and beginnings.

Three

On board the S.S. *Victoria,* Lisa experienced a deep dismay at her first sight of the dormitory accommodation allotted to steerage passengers which included every one of the children's parties. None of them was used to comfort, but these poorly lit quarters in the hold of the ship below the water-line were far worse than anything she had expected. Row upon row of tiered bunks took up most of the space, leaving narrow passageways in between. The one in the centre was slightly wider to allow space for the collapsible tables erected at mealtimes. A canvas sailcloth, fastened from a crossbeam to walls and deck, separated male from female passengers, in sight if not in sound.

Only in these depths was it possible to see what an old ship it was. Lisa guessed it had probably been named after the late queen when steam had first begun to dominate the scene at sea. Although the whole area appeared to have been recently scrubbed throughout, the damp smell of suds failed to subdue certain peculiarly unpleasant odours. The toilet arrangements were decidedly primitive. Chipped and rusty enamel sinks in a row would allow twelve people at a time to wash publicly. A screened-off section offered more private facilities, but after waiting such a long time to come aboard the children soon strained these to the limits, causing many of the younger ones to wet themselves before their turn came in a long line to reach the wooden-lidded buckets.

Yet on the whole everybody was remarkably cheerful. All the adult escorts were experienced in accompanying parties of children overseas, for the scheme itself had been in operation in varying degrees for over thirty years. Lisa was one of those briefed earlier on the train by Miss Drayton in the procedure of claiming bunks from the numbered label of each child, and she and Teresa and Myrtle became busy making sure that the younger ones knew in which end they would be sleeping, for not all would have a bunk to themselves.

As soon as the small bundles of possessions were stowed away under the bottom bunk where boards would prevent their sliding away when the ship rolled, the children throughout the quarters obeyed orders to stand by their sleeping places. Then the escorts came along with large paper bags containing currant buns, and there was one for everybody. Miss Drayton was the exception in not personally handing out this welcome treat to stem immediate hunger, but she preceded Lisa, to whom she had allotted the sticky task, and glanced back constantly over her shoulder to make sure that nobody was getting more than one bun, since she had purchased only the exact amount.

"Our buns ain't as big as what the other groups 'ave got," Minnie commented, eyeing critically the small one she had received.

"Shush!" Lisa said quickly. "Eat it up and be thankful." Apart from the danger of Minnie's bun being forfeited if Miss Drayton caught what was said, Lisa had no wish for the woman's ire to be spiked again that day.

Gradually it grew near the time for sailing. The escorts began to usher the children up the companionways in order for them to have a last view of England. Lisa, keeping hold of Amy's hand with Minnie tagging close behind, stepped out into the sunlight again to find the steerage area of the deck jam-packed, most of the bigger boys having grabbed the best places at the rails. The escorts, men and women, Miss Drayton among them, gathering together to renew acquaintance, were paying no attention, and discipline was being relaxed for the time being.

Lisa drew breath. She had fought too often for the bullied and oppressed at the orphanage to let a few hulking boys block the view for her charges. "Hang on to my waist, Minnie," she instructed, "and tell the rest to follow suit in turn to form a snake. Right? Here we go!"

Propelling Amy in front of her and with elbows flailing like the wheels of a paddle-steamer, she reached the rails. With a few shoves, she managed to secure some space, ignoring pithy comments.

"There we are!" she exclaimed triumphantly, taking her place protectively to the rear of her band. "Now each one of you can see when we leave old England."

There was a great bustle of activity prevailing on the dockside. A few latecomers among the more affluent passengers were ascending the gangway reserved for First Class, the women in feathered hats and soft furs, the men agleam with gold tie-pins and silver-headed canes. Porters ran with their baggage, two, and sometimes three, needed to trundle the huge cabin trunks, all of it of finest leather and clearly monogrammed.

"All visitors ashore!" The call echoed in every part of the ship. There were no visitors in the steerage quarters, but the announcement electrified the air. The time of sailing was imminent!

Quite a number of people streamed off the ship to join those that had already collected on the dockside to see relatives and friends sail away. Judging by the merriment of some of those that had been aboard, it appeared that earlier arrivals in First Class had been holding champagne parties in their cabins.

Slowly the gangways were swung away. Ropes were released from bollards and the deck vibrated underfoot from the ship's engines. Suddenly there was a scuffling somewhere at the back of the crowd on the quayside and a shrieking woman burst into view, her hat awry from the physical struggle she had had with the officials to get through, her lanky hair streaming from its pins.

"Wait! Wait!" she screeched, running towards the ship. "My kid's on board! I want 'er off!"

At the rails, Minnie gave an exultant yell. "It's my Ma! Ma! I'm 'ere! I don't want to go no place! I want to be with you!" In her eagerness, she attempted to climb the rails. When Lisa restrained her for her own safety, she waved frenziedly through them to catch her mother's attention. Six months had gone by since her father had died and her mother, left with twin babies and no means of support, had taken her to the orphanage, sat her down on a bench in the hall and told her that she had to stay there, for there was no money to feed her at home any more. She realised she should have known that one day her mother would come back for her.

"Ma! Ma!"

"Minnie! Minnie!"

Her mother had seen her and was darting along to come level with the soaring spot on the ship from which she looked down. Minnie began to feel frightened. Before her eyes her mother appeared to be going crazy, simply crying her name over and over again in the midst of breast-beating and hair-tearing. All the time the cobbles of the dockside seemed to be moving away beneath her parent's ill-shod feet. Then Minnie saw a gap was widening between ship and shore. The blast of the ship's siren drowned her panic-stricken shriek, and when the reverberating notes faded away she was stretching out her arms between the rails, sobbing pathetically. By that time the cheers and last farewells being exchanged between the more well-to-do passengers and their well-wishers was at its height.

Minnie's mother dropped to her knees, sat back on her heels, and threw her arms over her head, rocking in despair. Then, as those waving to the ship moved along in front of her, she was lost to sight. Lisa drew the sobbing child away from the rails, letting others crowd forward, and held her tightly in comfort.

As they stood there, locked in the press of those excitedly unaware of the drama that had taken place, Lisa watched the roofs and towers of the port buildings sliding away at a steadily increasing pace.

"Goodbye, England," she whispered emotionally in farewell. "God bless my homeland."

As the ship continued to head out along the Mersey estuary,

she was able to see that Peter's vessel was in the last stages of departure on the tide. She wondered if he was at the rails watching the S.S. *Victoria* sail away. Just in case he was, she raised an arm and waved. He could never have seen her, but it pleased her to do it.

That night as she lay awake, her thoughts drifted to him again. He would be in a bunk exactly like the one in which she was lying and amid similar surroundings. Probably he was asleep and untroubled. She was more than grateful for the candies he had given her for the children. He must have learnt to call them caramels from gentlemen with a sweet tooth who went salmon-fishing on the Namsen. It was an elegant name for good, plain toffee. One had been wonderfully effective in consoling Minnie, at least for the time being.

How the ship creaked and groaned! So far the swell had been gentle and everybody had been able to eat the supper of bread and cheese given out from the steerage galley. All around her the children slept, some whimpering as though they dreamed, and a few snored as if to match that which came from the other side of the sailcloth. Somewhere in the gloom an emigrant woman, one of the independent travellers in the hold, was trying to soothe her baby who had awakened. The thin cry stopped abruptly as the infant was put to the breast, and all was still in that direction again. With the exception of the Herbert Drayton group, every party had its adult escorts sleeping in the steerage quarters. Miss Drayton had simply bade hers good night and gone up the companionway to a cabin on another deck.

Turning on her side, Lisa pulled the thin blanket closer about her ears. It was as well that the younger ones were sharing bunks, for it was cold below the water-line. She thought she heard a scuttling and tried not to think of rats. In the morning the caramels were gone and only shreds of the paper cone remained.

Nothing went right on the voyage after that. The weather changed; most of the children were seasick; and the food dished out from the galley was of the poorest quality. Lisa tried to get her charges up on deck whenever the rain and rough wind eased enough for them to be able to take some exercise in the fresh air. It was always cold and they shivered in their inadequate clothing, but she organised singing games for them to play which kept them moving. Children from other groups joined them and sometimes the deck was teeming with a skipping, dancing throng. Passengers from the better part of the ship came to the rails of an upper deck to watch. It was when Lisa and her own little circle were taking a rest that she heard an expression used to describe them that was to alert her to the possibility of prejudice awaiting them in Canada. A Canadian woman in furs was asked by her well-clad young daughter why there were so many children on board. Her disparaging reply was clearly heard.

"They are Home children, Prunella. That is to say they come from the streets or from dreadful institutions into the homes of decent people in Canada. Come away, dear. Even at this distance, there is no telling what infection one might catch from that type of person."

Since Miss Drayton was so rarely available, making an appearance only briefly once a day from her First Class accommodation on the top deck, Lisa asked another of the adult escorts, whose name was Mrs. Plum, which suited her comfortable appearance, about what she had overheard. Mrs. Plum, who was escorting a group of girls for the Dr. Barnado charitable organisation, was liked and respected by the girls under her supervision. She tried to be reassuring.

"I'll be honest with you, Lisa. You will meet hostility and suspicion just as you will meet kindness and friendliness. It is fortunate that not so many Canadians these days view Home children in the light you have described to me, but mud sticks from the days in the beginning of the movement, when the British Government seized the chance to rid themselves of hundreds of guttersnipes and thieving young street urchins under the cloak of emigration. The truth is that many of those children did well in their new lands, whether it was Canada, South Africa, or Australia, but the bad ones tainted the good name of the rest and some of that still lingers on today."

She did not add that, human nature being what it was, the

Home children of that time, as in the present day, were as much abused and sinned against as they had ever sinned themselves. Some charitable organisations were far too lax in making sure that suitable homes were found, merely eager to unload the children on the assumption that anything was better for them than whatever they had known previously. Thankfully Dr. Barnado was not of that ilk. He took a personal interest in the fate of every child, boy or girl, and not only had he visited Canada himself more than once, but his charter for the vetting of character and the health of Home children, plus the need for reports on their whereabouts, progress and welfare after they had been placed in a home or employment, had been adopted by the Canadian Government. Yet the loopholes remained. Far too many children slipped through them and were lost to any of those who would have cared for their well-being.

"Thank you for your explanation, Mrs. Plum."

"I hope I have put your mind at rest. At least you and the other young emigrants today have been prepared for your new life. There you have a great advantage over your predecessors. In the early days they came in ignorance, having known only crowded slums and the constant rumble of traffic, to find themselves in isolated places miles and miles from the nearest neighbour, which must have been mental torture for many of them. You will know what to expect from such circumstances and will be ready to adapt."

"We had two geography lessons, and the superintendent of our orphanage loaned us older girls some books on Canada, which I read. Not everybody did."

Mrs. Plum looked perplexed. "Do you mean that Miss Drayton did not give you a talk herself on the subject?"

"She probably did not deem it necessary since we are to be in Toronto, which from what I read is a city, like any other city."

"All of you? In Toronto, I mean. But I thought the Herbert Drayton Memorial Society usually sent some children west to the prairies."

"Western Canada has never been mentioned to us."

"Oh. Then I must be mistaken. I have never visited Toronto

myself, but I believe it has a pretty location on the lake. I'm sure you will be happy there."

Lisa pondered over what had been said. She could not endure the thought of the little ones she knew so well being scattered out of her range, at least not until they were thoroughly settled with their adoptive families. No, there was no need to worry. They would all be in Toronto. Even Mrs. Bradlaw had been sure of that.

There was more rough weather and a good deal more seasickness before Canada loomed on the horizon. The new would-be Canadians streamed down the gangway in pouring rain to the noise and bustle of the Halifax dock area. Some emigrant criminals, about to be deported, jeered at them through the bars of a stone building. Trains with vast black locomotives hissing steam were boarded by individual parties, who occupied special original "colonist" cars, which had wooden seats with no leather padding. A pot-bellied stove with a scuttle of fuel beside it at one end of these carriages gave facilities for cooking. It was cosily alight and gave out a welcome heat as Lisa and the others in the Herbert Drayton party came aboard their car.

The windows steamed up as they divested themselves of their damp outer garments and hung them on wooden pegs. The younger ones knelt on the seats to wipe hands across the glass and peer out. The older girls were receiving instructions from Miss Drayton.

"You will take turns in preparing the meals in pairs. I have brought food supplies from the ship to last until tomorrow. Whenever the train stops to take on water and coal, I shall alight to purchase bread and anything else that is needed from the local store or from people who bring their wares to the passengers. It is a long time now since breakfast, so two of you may start a meal right away. Rosie—and you, Lisa."

Outside in the rain there came the sing-song call of the conductor. "All aboard!"

"We're off!" Rosie exclaimed. The brass bell on the locomotive clanged an announcement of departure as the great train began to pull out. Rosie and Lisa would have liked to join their companions in looking out of the windows, but Emily had opened a hamper and was handing them two cans of stew to heat up on the stove.

It was a long journey and there was plenty of chance to observe the passing landscape before they reached their destination two days later. The nights were particularly uncomfortable, since they had no pillows and had to cover themselves with coats. Miss Drayton retired to a sleeping compartment and took her meals in the dining car.

At Union Station in Toronto, they trailed after Miss Drayton to waiting cabs. The city met them with warm May sunshine and an abundance of fresh green foilage. To Lisa it was as if a forest of maple trees had been trapped within the city from the time the first foundations were laid. Shady branches made lace patterns everywhere over doorways and open lawns and wide streets, the nomenclature of which proclaimed loyal monarchical tribute to the mother country. The architecture was elaborately pinnacled and porched with cupolas abounding, the Parliament buildings in Queen's Park a veritable feast of ornamentation, and church spires piercing the sky at many points. Lake Ontario, which the whole party had glimpsed while being bowled along, shone a sharp silvery blue, the harbour busy with shipping and an island lying offshore like a soft rug spread upon the surface of the water.

At Sherbourne Street, in a residential area, the girls alighted outside the house that the older ones recognised immediately from the photograph they had been shown far away in England. If anything, it appeared grander in reality, in keeping with the rest of the houses in the street, and had every sign of having recently received a new coat of paint. There were rich damask drapes at the window. A housemaid in cap and apron opened the front door, revealing a vestibule ashimmer with blue flock wallpaper, as Miss Drayton was paying the cab drivers and giving instructions about taking her cabin trunk to the back entrance. Almost at once another woman appeared from the interior of the house, a smiling, fluttering creature with an ageing, doll-like face, her greying hair coiffed upwards into a pompadour and fastened with a tortoise-shell comb that had come slightly adrift, giving her head an untidy appearance.

"Dear, dear, Emily! Welcome back again!" she exclaimed, coming down the porch steps.

"How are you, Mavis?" Miss Drayton put a cheek coolly against the other woman's in greeting. "The house looks nice. When did the painters leave?"

"A week ago." An anxious note crept in. "It is exactly the magnolia colour that you wanted, isn't it?"

"Yes, Mavis. Please do not fuss. I have had a most exhausting journey." Miss Drayton flicked a hand wearily in the direction of the new arrivals clustered in a bunch on the path behind them. "Look after those children. I'm going up to my room to rest. Have tea sent up to me." She swept into the house.

Mavis faced the group, linking the fingers of her restless hands together and smiling vaguely. "You may tell me your names later. I have a dreadful memory and would never remember them now. I'm Miss Lapthorne, Miss Drayton's deputy. Follow me."

She did not take them into the house through the porch as they had expected, but led them around by a side path to the rear. There they entered by the back entrance to mount three flights of a servants' staircase to attic accommodation, which consisted of four large rooms under the eaves, one with some old horsehair sofas and a table to serve as a sitting-room. The sleeping quarters were sparsely furnished with beds and cupboards. Apart from there being more space, they could have been back at the orphanage.

"Do we eat up 'ere?" one of them asked in a choked voice of disappointment. It was Myrtle, who had been so impressed by the photograph, and throughout the journey had pictured entering into a lap of luxury.

"No. You will take your meals in the kitchen."

"Don't it get 'ot up 'ere in summertime?" Rosie inquired suspiciously.

"Oh, you won't be here until then," Miss Lapthorne replied, shaking her head in mild amusement. "Some of you older girls will be leaving before the end of the week. Everything has been arranged." She turned to leave, looking back over her shoulder from the head of the stairs. "You are not allowed beyond the baize door of the kitchen into the rest of the house to bother Miss Drayton with your presence. However, I have a study on the second floor with access from this staircase. You may seek me out whenever you wish."

Lisa stepped forward. "I don't understand about everything being arranged. What of the meetings we are to have with our employers?"

Miss Lapthorne's eyes were a lilac-blue and could have been quite lovely if she had not had a nervous habit of shifting her gaze. "Be pleased that the orphanage references, posted to me by Miss Drayton, were good enough to gain some of you employment without personal interviews."

"What of the young ones who are to be adopted?" Lisa persisted. "Are they to be taken sight unseen?"

Miss Lapthorne flapped her hands. "Not so fast. All in good time. Get unpacked and then come downstairs to eat."

Miss Drayton rested until the next day. By then it did not matter what previous arrangements had been made, for everything had to be postponed in any case. Amy came down with a fever which swept through the household with such ferocity that almost all were laid low in turn. The doctor believed it had been contracted on the ship and, not being sure what might develop, put the whole building into quarantine. Lisa, with her natural resilience, and Mavis Lapthorne, for all her fragile appearance, remained on their feet, working together to look after the others. It was during this period that Lisa discovered that Miss Lapthorne resorted to the bottle to sustain her in moments of stress. The only time she was not on hand to help Lisa was when she had passed out completely after indulging herself too generously.

When Mavis Lapthorne discovered afterwards that Lisa had held her tongue about the matter, she was singularly impressed. Not as much as a giggling whisper had been shared with the other girls, which—horror of horrors—might easily have reached the ears of Emily Drayton, with disastrous results. On the contary, Lisa had actually covered up for her. When serving beef tea to Emily Drayton in her sickbed, the girl had made some excuse as to why she had made it instead of her superior.

What was more, it had been made deliciously, just as Emily liked it, and Emily was hard to please. Mavis Lapthorne resolved that Lisa should not go into domestic service elsewhere. She would make the girl her right-hand assistant. She needed someone who could be trusted to keep silent about her little need of a swig or two now and again. What was just as important, Lisa knew how to manage children. The most feverish of the patients became calmer in her presence, and querulous convalescents gave up squabbling to gather into whatever word game she had organised. What a boon it would be to have Lisa to take charge whenever unmanageable children were brought to the Distribution Home.

It took courage to make the request to Emily Drayton. Miss Lapthorne chose a suitable moment. Inclined to be forgetful, she had made a list of good reasons why Lisa should remain in Toronto and not be sent away with the rest of the older girls. Only her personal reason about her drinking habits was not written down.

"Nonsense, Mavis!" Miss Drayton reclined back against the cushions of the swing-seat on the shady veranda. "You know how much in demand my girls are these days. I like to keep up a steady supply."

"But you can send the other fourteen as arranged. Lisa does not need to go. It would be an economy, too."

"An economy?" Miss Drayton was always interested in cutting expenses when her own comfort was not affected. "What do you mean?"

"I could get rid of the housemaid. That would be a saving. Lisa could take her place. What better than that one of our own emigrants should receive visitors to the house. I think it would make a good impression. And you wouldn't have to pay her any wages."

Miss Drayton looked thoughtful, mulling over the suggestion. "Hmm. It is not often that you have any good ideas." She gave a nod. "Very well, but it will mean hastening a decision on the placing of those two little children she guards protectively. What are their names? Minnie and Amy? Yes, that's right. They would take up far too much of her time if they remained anywhere in the vicinity. She would want to go darting off to visit them every five minutes."

"But that nice Mr. and Mrs. Lawson on College Street want to have Amy! They were touched by her sad background when they read the information sheet I gave them."

"All the children have wretched backgrounds, Mavis. Please do not start getting sentimental. The Lawsons can have one of the others." Seeing that further protest was about to be forthcoming, her eyes became steely. "Well? Do you want to keep Lisa, or do you not?"

Miss Lapthorne capitulated quickly. "Yes, I do. It shall be as you say. Only I think there will be trouble. Neither child will want to be parted from her."

"Then we shall follow the usual procedure as when parting sisters from each other."

Lisa was pleased when Miss Lapthorne took her out in the buggy to visit the home of a couple who had offered adoption to two of the children. They drove out through the suburb of West Toronto Junction and into the countryside where there were orchards, villas, farms, and densely wooded stretches of oak and yellow pine. The whole drive took much longer than Lisa had expected and they ate a packed lunch on the way. The farmhouse, when they reached it, was a log building erected by early settlers and enlarged at a later date. The farmer and his wife proved to be dour folk and there was a subdued look about their own offspring. Miss Lapthorne shook her head as she and Lisa left again.

"All that farmer wants is another couple of pairs of young hands that he can train to work on the land. Farmers are always desperate for cheap labour, and taking little children is a good investment for them."

"Nobody will be sent there, will they?" Lisa asked anxiously.

"Not if I can help it," Miss Lapthorne replied, looking straight ahead. "That man rules by the strap of his belt."

The woman went up in Lisa's estimation. Miss Lapthorne was a weak and muddled creature in many ways, but she had kindness in her. It was evening when they arrived back at the house and as Lisa ascended the staircase she did not hear the usual chatter. With a sudden wave of foreboding, she dashed up the rest of the flight and threw open the door. The sitting-room area was deserted. She saw it was the same in the bedrooms until she came to where the young ones slept. Only eight of the ten beds were occupied and the children sprang out of the covers at once to rush to her, showing they had feared she would not return.

"They've gone!" Gertie squealed.

"Where?" Lisa demanded.

"I dunno. Everybody's gone 'cept us."

"Amy and Minnie, too?"

"Yes."

Lisa flew downstairs again. Breaking all rules she burst through the door that led into the main part of the house. Miss Drayton was about to go out to some social function. She was in blue silk with pearl-drops in her ears and a wrap about her shoulders.

"What has happened while I've been away today?" Lisa cried out. "Where are Amy and Minnie? Where is everybody?"

"Your companions left today for the prairies in the charge of my representative, Mrs. Grant, whom you have not met, but who is a tower of strength to this organisation." Miss Drayton smoothed her elbow-length white gloves and fastened the tiny buttons at the wrist, her tone a trifle bored, as if she were in no mood to discuss mundane affairs. "Amy and Minnie are travelling on the train with them as far as a certain point where they will be collected by the husband and wife who are adopting them. They have not been parted."

"I don't understand anything that is happening here! When we first arrived Miss Lapthorne said that *some* of us were to get work on the strength of our orphanage papers alone, but she did not say everyone. And why have I been left out? Were mine against me?"

"Due to the delay caused by the fever, Mrs. Grant had extra time to secure employment for everyone of the right age. Some will be in towns, other with homesteaders. As for you, Miss Lapthorne wishes you to remain here as her permanent aide, and I have given my permission."

"What are homesteaders?" Lisa was puzzled.

"They are people who take up government land and farm it. Many of the men's wives have been used to being waited on by domestic servants before coming to Canada, and Mrs. Grant deals with requests for orphanage girls."

Lisa stepped closer, hands balled at her sides in desperation. "I want to see Amy and Minnie with the family you have chosen for them. It won't be easy for them to settle in, I know!"

Miss Drayton eyed her dispassionately. "You really are ridiculous. Do you not realise yet what a vast country you are living in? The whole of the British Isles could be swallowed up in this province alone. I cannot afford to pay unnecessary fares for you to go jaunting far across Ontario. In any case, when children are adopted it is a generally accepted rule held by all societies that links with the past should be severed."

"That I can accept, but in this particular case you have been cruel! You have sent them away far too quickly!"

"Do not dare to speak thus to me!" Miss Drayton was shaking with temper, her face patchy with colour as she pointed to the baize door. "Go back to the part of the house where you belong! Never again come in here unless at Miss Lapthorne's instructions, or with my permission!"

Raging inwardly, Lisa made no move. "What of writing to the others who have left today?"

"If they decide to correspond with you, that is another matter. I never divulge addresses."

As Lisa flung the baize door shut behind her, she heard a movement at the top of the stairs and caught the flick of Miss Lapthorne's skirt. The woman had been eavesdropping.

"Why didn't you tell me what was to happen today?" Lisa called out accusingly, darting to the foot of the flight.

Slowly Miss Lapthorne returned to the head of the stairs to look down at her. "I wasn't allowed to," she confessed shakily, twisting a handkerchief in her hands as if she would tear it. "It would have been too upsetting for you and the little ones to part knowingly. Miss Drayton was only doing what she thought best." She smiled with forced brightness. "Never mind, you won't be kept in ignorance of anything now that you are to be my assistant."

When Lisa made no response, merely setting a hand on the newel post and leaning her forehead wearily against it, her shoulders bowed dejectedly, Miss Lapthorne had the grace to look shamefaced. She hastened into her own room and closed the door. There came the clink of bottle and glass.

During the next few weeks the remaining children were adopted one by one. Gertie went to the kindly Mr. and Mrs. Lawson on College Street and their troubles began. Gertie stole, swore, smashed valuable bric-a-brac, and finally ran away. She was not caught, being well used to scrounging a living on the streets and escaping authority, a way of life only stemmed when she had been taken to the Leeds orphanage a few months before being brought to Canada. Then, unexpectedly, she returned of her own free will to her adopted parents. Being an exceptional couple, they accepted her back as if nothing had happened and afterwards there were no more disruptions.

Lisa had no knowledge of the fate of the rest of the orphans, all of whom went farther afield. No word reached her of how Amy and Minnie had adjusted to their new surroundings. Miss Drayton kept such information locked in her files and not even Miss Lapthorne had a key.

When Miss Drayton left Toronto, it was to sail for France and take a short holiday on the Riviera before returning to England for some fund-raising and to collect a further consignment of children. The house on Sherbourne Street became a quiet place. Lisa was given the task of cleaning it from attic to basement, laundering every blanket and item of bed linen and airing every mattress in readiness for the next influx.

Miss Lapthorne rewarded her hard work by allowing her to go for walks on her own, which gave her the chance to get to know Toronto as once she had know Leeds. She would have welcomed the privilege of being allowed to play sometimes on the grand piano in the drawing-room, for she had been taught by one of the teachers at the orphanage, who had spotted that she had some musical talent. But the piano lid at Sherbourne Street was kept locked and remained that way. She could only assume that the fine instrument was there to give an additional touch of oppulence to the over-decorated room, and to set off the silver-framed photographs of Miss Drayton's father that were displayed upon it.

On Sundays Lisa accompanied Miss Lapthorne to the Baptist Church on Bloor Street. The congregation was quite grand, arriving in fine carriages, the gentlemen in silk hats. A few people looked down their noses at having a Home girl in their midst, but on the first Sunday the minister had made a point of welcoming her from the pulpit, and the friendly smiles and nods of others made up for the slights she received.

Although Miss Lapthorne was usually amiable, somehow Lisa could not trust her. It was not just the deceit over the banishing of Amy and Minnie. The woman was too indecisive and lacking in character to be relied upon at any time. It was in keeping with everything else that the spinster should constantly uphold the pretence of abhorring alcohol, saying that she only kept brandy in the house for medicinal purposes. Yet it was ever her refuge, for she could not endure any kind of tension without it. A drinking bout always followed a government official's routine call at the house. She would fly into a flurry of agitation, getting Lisa's assistance as soon as he appeared on the doorstep, entrusting her with carrying the books of entries from the specially unlocked drawers in Miss Drayton's study into the drawing-room where he awaited them.

Everything would be in order, and the official would always approve the spotlessness of the house when looking over the attic quarters waiting in neat order for the next batch of new arrivals. He never left the house in anything but an agreeable mood, but Miss Lapthorne was completely distrait when Lisa closed the door after him. That same night the spinster always shut herself away in her room with a bottle and did not emerge until noon the next day, looking pale with a headache that was troubling her.

Lisa once asked her why these official visits upset her. Her gaze shifted as she blinked nervously. "I'm merely anxious not to let Miss Drayton down on any count. We are old friends from our schooldays. I have her interests always at heart."

That was apparent. It explained why somebody as efficient as Emily Drayton should tolerate Mavis Lapthorne as her deputy. At least when sober, which could be for weeks at a time when Lisa smoothed out minor domestic troubles for her, she kept the records and housekeeping ledgers in a beautiful hand. She also had the kind of prim looks and general appearance in public that only reflected good on the reputation of the Distribution Home if anyone should have any doubts about its reputation.

Autumn came. Everywhere the trees were scarlet, crimson, orange, and yellow, the violence of colour tinting the interior of houses and filling Lisa with wonder at their splendour. Then suddenly Miss Drayton returned, disrupting the quietness with no fewer than fifty girls to be placed in domestic service, all between the ages of fifteen and seventeen. Mattresses had to be placed on floors to accommodate them in the attics, for Miss Drayton would not have her own part of the house invaded, and meals had to be taken in shifts at the kitchen table. Some of the girls were orderly, but most were on the wild side, quick to quarrel and, on occasions, fighting and hair-pulling.

Miss Drayton lost no time in shipping them out. Mrs. Grant, of whom Lisa had heard previously, arrived to escort them. She was a tall, grim-faced woman, and her authoritative manner quelled even the most unruly. Lisa tried to gain some information from her about Amy and Minnie.

"Don't question me," the woman retorted. "My reports are not for the likes of you."

Before the girls left, Lisa was able to gather that the majority had been in domestic service in workhouses and institutions, and she could guess how glad the authorities were to get rid of them in order to fill the vacancies with others desperate for work. She gave several of them a list of the names of those with whom she had come to Canada, requesting that if they met up with them to say how much she would like a letter. She had long since come to the conclusion that those who would have written had decided she had gone to work elsewhere as they had done. She could well imagine Rosie, in particular, supposing her to be favoured because she had sought to educate herself by extensive reading. How wrong that supposition was.

The irony of it came home to her still further when she found the state of the girls' quarters after their departure. Filthy rags and unemptied slops and rubbish of all kinds had to be cleared away before she could start washing and cleaning the rooms. It made her more grateful than ever for the tiny box-room that Miss Lapthorne allowed her to occupy as a mark of her promotion to deputy's assistant.

Everything was spick and span again when she was giving a final polish to the attic windows and saw Miss Drayton departing once more for England, with Miss Lapthorne bidding her goodbye. Caught off guard, Lisa was suddenly assailed with a longing for a glimpse of English hills and an English sky, but she crushed it down and diverted her mind elsewhere. From the time she had first been taken into the Leeds orphanage, she had learned to live each day as it came and not to waste time in useless regrets.

Winter set in and the snows came. On the first day of the New Year of 1904, Lisa reached her fifteenth birthday. Miss Lapthorne kindly made her a cake. It was the first celebratory delicacy she had ever had.

Miss Drayton returned in the spring with a party in tow, and the pattern of coming and going was resumed. Lisa knew by now that the majority of the children went to faraway rural areas in Ontario. According to Miss Lapthorne, Mrs. Grant was responsible for checking the homes into which the children were to be received, but as it was impossible for her to meet every family personally, because of the distances involved, others were designated by her and the collective reports presented for Miss Drayton's final approval. The fact that there never seemed to be any delay in the distribution of the children caused Lisa much anxiety. From all she had seen and observed since being drawn into the Herbert Drayton Memorial Society, she felt they were simply being got rid of as quickly as possible. The thought of their being exploited or treated cruelly haunted her.

In desperation she went to see Mr. Lawson, who had adopted Gertie and whom she knew to be a good man. He listened to her patiently and then dismissed her worries out of hand, having implicit faith in the society.

"Take my own case, for example," he said. "My wife and I were extremely disappointed not to be able to adopt Amy. Mrs. Lawson had taken the child to her heart. But when it was explained to us that Amy had the chance to rejoin a sister, already adopted, we had no wish to stand in her way."

"But that wasn't true!" Lisa burst out. "Amy had nobody in the world! Her whole family was wiped out by cholera."

"All except one sister," he corrected pedantically. "You cannot be expected to know the complete background of every child passing through the society for adoption. Be assured that everything is being done for the best. I shall not mention your visit if I should see Miss Drayton again. It would hurt her feelings to know she was being doubted. At the same time I commend your concern for the weak and helpless. I thank God there are no grounds for such misgivings."

She returned to Sherbourne Street in a fury of frustration. Not long afterwards she had cause again to rage against dubious circumstances. A widower came to collect an exceptionally pretty child for adoption. Well dressed and with a cultured voice, he made a generous donation to the society in appreciation of its charitable work, but Lisa felt an instinctive abhorrence for him. Shut out by Miss Drayton, she implored Miss Lapthorne to intervene on the child's behalf and not let her be taken away by him.

"Don't be foolish, Lisa. He's a gentleman," Miss Lapthorne replied inanely. "He has a fine home in Ottawa and our fortunate orphan will lack for nothing. There's no need to worry that he has no wife. He has assured Miss Drayton that his housekeeper is a most motherly soul."

Lisa trembled for the fate of that child. She had not grown up in an orphanage without learning a great deal of life through the experiences of other inmates. Her loathing of Miss Drayton increased, knowing that the woman must have closed her eyes to the obvious. Miss Lapthorne, on the other hand, was curiously innocent. For that reason alone, Lisa was able to forgive her for many stupidities.

Another year dawned. Lisa passed her sixteenth birthday. The mirror in her room had reflected changes in her face and figure. She put up her hair into a knot at the top of her head. She sewed her own clothes. Although officially she still received no wages, Miss Lapthorne, perhaps fearful that she might leave for fully paid employment, made sure she received a small amount of money regularly out of the petty cash. If Lisa had not known herself to be a comfort and a refuge to many of the bewildered children who arrived at the Distribution Home, she would not have stayed. In moments of depression, she could see herself ending her days as another Miss Lapthorne. At least she had no desire to marry. Her single terrible experience had closed such doors for her.

She often wished she had someone to talk to about everything and knew whom she would have chosen. In her little room she had a small Norwegian flag tucked into the corner of a framed text on the wall. She had cut it out from an old magazine illustrating in rather gaudy colours the flags of all nations. It kept Peter Hagen in the forefront of her mind. Not that she thought that she would ever forget him. More than that, the proximity of the flag to the words of blessing seemed to her to be a means of ensuring his safekeeping wherever he might happen to be.

Four

Peter Hagen had been in the United States for more than three years on the late August day in 1906 when he alighted from a train that had brought him to Toronto from Buffalo. If there was any difference in his appearance, apart from his being much better dressed, it lay in his muscular development, the last trace of the ranginess of youth lost in the full physique of a powerful man. There was little that he had not done in the way of heavy work since being pushed around and kept waiting and hustled along in the sheds of Ellis Island. His fierce Viking pride had made it difficult to tolerate the arrogance of officials, but once he was on the mainland he forgot his resentment in his interest in all there was to see. He had thought Bergen a big city, but New York was the size of many Bergens, and noisier by night and day than any avalanche he had ever heard.

With his box on his shoulder, his homespun attire marking him out as a newly arrived immigrant, he had stared at everything from the windows of the stores to the handsome mansions on Fifth Avenue. He had an address in his pocket. There probably was not a Norwegian anywhere who set out on a journey, either at home or abroad, without a list of hospitable anchorages where he would be given a meal and a place to sleep by a relative, friend, or somebody recommended by either of the former. It was hospitality that was gladly returned in full measure when the opportunity arose, and Peter did not have the slightest doubt of his welcome when he knocked on the door of a third-floor apartment in a tough-looking section of the city.

The family who lived there were cousins of his cousin, their origins in Sognefjord, and his hand was nearly shaken off his wrist in their joy at seeing someone from the old country. They sat him at a table, plied him with food and strong coffee, and all sat around to watch him eat while they fired a ceaseless barrage of questions. He wondered if in them he was seeing himself in the future, well satisfied with life in America but unable to lose a gut-wrenching homesickness for what had been left behind. For the second generation, American-born and regarding him quietly with the natural good manners of contented children, there were the links of heritage, but never would they know an unappeased yearning for the breath-taking beauty of a fjord-riven land.

He slept the night on the sofa and the next day took a room of his own in the neighbourhood. His cousin's cousin was a carpenter and told him where to apply for work. For six months he worked on a building site in downtown New York. Mountains had given him a head for heights and from the first day he had walked along scaffolding without a qualm. He bought himself a good suit of clothes and enjoyed himself in hours of leisure. Pretty women were attracted to him and he lacked for nothing in his personal life. It irritated him that he was frequently taken for an Englishman by the way he spoke the language with what was called an English accent. No one could be more thoroughly Norwegian than he. Nevertheless, his fluency was admired and he was invited to teach English to two Scandinavian immigrants who were finding it hard to make themselves understood. When he arrived at the place of venue, he found that six more had come along to take advantage of the opportunity. When the numbers swelled to twenty-six by the next session, he divided them into two classes on separate evenings and soon had the same number again in each. He charged them a small fee, which helped his finances, and before long he was giving lessons for five evenings of the week. Saturdays and Sundays he kept free for his own affairs.

Gradually the novelty of city life began to pall. He was a countryman at heart and he had not come to the United States to turn into a New Yorker without keeping to his resolve to see as much as possible of the country before striking roots. His brother, Jon, with whom he was in spasmodic correspondence, suggested he go out West to join up with him, but he was not yet ready to leave the East. He packed his good clothes into his travelling box and donned some practical wear, his emigrant suit long since thrown away. He said goodbye to his cousin's cousins and left the city. During the next two years he worked on farms and in forests, never staying long in any place. The wages fluctuated, sometimes little more than a pittance, but he was breathing pure air, liking the experience of new horizons, and went cheerfully about the most arduous and back-breaking tasks. Travel never cost him anything. He became expert at judging the right moment to leap a wall or break the cover of a bush as one of the great trains began to pull slowly out of a railway station, or from a coal and water halt. On reaching one of the unlocked boxcars, he would shoot back the door and throw in his travelling box before heaving himself up and aboard. Sometimes the car would be occupied already by one or more men, and although there were always the villains who had to be watched, there was on the whole a curious camaraderie among those who rode the rails. Many boxcars were padded with wads of paper and from the others he learned how these could be pulled off and used as wrappings for warmth when the weather was cold. At junctions they sometimes all jumped off and made a short camp, brewing coffee over a fire. Those with nothing begged a hand-out from local people and usually returned with something to eat or drink. Peter made sure he was never in those straits and, as a precaution against thieves, kept his money in a wallet-belt inside his shirt.

He had worked in areas of New England and Ohio before he arrived on the outskirts of Buffalo and secured employment in a large stable where horses of every type were bought and sold. His uncle in Norway had kept a pair of carriage horses for the English visitors, and a number of gentlemen had always brought their own riding horses with them, which meant there was nothing he did not know about grooming and caring for fine bloodstock. On the farms and in the forest work he had done more recently, he had dealt with big draught horses. At a stud-farm he had met up again with some of the fine shire horses that had aroused his admiration when he had first seen them on the streets and in the fields of England.

It was his good fortune that the stud groom was a gnarled old Englishman who warmed to a shared interest in the magnificent animals and was willing to pass on knowledge to a keen young stable lad. From him Peter learned the points to look for in order to judge quality of breeding in addition to working ability. Not only did these great horses have to have a commanding appearance, but the well-balanced head must be lean with a certain breadth between large, docile eyes, the ears sharp and sensitive and necks slightly arched. Shoulders were all-important, as were full-muscled hindquarters and legs with sinews like fine cords. Girth was anything up to eight feet, and the weight of a good horse varied between seventeen and eighteen hundredweight.

His knowledgeable approach to horses and his energetic attitude soon earned him promotion at the Buffalo stables. He began to accompany his employer to sales. Now and again they went to New York to meet special shipments. After deals were completed, it became Peter's responsibility to ship anything from a hundred to two hundred horses on a special Wells Fargo Pacific Express train to Nebraska and elsewhere. Before long, he was being entrusted to buy and sell on his own, earning himself commission on top of his wages.

He was representing his employer on a mission to Toronto when he emerged from the portals of the railway station and looked about him. If any one from his native land could have seen him in his well-cut suit, a heavy gold watch-chain looped across his waistcoat, and a wide-brimmed Panama hat shading his eyes from the August sun, they would have thought he had become a millionaire. Recently he had had his photograph taken for his aunt, knowing it would please her to see him looking well and prosperous. He could imagine it framed and set in a place of honour, probably beside a picture of the new King Haakon of Norway.

Remembering directions he had been given, he walked along to book in at Walker House, a hotel on the corner of Front and York streets, which had been recommended to him. His only luggage was a leather valise which he carried whenever he went on business trips. At his Buffalo lodgings his old pine travelling box, much battered by its rough journeyings, was handy for storage. He did not expect to use it again until travelling some far distance after leaving his present employment, for already he was forming plans for going into business on his own. He expected to learn a great deal about the Canadian trade in heavy horses when he attended a sale on the morrow. His employer wanted some good Percherons shipped in via Montreal from France, which meant that his own preference for English shire horses would have to be put aside.

In his hotel room he unpacked a few things before setting off to an address in Shuter Street. There he spent a long time viewing the horses for sale, making notes for reference during the auction on the morrow, and gradually making up his mind which of the horses should earn his bid. Afterwards, with time on his hands, he decided to have a look around the city which he had never visited before. Soon he found himself in the busy commercial area of Yonge Street. When he paused to look at some pens in the window of a stationers' store, he had no idea that inside a customer, waiting for her change after making a purchase, had sighted and recognised him. As he strolled on again, he did not pay any attention to footsteps running after him until his name was spoken.

"Mr. Hagen! Peter!"

He swung around in astonishment, acquainted with no one in Toronto and at a loss to suppose who might know him by name. It added to his bewilderment when he saw that the girl who had addressed him was a complete stranger as far as he could tell. Or, on second thoughts, was there something vaguely familiar about her that was striking a chord at the back of his memory? Politely he raised his hat.

"You have the advantage of me, Miss—er—?"

"Shaw. Lisa Shaw. Don't you remember me? We met at Liverpool docks when you were sailing to New York and I was bound for Canada." She smiled. It was a beautiful, happy smile that gave an additional sparkle to her fine hazel eyes. "I never had the chance to thank you for the candies you gave me for the children."

It all came back to him. He recalled his compassion for the ill-clad waif saddled with the responsibility of looking after far too many children on her own—in his opinion. Then a sour-faced woman had attacked her for talking to him. "Yes! I remember. Of course I do!" He took her hand and shook it in reunion. "What luck to meet you again, Lisa."

He meant it. She was no longer so painfully thin, and although still slender, she had filled out into soft curves of breast and hips with a narrow waist. Her hair, no longer straggling, was pinned up prettily under a hat of coarse straw, a curling tendril or two by her ears. Her dress was of cheap cotton, indicating that her circumstances had not vastly improved in the interim of their two meetings. But she was one of those fortunate girls who made anything they wore a natural enhancement of figure and grace and sexual allure.

"I was in that stationers' store," she said, half turning from the waist to indicate the location, "when I spotted you. What are you doing in Toronto?"

"It's quite a tale," he said, "and I want to know what has been happening to you. Here, let me take your parcel from you. That's better. It's too heavy for you to carry. Tell me where we can sit and talk without interruption."

Lisa thought for a moment before suggesting the Horticultural Gardens. Although Sherbourne Street flanked one side of its ten acres, Miss Drayton was back in England doing some fund-raising and collecting another consignment of children, which meant there was no danger of abuse through being seen in his company.

They found a park bench in the shade. He rested an arm behind her along the back of it as they sat down. All around them were colourful flower-beds and the air was fragrant. He inhaled deeply in appreciation.

"That scent reminds me of the Molde rose," he said nostalgically.

"What rose is that?" she asked, removing her hat and combing her fingers into her hair to lift it slightly where the crown had flattened its softness. "I've never heard of it."

He smiled. "It's a dark red bloom with a heavy fragrance that grows exclusively in a little place of a few hundred inhabitants on the south facing slopes of the Molde fjord. Town of the Roses is the name most commonly used. I know it well. It lies only a matter of miles from the valley where I was born."

"It must be a beautiful spot."

"Once seen, it can never be forgotten."

She tilted her head inquiringly. "You're not homesick, are you?"

He laughed. "No! There's too much to see and do all the time. In any case, I can say truthfully that I feel I belong to this part of the world now. My whole attitude has changed. I'm a Norwegian-American. What about you? Have you settled down?"

She considered carefully. "I miss the gentleness of an English spring, but then, nothing can surpass a Canadian autumn. I suppose I still have divided loyalties."

"Tell me about yourself, Lisa."

"Not yet." She was adamant. "You first."

He made no protest and related his adventures, describing the work he had done and mentioning the distances he had travelled. He concluded by explaining his purpose in coming to Toronto. She listened attentively, his manner of speech still enhanced for her by his Norwegian accent. Her gaze never left his face. She had thought him fine-looking when she had first set eyes on him. Now she found him truly handsome. How very relaxed he was, and how quick to smile and chuckle. It was easy to see that all was going well for him, and she would have liked to have matched his new worldliness with some poise and sophistication. But she always had to be herself, just as she was. It never occurred to her that therein lay her particular charm.

"Now it's your turn to tell me what has happened since you left Liverpool," he urged. "Where are you working?"

"I'm still at the Distribution Home. I've never left it." She described how it had all come about and said what a strange existence it was for her. She was either passing the time quietly alone in the house with Miss Lapthorne, or else she was being rushed off her feet trying to do a dozen chores at once. It did happen more frequently that there were spells when the children for direct adoption stayed much longer than they had done previously. The Canadian authorities had tightened a number of restrictions and Miss Drayton was not able to place them quite as speedily as before, which Lisa thought was all to the good. She had never seen any one of them who had left Sherbourne Street, with the single exception of Gertie Lawson, whom she sometimes glimpsed from a distance. She paused for a few moments, compressing her lips in an almost secret smile before she spoke again. "It hardly seems possible that I'm sitting here talking to you. I've wished so often that it could be."

His whole face showed pleasure. "Do you mean that you've actually thought about me sometimes?"

She almost told him about the flag she had cut out of the magazine, but decided against it. "Yes, although I never thought we should meet again."

"Maybe I find it less surprising."

"You do?"

He grinned. "It's a national trait on my part. We Norwegians are not so many in number, but wherever we go in the world we always meet a neighbour from home or someone else we know. Therefore I find it perfectly natural that you and I should find each other again."

Then suddenly it seemed natural to her, too. She realised that deep in her heart there had always been an unacknowledged conviction that their paths would cross again, however briefly. It was as if the knowledge had existed since the time of her birth that there would be one man to find and love and lose, only to find again. For it had been love that he had awakened in her on that far away dockside. She had not recognised it at the time, but she had cherished the tenderness ever since and now being with him was like a home-coming.

"Have you found the place yet where you want to strike roots?" she asked.

"Far from it," he answered firmly. "America is still my oyster. Jon, my brother, has moved from Oregon to the neighbouring state of Washington and says Norwegian settlers are everywhere there. It must be that the mountains and the forests remind them of the old country."

"Will your brother stay there, do you think?"

"No, he is still set on returning home one day to take over the family farm. He wrote in one letter that nothing gladdens him more than when he receives a lumber season's wages in golden dollars because each one is going to enrich the soil of his own land for himself and his son one day."

"How old is his boy?"

"Three. He has never seen him."

"That must be hard. And it is surely a lonely life for Jon's wife."

"Not exactly lonely. In some ways the pattern of Ingrid's life is akin to yours. She is kept extremely busy for weeks at a time and then there are lulls. She either has a houseful of my brothers to cook for or else it is just she and my father and her child at table. Then there is all the farm work she does, outside all day at harvest time and back to tranquility in wintertime with her spinning wheel and knitting needles and snow up to the windows."

"All without the man she loves."

"That is the fate of many Norwegian women whose men come solely to make their fortunes in the New World. Some wait many years for their husbands to return. Not long before I left Norway, a man from our valley returned after seventeen years away."

"Had he become a rich man?"

"No, but he had enough in his pockets to strut about and boast a great deal," Peter answered wryly.

"Shall you do that if ever you go back on a visit?" she teased.

He shook his head, amused. "No. The truly successful never boast and that's what I intend to be. Shouldn't you be thinking of breaking away from your present job?" His glance flicked admiringly over her. "With your nice appearance you could start working in a store or hotel or a restaurant where there would be a chance of promotion."

She looked down at her hands in her lap, lacing her fingers together. "I have thought about it," she admitted frankly, "but it's out of the question." Briefly she summed up everything for him. "I'm not being a martyr. Please don't think that. I just happen to believe that money isn't everything."

He had been of the same mind about money during the months after leaving New York when he had gone around taking whatever casual work came his way, but basically it had been for the sheer enjoyment of total freedom and not for any commendable purpose such as hers. She was no ordinary girl. Somehow he had known it when he had singled her out of the crowd in a teeming embarkation shed, even though his interest had been aroused out of the boredom of waiting to go on board ship and not from the far more agreeable sensation he felt now in her presence.

"Do you know many people in Toronto?" he questioned, more sharply than he had intended. He had a sudden fear that she might have a romantic entanglement that would leave no room for him.

She turned her face quickly towards him in mild surprise at his tone. "I'm acquainted with many. I belong to a youth group and a sewing circle at the church, although there is only time for those gatherings when the centre is empty as it is at the moment."

"No special beau?" he probed.

Her eyes gave her away, showing that there had been those who had aimed to monopolise her company. Still more had had ulterior motives simply because the stigma of her being a Home girl suggested she would be easy game. She had avoided all of them. That came through in her ringing reply. "No one."

He saw he had embarrassed her and sought a diversion. "Are refreshments available anywhere in these gardens?"

They strolled to the pavilion, an ornate building with much white-painted ironwork, which dominated the gardens. They sat at one of the tables on the veranda and were served ices in rose-china dishes and lemonade in frosted glasses. Already it was late afternoon. He could not bear that the time was flying past with such speed. After they had talked generally for a while, she revealed that she was also aware how the minutes were ticking away.

"Did you say you were leaving the day after tomorrow?" she asked quietly.

He reached out his hand and took hers into his, looking seriously at her. "I have no choice. Whatever horses I buy have to be shipped without delay. My employer will not tolerate extra stabling fees." There was a pause. "But we have the rest of today and tomorrow evening when the sale is over. If I'm lucky you might even come to the train and wave me goodbye!"

"I did that once before from the deck of the S.S. *Victoria,* although there was no chance that you'd see me."

"I think I knew. Anyway, I waved until your ship was out of sight."

A tremor went through her. "I don't like partings. I've had so many of them."

The pressure of his hand increased, firmly and surely. "It won't be goodbye this time. I'll come back to Toronto again to see you, if you'll let me."

Her response was eager. "Oh, yes!" Then she added on a more subdued note: "But it is a long way away."

"There will be other sales to bring me here on business and I'll get a vacation sooner or later. In the meantime, we can write to each other." He whipped out a notebook from his pocket and took down her address as she gave it to him. Then he wrote down his own before tearing out the page to hand it to her. "Now we shall never lose touch again."

She took the page and folded it away carefully into her purse. Letters were rare events in her life, although during the past few months she had received two of special significance, one from the town of Lauder in Manitoba and the other from Raymond, Alberta, a place that had been recently settled on the prairies. She had looked them up on a map.

On the strength of the contents of the letters, she had written to Mrs. Bradlaw at the old orphanage in Leeds, unable to think of anyone else to whom she could communicate on the matter. No reply had been forthcoming.

She realised she had counted too much on that brief spell of mutual respect between them. Her letter had most surely ended up in a wastepaper-basket. But in Peter Hagen she had someone at last to listen to her. Already he had shown compassionate understanding when she had explained why she did not feel able to leave the Distribution Home.

"Would you be surprised," she questioned keenly, "if I told you that Miss Drayton supplies brides to western Canada?"

He gave her a long look. "My brother has mentioned a sad shortage of women in some areas where he has been working. It would be the same on this side of the border. If the girls are willing I see no harm in such an arrangement."

"I agree with you there. While I was at the orphanage I heard about a society taking brides to Australia, but they were properly chaperoned and looked after until married to the man of their choice."

"Then where is the problem? The law these days prevents any female from being forced into a marriage."

"But officially Miss Drayton sends the girls as servants. The men out West pay her a thousand dollars each in advance as a domestic agency fee. It seems that Mrs. Grant, who is Miss Drayton's representative, delivers the girls haphazardly to whoever happens to meet the train as it crosses the prairies, or takes them direct to a given address where supposedly employment is awaiting them. If the man is refused when he proposes marriage, he is the loser on two counts, whereas Miss Drayton is always the winner, with his money safely in her grasp. The inspectors are always entirely satisfied with the records whenever they call and so on the surface at least there is nothing illegal to be pin-pointed."

"It still sounds entirely crooked to me."

"Oh, I'm so glad you share my opinion. Apart from any more serious aspect, it is entirely unethical as well. You see, funds raised in Great Britain for the Herbert Drayton Memorial Society should be divided equally between finding homes for orphans and securing good employment in a family environment for older girls. That is the published aim. All too often the older ones outnumber the younger children, except when there is a spate of infants, and even babes in arms, which is a sign to me that Miss Drayton is covering her tracks for a while."

"When did you first suspect this state of affairs?"

"I began to notice that although Toronto people came to the centre with a willingness to take an immigrant servant, which is what we had all been led to expect, there were never any girls available. They were all going to the West."

"Do you have any proof of what you believe to be happening?"

"Out of all the girls only two have ever written to me. One appreciated my forewarning her of what might lie ahead, and she had found out about the fee-paying. The second girl, named Alice, found herself alone on a prairie homestead with a brutal man who already had a wife somewhere. When the travelling threshers came for the harvest, she ran away with a thresherman. He deserted her in a small town somewhere. She was near her time with the homesteader's child and without a cent. She was begging in the streets when a covered wagon came through. A Mormon widow was on her way to make a new home in Raymond in the same province. The kind woman befriended her, tended her at the birth, and drove mother and baby with her to the new settlement. Alice has since married a Mormon herself and wanted me to know she has found happiness with a good man." Lisa paused thoughtfully. "Although she was lucky in the end, it is impossible to measure the misery and hardship that many of the other girls have surely had to endure."

He spoke bluntly. "Has it occurred to you that some might have ended up in sporting houses?"

She had not heard the expression before, but she understood its meaning. "Yes," she replied with equal frankness. "The tragedy on that score is that remarkably few of those whom Miss Drayton brings are of a wayward nature. Although occasionally there is a rough group, they are on the whole quite ordinary girls, as nervous and upset by the strangeness of everything as the young children that come to the centre."

"Do you still have the letters?"

"Not anymore. They were stolen from my drawer."

"By whom?"

"This is difficult to say. I fear there is pilfering by some girls and I lost a scarf and a blouse at the same time."

He frowned. "That's a great pity. I realise that without any proof it would be virtually impossible to instigate an official investigation. Let us hope you hear from another of the girls soon."

"I'll make sure I don't have the letter stolen from me, too." She took a glance at a clock at that point and said she had to leave.

He walked with her to the gates of the garden where she took her package of stationery from him. With all arrangements made to meet later that evening, she turned away down the street. She had covered no more than a few paces when he called after her. "Lisa!"

She turned round and stood with the package weighing down her arms, her expression inquiring. "Yes, Peter?"

His expression was intense and serious, almost threatening in the force of feeling that reached out to her. "Thank God you have never been sent away!"

Her lips parted on a sharp intake of breath. She was excited and frightened as much by the vehemence of his words as by her own reaction to them. It was as if her heart flew to him while physically she was possessed by panic. She stammered an answer. "I never will. Not now. Nobody can make me. It would only be by my own free will."

"That's what I'm counting on."

He was saying too much and saying it too soon. She had never known that exultation and fear could go hand in hand. His eyes continued to hold hers as she took a step backwards and then another in the direction she was to go. Then abruptly she broke the visual contact between them, whirling about to continue on her way.

At the house she was met by Miss Lapthorne in a tantrum at her lateness. "Where have you been, Lisa? Why weren't you back long ago?" Her tone became self-pitying. "I have been waiting for you to make me a cup of tea."

It brought home to Lisa as never before how Miss Lapthorne had come to depend on her for every little thing. Although originally her chores had been that of housemaid and cleaning servant, it had changed gradually to make her housekeeper as well. It was she who decided the grocery lists, dealt with the gardener, sorted the laundry, ordered fuel for the furnace, and saw to the rest of the household chores. Although a temporary cook came in when the house was full, since Lisa then needed all the time available to look after the new arrivals, she did the cooking for Miss Lapthorne and herself at all other times. She replied to the woman's question with one of her own, being in no mood for explanations.

"Did you want any of this stationery in your own room or is it all for Miss Drayton's shelves?"

"Put it in the study for now. It can be sorted another time."

Lisa waited while Miss Lapthorne took a bunch of keys from her pocket to unlock the study door. Lisa put the heavy package down on the desk and left it there. As the woman locked up again, Lisa went to make the tea. Putting on the kettle, she thought about the evening ahead. Although Canadian households were probably more lenient, Miss Drayton's rules were the same as those governing English abodes. Servant girls were not allowed "followers," as any prospective suitors were called. Miss Lapthorne, having discovered that Lisa showed not the slightest inclination to be "followed" had become quite lenient in Miss Drayton's absences, allowing her to attend minor social events at the church hall. There was one this evening that would cover her absence without any explanation needed. She could leave and come home again as she pleased without question. It also meant she could curtail her time with Peter whenever she wished, for if he became amorous, attempting to embrace or fondle her, she feared she would lash out at him instinctively as she had with anyone else who had mistakenly thought to take liberties. The irony of it was that inwardly she would be yearning for what she was rejecting. The past was inexorably blighting and warping her chance of a true relationship with the one man she admired more than any other.

He was waiting for her as arranged. They met with smiles, each happy to be together again.

"I'm glad you're on time," he told her. "If you had been late I would have started to fear you were being prevented from leaving the house."

"I might have been if Miss Drayton had suddenly turned up. But fortunately that didn't happen."

"Do you always know when to expect her?" he asked as they began to walk along together.

"Sometimes she doesn't bother to write to Miss Lapthorne and simply sends a wire when she lands at Halifax. On occasions we receive no advance notice at all. She believes we should always be ready for new arrivals at any time, a policy contrived to keep us on our toes. It certainly keeps Miss Lapthorne in a constant state of tension when it's about time for Miss Drayton to come again. She's like that now, as a matter of fact."

Lisa was aware of being a trifle more tense herself at that moment, although for an entirely different reason and only towards him. She was nervous in his presence as she had not been that afternoon. He did not appear to notice, but when he would have linked his fingers with hers to walk hand in hand, she withdrew hers on the pretext of adjusting the chain of her purse on her other wrist. Then she was conscious that he glanced askance at her. He did not make a second attempt, although he did support her by the elbow when they boarded a streetcar to go down to the lakeside.

He took her to dine in a restaurant overlooking the bay. For her it was the most exciting occasion, for she had never eaten in a place of any style before. Her eyes sparkled and her natural enjoyment of everything was a delightful spectacle for him. Afterwards they strolled along the planked boardwalk, and when he suggested taking a row-boat out on the bay she felt quite overwhelmed that so much could happen all in one evening.

"This is fun!" she exclaimed as he pulled strongly at the oars, drawing her out across the water that was lapping reflected lights. "The last time—indeed the only time I was ever in a boat of any kind—was on the S.S. *Victoria.* What a dreadful voyage that was!"

"Describe it to me," he said, wanting to know everything that had ever happened to her while not wishing to spoil her light-hearted mood. "In fact, I'll challenge you! My trip was much worse than yours."

She entered the game, laughing. "It couldn't have been. We had poor bedding, cramped conditions, and little ventilation."

"We were two hundred and eighty men packed like sardines in the bow."

"We were below the water-line."

"So were we—except in rough seas when the bow rose and fell like a swing, making most people seasick."

"There were rats! They ate the caramels you gave me." Her fingertips flew to her lips as if she would have held back what she had said. "Maybe I shouldn't have told you that. You spent hard-earned money to buy them."

He was entertained by her discomfiture, which he found appealing. "The rats wouldn't have eaten the food dished out to us from the galley. It was so foul that it caused a riot. Men threw it back at the cooks, broke up tables, smashed lamps and finally stormed the galley to grab what they could for themselves."

She was aghast. "You win. Is it really true?"

"Every word. But that's nothing compared with some tales I've heard of conditions aboard emigrant ships. You and I can think ourselves lucky that we fared as well as we did."

It was refreshingly cool on the lake away from the heat of the city. Lisa trailed her hand in the water now and again. Sometimes he rested on the oars as they talked, sharing thoughts, giving opinions and indulging in friendly arguments. It seemed impossible to her that the time they had spent in each other's company would still add up to less than twenty-four hours. It was as if they had known each other forever.

When they came ashore again and he had surrendered the hired row-boat, they returned at a leisurely pace to the corner of Sherbourne Street. There they faced each other in the glow of a street lamp.

"Can you meet me tomorrow evening at the same time?" he asked her.

She nodded. It had been a blissful evening. Not once had he attempted any kind of advance that would have made her shy away. He must have taken more notice of how she had withdrawn her hand than she had realised. She was grateful for it.

"I'll be here," she promised. "Good night, Peter."

"Good night, Lisa."

She reached the house and went up the porch steps. The door was always left unlocked for her when she was out, since Miss Lapthorne liked to retire early. She went indoors quickly and fastened the bolt behind her.

It was all she could do not to run to him the following evening. She thought she greeted him with restraint but her face was radiant and her eyes ashine, leaving him in no doubt that nothing would have stopped her from meeting him. Had he not been extremely busy all day the time until seeing her would have dragged tediously.

"How did the sale go?" she inquired eagerly as they fell into step. He made no attempt to take her hand.

"Very well. I bought sixteen good horses."

"Where are they now?"

"I've moved them to stables near the railway station. Now I'll tell you something that I hope you'll be glad to hear. Instead of shipping them out early tomorrow morning, I have booked their transportation on a late evening train. That means we have an extra day." He could see for himself that she was overjoyed. "How shall we spend it? Where would you like to go?"

"Let's take a picnic to the island on the lake!" she exclaimed. It was something she had always wanted to do.

"Then leave everything to me. I'll get a store to pack a basket for us." He pulled two theatre tickets from his pocket. "As for this evening. I've booked two seats for *The Pirates of Penzance.*"

She halted with such abruptness that he took another pace or two before turning on his heel in some surprise. Her hands were clasped together in her exuberance and he thought he would never get used to her enchanting response to any small treat that came her way.

"I've never been to a show, Peter," she exclaimed.

He smiled, jerking his head in the theatre's direction. "Come along then. You don't want to be late, do you?"

"No!" She broke into a run, giving him a mischievous glance as she shot past him and he had to race after her to catch her up.

In the foyer he bought her a box of chocolates trimmed with a blue satin ribbon and presented it to her when they had taken their seats. "These should make up for the caramels you lost," he teased.

She opened the box with such care that it was easy to tell it was the first she had ever received. Yet she would not make a selection for herself until he had made a choice. Then she bit into one and closed her eyes at its delicious taste. He watched her profile and found her extraordinarily beautiful. Her chin was tilted a little higher as she savoured the chocolate; her throat was white and graceful; and her lashes lay long and curling. He was gratified to be making many things happen for the first time for her. And because he was lusty and virile, capable of enormous passion, it was inevitable that his private thoughts about her became more sensual.

As the orchestra burst forth into the rousing overture, the corner of the chocolate box struck in his chest. "Have another chocolate before the curtain goes up," she whispered excitedly, popping one into his mouth. She took one more herself, put the lid carefully on the box on her lap, and turned her attention towards the rising curtain.

She was enraptured by every moment of the performance, applauding enthusiastically and consulting her programme for every detail. Afterwards when he walked her homewards she enthused over the highlights of the production. At the corner of Sherbourne Street in the lamplight they drew to a halt. "It's been an evening I'll always remember, Peter."

"We still have tomorrow to spend together."

She nodded happily. "I think I had better meet you on the steps of the library. I'm allowed to spend hours there amongst the books. Miss Lapthorne would never let me out for a whole day if she thought I was anywhere else."

It was agreed that they should meet at ten-thirty. She bade him good night and hurried away. She was about to turn the door handle when he came after her up into the shadowed porch.

"You forgot the rest of your chocolates, Lisa." He had carried the box from the theatre and held it out towards her.

"So I did." She took the box with both hands and held it upright against her chest. Like a shield. Her breathing quickened, as did her pulse. He came closer, looming dark against the street lamps, his intention clear. Her own forgetfulness had given him the opportunity to seek her lips where they could not be observed. In her head she heard the rustle of hay and the snap of a lantern being shut. She became rigid, possessed by a paralysing terror that she tried in vain to fight against, a violent shaking taking possession of her. If he touched her in her present state she would scream. Scream and never stop. She heard him gasp in dismay at her fear-distorted expression.

"Lisa!" His voice was thick with shock and outrage. "Don't look at me like that! What sort of man do you think I am? Surely you know that I of all people would never want to displease you. I love you!" He spread his hands out palm uppermost in a vigorous gesture of supplication. "Do you hear? I've fallen in love with you!"

Love. It was a word warm and golden as the sun with an extensive range that she comprehended well. She loved little children. She loved her homeland. And, vitally and overpoweringly, she loved Peter. There was no cruelty in love. No brutality. The box she was holding dropped to the porch floor, spilling its contents across the boards as she covered her face with her hands.

"There's no need to cry." He was frantic to reassure her but she appeared unable to cease her dreadful weeping. The tears came glinting through her fingers in an outpouring that had him completely at a loss. He wanted to put his arms around her protectively, but feared to make matters worse. Finally he tried persuasion. "Listen to me, Lisa. Just take your hands away from your face. You have such a beautiful face. There's no need to hide away from me. Ever." He shrugged in desperation, although she could not see. "Maybe I have spoken of love before I should have, but since I have such a short time in Toronto on this visit, I can't regret having spoken out. It is my hope and belief that there is something between us that is as important to you as it is to me. If I'm wrong then you have every cause to turn away from me. If I'm right, then look at me again as you did when we met in reunion earlier this evening."

For an inestimable time he thought that nothing he had said had had any effect. Then, to his relief, she obeyed his request, lowering her hands and raising her head, her eyes still awash with tears. She spoke in a whisper.

"I love you, too, Peter."

He drew breath. "Then all is well," he said gently. Fleetingly he had glimpsed the despair that would be his if he should lose her.

Neither made any move. Both were perfectly still as they looked into each other's eyes, softness and wonder in their locked gaze. All around them were the quiet night sounds of whispering leaves and the distant clack of hooves. Now and again there was the rumble of a distant streetcar. The porch had become their haven. Each was drowning in love for the other. It was as if they had been born for this time and this moment.

Almost imperceptibly at first she began to draw nearer until she came to where he stood. Her eyes remained open as he bent his head to meet her lips with his own, no other physical contact between them. Then as she became lost in the ensuing tenderness of his kiss, her lids drooped and she swayed against him. His arms went about her and she herself reached up to put her hands at the sides of his face. They were united in a marvellous gladness.

It was a long kiss. She supposed that he was surprised when they drew apart that she should return her lips to his almost at once to kiss again. But there was such benediction in his loving mouth, and it was wonderful to feel safe in his arms, something that had been beyond her imagining. So much dread in her had melted away. She knew she would have adored him forever for just that alone. At last she was free to begin to feel pride in her own femininity, to be a woman in love without any sense of shame or degradation. With Peter there would never be anything to fear. He had promised it and therefore she knew it to be the truth.

Her lips left his and they smiled fondly at each other. He took her hands and raised them to kiss her fingers as he held them. "Tomorrow we shall have so much to talk about, my sweet Lisa."

She sighed at having to leave him. "I must go in now."

As she took a backwards step to the door, her foot sent one of the fallen chocolates spinning away down the porch steps. She had forgotten them for the second time. Together she and Peter stooped down to gather them up from the dusty boards and tumble them back into the box. He said he would throw them into a trash-can along the street.

"I would like the ribbon from the box," she intervened quickly, the practical streak in her showing through. She knew too much about poverty to tolerate unnecessary waste. "It will look pretty on a hat."

He pulled it off and gave it to her, amused. "One day I'll buy you miles and miles of ribbons. I'll take you home on a visit to Norway and you shall have a beribboned hat for each day of the week while I take you around to meet everybody."

"And you shall show me the Molde rose!" she said quickly, pleased by the compliment he had paid her.

He put an arm about her waist and hugged her close, looking down into her joyous face. "I'll give you a whole bouquet of them."

They kissed again lingeringly. Then she slipped from his embrace and into the house.

He was on the library steps when she arrived next morning. In his hand was the strap of a picnic box which bore the name of the city's best store. When they had exchanged greetings, he asked her if she would like to see the horses he had bought, as they had plenty of time before the ferry sailed.

"Yes," she replied, interested to learn more about his trade.

He had been to the stables once already that morning to feed and water the horses. At his advice she did not enter the stalls. Any casual shift of movement by any one of the huge animals could knock her flying, for as yet they were still nervous from a constant change of surroundings during all the transportation they had endured. All were Percherons, fifteen of them black and the sixteenth a beautiful dappled grey. Peter gave them apples that he had bought on his way there, patting their necks and talking encouragingly to them.

"Aren't they beauties?" he remarked over his shoulder to Lisa as he fed the dappled grey with the last of the fruit. "The Percheron is the best heavy horse to come out of France. Its origins go back to the province of La Perche, hence the name. Black is most favoured nowadays, but this particular stallion is the colour of his ancestors. They must have looked just like him in mediaeval times when they were war-horses charging into battle with their armoured riders in the saddle."

"What a thunder of hooves there must have been!"

"You're right. Each one of these horses weighs almost a ton. I should think the ground vibrated for miles under their weight. Do you like horses, Lisa?"

"Yes, I do. But I've never had anything to do with them."

He gave a shake of his head as he left the stall. "I find it difficult to visualise a life of growing up without horses of one kind or another."

They caught the ferry with time to spare and stood by choice at the rails for the whole of the short voyage to the island; the water was full of yachts and every kind of rowing craft. They watched the five-mile spread of Toronto recede to become a city of toylike dimensions and then they were at the island. Everywhere it was lush with trees and foliage. Since this was a favourite summer resort for city-dwellers, there were any number of pretty villas with flower gardens in full bloom. They took a winding path that led them beyond the fishing boats at Hanlan's Point and came to a leafy grove with a sloping bank that went down to the water's edge. They had an unhindered view of the glittering lake with no sign of habitation.

Then, as she had anticipated, they shared their first kiss of the day. After putting down the picnic box, removing his jacket and tossing his Panama hat aside, he had held out his arms to her, letting her come freely to him in her own time and at her own will. There was a new development in his kissing, the first thrust of passion that he had restrained the previous evening, and although briefly her eyes fluttered open on a start of the old panic, the second of fear passed as swiftly as it had come. This was Peter, whose strong and tender hands were stroking her back as he held her close. And it was his mouth, and no one else's, that was becoming bolder, loving all of hers in a manner that stirred and excited her quite deliriously.

They wandered for a little while hand in hand along the water's edge before the undergrowth became thick and they turned to retrace their steps at the same leisurely pace. He outlined for her his hopes of eventually opening stables of his own, not only for buying and selling, but for breeding as well. He explained that in the shire horses there were clear distinctions, such as the Suffolk Punch, the Clydesdale, the Shire itself, which through its fame had given its name to heavy horses generally, and the French Percheron, which he also admired as she knew. All those soundly bred had a courageous spirit and a will to work that made them greatly sought after in the western states of America as they were in the parallel provinces of Canada.

"There is an insatiable demand for heavy horses. They are the pivot around which whole economies turn, not only in farming and the timber trade, but in the rapid building of the railways that is going on everywhere. There are fortunes to be made by men known to be reliable dealers with good horses in regular supply. I intend to move into the field on my own at the first chance I get." His attitude was one of serious determination.

"When will that be?" she asked.

"A trifle longer than I would wish, now that I have met you. I should have followed my brother's example as soon as I reached New York." He released a regretful sigh.

"What do you mean?"

"Jon has saved every cent since he landed in the States. I've spent freely thinking I had no one to think about except myself with all the time in the world to do whatever I wanted. You've changed all that."

She spoke quietly. "Since yesterday?"

"I believe it was the day before that. I look back to the moment when I heard my name spoken and I turned around to see the girl who was to change my life." He came to a standstill and took her by the shoulders to turn her towards him. "You know what I'm saying, don't you? I have nothing to offer you yet, but if you will be patient and bear with me, all that will change."

She understood him so well. For herself, she would have tramped beside him along the roads between horse sales if it had been deemed necessary, wanting only to belong to him. He could not hold that attitude. Although he did not realise it, he was still steeped in the heritage and tradition of his homeland where a man who married must be the provider and protector in every sense of the word. His male ego would not tolerate anything less. Her love outpoured for him without question or criticism.

"I'm a patient person," she said softly.

"My darling Lisa."

They put their arms about each other and kissed. Still linked, they resumed their returning stroll at the water's edge until they came back to the glade. There they sat down to enjoy their picnic under the trees. The box included a check cotton cloth which she spread out before unpacking the food. He watched her, leaning his back against a tree trunk, his long legs stretched out before him and crossed at the ankles, thumbs hooked in his waistcoat pockets. There had been times before when with the brashness of youth he had imagined himself to be in love. More recently, liking and affection had enhanced certain sexual encounters, but love as he knew it now had not come into his life before. He loved Lisa with a force and a possessiveness that made his head reel. Any cynicism he might have nurtured in the past had melted away completely in the revelation of what love really meant.

She had removed her hat, and the sun, dappling through the foliage, played across the sheen of her hair. He intended that before the day was over he would see it hanging free, drifting across her full breasts which moved so enticingly under the thin muslin of her dress as she set out the picnic. At times he could just discern the nipples and could imagine how embarrassed she would be to know their shape was being revealed through whatever stout camisole top kept their beauty hidden from direct sight.

Her modesty intrigued him. He had not minded being kept at a distance at first. It was what any man expected of a respectable girl, no matter how much he might try to undermine her resistance later. If he had not been compelled to leave Toronto so soon, he would not have followed her up onto the porch last night, but would have waited through a due number of meetings until proprieties permitted the first advance. He had truly expected her to see the situation in the same light. Her terrified expression had stopped him in his tracks. If she had not talked to him previously in an open manner about the possible fate of the pauper girls sent westwards, he would have thought her one of those innocents who imagined the sharing of a kiss could induce pregnancy. Instead, he realised it was an excessive shyness combined with a personal modesty. To her a first kiss amounted to a violation of all she had screened around her own femininity. It was no wonder she had reacted with tears at the prospect. The fact that she had overcome what must have been a long held retreat, to kiss him of her own volition, was an intoxicating measure of her feelings for him. As if that were not marvel enough, there was the certainty that when he had won her truly he would discover depths of passion in her that would make their marriage bed a place of joy throughout all their lives together. He felt intoxicated by love.

"The picnic is ready," she announced, sitting back on her heels. "What a spread!"

When they had eaten, she refused to let him help her pack up the remains, wanting to do it on her own. He lay full length on the grass, well content, and closed his eyes. When everything was tidied away, she looked at him and smiled that he slept.

He did doze, but only for a minute or two. Lifting his head he saw Lisa sitting on a rock down by the lake. She was peeling down her black stockings, one leg already bare, and when her toes were free she swung both feet into the water and splashed lightly. He raised himself on one elbow. From the shadows where he lay he thought he had never seen a lovelier sight than Lisa there against the diamond sparkles of the lake beyond.

She was singing softly to herself as she came back up the bank, her stockings trailing from her hand. When she saw he was no longer asleep she coloured shyly, and hesitated for a moment or two before coming to sit down on the grass beside him. Her hat lay nearby and she thrust her stockings out of sight under the crown of it. He smiled to himself. Did she imagine he had never seen a pair of discarded stockings before?

"The water was colder than I had expected," she said, as if to explain why she had left her toes bare to the warm sun as she smoothed her skirt hem over her ankles.

"It's deep there by the rocks." He sat up and rested an arm on an updrawn knee. "Lisa."

"Yes?" She did not look at him, her lips parting slightly as she drew in a breath at the intimate tone of his voice.

"Release your hair from its pins."

"Why?" A whisper.

"I want to see you as no other man has seen you."

Slowly she put up her hands to begin drawing out the pins and setting them in a little pile on her hat brim where they would not get lost in the grass. The guilelessness of her actions, which he had seen performed in wantonness by other women many times, emphasised the virginal look about her that he longed to dispel in an awakening. Her hair, soft and shining as pale yellow silk, slipped free to swing down around her face and to cover the length of her spine. When he made no move, she turned her head to meet his eyes. She had never thought to see such amorous worship in any man's looking. She felt herself melt.

He leaned over and bore her down onto the grass, their limbs alongside. His mouth was on hers in kissing that blotted out the trees and the sun and everything else beyond their embrace of each other, for she clung to him as if to hold forever this last hour before they had to leave the island.

She did not know how or when he managed to unfasten the

buttons down the front of her bodice but when his lips, having covered her face and throat with light and loving kisses, began to move downwards, she saw that her camisole top was also loosened, revealing half curves of her breasts, the aureoles of her nipples just visible.

She had thought the past completely banished, but it was all she could do not to follow an instinct to cover herself. It made her realise that each stage in love-making must be met anew until all the shadows were gone. Peter's caressing touch as he cupped one breast and then the other to kiss the nipples with lips and tongue made her catch her breath erotically at such sensual delight. She murmured loving words to him, burying her fingers convulsively in his thick hair and then letting them trail down the back of his neck to reach his shoulders with a sweet restlessness. She was filled with a delicious sensation, all else lost beyond the realm of loving and being loved. When he made a bracelet of his hand about her bare ankle to travel slowly and exploringly upwards, taking her skirt in folds about his wrist, she lay still in utter bliss until his stroking, amorous touch was on her thigh. Then suddenly she was afraid. Involuntarily she gave a great start, jerking herself away from him, and covered her face in the crook of her arm.

It was a measure of his wish to cherish and care for her that enabled him, against his own highly roused personal desires, to pull her skirt down into place again. Moving up on his elbow, he leaned over to bring his face above hers. Gently he took her arm away and looked down at her with tenderness and reassurance.

"I'm not hastening you into anything, my darling Lisa," he said softly. "You're more beautiful than you could ever realise, and I'm half out of my head with love for you. But don't be afraid of me." His fingertips brushed some curling tendrils away from her eyes. "I'd never hurt you or go against your wishes. You're everything to me."

She sat up and put her arms lightly about him, her trembling still of such violence that it passed through her into him. "I'm not frightened of you, truly I'm not," she insisted, leaning forward to press her cheek briefly against his in emphasis. Then she looked downwards and spoke falteringly. "There are other fears."

He thought he understood. "I'm not irresponsible. You can trust me to take precautions against that outcome."

"It's not what you're thinking. I do trust you. Completely. It is old fears from England that are troubling me and have nothing to do with us." Her eyes searched his. "I love you. I want to belong to you, but I need more time."

"Is that why you shrank from me last night when I came onto the porch to kiss you?"

She nodded. "I'd never been kissed with love before."

His eyes smiled at her. "I did guess that. Then what are these fears? Maybe if we discussed them together, you could put them away and forget them forever."

She shook her head quickly, not altogether sure how she had been drawn into this conversation and wishing to end it. "Let's pretend I never mentioned them."

He was not to be brushed aside and became lovingly and endearingly persuasive to her. "If we do, they'll always be there between us. Come, my sweet, tell me. Let's set the pattern of our future, always able to talk and open our hearts to each other."

He thought he was to hear of ill treatment at the orphanage. She had related enough of events throughout her days there for him to gather that she had had a cheerless childhood, and he knew how difficult it was for those persistently shut out to accept affection spontaneously in later life. Never once did he expect to hear anything of a sexual nature. Encouragingly, he enfolded her in his arms, drawing her to lean against him with her head resting on his shoulder. For a few moments she closed her eyes, savouring his nearness and the feeling of being cosseted and protected against all things. Then she began to recount how she had run away and everything that had been entailed until she came, shudderingly, to the assault upon her, giving minimum details, but enough to convey the horror she had endured. Her heart became marvellously light after all was said. She nestled closer to him, knowing that through his listening he had swept away the last barrier between them.

There was a silence. Then he spoke harshly. "Payment for your supper, was it?"

She felt her blood freeze. Drawing back, she looked into his face which had a strained, angry expression. "What do you mean?"

"It's obvious. You were hungry and the farmer's son arranged that you should have food in return for a certain favour in the barn."

"No!" She sprang to her feet, clutching her bodice together.

He looked up at her in torment. "I'm not blaming you. It must be terrible to be nigh to starving."

"But I wasn't starving. Not then. I had a piece of bread and cheese that I'd bought with some money a gentleman gave me." She saw his eyes narrow and cried out defensively: "I opened a gate for him, that's all!"

His elbows were resting on his updrawn knees and he dropped his head into his hands, his shoulders slumped. "I don't doubt you," he said with desolate bitterness. "I'm speaking out of my own jealousy."

He was consumed by it. Its effect was all the more devastating because it was something he had never experienced before. The thought of another man laying hands on her nakedness and possessing her was a knife blow he did not know how to survive. Everything about her had led him to believe she was physically innocent, the kind of girl he had always expected to marry. The worldliness and broadmindedness that had come to him through his travels and new environs, fell away from him like a cloak. He had reverted completely to his early prejudices. His background, his upbringing, and his culture had instilled in him the rule that any self-respecting man chose a virgin to be his bride. How else could the steadfastness of his home and the health and well-being of his children be ensured? The conviction was linked to the importance of heirs and the entailing of land over many generations and, although in his case it had no immediate relevance, he was powerless to go against his conditioning in his present, seething state. Logic and reason had been swept away by her shattering disclosure.

She was watching him in an agony of apprehension. "There's

no need to be jealous," she cried out, her mouth tremulous, her throat tight. "It was hateful and loathsome. I thought I should never be able to face marriage. You changed everything for me."

He believed her. The trouble was that believing her made no difference. He loved her too much, which paradoxically made it impossible for him to remove the blame from her for having allowed the circumstances to come about in the first place. Rising to his feet, he gave vent to retaliation out of his own raging jealousy. "I can't say I noticed it. You lay shaking on the grass as if inviting rape. How do I know it was not like that before?"

Anger gushed through her. With a cry of outrage she struck him hard across the face. His head snapped back after the stinging impact and his eyes were flinty in his temper at her action. Her bodice had fallen once more into disarray and the almost unbearable beauty of her breasts was revealed again to him. Stunned by what she had done, she placed her spread fingers lightly over her parted lips and took a step backwards, to stand drained of rage and touchingly forlorn, forgetful of her half-nakedness.

He reached for his jacket, which earlier he had suspended from a branch, and put it on. "You had better tidy yourself," he advised without expression, his lips thin and a pulse leaping in his temple. "It's time to leave."

She turned away to fasten her buttons, unable to see them for the tears that had begun to cloud her vision. Her stockings were twisted as she pulled them on, but nothing seemed to matter anymore. When she had pinned up her hair and secured her hat, she turned to see him looking out towards the lake, his back towards her, the empty picnic box under his arm.

They walked in silence. He tossed the box into a trash-basket before they went on board the ferry. As before they stood at the rails. She saw nothing. Now that they had lapsed into silence, neither of them could find a way out of it. The gulf between them was getting wider and wider.

They stepped from the ferry back into the noisy bustle of Toronto's early evening. Originally they had both assumed that she would wait while he took the horses on board and afterwards they would have the last minutes together before he sailed. That was now out of the question. Neither wished to prolong their mutual anguish.

"Goodbye, Peter," she managed to say unfalteringly with her chin high, although to add anything else was beyond her.

"Goodbye, Lisa." His face had a white look and his cheeks were hollowed.

She turned quickly and hurried away, her spine and shoulders very straight. He wished he could have called her back, but the fit of choking temper that had immobilised his vocal cords all the way from the glade continued to throttle him and brought a new anger.

One by one he led the horses aboard the waiting train. Some gave him a little trouble, but he soothed and patted them as he urged them forward and eventually all sixteen were safely in their places in readiness for the journey to Buffalo. He took his watch from his pocket. Five minutes left before departure time.

He prowled restlessly about the platform. Beyond the railway station Toronto was a city of lights beneath the stars. He lit a cheroot, smoked it for half a minute and then threw it down to crush it underfoot. Lisa, Lisa, Lisa. Her name rang through his brain, his jealousy unabated, but his fury fast subsiding.

"All aboard!"

He hesitated. In a flash of enlightenment he knew that to step aboard the train was the last thing he wanted to do. How could he ever have thought of leaving Lisa? Why had he let her go from him in anger and with words that should never have been said. The foolhardiness of what he had done began to sink in with an awful finality, the pain of loss driving him back to reason. Through petty jealousy, the basest of human emotions, he had turned away from the only girl he had loved or ever wanted to love. He must have been mad! His selfish disappointment had been such that he had failed to see how much greater was her anguish. He had encouraged her to disclose her secret and then rejected her through his own crass stupidity.

He saw then that if they had had more time together without the imminence of his departure, their lovers' quarrel could have been resolved. God! What a fool he had been. He couldn't live without her. He thought of everything he loved about her. Her liveliness, her beauty, her courage and her unaffected joy in all the fun they had shared. She had looked to him to erase through love the darkness of the past for her and he had failed her.

The train was ready for departure. All doors were slamming. For a moment he was prepared to let it go without him but he could not desert the horses. There would be no one else to look after them throughout the long journey. With reluctance he boarded the train, deciding he would send Lisa a wire from Buffalo. Then as the wheels began to turn common sense prevailed. He queried how he could convey the regret that assailed him for all he had said to her or tell her of his longing for her to put her arms around his neck and show her forgiveness. For he was sure she would forgive him. With her warm and generous nature she would accept his apology and never hold back from him what he wanted to hear from her. She would wipe out the terrible quarrel that was of his instigation, knowing that the like of it would never occur again.

He knew what he would do. As soon as he reached Buffalo and had delivered the horses, he would return to her. If time off was refused by his employer, he would quit the job. Nothing was going to stop his reunion with Lisa. When all was well between them again, he would ask her to share his somewhat uncertain future, for he would not risk losing her a second time while he gathered some money into his bank balance, which had been his original intention before asking her to marry him. With what he knew of her character, she would not mind facing hardships at his side. One day he would buy her silk dresses and a shining new automobile to ride in, and in the meantime they would get along somehow. The train was gathering speed. The last lights of Toronto twinkled out of sight like a dying spark.

Lisa rose from the seat in the railway station where she had been sitting. Right up until the last minute she had hoped that Peter would realise she would not go far from him all the time there was still a chance that he might find a way back to her. She loved him. Nothing had changed that and, strangely, she understood that it was the depth of his feelings for her that had created the awful impasse. If he had not loved her, he would not have cared about any previous incidents in her life. That was why she had hoped right up to the last minute that he would come looking for her and rush her onto the train with him. It had proved to be a foolish dream. Yet she would have gone anywhere with him. Anywhere at all.

Five

When Lisa entered the house she saw that Miss Drayton's study door was open. In the room the desk was a litter of papers and entry books as if Miss Lapthorne had been turning out everything, the drawers left open. Lisa, who had expected to be met by a reproach and was not sure how she would endure an upbraiding for lateness in the depth of her own sorrow, decided she had better find out what was happening.

There was no sign of Miss Lapthorne anywhere downstairs. Upstairs she found her lying drunk across the bed, an emptied brandy bottle and a fallen glass on the floor. Lisa removed the woman's shoes, put a quilt over her, and left her for the night.

Lisa found it impossible to sleep herself. She had learned a bitter lesson. There were some secrets that should never be told, although if Peter had carried through his obvious intention to make love to her, he would have known anyway that she was not as he had supposed her to be. His reaction would have been the same.

Through the night hours she sat up in bed, hugging her knees through her nightgown, and rocking sometimes in her misery. Maybe it would have been better if he had found out that way. At least for a brief, halcyon time she would have known his love and his loving body, a memory to cherish and hold, no matter what came afterwards.

By dawn she was up and dressed again. She set about her house-cleaning chores, cast down by her own listlessness. Normally she went vigorously about her tasks, but today everything was a burden. Her thoughts dwelt on Peter all the time and there was a drumming awareness in her of a new yearning he had created that made her ache for his arms and his nearness. She had glimpsed how it might have been between them and it made the agony of losing him all the greater. For the first time she began to suspect how passionate she might have become in meeting his love-making if only everything had not gone awry.

At the study door she hesitated. She was never in there alone. Miss Lapthorne unlocked it and remained in the room while she swept and polished, but with Miss Drayton due back in Toronto any day, it would not do for dust to be lying there when she arrived. Entering, Lisa set about her work. When it was done, she looked at the desk. Usually that was dusted, too. It would be impossible to attempt to sort the papers, which were no concern of hers anyway, but at least she could shut the drawers and polish all around it.

She had given a good shine to most of the carved woodwork and was about to push in the last drawer when she caught sight of her own name on a postmarked letter in it. She recognised Alice's writing, and it had been posted in Raymond over two months ago, which was shortly after Miss Drayton had last left for England. That meant that Miss Lapthorne had kept and concealed it.

With a rush of anger, Lisa picked out the letter and saw that there was another addressed to her underneath it. And another below that. All three were unopened, but that was no commendation. It was obvious that they were being kept for Miss Drayton's perusal and censure and her ultimate destruction of them. It certainly explained to Lisa why correspondence had been so sparse over the years. The post was caught in a closed box when it came through the door. It could only be unlocked by a key that Miss Lapthorne kept on a ring. Lisa had never considered this to be unusual, for it had been the same at the orphanage, and she understood that in many strict households the husband kept the key in order to keep check on whatever mail came aimed for his sons and daughters. On the two occasions when she had been handed a letter by Miss Lapthorne, it was when she had happened to be working close at hand, and no doubt the woman was not going to risk her having glimpsed her name. No wonder they had vanished again from her drawer afterwards. She had been wrong to think it was anyone other than Miss Lapthorne who had removed them.

Footsteps were shuffling down the stairs. Lisa went to lean against the desk and face the door with the three letters displayed in her hand in a fan shape. Miss Lapthorne, appearing in a silk kimono and slippers, was already so pale and sickly-looking that her reaction at seeing the discovered letters made little difference to her haggard expression.

"Oh dear," she said weakly, sitting down in the nearest chair. "I have always been afraid you'd find out one day." She peered in disbelief at the desk. "Did I really leave everything in such a mess? I couldn't remember whether or not I had locked up again, which is why I came straight down here."

Lisa shook the letters angrily. "Why did you withhold my mail?"

Miss Lapthorne pressed fingertips to her throbbing temples. "I was only obeying rules. Miss Drayton discourages correspondence for her girls' own good. If one wrote of discontent it could upset others unnecessarily."

"Particularly if they should write of being sent out West primarily as brides, having had no previous notification! Some of the girls are only fourteen and fifteen!"

Miss Lapthorne clapped her hands over her ears. "Mrs. Grant is entrusted to put the younger ones with families."

"You have no proof that she does that," Lisa retorted.

"Don't let us talk about it any more now," the woman implored. "My head is splitting in twain. Please fetch me a nice cup of tea and one of my headache pills."

While Lisa was waiting for the kettle to boil she opened her letters. Alice wrote that she was expecting a second child and was full of praise for her husband who cared for her first-born as if the boy were his own. The other two letters were from young women whom she had never met, both having passed through the Distribution Home a long time before she had come to Canada. Each had been given her name by a former companion of hers from the Leeds orphanage, who had heard indirectly that she was still at Sherbourne Street. The girl in question was Teresa Dutton, with whom Lisa had grown up and whom she had always liked, although they had never been close friends. She recalled that Teresa had been the only one to give her a helping hand with the young children in organising games on the ship's deck, and more than once on the train journey had taken over in keeping them amused to give her a rest. From the letters it appeared that Teresa was now living in Calgary, Alberta, and since both correspondents travelled a great deal she had offered her address and would forward Lisa's replies on to them. Both young women, although they had probably conferred, had written independently to put the same request to Lisa. As their letters to Miss Drayton and Miss Lapthorne had gone unanswered, they wanted to know if she had access to the files and could give them any guide at all to the present whereabouts of their sisters, from whom they had been parted through the Herbert Drayton Memorial Society. The names were enclosed, and each writer, in spite of the poor writing and ill spelling, conveyed a desperate longing to find her own kin again. One was a twin, and it was easy to discern that the cruel separation had left a scar.

Lisa carried the tea and the headache pills into the study. Miss Lapthorne was seated at the desk, making an effort to tidy up the papers into order and put them away. As she closed an entry book to lift it from the desk, Lisa startled her by slamming a hand down on it and holding it under pressure.

"How far does that book go back, Miss Lapthorne?" she demanded furiously. "Ten years? Twelve? Does it record where Miss Drayton sent a twin named Esther Hastings or the whereabouts of the five Hamilton sisters ruthlessly separated from the eldest, who still seeks for news of them?"

The woman groaned faintly in exasperation and made a dismissive gesture. "Is that what your letters were about? Silly girls bother us sometimes with inquiries about their families, wanting to know if their parents are still alive or if we know where their brothers and sisters are to be found and so forth. Often those placed in this country by other charities write to us—grown women with children of their own—all with this mad desire to trace kith and kin."

"I consider it perfectly natural."

"Do you?" It was said with sarcasm. "Your opinion is not rated very highly in this house. Every Home child is given a new chance in life in this country and hankering for past associations is not to be encouraged. Letters of that kind are thrown away." She reached out for her tea, which was on the desk, but Lisa stayed her wrist, determined to see this issue through.

"I think it is simply that your records don't go beyond the first week or two of any foundling's placement. On paper, Mrs. Grant's check-list looks excellent to the inspector, but neither you nor Miss Drayton have ever seen for yourselves whether things are well with the waifs and strays you've scattered indiscriminately throughout the land. That's why you're always in such a state of anxiety whenever he comes. You're afraid that one day he might pounce on some small point you've overlooked."

"How dare you!" Miss Lapthorne's flurry of outrage was short-lived for her head ached too much. As Lisa released her wrist, she put a limp hand to her brow. "I have enough to think about without you becoming obstreperous, Lisa. Worse still are these delusions about the integrity of your benefactresses, because I include myself in that category with Miss Drayton. If it had not been for me, you would have left here long ago, as I have mentioned on many occasions, and now it seems we are all to move West together."

"Move? What do you mean?"

"I mean that I had a wire from Halifax yesterday in your absence. Miss Drayton sent it upon disembarking there. I'm to have papers and books packed up together. She thinks that in future the Distribution Home should be in Regina, Saskatchewan, where she owns some property. That is prairie country, you know. Very different from anything you have seen so far." She took up her tea at last and drank it thankfully as if it were a restorative. "You shall continue to be my assistant, Lisa. I'm prepared to overlook your impertinence to me."

Lisa decided, not for the first time, that Miss Lapthorne was quite impossible. "Do you want to leave Toronto?" she asked her, greatly taken aback herself by the prospect.

The woman lowered her teacup. "Upheavals of any kind disturb me," she admitted carefully, in the pretence that her listener was not aware of it. "I was quite distraught yesterday when I received the wire and you were not here to run errands on my behalf, such as telegraphing Mrs. Grant from the post office and so forth." Then her whole face softened on inner thoughts and she spoke tremulously and sentimentally. "But I go wherever my dear friend, Miss Drayton, goes. I left England to come to Canada with her. It is a much smaller step in every way now to go from Toronto to Regina. Home is where the heart is, Lisa."

"I'm sure you're right," Lisa agreed quietly, thinking in terms of an entirely different relationship.

Miss Lapthorne had found sufficient stimulation in the tea to start issuing orders. "Now as much as possible in the way of preparations to leave must be done. Get your belongings packed in readiness. Afterwards pack mine into a large trunk you will find under the stairs. It's not seen the light of day since I first arrived in this country fifteen years ago. I expect it will be dusty."

Upstairs, Lisa crossed the floor of her little room to hold back the lace drapes at the window and look out. She could see as far as the corner where Peter had waited for her. It was as well that she was leaving Toronto, for otherwise memories of those three wonderful days would meet her everywhere, and the like of them would never come again. The lace became crumpled in her grasp as she covered her face briefly, fighting back the anguish that kept engulfing her.

It did not take her long to pack her possessions into a tapestry valise she had made herself during one session of church sewing evenings. Last of all she took the cut-out Norwegian flag from the frame on the wall and tucked it into a book of poems which she placed on a folded piece of tissue paper that held the blue satin ribbon from the chocolate box.

Miss Drayton arrived the next day. As always prior to her arrival, when known, Miss Lapthorne was almost beside herself with excitement, going constantly to the window to look down the street and fussing over the final preparations. In the early days she had gone running down the porch steps to welcome her friend before the hackney cab had drawn to a halt, but Miss Drayton had put a stop to that, saying it was unseemly and undignified. Now it was with carefully maintained restraint that Miss Lapthorne moved out onto the porch after Lisa had opened the front door as the usual cavalcade of hackney cabs from the railway station drew up outside.

It was easy to see at once that Miss Drayton was in a savage mood. She barely tolerated Miss Lapthorne's fond kiss and gave her quite a forceful thrust in the direction of the thirty girls alighting from the cabs.

"Get those creatures settled in as quickly as you can, Mavis. Then come to me at once. There is much to talk about and arrange." She stalked into the house. It was rare for her to give as much as a glance at Lisa, and today was no exception.

Miss Lapthorne saw the girls up to the attic rooms, explaining they would only be there overnight and left them to Lisa's charge. They were from workhouses and institutions in south London, and were friendly and eager to talk to Lisa as the groups usually were. It always came as a relief to them to find someone young in the house to whom they could put their questions. The buzz of chatter continued down the stairs as she led them to a prepared meal in the kitchen.

Emily Drayton was lying against satin cushions on the chaise longue in her bedroom when Miss Lapthorne arrived bearing a silver tray of light refreshments daintily arranged. She ignored her deputy's chatter as the tray was set into place on a low table at her right hand. It was the usual flow of delight that she was back again, the expressed concern that she should get adequate rest after the journey and all the unnecessary fussing that occurred on these occasions. When they had been young their relationship had been pleasing to Emily Drayton, but those feelings were long since gone, although Mavis was too stupid and too devoted to realise it.

"Sit down, for mercy's sake, Mavis," Emily Drayton exclaimed in exasperation. "My cushions are perfectly comfortable and do not need rearranging. There is scarcely time as it is for all that has to be said and done. First of all I have to tell you what happened while I was in England."

Miss Lapthorne sat down quickly in the nearest chair facing her. "Yes, Emily dear. I'm listening."

There followed a disturbing account to the sympathetic ears of the listener of an official investigation into the financial affairs of the Herbert Drayton Memorial Society. It had been an embarrassing ordeal, which Emily Drayton thought she had countered to a certain extent, but it was clear to her that she was by no means out of the woods. The inquiry had been instigated by Mrs. Bradlaw of Leeds and persons unknown. "I say unknown, but I have reason to believe that some of the information came from this very house."

For one panic-stricken moment Miss Lapthorne thought she was being falsely accused. "No! I took an oath on the Bible that I would never reveal anything of our affairs, business or otherwise, to the outside world!"

"I do not mean you," Emily Drayton snapped, almost at the end of her tether. "I suspect Lisa Shaw."

Miss Lapthorne caught her breath. She had never revealed to Emily that she had broken the Home's rule about giving no incoming mail to any girl in her charge, but she had not been quite sober on those occasions. Afterwards, she had filched the letters back again. It would never do in the present circumstances to let Emily know that only the day before Lisa had claimed three letters that were rightfully hers. At all costs the girl must be persuaded to keep quiet about them. "You are linking Lisa with Leeds, I suppose?" she questioned cautiously.

"Yes. Not that the Bradlaw woman had any time for the girl. I could see that. It is far more likely that one of the other Leeds girls wrote to her and she started stirring up trouble for me as a result of it." She frowned uncertainly. "Yet I usually have an instinct for these matters."

"Are you going to question Lisa?" Miss Lapthorne was on tenterhooks.

"Certainly not. Do you ever use your intelligence? If Lisa is the culprit, having received messages or communications of which you have been unaware, the last thing I want is for her to write about being cross-examined by me."

"You're right, of course."

"My main concern at the moment is not the cause of my present difficulties, but the cure. What has happened means I must make an entirely new beginning. At any time now news of the inquiry in England could leak through to local authorities here in Toronto, which is why it is essential to move swiftly. I have found loopholes before in conditions laid down for the placing of children in this country, and I shall find them again, but I need time to rethink and reorganise without officials breathing down my neck. A short sojourn in the United States should give me time to regather my strength and replenish my fortitude."

"I'll do anything I can to help."

Emily Drayton did not look impressed by this offer. She continued speaking as if it had not been made. "Apart from the inquiry, I had to contend with the most accusative letter sent to me in England from a minister in some far-flung corner of Ontario. It is certainly true that troubles never come singly. Why I bother myself with the welfare of others for so little reward I do not know."

"What sort of trouble was this?"

"It was about a bad home. One of two children placed there through the society had died. I had to write to Mrs. Grant about the matter and I can trust her to have the affair in hand. When is she due to arrive?"

"Early tomorrow morning."

"Good. That means we can all be out of here by noon. Mrs. Grant has used my property in Regina as a subsidiary Distribution Home for a long time. When my new arrangements are finally completed, it will become my headquarters."

"What will happen to this house?"

"I shall close it up. It will come to no harm. In a few years' time, when everything has died down, it would be pleasant to take up residence here permanently. I have always liked this house."

"So have I," Miss Lapthorne enthused, glancing appreciatively about her and thinking contentedly towards the day when she and her dear friend could drift towards old age together without any outside harassment. A thought struck her. "What is to become of Lisa? If you suspect her of tittle-tattle, she can no longer be my assistant."

"She will be placed somewhere by Mrs. Grant, but in the meantime keep quiet about that. I want her safely on the train out of Toronto without any unnecessary nonsense."

"An excellent idea." Miss Lapthorne could not get rid of Lisa fast enough. She completely forgot her liking for the girl and the many times she had been grateful for the competent management of the house. It should be easy enough in the short time that was left to prevent Lisa from blurting out to Emily anything about the letters, or making demands as to the whereabouts of the sisters of the correspondents that had communicated with her. Once Lisa was on the train for the West and Emily bound for the United States, everything would be over and done with.

That night Lisa heard the basement door open and close several times. She went to investigate. Looking over the bannisters, she saw Miss Drayton and Miss Lapthorne feeding papers and entry books and ledgers into the basement furnace, which was roaring away as it turned everything into ashes.

Long before noon the next day the house was shuttered and ready for being closed up. The carter came to transport luggage to the railway station, and Miss Drayton's trunks and boxes were piled high. Lisa and the other girls were to take charge of their own small items of baggage.

Mrs. Grant had arrived early. She was immediately closeted on her own with Miss Drayton in business talk. Miss Lapthorne was thoroughly put out by not being included and went about the many things there were to do with two high spots of colour in her cheeks. She tried to console herself with the thought that they were probably sorting out the trouble that had been made by the Ontario minister, but as her friend's deputy she felt she should at least be present at any business conferences.

Mrs. Grant emerged from the study and took a glance at the gold watch she wore on a chain around her neck. "The hackney cabs should be arriving in two minutes' time," she said to Lisa, who as senior Home girl was to share the responsibility in looking after the group. "Get the girls out on the lawn to wait. We want no delays."

It had been arranged that the Home party should be transported away from the house in plenty of time for Miss Drayton and Miss Lapthorne to complete the locking of doors and make a last-minute inspection of the property before leaving in a cab. When Lisa and Mrs. Grant had seen the girls into the vehicles, they took seats themselves. Lisa did not look back at the house as the cab moved away. It had been a place of heartbreak, not only for herself but, in another sphere, for many of the frightened, lonely, and homesick children that had passed through it.

Both Miss Drayton and Miss Lapthorne had been too busy making final checks for security to see the hackney cabs leave. They met in the hall, the open door giving the only light into the house.

"Do I have all the keys?" Miss Drayton asked.

"Yes." Miss Lapthorne knew her reply to be a white lie. Once she had lost a front door key and had two recut, one being on the ring of keys in her friend's hand, the other reposing in her purse as a sentimental keepsake towards the day when the two of them would return to make this house their home together.

"Then go ahead," Miss Drayton said. "I will close the vestibule door and then lock the front door after me."

Miss Lapthorne emerged into the sunshine and waited on the porch steps. She thought it fitting that the two of them should descend side by side. At the kerb two hackney cabs waited, and she tut-tutted to herself that there had been a mix-up, causing two to be sent instead of one. Then with some surprise, she saw her solitary trunk was loaded onto the cab standing to the rear of the other and wondered why the carter had not taken it with the rest of the baggage. She turned as her friend withdrew the key from the locked front door and something about Emily

Drayton's whole demeanour suddenly struck a warning knell as nothing else had done.

"This is farewell then, Mavis."

"What did you say?" Miss Lapthorne stammered. Her heart had taken a lunge and was beginning to pound terribly in alarm. "We're travelling to the railway station together, aren't we?"

Emily Drayton dropped the ring of keys into her purse. "I had no idea what your plans would be, hence the two cabs."

"But am I not to go to Regina?"

The reply came coldly. "Did I ever mention that you were? Mrs. Grant has always been in charge there. I simply have no need for two deputies."

Miss Lapthorne's whole face was working. Her twitching lips seemed barely able to form the words she spoke. "How could you play such a cruel joke on me? I don't think it's amusing."

"I am not in the habit of joking about anything. You should know that. You know also that my policy has always been for the quick, clean break when separating two people from each other. Thus it is only to be expected that I should apply the same method to our parting." Emily Drayton dived her hand into her still open purse and drew out a thick envelope, which she pressed into the other woman's nerveless fingers. "You will find a handsome financial gift enclosed, Mavis. It will recompense you for any temporary inconvenience and, if you get good advice on how to invest it, you will be kept in moderate comfort for the rest of your days. Now you cannot say I am ungenerous." Snapping her purse shut she went down the porch steps onto the path. She stopped impatiently as Miss Lapthorne flew after her.

"Are you saying we are never to meet again, Emily?" The cry was frantic.

"I am." Fastidiously Emily Drayton plucked the other woman's clutching hand from her arm. "Please do not maul me, Mavis. You know I have never liked being mauled."

"What of our friendship? What of all we have meant to each other?"

Emily Drayton fixed the frantic woman with an icy glare. "Over and done with a long, long time ago. Now let us shake hands in a dignified manner." She extended her white gloved hand.

Miss Lapthorne stared at it as if in disbelief. Then with a terrible wail like a wounded animal, she clamped both arms about Emily Drayton and kissed her hard on the mouth. There were a few moments of struggle watched with interest by the two cab-drivers and several passers-by, who paused on both sides of the street. Finally Emily Drayton freed herself with a force that flung her former companion to the ground.

"You disgusting wretch!" she shrieked hysterically. Snatching a lace-trimmed handkerchief from her jacket pocket, she wiped her lips furiously as she ran down the path and sprang into the foremost cab. The cabby whipped up his horse and drove away.

The other cabby came to where Miss Lapthorne still lay on the grass where she had fallen. "Are you all right, ma'am?" When she muttered that she was, he helped her to her feet. Seeing that she seemed to be in a daze, he tried to bring her out of it. "Where do you want me to drive you, ma'am?"

She looked at him dully, not comprehending what he had said. "Drive?" she echoed.

"Yes, ma'am. Your trunk is on my cab. I'm waiting to take you wherever you want to go."

"Oh, yes." With an effort she gathered herself together. "I'm not going anywhere after all. Take my trunk off the rack. I'll open the front door for you."

He unloaded the trunk and shouldered it into the house. He found her sitting listlessly on a hall chair, staring blankly before her. "Where do you want the trunk, ma'am?"

"Please put it upstairs in my bedroom. The first door on your right at the head of the stairs."

Enough light glimmered through the closed shutters for him to be able to find his way. The key was in the lock and he turned it. When he came downstairs again, she was on her feet. He took the tip she gave him. As he departed, he heard her shoot home the bolts of the front door.

Miss Lapthorne found she was still clutching the envelope Emily had given her. Going through into the kitchen, she found matches and set fire to it and its contents over the sink for safety. Then she went to the basement door, unlocked it, and went down the iron stairs. It did not take her long to find what she was looking for and then she placed a chair directly below one of the ceiling beams.

As she began to knot a noose in the length of rope, she thought how surprised Emily was going to be one day in the future upon her return to Sherbourne Street. She, Mavis Lapthorne, would be waiting for her.

Several times the doorbell rang through the house in the next few days. Its clanging reached the basement but was unheard. Among the would-be callers was an irate representative of the local authorities, intent on investigating some rumours that had reached his office about the Herbert Drayton Memorial Society. Another who came was Peter Hagen. He arrived with a bouquet of red roses and a betrothal ring in his pocket.

Shock chilled through him when he saw the shuttered windows. He hammered on the door and rang the bell fiercely. At his failure to get any reply, he walked around the house in the vain hope he might find someone in the garden at the rear, or a kitchen window open to show the place was still occupied. Then he made inquiries at every one of the neighbouring houses, including those on the opposite side of the street. All he was able to gather was the Distribution Home was closed, the two women in charge had gone away, and the girls had departed in hackney cabs.

"Have you any idea where they might have gone?" he asked desperately. The reply was always the same. Nobody knew.

For a while he sat on the porch steps, writing a letter to Lisa. One of the neighbours had obliged him with a sheet of paper and an envelope. When he had sealed it he put it through the door in the hope that when somebody returned to the house, the letter would be forwarded on to Lisa wherever she was. Standing on the porch, he rubbed his chin with his thumb as he considered where he might get a firm clue to her whereabouts. Then, balling his hand, he gave a thump against the porch pillar and leaped down the steps to hasten away in the direction of the local administrative offices of the Parliament buildings. He was again out of luck. All he gathered there was that the closing down of the Distribution Home had come as just as much of a complete surprise to the officials there.

He did no better at the railway station. Booking clerks shook their heads in answer to his questions. Since he was unable to find a porter able to remember a party of girls, he could only conclude that if they had travelled by train then each one had carried her own luggage. Determined to leave no stone unturned, he went last of all to the steamship companies' offices at the harbour.

Nobody was able to help him with any information. Coming out of the last of the buildings, he paused in the entrance hall to study a framed map of Canada on the wall. The only clue he had came from what Lisa herself had told him, her impression that the older girls were always being sent westwards. She could be anywhere in that vast area of land west of Winnipeg. But he would find her. Somehow and somewhere he would find her again. It was a search he would never surrender.

The bouquet of red roses he had bought lay forgotten on the porch of the house in Sherbourne Street.

Six

Lisa sat looking out of the colonist-car window at the passing Ontario farmland and forest and rivers. Days of rail travel stretched ahead. For the first two hours of the journey she had supposed Miss Drayton and Miss Lapthorne to be in First Class accommodation in another part of the train. Then she had been called over to the vacant seat beside Mrs. Grant to be informed that neither woman was accompanying the party to Saskatchewan.

"I'm Miss Drayton's new deputy," Mrs. Grant continued, "since I know the West and Miss Lapthorne does not. Unlike my predecessor, I'm accustomed to managing without a personal assistant. However, I know you are used to young children, and therefore I'm going to entrust you for the time being with a special task. At one of the halts along the line, I shall be taking on board the train an eleven-year-old. She will need your undivided attention. The home into which she was placed was not as I had been led to believe. I want you to calm and reassure her in readiness for her next placement."

"When will that be? If she has been through an unhappy experience, as you say, you can't expect her to recover quickly. I remember at the orphanage in the mother country it sometimes took months before such children began to adjust to disciplined surroundings."

"Fiddlesticks! Children adapt quickly. She will be going to a prairie homestead in about two weeks' time. In the meantime, do as I have instructed you."

Lisa returned to her own seat. There was much to think about which was a good thing, for it enabled her to keep heart-tearing images of Peter at bay. Mrs. Grant had said enough for her to realise she could no longer expect to remain in employment at the Distribution Home. In other words, she was in exactly the same situation as the other girls in the party.

Her gaze flicked over them. Some chatted together and a few bent their heads over tattered copies of romantic tales; others played cat's cradle with a piece of string, or amused themselves and one another with "I Spy" games linked with the passing landscape. Before leaving Sherbourne Street she had given them the customary eve-of-departure talk as she had to all other groups of similar age going westwards. After urging them to adapt as soon as they could to the customs and ways of their new land by thinking of themselves as part of Canada already, she prepared them for proposals honourable and otherwise if they should find that their employer was a man living on his own. The reaction was the same as that of others before them. Since the majority hoped to marry eventually, not many were unduly disturbed, and almost without exception the girls boasted that they knew how to take care of themselves. Yet, as on previous occasions, the bravado wore thin with several of them in the night. Lisa had made a pot of tea many a time in the dark hours, sitting with nervous girls in the kitchen lamplight while counselling courage and fortitude in addition to the use of wits to get out of any unpleasant situation. After all, she had often added silently to herself, none knew better than she what it was like to be caught unawares by male violence and, in her case, to the most terrible cost of love itself.

Now, from what she had deduced from Mrs. Grant's words, it would soon be her turn to face an employer as yet unknown. It would happen when the child soon to be committed to her care was judged ready by the woman's definition of fitness to be taken to a new home. Within her own mind, Lisa had already decided not to be thrust again into a domestic post not of her own choosing. She had had enough of being subjected to the petty rules of others without being allowed a voice in the shaping of her own future. Well, that state of affairs was about to change. The West of this great continent was not England, where references to character and working ability were demanded before a threshold could be crossed. It was not even Toronto where the same conditions were maintained. The West was open to all who came there seeking work and adventure and new horizons. She would seize her independence as soon as the right moment presented itself. Prudently she had saved a little money out of the minuscule wage Miss Lapthorne had paid her, which meant everything would be vastly different from the last time she set out for freedom, along an English road.

It was sometime during the afternoon of the following day when the train was slowing down towards a station that Mrs. Grant made ready to alight. This time it was not to buy provisions from local people proffering wares, but to meet the child being delivered once more into her hands. The girls in the party, always eager to get out into the fresh air, however briefly, crowded out after her to throng about looking at everything. Lisa took her turn last of all and waited by the steps of the car for the child to be brought along. From a distance she saw that a woman was handing the little girl over to Mrs. Grant. Some conversation was exchanged between the two adults, although not a word was addressed by either of them to the child, who stood silently, a thin scrap of humanity with hanging dark hair and garments too big for her. After nods of goodbye, Mrs. Grant and the woman parted company, the former to retrace her steps towards the door of the car, the wrist of her charge gripped firmly in her hand.

Lisa watched them approach. As they drew near it seemed to her there was something vaguely familiar about the child, who was looking warily up at the train. She took a step forward and then another.

"Minnie?" she called softly, still unsure.

The child turned her gaze sharply at hearing her name spoken. For a moment there was a blank stare. Then there came a sudden transformation in the pinched features. A great sob burst from Minnie's throat, mangling her shout. "Lisa!"

She hurled herself forward, tangled hair streaming behind her. Lisa, running to meet her, caught her in outstretched arms. Both of them cried, Lisa cupping the child's head against her. Mrs. Grant watched them for a few moments and then prodded Lisa in the shoulder.

"I had never expected that you two would know each other."

"We came to Canada from the same orphanage in Leeds."

"What a stroke of luck. That means your task is half done for you. I expect to find Minnie as right as rain in no time at all." She went bustling off to round up the Home girls and get them back on the train.

In the midst of joy there came the thought of another child. Lisa drew back a little to take Minnie by the shoulders and look searchingly into her face. "Do you know anything about Amy? Where she is or how she is?"

The reaction to her question was a stark look, huge tears overflowing. "She's dead. We was together and she's dead." Minnie's voice was rising in pitch to a quavering note of distress. Lisa, hiding her deep sense of shock, quickly put gentle fingertips against the child's lips.

"You can tell me about poor Amy another time. Not now, my dear. Let's get into the train and take our seats. I'll tell you a story if you like. Do you remember how you used to like my stories?"

As they were about to step up into the car, Minnie clutched frantically at Lisa's sleeve. "Don't let Mrs. Grant take me away from you ever again!"

Lisa looked down into the wan and desperate face upturned to hers. She had seen far too much sadness in children's faces and had raged in frustration countless times against those who used authoritative power or sheer brute force to inflict misery into their lives. This was one case she might be able to amend. "Just stay close to me, Minnie," she advised. "I'll find a way to prevent it somehow, I promise you."

The wheels of the train began to turn again, the bell of the locomotive clanged in its pattern of announcing arrival and departure, and the passengers settled down once more to the routine of the journey. Lisa was engaged in telling Minnie a Hans Andersen story and was listened to either surreptitiously or openly by the older girls sitting nearby. At the back of her mind she was readjusting the plan she had formed towards her break for freedom. She had been right in her first assumption that this escape would not be in any way like the last one she had attempted. This time she would have Minnie with her.

The nights were long for those who found it hard to sleep, unlulled by the endless rattle of the wheels. Blinds were drawn down when night fell, but occasionally Lisa would lift the one by her away from the window to look out into the darkness. It was somehow comforting to catch sight of a lighted window or to see bright clusters of them lying like glow-worms to denote a number of habitations. These became more and more scattered and sparse as Ontario was left behind and Manitoba spread out under the wheels. There, after leaving Winnipeg, even the trees fell away and the morning dawned when the Home girls awoke to find nothing but prairie stretching away into the distance as far as the eye could see on either side of the train. They stared aghast as if hypnotised by such vastness. Even Lisa felt herself quail.

"Oh my God," one London girl finally groaned expressively.

The exclamation acted like a signal. All the rest began to snivel, weep and sob out loud, continuing to stare out of the windows as if clinging to a faint hope that surely somewhere a forest or a hill or a mountain would rise up to break the endless monotony of the strange landscape spread in every tawny hue that could be derived from dried grass and tumbleweed and stubble. Lisa, suppressing her own apprehension, had difficulty in rousing two of the tearful community into helping her serve the simple breakfast. Mrs. Grant did not take the least notice, sipping her coffee when it was served to her, and reopening a book where she had closed it the night before. It was easy to see that these weeping sessions at first sight of the prairies were commonplace to her.

This was confirmed for Lisa in a general way by the conductor. When he came through selling tickets to those newly come aboard, she followed him through to the platform between two cars where she could speak to him unseen by Mrs. Grant. She asked him about the number of halts, including those for taking on coal and water, that the train would make before reaching Regina. He knew the Home party would be alighting there and assumed that Lisa was getting anxious for the journey to be done for the sake of the weeping girls.

"Immigrant women who have never seen the prairies before always cry at this point," he informed her phlegmatically. "Even those who have come from Russia or some of the mid-European countries where they've only known privation and persecution often bawl like the rest. It gets worse for many of them when they learn that for days more they're not going to see anything else but prairieland. Some of the refined ladies have hysterics when they get off the train at their stop to find its only mark is the name of the place on a board by a water tank and nothing more. They're the ones used to house servants and streets full of shops. Why their crazy husbands bring them or send for them, I don't know. They have with them trunks full of fancy clothes and white gloves and fine china, and then find themselves in sod-roofed shacks on homesteads miles from their nearest neighbour. Sometimes half their precious possessions have to be dumped before they get there when the horses tire along the way. You going far from Regina?"

"Not until we Home girls go our separate ways," she answered.

"Well, don't you worry too much about that weeping and wailing in there," he advised her, giving a nod of his head towards the car. "I tell you that for every woman who continues to fear the West, there are thousands who overcome every hardship and raise their families and prove themselves to be the very salt of the earth. Those girls will be the same before long."

"That's good to know," she said before thanking him for the train information he had given her.

"You're welcome." He touched the shining peak of his cap and moved on to the next car while she returned to take her seat by Minnie again.

It had not been easy for her to restrain the child from following her onto the platform. Minnie wanted the constant reassurance of her presence and did not like her to be out of sight. Knowing from the past that Minnie was tough and resilient by nature, Lisa hoped that her spirit had not been entirely broken, but it was too early to tell yet, for she whimpered constantly in her sleep and turned away when others spoke to her. At least there was an improvement in her general appearance. Lisa had brushed the tangles from her hair, sewn some missing buttons onto her clothes from a sewing kit, and replaced the string in her boots with a pair of laces. It did seem to Lisa that she might have found a turning point when she took the chocolate-box ribbon from her valise and used it to tie back the child's hair.

Minnie seemed awed by it. She kept eyeing her reflection in the window, putting up her hand now and again to touch the smoothness of the satin reverently. Lisa, seeing this first stirring from a terrible listlessness, thought the ribbon could not have been put to better use.

By now Lisa had gathered enough facts from Minnie to form some picture of what life had been like on an isolated farm for her and Amy during the three years and more since they had been taken from the house in Sherbourne Street. There had been no schooling, no play with other children, only grinding work from morning until night on the land and in the house. The farmer and his wife, fraught by failed crops and sick cattle, had been unable to afford hired help and with no children of their own had taken Home children to slave for them. "They're cheaper to feed than chickens," the farmer had said once in the children's hearing, "but as senseless if wits ain't beaten into them." Two older Home boys ran away. One was recovered and bolted again six months later with weal scars on his back that he would never lose. The girls had missed the company of the second boy, for he had been a kind lad, taking over some of Amy's heavier chores and sharing berries or any extra victuals he managed to scrounge, for they were always hungry. Amy, terrified of everything in her timidity, seemed to lose the power of speech after a while. People who called at the farm thought she was dumb. As time went by most of the callers were those trying to extract money owed to them, and there would be shouting and swearing and ugly scenes. The girls dreaded these occasions, for afterwards the couple became even more bad-tempered with each other and with them. Minnie became deaf in one ear after a session of being hit about the head.

Conditions deteriorated still more. When there was little food on the table, the girls went without. There was more trouble when a kindly minister, perhaps alerted to their state by some report, wanted to remove them from the farm then and there. He was shown adoption papers to prevent his action and was seen off the land with the threat of a shotgun. Then Amy fell ill. She had ailed before, but this time she could not rise from the straw on which she slept. Two days later she died. Minnie did not know if there had been a proper funeral, for the same day the woman sent by Mrs. Grant had come to the farm. She had declared the adoption papers to be null and void, which Lisa concluded could easily have been bluff more than truth, and had taken Minnie away with her. After two overnight stays they had come to the railway station where Minnie had found Lisa again.

The journey continued. Lisa, who had written down the times of halts that the conductor had given her, made a careful decision as to at which point she and Minnie should leave the train. She made final preparations, tucking away into her valise some portions of her daily allowance of food that would keep wholesome for a few days. Then she told Minnie exactly what they were going to do when the moment was right for their dash for freedom.

Everybody was sleeping when the train began to slow down in the blackness of the prairie night. Lisa, who had no watch, had drawn Minnie with her out onto the car platform in good time. Nobody had seen them slip silently out of the door. Leaning over the platform railings to peer ahead, Lisa saw with relief there were no station lights approaching. Her one fear had been that she might have miscalculated her stop. Still watching as the train came to a halt, she could see the great hissing locomotive had drawn level with a water tank and coal bunkers. Such was the length of the train that she knew there was no chance of being spotted by the engine driver or his fireman as they moved around in the firebox's red glow and the light of half a dozen lanterns. Clutching the handle of her valise, she descended the steps of the car platform and helped Minnie down with her.

"Now let's run," she instructed in a whisper.

They ran as hard as they could away from the train, stumbling over rough ground and through high grass which whispered and rustled around them as they plunged on. Finally they flung themselves down and lay gasping for breath.

"The train's going," Minnie said, sitting up.

Lisa sat up beside her. Together they watched the train pull away and for a long time afterwards they could still hear it rattling in the far distance. The last contact of sound was a blast from its whistle as it approached a crossing somewhere. It sounded almost eerie in the prairie night.

Then, except for the far-off yip, yip, and squealing cry of coyotes, the only sound was that of the breeze stirring the tops of the grass.

They slept huddled together, keeping their faces covered against mosquitoes. The night was warm from a sun-baked day, but there was no comfort in the hard ground. At dawn Lisa stirred into wakefulness with a start to see an old man with a weather-beaten face, white hair, and an unshaven chin looking down at them. He was clad in working overalls and a faded check shirt.

"I'm Jim Chivers," he drawled. "Wanna cup of coffee?"

"Thank you. Yes, I would." She scrambled to her feet, looking quickly about her, but there was no one else to be seen. Minnie was still sleeping.

"What's her name?" He indicated the child with a nod.

"Minnie. I'm Lisa, Mr. Chivers."

"Call me Jim. Everybody does. Wake your sister up and follow me." He began to trudge off.

Minnie awakened sleepily. She nodded on being told they would pretend to be sisters. Yawning and rubbing her eyes, she plodded along beside Lisa in the wake of the old man who was surprisingly sprightly and moved at a swift pace. Near the tank and the bunkers was a railroad shack that had not been visible in the dark. When Lisa and Minnie entered there was the inviting aroma of coffee mingling with that of frying ham and eggs.

"Sit yourselves down," he invited, busy at the stove. "It ain't often I gets company for breakfast."

The food was roughly served on chipped enamel plates, but Lisa thought she had never tasted anything more delicious. She and Minnie did justice to it with thick slices of bread that he cut for them. The coffee was strong and black, but Jim found milk for Minnie, saying that she looked as if she could do with some fattening up. He ate less than they did and filled his pipe, tamping down the tobacco as they finished the loaf between them.

"You jumped the train last night." It was a statement, not a question. "How come? No money for a ticket?"

"That's it." Lisa seized on the excuse.

He put a match to his pipe, puffing on it. "The conductor about to catch up with you, was he?"

"Yes."

"In the middle of the night? When the last stop was early evening and he would have been up and down the length of the train knowing just who had come aboard long before folks settled down to sleep." When Lisa made no answer to this probe, aware of being caught out, he pointed the stem of his pipe at her and then at Minnie. "My guess is you're both on the run."

Lisa sat back with a sigh. "We are, but we're not criminals, if that's what you're thinking."

"Home kids, are you?"

"Oh dear." Lisa put an arm protectively around Minnie, who had slipped from the neighbouring chair to stand close to her. "Is it so obvious? How did you know?"

"Just a hunch. You talk with an English accent as if you're right off the boat, although she's a bit better." He indicated Minnie again with the stem of his pipe. "Immigrant girls don't jump trains at night-time to land themselves in the middle of nowhere. I reckoned you must be desperate and I know a runaway when I see one."

"All right," Lisa said, feeling she could trust him with their story. "I'll tell you what happened. We couldn't risk getting off near a station because if we had been sighted and dragged back onto the train by the woman in charge of our party then all chance of getting away would have gone."

He listened with interest as she recounted meeting Minnie again after all the child had been through and of the decision she had made to look after her. His job of track maintenance with the Canadian Pacific Railway was a lonely one and he had heard some odd tales from travellers in his time. "Now where are you aiming to go?" he asked when she had concluded.

"To Calgary. A girl I know lives there. We were friends and I think she would be able to advise me about getting work. Minnie knows her, too."

"Calgary is a long ways from here."

"We'll travel in a boxcar. That's what I've planned. I know freight trains travel East full of grain at this time of year, and back to the West with the boxcars empty as often as not. We shall have to wait until one of the west-bound freight trains halts here for coal and water. You see, Jim, apart from anything else, I didn't know whether I would be able to evade railway police near a station and get Minnie as well as myself into a boxcar when the train was gathering speed as the men do." She was thinking of Peter, whose descriptions of some of his adventures had put the idea into her mind once she had committed herself to keeping Minnie with her. "At least, not until I've tried it the easy way first."

Old Jim guffawed. "Women don't ride the rails."

"I don't see why not."

He saw how determined she looked and was no longer amused. " 'Cos it ain't safe for females, that's why not."

"I'm aware of the dangers. Minnie and I will stay hidden all the time. If the worse comes to the worst, I'm not unarmed. I have a pair of strong scissors in my valise and a sharp knife that I kept back from preparing food on the journey."

"You're crazy."

"Maybe, but it's important to get Minnie as far away as possible from any chance of recapture, and Calgary seems a good chance to me. All the money I have in the world amounts to two dollars and twenty cents and that won't buy us tickets. So we're going by boxcar and nothing is going to stop us getting to our destination."

He puffed twice on his pipe before he began to guffaw again, his shoulders shaking with mirth, and abruptly he slapped his knee with approving glee. "Well, I'll be damned! I reckon nothing will."

To her astonishment, Lisa heard Minnie chuckle. The child was finding the old man's amusement infectious. It was the first time she had thawed from her bleakness into any kind of lighthearted response. Lisa laughed a little herself in sheer relief. She hoped it was a good portent for all that lay ahead.

Jim then gave her some helpful information. That evening a transcontinental freight train from the East would be going through on its way to Calgary. It would stop for water and coal between eight and nine o'clock. He would be up by the locomotive when it stopped and she and Minnie must get aboard as near to it as was possible. This was because those boxcars were less in favour with men who rode the rails, for risk of being seen by the driver and fireman was greater there, and also when a train was gathering speed the rear of it was often all that was available to those forced to wait until the last minute before climbing aboard. The girls would have the advantage of darkness and a certain amount of time in which to make their choice.

During the morning Jim made four stout props of wood. These were to be braces for Lisa to wedge on the inside of the boxcar to stop the two sets of doors being opened from outside by others when the train stopped somewhere. Lisa appreciated his thoughtfulness. She and Minnie spent a pleasant day at the halt.

Jim told them where to look for the berries known as saskatoons, and they picked some and put them into a bowl. Afterwards Lisa baked them into two pies for him, but he insisted that they put one aside for the journey. He made them a meal of prairie chicken, which proved to be a species of grouse, and told Lisa to put a whole cooked one that had not been cut with the pie. He provided a basket for their provisions and included a lantern, some matches, and a flagon of drinking water and some dried food, including grits. He took her knife and scissors and sharpened them on a grindstone until they had a razor edge. He returned them to her wrapped in a piece of sacking for safety, and she put them away carefully.

As darkness fell the last few hours of waiting seemed long. He heard the train before they did and escorted them across the tracks to wait on the side opposite to the tank and bunkers where all the activity would be.

"I can't thank you enough, Jim," Lisa said gratefully. "I'll never forget your kindness."

He became gruff and irritable, embarrassed by her thanks, but he shook her hand and then Minnie's in a hard grip that expressed his good will. "S'long," he said. "Don't forget nothing I've learned you about riding the rails."

He stumped back across the tracks. They crouched down to hide in the grass. The train drew nearer at a steady speed. Then with a sound like thunder and a violent hissing of steam the locomotive passed them and came to a halt a short distance away. Following Jim's instructions, they waited for a few heart-thumping moments to see if any unofficial riders alighted for a breath of fresh air, but not a door slid back.

"Come on," Lisa whispered. They hurried along by the side of the train and were out of luck with the first half-dozen box-cars, which were padlocked to protect cargo inside. Soon they came to the first of the empty ones that made up the rest of the stretch of the long train. Lisa found that the door slid back more easily into its outside slots than she had expected and the interior had a dusty, grainy aroma that was not unpleasant. She loaded on her baggage and a bucket that Jim had given her without comment, its essential purpose fully understood. After helping Minnie up with the provisions, she ran back to collect two of the heavy props and shoved them aboard. When Minnie had pulled in the other two, Lisa tucked up her skirt and climbed up herself into the boxcar. She closed the door shut and laughed softly in the darkness.

"Calgary! Here we come!"

Minnie clapped her hands. "Let's wave goodbye to Jim," she requested eagerly.

They opened the opposite door cautiously to look out when the train began to move again. They could see him in the light from the railroad shack. Although he must have seen the glimmer of their waving hands, he made no acknowledgement, which they realised was a sensible precaution against attention being drawn to them from another part of the train. Soon the halt was left far behind. Ahead lay a three-day journey. Lisa lit the lantern briefly in order to see where to brace the props securely against the doors. In darkness again they settled down to sleep.

In the warmth of the following day they kept a pair of the doors apart in order to break the monotony of being shut in. Now and again a herd of cattle would stream away from the train in alarm. Once they caught sight of grazing buffalo in the distance. Derelict shacks bore witness to homesteaders who had failed and departed. It was cheering when they did sight smoke from a cooking stove rising bravely above a sod roof, although usually too far away to glimpse the inhabitants. And always the endless prairies rolled on and on under a blue sky greeting the first day of September.

As if in warning that everything had been going too easily, that night turned bitterly cold. In the morning there was no sun and the draught through the open doors was fierce enough to make them sit well out of range. Jim had told them that the weather could be unpredictable around this time of year, although a cold snap did not mean that mild days were necessarily at an end. Lisa found an extra shawl in her valise for Minnie, who was already draped in a borrowed jacket.

It was early evening when the train stopped. Lisa had no idea where they were, but she hoped that by now they had covered some of the territory of the province recently established as Alberta. Although alert every time the train was at a standstill, she had begun to feel confident that in following Jim's advice to keep as near to the front of the train as possible they had escaped any intrusion and would continue to be left in peace. Therefore it came as a great shock as the train began to move on again for the doors at the right hand side to shake against such a violent pull of strength from the outside that one of the props, perhaps not as secure as it might have been because of her fingers being chilled when she set it back into place, leapt and fell with a clatter. In the resulting aperture the ugly, unshaven face of a man appeared as he poised for entry. His eyes widened at the sight of Lisa, who had sprung to her feet, and he registered the flurry of another skirt behind her. Instantly he turned his head to bawl an announcement gleefully over his shoulder.

"Women! In here!"

Lisa did not hesitate. She snatched up the empty bucket by the handle and dealt him such a blow in the face with it that he fell back, a cut from the base rim opening above his eye. She slammed the door shut again and rammed the prop into place before she realised that she was trembling with fright from head to foot. The train was gathering speed. She leaned back weakly against the wall and managed a shaky smile at Minnie, who had rushed to her with a cry.

"It's all right. We're safe now. Let's forget that it happened." She felt it was important to distract the child quickly. "What about something to eat?"

As she lit the lantern, which hung for safety on a nail in the wall, Minnie went to the provision basket. They had allotted so much food and water for each day of the journey, and the amount was getting low. They soon finished their meagre supper and were putting what was left of the bread and some other items back in the basket when Minnie lifted her head, listening attentively.

"Is that thunder?"

Lisa listened as well. For a moment or two it did sound somewhat like thunder until there came a scraping sound. She felt the colour drain from her face. "That man is on the roof!" she exclaimed in horror. Minnie whimpered with fright, drawing close, and Lisa put protective arms about her as they stood listening.

Both started in alarm as the doors that had been tried previously began to shake. Lisa realised he had climbed down to the side and would be hanging on to the vertical handrail as he tried his strength on the doors. He used short, sharp jerks, trying to dislodge whatever wedged them.

"Quick, Minnie! Lean against one of the props for added support," Lisa instructed. "I'll take the other."

While the child did as she was told, Lisa paused only to unwrap from its sacking the sharp knife that she kept on a convenient ledge from which it could easily be snatched up. Hardly had she put her weight against the other prop when the doors on the opposite side of the boxcar began to shake and jerk in a similar fashion. The would-be intruder had with him whomever he had addressed upon first sighting her and Minnie. Even as Lisa grabbed the knife and advanced to check the other props, one of them gave way, and the door shot open. The man who lunged in was not the one she had seen before. Red-haired and red-bearded, short and thick-set, he would have thrust her aside to gain admittance for his companion through the other doors if he had not seen the knife glinting at him, the point long and dangerous.

"Get out!" Lisa ordered. "Go back the way you came!"

"There's no need to be hasty." He showed his tobacco-stained teeth in a twisted smile, his hard eyes ranging over her in lustful appreciation. "We could have a fine little party here. I've some booze in my pocket and my pal outside has a bottle of good Scotch whisky." His leering gaze went to Minnie, who had forgotten her task of leaning her weight against the prop and stood huddled in terror back in the corner. "How old are you, honey? Old enough I guess. You'll get your turn."

"Keep away from my sister!" Lisa stepped swiftly between him and Minnie. She felt sick with loathing and disgust. His face, his threatening presence, the lantern that swayed with the movement of the train making their shadows dance, had combined into a situation horribly reminiscent of one that had occurred thousands of miles away in another country. In her racing mind she judged him stupid for having given away that he had only one companion outside, which meant she knew exactly the odds against her, and she felt that all the time she could deal with them singly she would have a good chance. "I'm not telling you again. Get out!"

In fury she made a threatening gesture with the knife, intent on making him back out of the still open door. The blade came close enough to his face for him to dodge instinctively. It was also not the first time he had been menaced with a knife. His hand shot out in a slicing movement, catching her a sharp blow across the wrist that released her grip. As the knife clattered and spun across the floor, he added a kick to send it whirling outside into the speeding darkness. Grinning mockingly at her, he reached behind him and pulled the door shut.

She stood defensively. There were still the scissors on the ledge near Minnie. If only the child would have the wit to remember they were there and dash them to her she would not be caught by his trick a second time. But Minnie was paralysed with fright, standing as if glued against the wall, eyes starting from her head. The man wagged a finger in her direction.

"Listen to me, young 'un. I'm keeping my pal outside a while longer. First come is first served in my reckoning. If you move out of that corner or make a squeak at what I'm going to do to your sister, I'll throw her off this train and you'll never see her again. Get that?"

Minnie shrank still further into herself, looking almost as if her senses had been knocked out of her by the enormity of his threat. Lisa raged inwardly. If he had been in possession of all the facts about the child, he could not have said anything better guaranteed to crush her into terrified obedience. Minnie gave a nod, closing her eyes and turning her face away, her jaw shaking as if her teeth chattered in her fear. Still grinning, the red-haired man returned his attention to Lisa, beginning to unbuckle his belt. Outside his companion, in spite of the rattle of wheels and the rush of air, must have heard something of the voices inside, for he stopped jerking on the doors and thumped a fist for admittance instead. It gave impetus to the red-haired man's actions, showing that he knew a lack of response would send the fellow up over the roof to try the other door. Lisa threw herself towards the only weapon of defence within reach, but before her outstretched fingers could grab the lantern, she was seized and brought crashing down in a tangle of her limbs and his.

She fought wildly, hitting and struggling as his awful weight pressed her down on the hard floorboards. He swore at her vilely, finding her stronger than he had expected, and with a free hand he jerked her head upwards by a handful of hair and crashed it down again, stunning her almost into oblivion with pain. The resulting second or two of near unconsciousness lessened the impact of the strange sound he emitted that was more gasp than grunt as he was struck across the back of the neck. All she knew was that he had become quite motionless and his weight had increased to an extent where it threatened to impair her breathing.

"I think he's dead, Lisa," Minnie's voice uttered in high-pitched tones not far from hysteria.

Gripped by fresh horror, Lisa pulled herself free and away from the man who lay with one of the displaced props across his shoulders. Minnie had forgotten the scissors, but she had thought of the prop. She remained standing where she had hurled it down, her hands drawn back and clasped together against her chest as if she had become transfixed after her timely action. Overhead boots slithered and scraped as someone came across the roof. Scarcely able to think, guided by an instinct for survival, Lisa turned out the wick of the lantern and grabbed up the prop.

"Don't make a sound," she whispered to Minnie, giving her a swift thrust into the safety of the deepest darkness. Then she herself drew back, balancing the prop horizontally in both hands.

The door was shot back. The new arrival was revealed in silhouette against the stars. "What's the big idea—?" he began. Then, puzzled at there being no sound within and thinking for a moment of disbelief that maybe he was in the wrong boxcar after all, he peered into the blackness of the interior and spoke his companion's name inquiringly: "Matt?"

There was a rush of movement. The end of the prop caught him full in the chest and he went falling backwards to roll over and down and far out of sight as the train rushed onwards, the prop left askew by the side of the track. Lisa, who had barely saved herself from falling with it by grabbing at the door, reeled back out of danger.

Filled with abhorrence, she forced herself to return to the

prone figure on the floor. There was no pulse. She guessed the neck had been broken and knew what must be done. Using all her strength, she dragged the body across to the open aperture. There she dropped to her knees and with a final effort pushed it outside.

Shudder after shudder went through her. Quickly she closed the door and had to wait until a feeling of nausea passed. Stumbling to where the matches were kept, she relit the lantern, her hands shaking so much that it became a difficult task. The fitful light revealed Minnie still in a state of shock, crouched down with her arms flung over her head. Lisa went to sit down beside her.

"He wasn't dead, Minnie," she lied in a cracked and husky voice that echoed the strain of what she had done. Her main concern was that the child should not grow up with a man's death on her conscience to plague her in years to come. "You had just knocked him unconscious."

Minnie lowered her arms, her face tear-streaked. "I 'ate him!" she cried out wildly. " 'E 'urt you."

"He didn't hurt me as much as he might have done. You prevented that." Lisa leaned her head back in utter exhaustion against the wall. She was scarcely able to lift an arm as Minnie fell sobbing against her, but she cradled the child's head soothingly against her shoulder. All her plans to make a new start in Calgary must be revised. She had no idea if a police investigation would follow the discovery of the red-haired man's body on the line. It would depend on whether his travelling companion lodged any sort of complaint, although that was doubtful considering the circumstances. Nevertheless the risk remained to combine with the ever present possibility of Mrs. Grant's conducting an independent search for her and Minnie. The sooner the two of them moved on from Calgary, the better it would be.

They arrived there in the afternoon. Lisa looked out of the boxcar before they alighted to make sure they would not be seen. Unexpectedly she found herself catching her breath with pleasure at the sight of the foothills of the Rocky Mountains making dramatic impact against the sky. Quickly they darted across the tracks to reach the shelter of some warehouses. Nobody had spotted them.

Calgary was a thriving, bustling place with wide streets, where stables and saddle-makers and smithies gave a horsy aroma to whole areas. Architecturally it was a conglomeration of styles from the imposing sandstone banks and stores incorporating cornices and balustrades and Ionic pillars to the impressive mansions of the rich and the veranda-fronted houses that flanked wide streets. At a humbler level there were the log cabins on the outskirts, the sod-roof shacks from the city's early beginnings, and the canvas shelters erected by those in the process of building their own simple dwelling place or merely passing through. Most people were going about their business in stout working attire, but the well-dressed women followed fashion in large-crowned hats and the low-busted sheath silhouette with the ankle-length skirts that would have been at home in Paris, London, or New York. Their prosperous menfolk were in stiff collars and natty suits, diamond pins sparkling in cravats, gold watch-chains sporting fobs for gold dollars. Streetcars rattled and automobiles bleeped horns and carriage wheels followed clattering hooves. The steps of the Hudson Bay Company appeared to be a meeting place for Indians, who sat there leisurely watching the world go by.

Minnie was fascinated by a stuffed goat above the entrance to a meat market, which Lisa thought was a strange choice of trade advertisement. Yet she was glad that her charge was showing interest in everything, seeming to have recovered remarkably well from the experience on the train. Not for the first time Lisa felt that she and Minnie could truly have been sisters, for they were both survivors, each with a will that matched the other's to get through everything somehow.

Only men with an alert eye for a pretty face and figure took notice of Lisa as she led Minnie along the streets with her, her battered valise in her other hand. On the corner of Seventh and Centre streets, which seemed to constitute the hub of the city, she consulted one of the strangers' letters that she had salvaged from Miss Drayton's desk drawer, checking the address she sought. "It shouldn't be far from here," she said to Minnie as they set off again.

The house, when they came to it, was large with heavily draped windows, giving it a secluded look. Lisa went up the porch steps, Minnie following her, and rang the doorbell. It was opened smartly by a maidservant in cap and apron. She and Lisa recognised each other instantly.

"Teresa!"

"Lisa Shaw! Lumme! Come in quick. Who's the kid? Cor? Minnie ain't it?" She half pulled them into the house, exclaiming every word in surprise, and hugged them both in turn in her delight. "Visitors don't usually call at the front of the 'ouse at this time of day unless they're strangers passing through town, or other right randy devils what don't care who sees them. Local gents prefer the side door for admittance. You could 'ave knocked me down with a feather when I saw you two on the doorstep."

Lisa and Minnie stared around them in amazement at the gaudy opulence of the hall in which they found themselves. Crimson silk panelled the walls, velvet drapes with gilt fringes framed archways, and an ornate staircase of marble and ormolu curved upwards to the floor above. Chandeliers, as yet unlit, sparkled gloriously in the dimness and the carpets underfoot were luxuriously soft in rich jewel colours.

Beyond the door through which Teresa guided them, the house became commonplace and ordinary with broom and storage cupboards lining the passageway, which opened in turn into a large and comfortable kitchen. A fire burned cheerfully in the black range and plenty of polished saucepans reflected the glow through the grating.

"Is this a palace you're living in, Teresa?" Minnie asked with awe.

Teresa became convulsed with mirth. "No, love. There ain't no palaces in Canada that I know of, although the madame that reigns over this 'ouse 'as more airs and graces than any queen in a crown."

Lisa, who had guessed immediately the business of the establishment from Teresa's prattling, sat down in the chair that her friend had pushed forward. "How did you get here, Teresa?" she asked. "Did Mrs. Grant bring you to this house?"

"No. I was pushed off the train at some place on the prairie where a family was waiting for me. They were ranchers, which means they raise cattle only, and they were kind folks. I did better than many of the girls. I've tales to tell about what happened to some of 'em that would make anything that goes on under this roof seem like a vicarage garden party. 'Alf the men what met them thought they were getting a wife to knock about and a farm 'elper and a 'arem slave all rolled into one. The other 'alf were good men. They dressed themselves up in their best clothes to meet the train and were new shaven and shy and real nice. So I don't blame the men as much as I blame Miss Drayton. She grabs in money 'and over fist for sending nubile girls out to the West to end up anywhere, and I've figured out that all the time she's using the charity as a shield for her private deals."

"That's what I discovered for myself after a while. Nobody would listen to me. But I had the feeling when I travelled West now that Mrs. Grant was not at all sure when any more girls would be coming." She went on to tell Teresa about the time she had spent in Toronto and how the surprising announcement had come that the house was to be closed. She also told Minnie's story and how they had escaped to ride the rails to Calgary. Minnie sat silent throughout. Lisa had impressed upon her that they must never mention the train incident to anyone.

"Maybe the truth about Miss Drayton 'as come out," Teresa said hopefully. Then she went on to explain that the loneliness of the ranch where she had lived first of all had been too much for her. Unlike some girls, she had received regular wages for her domestic work, and although it had been hoped that eventually she would be a bride to the son of the family, neither the rancher nor his wife had stood in her way when she expressed a wish to leave. She had travelled to Calgary where, hearing that a maidservant was wanted at the local brothel, she had taken the post as a stopgap and had been there ever since. "That's why you got those letters from the two former 'ome girls you mentioned. They're travelling whores, going from place to place by train and with no permanent address. I was told by

Rosie Taylor, who 'ad 'eard from somebody else that you was still at the Distribution 'ome in Toronto, and that's why they wrote to you and said to send your replies to me to keep for them."

"You've seen Rosie Taylor?" Lisa's mind flew back to their orphanage days.

"She's in this 'ouse. One of the girls. Now she *was* brought 'ere direct by Mrs. Grant." Teresa saw Lisa's expression and flapped a hand in a gesture of reassurance. "Oh, don't feel sorry for Rosie. She's a real slut and took to being 'ere like a duck to water by all accounts. Madame Ruby, who owns this place, looks after 'er girls and they're better off than most in this game, although they're not allowed out. That's the custom. Boredom makes them fight like wildcats with each other sometimes and Rosie don't 'elp by thieving and stirring up trouble. At least the travelling tarts see a bit of life, which is more than can be said for the little lot in this place."

"I'd like to see Rosie."

"That's easily arranged. First of all, where are you staying?"

"Nowhere yet. That's why we came straight here from the railway station. I hoped that you would be able to recommend somewhere cheap and tell me where I can get work at once."

"I can arrange both if you wouldn't mind doing the laundry 'ere. The washerwoman is away sick and the bed linen is mounting up. Minnie could give you a 'and and you could 'ave two beds in the basement in the room next to mine. Your wages would be less, but you'd get three meals a day."

Lisa accepted without hesitation. "Can we move in now?"

"Not so fast! You'll 'ave to see Madame Ruby first. I'll go and ask 'er."

Madame Ruby, a big-framed, large bosomed woman with triple chins and yellow hair, came to the kitchen with Teresa in her wake to interview the temporary washerwoman. What she saw surprised her. Her calculating eye ran over the girl's remarkably good points of appearance.

"Are you sure it's laundry work you want?" she queried speculatively. When Lisa nodded firmly, she did not press the point. "Hmm. You're in my employ then. Don't expect wages for the kid. She'll get bed and board and that's plenty." After stating the small amount that Lisa would be paid, she outlined the work involved and then left Teresa to show the new arrivals their sleeping quarters and where the wash-house stood in the yard.

Afterwards Teresa took Lisa upstairs to meet Rosie. Madame liked to keep the business section of her house entirely separate from the domestic quarters, and it was only because Teresa had to show Lisa the layout of the place for collecting laundry that she was able to be there at that hour. Although each girl had a room of her own, Lisa thought the accommodations would be better termed cubicles, with space for a bed and little else. She was introduced to those girls who were not otherwise occupied with a client, and all of them had fancy names. Rosie, however, had chosen to retain her own name and everything in her room was a bright rose pink with plenty of black lace. She was in black lace herself, lying smoking on the bed. Upon seeing Lisa she showed astonishment but no liking, all the old animosity of the past showing through.

"See what the cat's dragged in," she said pithily in answer to Lisa's greeting. Getting up from the bed, she looked Lisa's simple and travel-worn attire up and down contemptuously. "You've not gone far up in the world, 'ave you? The new washerwoman, eh? What 'appened to all that fine reading you did? Waste of time, wern't it? I'll 'ave you know I'm one of Madame Ruby's top girls. All the clients *I* 'ave are rich men. None of the hoi polloi for me."

Teresa interrupted. "Quit boasting, Rosie. Come on, Lisa."

Rosie's final barb followed Lisa out of the room. "I like my sheets ironed proper with no creases. Remember that or I'll 'ave 'em off the bed again and chuck 'em back at you."

During the next few weeks Rosie did carry out her threat several times simply out of spite. Fortunately Madame Ruby found out about it from Teresa and gave Rosie a forceful reprimand about wasting other people's paid time, which put a stop to any further harassment.

There was certainly enough work to be done without anything unnecessary being added to it. Lisa often thought that her daily routine had become much as it had been whenever she had been doing a stint in the orphanage wash-house, except that the bed linen was much finer, changed daily, and the garments came in the gaudiest silks and satins she had ever seen. Every day she stoked the fire under the copper, prodded the boiling linen with a soapy stick, rubbed at the washboard until her arms ached, rinsed in tubs and pegged wet washing endlessly on lines inside or outside according to the weather. Dust storms were what she dreaded most, for almost without warning they blew in from the prairie, gathering up more dust from the sun-dried dirt roads and turned all the washing grey, necessitating the return of everything to the soapsuds.

A chore from which there was never any respite was the ironing. Stacks of it were constantly replenished by Minnie, who gathered in whatever was ready for the irons heating on the stove. She was a strong and sturdy little worker, thriving on the good food provided and never shirking her allotted tasks. Whenever there was a breathing space, Lisa helped her with reading and writing and arithmetic. The child had had a basic grounding in the three Rs before leaving the orphanage, and it was a case of refreshing memory and picking up threads again. Lisa would have liked her to attend one of the local schools, but it seemed wise not to go anywhere or do anything that might attract attention. Here at Madame Ruby's they were safe in their isolation, never seeing and rarely hearing whatever went on in the rest of the house during the hours when the doorbell kept ringing and the phonograph played.

Once, when the phonograph broke down, Madame Ruby called Lisa from the wash-house to play the piano hidden by draped silken curtains in an alcove that led off the ornate reception hall. The woman had heard from Teresa that Lisa could read music and had played hymns at morning and evening prayers at the orphanage.

"There you are," Madame Ruby said, putting some sheet music in front of her at the piano. "Don't play loud. Just tinkle the keys to give atmosphere. I'll get that damned phonograph fixed later today."

The hour was eight-thirty in the morning. The girls, roused from heavy sleep after barely getting to bed, came tottering downstairs on their high heels in their thrown-on finery, yawning and with mascara-smudged eyes. Side by side they lined up in front of half a dozen rough, unshaven ranch-hands smelling pungently of horses and cattle. Lisa played away at the piano, tinkling tunes of the day while the selection took place. Those girls who were not chosen went thankfully back to bed on their own and Lisa returned to her washtub.

Whatever Lisa happened to be doing and wherever she happened to be, whether in the house or out of it, Peter was never far from her thoughts. She tried to keep her memories dormant, resigned to the fact they could never be banished, but time and time again they would flare into her heart and mind without warning, making her catch her breath despairingly.

After that first occasion at the piano she was called upon to play at other times, her rendering of the popular tunes of the day being easier on the ear than the wheezy note of the phonograph. To familiarise herself with the latest sheet music provided for her, she took to practising on an ancient piano relegated long ago to the basement. Madame Ruby grudgingly paid to have it tuned. From the start Minnie showed a keenness to learn and Lisa began teaching her. Before long she was playing simple pieces quite ably. As the child's talent developed, Lisa played little duets with her. Sometimes the other girls would drift down to the basement and sit around listening until Madame Ruby chased them out again.

Out of the first savings from her wages, Lisa bought Minnie some warm clothes and a pair of strong boots. She bought nothing for herself, having brought with her to Calgary the winter garb she had had in Toronto. Yet that did not stop her looking longingly at frocks and coats displayed in the store windows, which were always enhanced by hats with crowns deeper than ever before and an abundance of trimming. Sometimes she was asked to make purchases of chemise ribbons or similar small items by Madame Ruby's girls, who did most of their buying from dressmakers and clothes travellers who came to the house with cases full of wares. It was always a pleasure for her to go into a good store and look at everything before conducting her business there.

The first blizzard of the winter came on the second day of November. From then onwards, apart from the welcome Chinook winds that for a brief spell blew warm and dried everything on the clothes lines in no time at all, the freezing weather took full possession. Icicles fanged every roof, ledge, and porch, and the distant Rockies were as white as the surrounding landscape, magnificent and awe-inspiring. Plenty of social events lightened the winter months for those free to attend them, but in her own way Lisa was as tied to Madame Ruby's house as any of the girls following their age-old profession there. The ratio of two men to every woman in Calgary meant that the plainest of females in the city had a wide choice of beaux, and Lisa with her good looks had to fend off persistent attention wherever she went. For that reason she avoided all social gatherings. She would not take the risk of being picked out as a new face in the community and having questions asked about her. Although for the first few weeks she scanned whatever local newspapers she could get hold of, nothing was reported of a body on the railroad line. She soon learned that it was not uncommon for a drunken railroad bum to fall out and break his unfortunate neck. Yet even with the anxiety of a police investigation removed from her, she knew no peace. Fear of a chance sighting by somebody in league with Mrs. Grant was always with her.

She registered at a domestic employment agency run as a sideline by a storekeeper's wife who happened to have been born in Leeds. On the basis of this link, the woman was most helpful to Lisa and promised to let her know if anything came up to suit her requirements. Lisa had asked specially to be considered if there was a chance of good employment with anybody passing through to the Pacific coast. The woman also gave assurance that she would answer no stranger's enquiries as to Lisa's present whereabouts. It was not an unusual request that had been made to her. She had heard it before. Many people who came West were seeking to leave something in their past behind them. Only prospective bona fide employers should interview Lisa.

Spring came at last, banishing the last icicle and turning the streets into a mire. Lisa had a sharp moment of anxiety when she thought she was being followed one day. A sly-looking man appeared to be dogging her footsteps, keeping a steady distance all the time. As a precaution she doubled back through a side street and reached Madame Ruby's without further sign of him. The incident unnerved her, for she could not convince herself that Mrs. Grant would not have sent out spies in an attempt to track her down. Her instinct was to take Minnie and flee from Calgary, but she decided she should keep her head and remain on the alert for any more danger signs. Then as each trouble-free day went by she began to breathe a little easier. Some weeks later when she was taking in washing from the line in the warmth of a late May evening she saw the same man being admitted to the house by the side entrance. She almost laughed aloud in her relief that her fears had finally been put to rest. Far from his being a spy as she had suspected, he was just a client who had happened to be taking the same route to Madame Ruby's as she had been taking that particular spring day.

In the curious isolation that centred her daily existence in the region of the wash-house and the kitchen, she had no way of knowing that a search she would have welcomed was still in progress for her. Had she been free to take a stroll whenever she wished, she might have come face to face with a tall, strongly built Norwegian-American, who had spent several days in Calgary in the hope of finding her, a quest he had pursued unstintingly since handing in his notice to his horse-dealer employer after finding that she had gone from Toronto.

Peter, strapping up his single piece of luggage in the rooming house where he had stayed on Eighth Street, grimly faced the fact that he had failed again. Every enquiry had drawn a blank. He was sick and tired of Canada. He had nothing against the Dominion itself, which he would have found agreeable in other circumstances, but he had not left his homeland to live like a hobo, riding the rails in a country not of his choosing and doing labouring jobs for a few dollars to see him on to the next place. Not that he wouldn't do it all over again if he thought there was the slightest chance of finding Lisa. But optimism had gone for the time being, stamped out in Vancouver, Victoria, Edmonton, Winnipeg, and Saskatoon, in addition to many other towns and some settlements not yet on the map. Calgary was the last straw. For some unknown reason he had pinned high hopes on the place and they had come to nothing.

For all he knew Lisa had read and tossed aside the notices he had inserted in the "Lost Trails" columns of various newspapers, asking her to get in touch with him at his brother's address. Who could blame her for hating him after what he had said to her? On reflection, he knew she would never hate anybody, not even him, but such was his depressed and disappointed state of mind he was gradually becoming convinced that the damage he had done to their love would have destroyed all feelings she had had for him.

He picked up his leather valise and went downstairs to pay his bill. Out in the street he turned for the railway station. He was on his way back to the States to earn a man's wage in a trade that was his own until such time as he had regirded himself to continue his search. He had not given up. He would never give up. It was Lisa that he loved and wanted. That was reason enough to go on looking for her.

Seven

With a note from the domestic employment agency in her hand, Lisa went to the Albert Hotel on Eighth Street. She had been told that a lady there was in urgent need of a travelling companion willing to stay on as house-help when the destination was reached. It sounded promising, and Lisa was full of hope as she gave her name at the reception desk. On this July day she had been ten months at Madame Ruby's and she longed to get away from the laundry tubs quite apart from any other reason.

"You are expected, Miss Shaw," the reception clerk informed her. "Room 10."

Lisa went up the red-carpeted staircase, a mirror on the wall reflecting her neat appearance. She wore a new dress she had made of sprigged blue cotton with a band of trimming around the ankle-length hem, a straw sailor hat adorning her pinned up pompadour hair-style. Eagerly she traversed the corridor and found the door she was seeking. She knocked and was told to enter.

Stepping into the room, she barely had time to register that whoever had spoken was nowhere to be seen when she received a savage push in the back that sent her staggering forward. Behind her the door was slammed and locked. She spun round to see that she had walked into a trap. It was Mrs. Grant in grey-coloured travelling clothes, who had been lying in wait for her and who now barred all escape by pocketing the key.

"You!" Lisa exclaimed in angry dismay.

"I've caught up with you at last." Mrs. Grant's heavy features were smug with satisfaction. "At this very moment, Minnie is being removed from that dreadful den of iniquity by the police. She will be brought here and handed over into my charge."

"I won't let you take her away from me! She's become a normal, happy child again."

"There is nothing you can do to interfere with my authority. I have the necessary papers giving me the legal custody until such time as Minnie is given over to new adoptive or fostering parents." Mrs. Grant shook a bony finger viciously at her. "As for you, I'm making sure you get what you deserve. The place you're being taken to should keep a smile off your face for a long time to come."

"You can't make me go anywhere against my will!"

"Indeed I can. You are only eighteen and not yet of age. Until you are, you are subject to me, since I am Miss Drayton's representative. Documents handing you into her charge were signed a long time ago by the orphanage governors in England. I have shown them to the local chief of police and if you dare to try any more tricks I'll have you arrested."

"You have no grounds."

Mrs. Grant glared at her in furious exasperation. "No grounds? What about abducting a child and endangering her morally by introducing her into a house of ill repute! I have been given all the proof I need."

There flashed into Lisa's memory the stranger whom she had originally suspected of being a spy, only to later dismiss the likelihood. So she had not been mistaken after all. He must have questioned whatever girls he had consorted with, but without arousing their curiosity or else she would have heard in their gossip that someone had been asking about her.

"Your informer must have told you that Minnie and I were employed there domestically, and she will tell you herself that I never allowed her to venture once into the other part of the house."

"What I might know and how it will appear to the police are two entirely different aspects of the situation." Crossing impatiently to the window, Mrs. Grant held back the lace curtain to look down into the street. Apparently Minnie and her police escort were in sight, for the woman watched steadily for a few moments before turning back restlessly into the room. "If you should wish me to elaborate on your crimes, Lisa, there is also your withholding from Minnie her right to the education she is bound to receive under Canadian law."

Lisa held back the retort that Mrs. Grant had not been unduly worried before about the children she had cast out into uncaring households. "I've been teaching her myself. She's quick to learn and is clever at most subjects. I don't think you will find that she lags behind anyone of her age who has been receiving formal education."

"Your gall is really astounding," Mrs. Grant said sneeringly. "Not the slightest sign of repentance." She threw up her large hands expressively. "When I think of the trouble you caused me by leaving the train as you did."

"How long have you known I was in Calgary?"

"Long enough to make arrangements that will ensure there'll be no more running away for you! The couple taking you into their home are in the full understanding that your moral salvation is in their hands. I spared nothing in my report on you. They are Mr. and Mrs. Fernley and true saints to take you, in my opinion."

"Where is this couple's home?"

"Many miles from here off the coast of British Columbia on the island of Quadra. Ever heard of it? No, I don't suppose you have. It lies at the back of beyond and can only be reached by boat."

"I'll go there on the one condition—that Minnie goes with me."

Mrs. Grant's complexion went patchy with angry colour. "You're in no position to make any conditions. You'll go there by yourself or you'll go to prison!"

"I think not. I'm prepared to lay a charge of my own before the police. It is that four years and two months ago, in May 1903, you took a fourteen-year-old girl named Rosie Taylor to Madame Ruby's house in the full knowledge of the nature of the business carried on there. You are a procuress, Mrs. Grant!"

"How dare you!" It was sheer bluster. The woman looked thoroughly alarmed.

"I can produce witnesses. Rosie herself will testify, I know. She did not like you and she is one who bears a grudge forever."

There came an authoritative knock at the door. Mrs. Grant hesitated uncertainly. "If I allow you to take Minnie with you, this nonsense about Rosie will be forgotten?"

"I'll not accuse you now, but if ever I'm called upon to give evidence I shall do so."

The knock came again. With a jerk of speed, Mrs. Grant went to the door, returned the key to the lock and opened it. Minnie stood there, white-faced with fright, the police officer's hand on her shoulder. She screamed out and cowered back at the sight of Mrs. Grant. Quickly Lisa ran forward.

"I'm here, Minnie!"

With a cry of relief the child rushed to her. Mrs. Grant had a few words of conversation with the police officer and then closed the door. "Your belongings have been packed up for you and will be taken to the railway station," she snapped at Lisa while pulling on gloves, her purse dangling by a strap from her wrist. "Things have gone through quicker than I dared hope. We can get the train leaving in ten minutes if we hurry, instead of waiting until tomorrow." It suited her to ignore completely that the situation was not entirely how she had planned it should be. The lack of delay was due entirely to Minnie's not having to be shipped elsewhere.

Teresa was waiting at the station with the valise. She looked anxious and became even more concerned when she saw them in the company of Mrs. Grant, whom she recognised instantly. "What's 'appening?" she questioned Lisa. "Where are you going with that old crow?"

"I've the chance to take Minnie with me to a new place of work. Don't worry about us. We'll be at Quadra Island."

"Where the 'ell is that?"

"When I have found out exactly I'll write and tell you. Goodbye, Teresa. Thank you for all you did to help us."

They hugged each other in farewell. Then Teresa embraced Minnie quickly, for the last passengers were boarding. Forbidden by Mrs. Grant to stay and wave them off, Teresa nevertheless defied the order and was still in sight when Lisa and Minnie were shoved away from the window by their hostile keeper.

There followed for Lisa a journey of breath-taking beauty. The train took them through the full grandeur of the Rockies and there were glimpses of azure lakes and tumbling rivers and snow-capped peaks that she watched tirelessly. Minnie was less interested in the scenery, but she was excited to glimpse a bear, an elk, and some mountain goats. If it had not been for the presence of Mrs. Grant, Lisa would have considered it a perfect journey. But the woman never left them alone for a second, even to the point of making Minnie accompany her to the convenience in case Lisa should make a break for freedom with the child if the train should make an unexpected stop.

At night, when the boards of the seats were pulled out into primitive beds, which was all the comfort available in a colonist car, Minnie had to sleep beside her against the wall. Lisa thought these unnecessary precautions quite stupid. They were indicative of the woman's own untrustworthy nature that she was unable to grasp that Lisa, having given her word that she would go to Quadra with Minnie, would never break her side of the agreement, no matter how easy a chance to get away might be.

When they arrived at Vancouver, there was no lessening of scenic splendour. The city lay in a setting of mountains with the blue waters of the strait asparkle in the summer sun. Lisa would have liked the chance to walk through the streets and look at everything, but she and Minnie were taken by cab directly from the station to the harbour. On the way she was struck by the predominance of men everywhere. Women seemed even scarcer by comparison than they had been in Calgary. Some of the men were well dressed, with the nonchalant air of having plenty of money to spend and a sophisticated knowledge of the best way to do it; the rest were clad in everything from flashy new suits to crumpled garments that had probably been slept in, judging by the drunken state of many reeling along the street. Some of the latter, in copper-riveted dungarees and spiked boots, made Lisa aware that she was in logging country. The men she saw everywhere were those who made their living in the lumber camps of British Columbia.

At the harbour, drunkenness was rife among those about to board ship to return to ports of call along the coast. Mrs. Grant explained that the steamship companies kept the cabins for women passengers, but should there be none aboard, which was more usually the case, then the accommodation would be let to the loggers wanting a bunk on which to lay aching heads, once the vessel had sailed. She was able to secure a three-berth cabin at the ticket-office and hustled Lisa and Minnie before her up the gangway. A seaman cleared a way for them across the deck and down companionways crowded with drunken loggers. Whistles and shouts and applause followed their route, much to Mrs. Grant's annoyance.

She kept the two girls in the cabin all the way up the coast, locking the door after her when she left it and having their meals brought to them on trays. Through the porthole they watched the passing shoreline of Vancouver Island, but had no glimpse of the mainland on the starboard side as the steamer sailed northwards. Drunken revelry prevailed at night, disturbing sleep, but Lisa preferred the cheerful noise to Mrs. Grant's heavy snoring. As the voyage progressed and men alighted at wharves and jetties on their way back to sawmills or to camps deep in the forest, the steamer became quieter by night and day.

In contrast, the weather changed and the waters of the strait became choppy. It was a wet and dismal evening when Mrs. Grant disembarked with her two charges and took them aboard a small mail-boat for the final stage of the journey. There were no other passengers in the tiny saloon with bench seating for six persons. Through its portholes they saw Quadra Island looming dark and forbidding in the gathering night. Fir and pine made black walls that closed in on either side of the narrows through which the vessel passed into the wide span of Granite Bay, which was their destination. The mail-boat gave a shrill blast to announce its arrival, but no answering response of any kind came from the shore. A solitary house on the rise overlooking the approach had a single window gleaming with lamplight like a watery eye in the rain.

Mrs. Grant led the two girls onto the deck and looked about in the darkness. No other lights were to be seen in any direction. "What a God-forsaken place!" she exclaimed with a shiver.

"Is that our new home?" Minnie asked, looking towards the distant window.

"That will be it," the woman replied.

"How can you be sure?" Lisa questioned. "Maybe there are other habitations over the rise."

"I doubt it. I was informed by Mrs. Fernley that she has no neighbours at all and her home is quite isolated. That house up there suits her description."

The mail-boat was slowing down, and it was time to leave the saloon. The halt would only be a matter of a minute or two to allow mail-bags to be unloaded onto the wharf and the two passengers to disembark. Mrs. Grant was remaining on board to return with the boat to the point where she changed back onto a steamer that was Vancouver-bound. She considered her duty done in delivering the girls to this place, no matter that she had shoved them off her hands sooner than expected. The Fernleys would be in for a surprise anyway when they discovered that they were to have two girls under their roof instead of one, but that was their problem and not hers.

Lisa and then Minnie stepped onto the wharf, assisted by a seaman. As he jumped back on board to continue chucking down the rest of the mail-bags, Lisa took Minnie's hand into hers, the rain lashing at them across the exposed wharf.

"Goodbye, Mrs. Grant," she said crisply. "I'm certain Quadra Island will look very different in daylight. I welcome being here. Minnie and I are free of you and your kind at last. That's what this place will always mean to me."

Mrs. Grant sniffed contemptuously. "You'll come to a bad end. That's all freedom will ever do for you. Good riddance to you both!" She turned on her heel and stalked back under cover. Already the mail-boat was on the move again.

Lisa called to the seaman still on the deck: "Do the Fernleys live in that house with the lighted window?" She was going to make sure before dragging tired Minnie all the way up to it in the darkness. The seaman shouted back to her as the distance between boat and wharf lengthened, his reply filling her with dismay.

"No. That's the Twidles' place. Don't know the name of Fernley in these parts!"

Lisa hurried Minnie along the wharf to shore. The first move must be to call at the Twidles' house and gather more information. She guessed that a Granite Bay postbox was no indication of the Fernleys' proximity, since distribution at this point probably covered a vast area. Mrs. Grant would have been well aware of that, but all she wanted was to see the back of them on an island that was as secure as a prison for those without the means to leave it. Yet Lisa's feeling of being free persisted in spite of this new development. She and Minnie would get through it somehow.

Rough steps formed by the trunks of trees sunk into the earth gave access up the rise to the Twidles' residence. They had only managed to get halfway up, having to guard against slipping and sliding backwards in the darkness, when a fan of light showed as the front door of the house was opened and closed again as two men emerged into the night. They were talking together as they approached in the bobbing glow of a lantern. Their voices were unmistakably English.

"Is Mr. Twidle there?" Lisa called out. There was an exclamation of surprise at the sound of her voice and the two men came hurrying down to where she and Minnie stood.

"I'm Henry Twidle," said the man with the storm lantern, holding it high to illumine her features as well as his own. He was around thirty years old and of energetic appearance, his roundish, clean-shaven face well formed, his eyes keen and a lightish blue under thick brows, his brown hair groomed neatly from a centre parting. The line of his mouth and chin denoted determination and a good degree of stubbornness. "You came with the mail-boat?"

"Yes, we did."

"We?" He swung the lantern towards Minnie and spoke with the abruptly cheerful tones of those unused to the company of children. "Good evening, young lady. I didn't see you at first." His attention returned to Lisa. "How may I be of assistance?"

"I'm looking for Mr. and Mrs. Alan Fernley's house."

"As it happens, this is Alan Fernley right with me." He shifted the lantern's rays again. She looked full in the face of the man who had previously been shrouded in darkness. He appeared to be a year or two younger than Henry and was by far the taller, topping six feet. When he doffed his wide-brimmed felt hat, the raindrops hung in his black curly hair. He was not by any means a handsome man, but a striking one with a fine prominent nose, a strong brow and jaw and a summer-tanned skin. His dark eyes were alert and intelligent, full of golden glints from the lantern light, and his mouth was big and generous as if never far from passion. She found him disturbing and interesting, but was not wholly sure at first sight that she liked him. Neither did it seem that he was prepared to like her.

"My guess is that you're Lisa Shaw, the young woman on whom my wife has set such hopes for help and companionship." There was a definite edge to his voice.

"That is my name, but I was given no details of what my domestic duties are to be."

"I understood that notification by wire was to be sent in order that we should know when to expect you."

"Everything happened rather suddenly."

"I should think it did! It's sheer chance that I happened to be here today."

"Then I'll count that as a much needed stroke of good luck," she replied evenly. "But before another word is said I must tell you that I only came here on one condition."

"Oh? What is it?" He did not sound as if he was prepared to accept conditions laid down by anyone.

"It is that I may continue to act as an older sister towards this orphan who came originally in the same Home party with me from England."

"Good God!" he exclaimed involuntarily. "Where do you think my wife and I live on this island? In a mansion? If you do, then you're in for a shock!"

His unbridled annoyance had the effect of chilling any remaining traces of amiability towards him that might otherwise have survived within her. "Then perhaps you would prefer us to go back to the wharf and wait there for the next boat to take us away again," she said stiffly.

"You would have a long wait. It is a week before a vessel calls again. In any case, I have signed guardianship papers for you since you are still not of age."

"Those could be torn up," she retorted.

"I assure you nothing would suit me better, but I happen to be a man who honours his commitments."

Henry intervened in what was developing into a lively dispute. "Why not let Agnes sort this out, Alan? Take the girls up to the house. They'll get soaked to the skin if they stand much longer in this rain. Here's the lantern for them," he added, handing it over. "I can see to fetch the mail-bags without it."

He went on down towards the wharf while Alan Fernley led the way up to the house, holding the lantern low for them to ascend the primitive steps without tripping. The house when they reached it was large and two-storeyed, set amid cultivated trees on a stretch of cleared land framed on three sides by the forest.

"Is the lady mentioned your wife?" Lisa asked Alan coolly as he opened the front door and stood aside for her to enter with Minnie.

"No," he replied in the same distant tones, entering the hall after them, "Agnes and Henry were married a while ago at Vancouver. My wife's name is Harriet. She is at our home on the east coast of the island and some miles from here. The whole purpose of your coming was to keep her company in my absences. She has suffered from spates of melancholia over the past few months, and I'm no longer easy in my mind about leaving her on her own, even though it's for no more than a few days at a time. However, now that you haven't come to Quadra Island on your own, the situation is once more in limbo."

He had taken her wet coat from her. As he hung it on a peg beside Minnie's and added his own, Agnes Twidle came hurrying from the sitting-room. "Visitors!" she exclaimed with pleasure. "What a wonderful surprise! Welcome to Granite Bay."

Lisa felt quite overwhelmed by her warm greeting and immediate friendliness after so much bleakness everywhere. Agnes was of medium height with pleasing features, brown wavy hair, and a wide smile. Her accent, unlike her husband's, announced that she was Canadian-born, and everything from her manner of speech to her movements proclaimed her to be well educated and gently reared. Briefly Lisa wondered at the romance that had transported Agnes from busy Vancouver to the isolation of Granite Bay. The sitting-room, with its plain and unpretentious mahogany furnishings, bore evidence of the couple's shared cultural interests by the number of books that crammed many shelves. Photographs abounded and glass cases of a collection of butterflies made bright splashes of colour on the walls. The single lamp in a silk-fringed shade gave a creamy interior glow that was far different from the dismal gleam the rain had made of it from the mail-boat.

"There is an unexpected complication," Alan explained after introductions had taken place. "Lisa has no wish to stay on Quadra Island without this child for whom she feels responsible, and naturally I wouldn't want to separate them. But, as you know, Harriet and I simply don't have room for a fourth person at our log house. If it means my making arrangements for them to be elsewhere, Harriet will be bitterly disappointed. That's the last thing I want."

Agnes gave a nod, summing up all aspects of the situation. "It's my opinion that no hasty decisions should be made. Lisa and Minnie can stay here if need be until another home is found for them. I suggest you leave matters to me for the time being. Henry will have taken the bags of mail on a hand cart up to the post office by now, and you were going to give him a helping hand with the sorting. Why not do that? I promise you I'll think of some way to solve this dilemma."

He thanked her. "It's no wonder that Harriet values your friendship as she does."

When he had gone again Agnes smiled, shaking her head. "Men are best left out of things like this," she said. "First of all, I'm going to give you both a good supper. Come into the kitchen and give me a helping hand."

They did it gladly, both liking her. "Where is the post office?" Minnie asked.

"It's in the store that my husband runs here for a Vancouver lumber company. Obviously you couldn't pick out the building in darkness when you came ashore. He is postmaster and deliverer of the mail in addition to being storekeeper. Granite Bay is a logging and fishing community, almost exclusively male, except for the Indian squaws. There is a large lumber camp four miles inland and a boom outlet in the bay—that's where the logs are floated out to the sawmills. Alan also works for the Hastings outfit—which is the local name for the lumber company. He is a highly skilled engineer and such qualified men are greatly in demand. His wife is an American. Recently she has been unwell. Therefore, you must not take too much notice if Alan seems short-tempered. It is only his concern for his wife that is the cause."

Lisa decided she must try and be more charitable towards Alan. It was odd to think of him as her guardian, quite apart from it being a ludicrous situation. If she had chosen to marry during her time in Calgary, nobody except her husband would have had any claim on her. Whatever the outcome, she hoped to meet Harriet. It would be interesting to see the other half of the Fernley partnership.

Since Agnes had already dined with her husband and Alan, she merely sat at the table with them while they ate, making sure they had plenty and listening while Lisa explained the circumstances of her own unofficial guardianship of Minnie. Afterwards, while Lisa washed the dishes, Agnes helped Minnie to dry them and the task was soon done. When they returned to the sitting-room, Agnes found some picture books for Minnie to look at while she and Lisa talked together. They learned that Agnes was Toronto-born and her family still lived at Brook

Street, which Lisa knew well. Agnes had met Henry while visiting relatives in Vancouver. He was a photographer by profession and had worked in the city since coming from Brighton in England to Canada, but upon marrying her, his aim had been to whisk her away somewhere on their own.

"It caused a great commotion at the wedding reception," she confided. "Just as we were about to leave on our honeymoon Henry announced that we should not be returning to Vancouver, but would be off to live far away at Rock Bay on Vancouver Island! A logging camp! I think my poor dear mother nearly fainted away!"

So Henry Twidle was possessive, Lisa concluded. And selfish? That was too early to say. His wife appeared to be a happy and contented person. Perhaps she did not miss city life. Yet she had spoken with such deep fondness of her parents and two sisters and brother that if a secret ache were there, it would be in having to live such a great distance from them.

"When did you move to Granite Bay?" Lisa inquired.

"Early this year."

"Did your husband take these splendid photographs?" Lisa glanced about the room. A number were of Agnes in picturesque settings; others were dramatic forest and river scenes. The exception was one of the Twidles' first home at Rock Bay.

Agnes nodded proudly. "His collection runs into hundreds. Personally I think his best ones are those he has taken when delivering mail and supplies to the lumber camps. He has captured exactly the hardships and dangers that those men endure every day of their lives. Would you like to see some of them?"

"I would indeed."

Agnes fetched a large album from a cupboard and placed it on the table, telling Minnie to draw up her chair to view them as well. "Alan Fernley is interested in photography, too," she said as she opened up the first page, "but not in quite the same way as Henry. He has built himself one of those cinematograph apparatuses for showing moving pictures. In fact, it is the second one he has made. The first was lost with everything else he owned in a fire during a performance of movies he was showing to an audience. That nitrate film is highly inflammable, you know. Fortunately nobody was seriously hurt, although poor Harriet suffered greatly afterwards through the upset of it all. Troubles never come singly, do they?"

Minnie, who had been leaning forward to look at the photographs on the first page of the album, gave an exclamation. "Oh, look at that!"

It showed two men balancing dangerously on a log suspended by a cable far above the ground, one with his arms widespread as if to emphasise the fact that neither was holding on.

"It's the spikes in the soles of their caulked boots that enables them to do that," Agnes explained. "Oh my! But it's still extremely risky to do!"

She turned the pages for the girls. It was easy to see that Henry had an eye for a spectacular picture. One of a great log falling into deep water from a chute showed the resulting fountain spraying hundreds of feet high. Another was taken at the dynamiting of a huge blockage of logs in a river and the massive lengths were being tossed aside like matches. There were loggers doing the madman's work of sawing the tops of the enormously high trees, and Henry had captured one as the tremendous whipping of the trunk resulted. Although the man was no more than a blur, the sense of speed and danger made the photograph thrillingly alive.

"There's Mr. Fernley," Minnie said, as another page was reached.

"Yes. He's at work on the maintenance of a steam donkey which pulls the logs to a landing. I think he's on the next page as well." She turned it. "There he is with a camera he bought from Henry. See how all the men have stopped work to pose for the lens."

"Mr. Fernley is interested in all aspects of photography then?" Lisa commented.

"He's interested from a commercial angle. People like to see themselves on a screen and he shows such pictures as lantern slides alternating with hired movies in a hall or a canteen or in a large room, such as the Heriot Bay Hotel, from time to time. Anywhere that a large audience can be accommodated, because these shows are always packed with standing room only."

When the last photographs in the album had been viewed, Minnie asked Agnes about the butterflies on the wall. The two of them went from glass case to glass case. Agnes was full of amusing little stories about misfortunes that sometimes occurred in her husband's pursuit of butterflies. And Minnie was highly entertained. She went eagerly to see some Indian beadwork that was kept in an upstairs room and Lisa could hear them laughing as the child tried on the necklaces and bracelets and headdresses. It pleased her to hear such happiness.

The two men returned to the house just as Agnes was bringing Minnie downstairs again. As they all regathered in the sitting-room, Agnes made her announcement.

"I think I've solved your problem temporarily, Alan. Lisa shall leave with you in the morning while Minnie remains here with Henry and me until such time as you have room to accommodate her." She tapped the child on the shoulder. "Tell Lisa that you are willing to stay at Granite Bay for a little while."

Minnie hesitated for a few moments, her expressive eyes showing in whose company she would have preferred to be, but she nodded firmly enough. "I'll stay."

Alan had fixed Agnes with a surprised stare. "Where do you suppose I'll find this extra accommodation?"

"You could divide off a small section of your large photography room." Seeing that he was about to give a strongly negative answer, she held up an admonishing finger. "Think of Harriet. If she and Lisa get on well together, as I'm sure they will, you wouldn't want the companionship split up simply because there was no room for Minnie. Remember that Lisa has her obligations, too."

"I'll see what can be done," he conceded, "but I'll have to give any alteration to that part of the house a good deal of thought."

"Not necessarily," she argued persuasively. "A dividing screen and a little wall-bed is all that is needed." Then, to stem further argument, she gave an encompassing smile to the girls. "I'll show you to your bedrooms now. You must both be tired after your journey. I'm going to retire at the same time. Good night, Alan."

"Good night, Agnes," he replied drily. "I knew I could rely on you to solve everything."

Agnes's eyes twinkled merrily. Ignoring Henry's scowl at hearing that Minnie was to stay on, she ushered the two girls before her up the stairs. Henry was jealous of sharing her with anyone, even a child, and for that reason Minnie's sojourn in the house could be for no longer than was absolutely necessary. In the meantime, she would enjoy the little girl's company. Tomorrow she would write to her sister Jessie at home in Toronto and tell her about the young guest. Her family did not like to think of her being too much alone, which was the fate of women in these parts, but she accepted it.

In the morning the rain had gone and the sun returned with a blaze of heat to set the whole of Granite Bay asparkle. The giant trees were revealed in all their full splendour in a luxuriant range of greens. Lisa, ready to leave with Alan after her overnight sojourn, came out of the house and looked about her, one hand shielding her eyes from the sun's brightness. She could see white pines and cedars, maples and firs and hemlock. Across on the far side of the bay a small gap revealed a skid-road made up of tree trunks laid side by side, which indicated the direction in which the logging out of the forest was being carried out in that area. Unlike the previous night when it had seemed that there was not a living soul anywhere but at the Twidles' home, there were several people about. Down by the shore, two Indians were repairing a canoe. On a bench outside the store some loggers lounged in the sunshine, waiting for Henry to open up there, and they stared across at Lisa, their jaws moving rhythmically as they chewed quids of tobacco, occasionally spitting out the juice. On the bay, in a row-boat, an old trapper enjoying summertime leisure, his dog sitting in the bow, was busy with a line and bringing in a silvery catch that glistened as it came out of the water.

Any second thoughts that Minnie might have had about being left behind had been dispelled by the discovery that the Twidles' cat had two five-week-old kittens. She barely took time to say goodbye to Lisa before returning to them.

"Don't worry about her," Agnes said as she walked down with

Lisa to where Alan had readied his long, narrow boat in which the journey was to be made. "I'll look after her and it will do her good to learn not to be entirely dependent upon you. After all, you're very young to have shouldered such a responsibility." She handed over a package. "Would you give this to Harriet? There are two novels in it that I'm sure you'll both enjoy, and a few other things that I think she'll like to have. I'm sure that you two will be good friends from the start. Harriet is a dear, kind person, as you'll soon find out for yourself."

The Twidles stood side by side on the wharf to wave to Lisa as Alan started up the engine and turned the boat in the direction of the narrows. Although Henry went to open up the store almost at once, Agnes was still waving when the trees finally shut her out of sight. Granite Bay was left behind, and ahead, beyond the narrows, lay Kanish Bay.

"There is something I should like to ask you, Alan," Lisa said. His attitude towards her was polite enough, but no less chilly than it had been the evening before.

"Yes?" He turned his head to glance at her, his eyes shaded by the wide black brim of the hat that had dried out since the rain of the previous evening.

"I was told by Mrs. Grant that she had sent a severe report on me to you and your wife."

"Didn't you deserve it?" He was faintly mocking.

Her shoulders straightened and she stiffened on the thwart where she sat. "No, I did not. I just wanted to know why you both still agreed that I should come here."

"The explanation is simple enough. Harriet's reasoning was that if we were going to open our house to a stranger, then it should be to someone in need of a good home. Her natural choice was a Home girl. The fact that we were informed that you were a deserving case in need of moral guidance sealed the issue. She is prepared to ignore the advice given that we should deal harshly with you." His mouth twitched sideways in faint amusement.

"I find it humiliating to be dogged quite unjustly by disgrace."

He shrugged. "Forget it. My wife will accept you as she finds you."

"What of you?" she challenged. "You have made it plain that you resent the intrusion of an outsider in your home."

"Two outsiders eventually," he pointed out sharply. "I'll remind you that you didn't come alone to Quadra Island. Since we are speaking frankly, I admit that I resented you before you even arrived, but I've managed to keep that from Harriet. If you and I are to get along at all with each other, I trust you will keep up my harmless deception for her sake."

"Such possessiveness appals me!" she burst out. "Can't you bear to share your wife's company with either kith or kin, no matter how lonely she might be?"

His expression became fierce, his nostrils dilating dangerously. "As it happens, my wife has no kin. She grew up in the care of her late mother's sister, and that lady has since died. Do you imagine that it pleases me to commit my wife to a hard and lonely existence? In normal circumstances, in a house in a town or city, I probably wouldn't even notice you under the same roof, but in the present confined quarters of our home I resent the prospect of never coming home to a meal alone with her and being unable to share a winter evening without the constant presence of another person!"

"I'll stay in the kitchen. I'll keep out of your way." She was as fierce as he.

"Wait until you see the house before you make any more such offers," he replied brusquely. His profile was towards her as he looked across at the passing shore where the seemingly impenetrable forest pressed down to the water's edge from the high slopes above. Its green luxuriance moved outwards across the surface in floating logs and twisted branches and mossy driftwood, which sometimes bobbed away in the wave created by the boat's bow. "This island and these forests would never be my permanent choice of habitation, although I appreciate the grandeur of it all. It's because at heart I'm a city man, having been born and bred in London. Harriet, on the other hand, is a country girl from a Connecticut farmstead and is happiest in the depth of nature. Because I believed it to be therapeutic for her to recover from a miscarriage amid surroundings of her choice, I agreed to try to recoup our finances by putting my engineering skills at the disposal of a prosperous lumber company as a means to an end of getting a cinema of my own again."

"You had a cinema? I didn't know. Agnes mentioned your interest in moving pictures."

"As so often happens, I had followed my father's footsteps into engineering, but from the start I was drawn to the bioscope and the technicalities of film projection. To gain wider knowledge I went to France to investigate the Lumière cinematographic equipment, and then came via Germany and the developments there to New York, which is the main centre of film-making and a magnet for anyone interested in that fast-moving industry. Harriet was working in one of the offices. We met and married within a matter of weeks. By that time I had designed and patented my own film projector, but so had a good many other people. Naturally I considered mine to be the best on the market. The one I've built more recently in my workshop outstrips the first, which I used when Harriet and I left New York. After a few months of putting on travelling picture shows, we set up our own movie house."

"Where was that? In the United States?"

He shook his head. "Nickleodeons had sprung up everywhere there in the wake of the earlier Kinetoscope Parlours and the Vitascope Halls. Canada had not expanded with the same rapidity and I felt the whole country was ready to be opened up on a grand scale. From my first beginnings in Winnipeg, I was already looking to the day when Fernley cinemas would be spread right across the continent. Then disaster struck in a fire and we lost everything. It was through shock that Harriet lost the baby she was expecting. That's why, through her choice, we came to British Columbia and to Quadra Island." His eyes hardened angrily on her. "So in future, Lisa, you may keep to yourself any other inaccurate suppositions you care to harbour about my attitude towards my wife, possessiveness included."

She coloured uncomfortably and forced herself to give a nod. No good would come of constant friction with him. Somehow she must try not to let him rile her. Perhaps it would be easier in Harriet's presence.

"Look!" he exclaimed suddenly, pointing ahead. "The whales are running."

There appeared to be a school of them. She could see them clearly as they rolled above the surface of the sparkling water and dived again, bursts of spray accompanying their harmless passage, for they were far from the boat and there was no danger. Somehow the sighting eased the tension and for a while he talked quite amiably, telling her of the salmon and other fish that abounded around the island as in neighbouring waters. Deer and grouse were to be had by any good shot in the forest, and fortunately the wolves and bears had long since gone from Quadra. Only the occasional cougar prowled in the deepest wooded depths as yet not approached for logging out by the lumber companies. As for shellfish, clams, and oysters, they were easy to come by along the boulder-strewn shoreline.

"Had I not been ambitious," he conceded, "it might not have been hard to settle on such an island with so much to offer, but you know my feelings there. Yet take Henry Twidle now. He is in his element. Only old age and infirmity will ever make him return to the mainland."

Lisa's thoughts went to Agnes. The island was as alien to a Toronto-raised woman as it was to a London exile. Both Agnes and Alan had come to Quadra Island through love for their respective partners. Alan, at least, had a chance of returning to his natural environs. Agnes did not.

It was late afternoon when he sailed the small craft into an inlet that must have been spectacular before it had been logged out by the lumbermen and then abandoned. New trees had sprung up, but the regrowth had been hindered by a forest fire at some time, which had left a blackened scar across the landscape. High on the bluff, a slender tawny-haired woman hurried into view, waving to the approaching craft. A large dog of mixed origins darted forward from her side to bark noisily in recognition of its master's return. Alan waved back vigorously to his wife, his expression transformed by the sight of her, all glowering looks completely banished. As soon as they were within earshot of each other, he cupped a hand about his mouth.

"I've brought you a surprise! This is your new friend-to-be here with me!"

She nodded to show she understood and, catching the dog by its collar, she turned for a nearby path that would bring her down to the shore.

Lisa glanced at Alan. "That was a kindly introduction. I appreciate it."

He shrugged. "I told you before," he said drily, "that all that matters to me is Harriet's peace of mind. So when I smile at you, Lisa, just make sure you smile back."

Oh, she would smile all right, she thought, angered by him again. But it would be with her lips only and not with her eyes.

As soon as the boat was beached and Alan had sprung ashore, he snatched his wife into his arms. They kissed with such ardency that Lisa busied herself getting out of the boat unaided, dismayed by the rush of physical yearning for Peter that had been unleashed in her at the sight of their passionate embrace. The dog, after an exuberant greeting of its master, had come across to await her without hostility. She patted its head, making friends.

"Leo has taken to you," Harriet said, smiling, having stepped across to meet the newcomer.

"Now he will have two of us to guard," Lisa smiled in return. Alan's wife was gentle-looking, kindness in the magnificent amber eyes and a sweetness about the pretty mouth. Her face was openly sensitive, full of the light and shade of vulnerability to the pain and joy of love. Lisa thought her beautiful, but too taut with inner personal distress, nerves frayed almost through to the surface.

"This is a great day for me." On impulse Harriet took both of Lisa's hands into hers, it being natural to her to give spontaneous and generous emphasis to her welcome. They faced each other in mutual respect and in the first stirrings of the friendship that each had hoped to share with the other.

Lisa felt quite moved. "You shall never regret letting me come to your home, Harriet."

"I believe that with all my heart. How did it happen that you were able to get here earlier than we expected?"

"It's a long story."

"Then it shall wait until you have rested. Let's go up to the house."

Alan, unloading crates of supplies he had brought in the boat, had already set Lisa's valise down on the sandy shore. She picked it up quickly, not wanting to be beholden to him for carrying it for her, and gave Harriet the parcel from Granite Bay.

"Agnes never lets Alan leave empty-handed," Harriet said, turning the parcel about in an attempt to guess the contents. "I know she will have remembered that I have had a birthday since he last called there." She made a bleak little grimace. "I'm two years older than my husband, and I was thirty. It feels like middle age when one has no children."

They reached the top of the path which continued across a slope to a single-storeyed cabin that had not been visible from below. Built of dark seasoned logs, it had a sloping roof and small windows. Harriet explained it was the property of the Hastings logging company for which Alan worked, which was why they had been able to rent it with its simple furnishings. Lisa paused on the threshold to look back over her shoulder in the direction of the scorched forest.

"How long is it since the fire took place?"

"It happened shortly before we came to live here, and the whole of the rest of the summer some of the stumps still smouldered. I used to pour water on those in the immediate vicinity right up until the snow came." She indicated the direction the forest fire had taken. "It was lucky that the flames missed the house or else we would have had to stay longer with the Twidles while we found somewhere else to live. By a lucky chance the orchard escaped as well, which means I can pick white cherries and apples and pears in season, and in spring its the prettiest sight with all the blossom. I have lilac trees as well and I always count the buds as soon as they appear."

Lisa was suddenly assailed by a wave of homesickness. "It was spring when I left England. In a way I haven't known a real spring since, because on the day I sailed I met someone and then parted from him again a while afterwards."

Harriet tilted her head with sympathetic inquiry. "Shall you tell me about him when we know each other better?"

"I think so. A little anyway." They smiled at each other again. Then Lisa followed Harriet into the log house.

The living room took up the greater part of the house, with a black range and kitchen facilities at one end and at the other an open hearth. A flight of steps led up to a sleeping loft, and through a side door below was Alan's workshop where his cinematographic equipment and tools covered every available scrap of space on the benches. Lisa could not see any room for a wall-bed to be made for Minnie. Her own sleeping quarters, entered by another door on the opposite side of the hearth, had once been a small storeroom and was far too narrow and low-ceilinged to accommodate a second bed or even a bunk bed above the one in which she would sleep. Lisa was thankful that it did have a small window for light and ventilation.

The only piece of furniture in the house that the Fernleys had brought with them to Quadra Island was the upright piano in the living room, which was a replacement for the one they had lost in the cinema catastrophe. Harriet explained that she had played accompanying music for the movies that Alan had shown and still played at the shows he put on for audiences from time to time. While she opened the package from Agnes, Lisa sat down at the piano and played from the sheet music on the rack. Harriet listened with appreciation.

"You're a pianist, too," she declared, coming across to show Lisa the unwrapped trinket box that Henry had made and carved for her. When Lisa had admired it, Harriet went up to the sleeping loft to transfer some pieces of jewellery into her gift from the Twidles.

That night the muffled sounds of Alan making passionate love to his wife kept Lisa from sleep. In her white cotton nightgown she knelt on her narrow bed, her hands pressed over her ears, and looked out of the window towards the moon-dappled water, where small islets lay like risen jewels upon the surface.

When eventually she fell back onto her pillow, she was racked by a physical yearning for the man she still loved and who was lost to her. Long after the lovers overhead had fallen asleep in each others' arms, she continued to lie awake, enduring her own personal torment.

Alan left again next morning. Harriet went down to the shore to see him off, Leo at their heels. When she returned to the house she stayed outside and did not enter. Lisa put away the last of the breakfast dishes she had washed and went out to her.

"Are you all right, Harriet?"

The woman nodded, pacing restlessly. "I hate this house more every time Alan leaves it. Take no notice of me. It's just that I never want to go back into it on my own when he has gone."

"You're not on your own now. I'm here."

"I know. I'm not used to the idea yet."

"Why do you have to live in this particular place? Wouldn't it have been better all along for you to have settled somewhere near Agnes at Granite Bay?"

"From here Alan has swifter access to most of the camps and outlets where his skills are needed. He can travel by sea, or inland by skid-road, or track or river tugboat. If he wants to get to the camp near Granite Bay he can even travel by an old lumber train from the Lucky Jim mine that lies a distance from here."

"Have you no neighbours at all?"

"There are some Lekwiltok Indians a few miles away, and an elderly missionary, officially retired, who still ministers to their spiritual welfare."

"Have you ever been afraid here?"

"Of Quadra Island? Never." Harriet seemed quite astonished by such an idea. "I was raised on a farm miles from neighbours, so isolation doesn't alarm me. In any case, Leo would savage any intruder who attempted to attack me, and I know how to use a firearm. But this is a peaceful place. These environs are more natural to me than bricks and mortar. When Alan is in a financial position to open up a movie house again, I'll adapt to city life as I did when I was younger." Her voice suddenly quavered.

"It's my own company that has become dangerous to me, particularly in the house. That's why I needed a companion and a friend, somebody else to think about in Alan's absences."

Lisa was moved by her distress. "How can I help?"

Harriet shook her head wearily. "By talking to me and hearing me out? The truth is that I've brooded and wept over a miscarriage for a long time now."

Lisa understood that Harriet, knowing she had not led a sheltered life, felt able to speak out more freely than she would otherwise to an unmarried girl.

"The shock you suffered through the burning down of the cinema in Winnipeg was no fault of yours," Lisa said consolingly.

"That was the first miscarriage. A second happened in this house. That's why I've grown to hate being under its roof without Alan. He had warned me never to clamber over the rocks in his absence, but I did, and I fell getting down the bluff to collect clams." She dropped her face into both hands in abject misery at the memory. "Somehow I managed to get back here and lost the baby that we both wanted so much. I've never told him about it. I can't. Only you know the truth of my present state of mind."

Lisa put a companionable arm about her shoulders. "Nobody can help an accident. We all do foolish things sometimes. I only know that regret can linger on against all common sense. At least I can understand what it is to feel as you do about wishing the past undone." It was then that she in her turn made Harriet a confidante of her secrets. She told her of the ordeal of being raped and how it had been instrumental in splitting her apart from Peter Hagen, whom she still loved dearly and could never forget. "So you see," she concluded, "I think you and I can help each other."

Harriet raised her head again with an attempt at courage. "I hope so, dear Lisa," she said. "Your suffering has been more than equal to mine."

They spent the rest of the day in the forest and gathering oysters from the shore, Harriet having taken a basket, stout gloves, and a knife for the purpose. During those hours together and in the days that followed, Lisa soon realised that her first impressions of Alan's wife had been correct. Harriet was a woman who was all emotion, guided by her heart and never by her head, loving her husband to distraction and as easily elated as she was cast down. At first it was not easy being a companion to her. Self-blame was a difficult conviction to shift, strengthened as it had been by hours of loneliness. Fortunately, throughout the rest of the summer and into the autumn there was plenty to do tending the vegetable patch, picking berries and other fruit, making preserves, and stocking up shelves for the winter months ahead. Yet there were still times when Harriet gave way to bouts of depression that seemed to drain strength and all will to move from her.

One day, unable to find her, Lisa rushed searching from place to place, gripped by rising panic at what might have happened. To her overwhelming relief, she found Harriet sitting on the rocks from which she had fallen on a certain fateful day, staring numbly and unseeingly in front of her. Clambering down the bluff to her, Lisa sat down beside her and simply held her hand. When finally the tears gushed forth, Lisa held her as if consoling a child. The incident seemed to cement a bond between them. Afterwards Harriet never again went off on her own. The improvement in the state of her mind was almost imperceptible for a long while, but gradually it became apparent to Lisa that Harriet had emerged at last from the threat of a nervous breakdown that had been far greater than ever her husband had suspected.

In spite of the isolation of the house, more people came to it than Lisa would have anticipated. A farmer's boy came once a week by boat with fresh meat, eggs, butter, and milk. Indians brought fish to sell, their squaws offering beadwork. Sometimes loggers travelling from one camp to another, on foot or on horseback, would notice the curtains at the windows of the cabin or washing on the line, and know that there were women there. Not once was there any trouble. They were without exception pleasant, ordinary men lonely for their wives or the sight of womenfolk, making some pretext to come to the door, hoping they would be invited to a meal. Harriet always found something for them, and they would wash their hands and slick down their hair before entering the house, reminding Lisa more of shy schoolboys than grown men engaged in some of the most dangerous work that was to be done anywhere. They were of all nationalities. More than once they were Norwegian. Their accents twisted a knife in her heart and she was always quiet and subdued after they had gone.

Henry Twidle arrived in his gas-engined boat with mail and news of Minnie. She had made friends with a girl of her own age, the eldest daughter of a manufacturer's representative who had moved into an empty house at Granite Bay. The wife had been a schoolteacher, specialising in music and the teaching of the piano. Minnie was attending the family lessons and enjoying sessions at the keys under expert instruction. The couple, whose surname was Jackson, were willing to take Minnie into the family until such time as she could rejoin Lisa, if that would be agreeable. The amount they wanted for her keep was negligible and Lisa knew she would be able to manage it by passing on the pocket-money wages she received from the Fernleys. She arranged with Henry how payment should be made through the post office and gave him letters to take back to Agnes and to Minnie.

While her friendship with Harriet strengthened and deepened, Lisa's relationship with Alan improved to a certain extent. A dangerous current reverberated between them. Lisa was uncomfortably convinced that Harriet was well aware of the tension that each brought about in the presence of the other, although she never made any reference to it by look or word. An open clash often occurred when Harriet was out of earshot. It happened when Lisa sought him out one day in his workshop to request once more that he make some accommodation for Minnie.

"I know you don't want her here," she challenged heatedly out of her troubled conscience at leaving the girl at Granite Bay indefinitely.

"You knew that from the start," he gave back, not taking his attention from the reel of film he was resplicing after removing a damaged length. "But I'll fulfil the obligation thrust upon me sooner or later."

"Minnie will be grown up and married by then!"

"That should solve the problem nicely," he stated drily, still at his task. "Would you like a motion-picture show this evening?"

"I'd rather have Minnie here."

"I'm not offering alternatives."

She swung out of the room. Trying to get the better of Alan was like beating one's head against a brick wall. Later she watched the one-reel movies, the projector of polished mahogany and brass lit by an inner lamp and hand-cranked. The reels were old, products he had bought outright very cheaply from a contact he had in New York, but they were a wonder to Lisa. There was a love drama, cowboys and Indians with plenty of arrows and smashing of furniture in saloon fights, and lastly a comedy that made her rock with laughter. Harriet shared Lisa's enjoyment, not having seen them before herself, and she had had Alan move the piano out in order that she could play accompaniments to suit the mood and pace of whatever was being shown on the screen, which was what she had done during their cinema days in Winnipeg.

Not long afterwards, the couple left in the boat with his cinematographic equipment to put on a movie show further down the coast at Heriot Bay. Lisa declined an invitation to go with them, since it had come from Harriet and not from Alan, and she remained with Leo at the house. When they returned they had given shows almost non-stop for three nights at the local hotel. The hired room had been packed for each performance, lumbermen and others having come from miles around. The mirth of those recognising themselves and acquaintances on the lantern slides that alternated with the movies sealed the enormous success of the enterprising venture.

For over a year Lisa lived on the east coast of Quadra Island. During that time she did visit Minnie, travelling with Henry and staying with Agnes and him. Although Minnie hugged her with love when she arrived and wept when she left again, there was no question of the child wanting to leave the Jackson family that was fostering her. Then the day came when Lisa made a special visit to Granite Bay.

"The Fernleys are moving to the site of one of the sawmills along the Puget Sound, in the United States," she told Mr. and Mrs. Jackson. "Alan Fernley has secured a highly paid position as chief engineer of a vast area, which means he will be away from home more than ever. That's why I'm going with them because, although the location will not be lonely, it has just been confirmed that Harriet Fernley is expecting a baby, and she wants me to be with her. I have come to give Minnie the chance to accompany me to this new place. There will be accommodation for her this time."

"Oh dear!" Mrs. Jackson exclaimed with dismay. "We don't want to lose her. She's become one of the family."

Minnie was called into the room. At the age of thirteen she was maturing fast, fulfilling an early promise of good looks. Under Mrs. Jackson's elocution instruction her speech had improved and she no longer dropped her aitches. Lisa was not sure that Evangeline Jackson, with whom Minnie had formed such a close friendship, was entirely the right influence, being a somewhat vain, flippant girl, but the steadying guidance of the parents seemed to be keeping a balance.

"There wouldn't be a school in the forests, would there?" Minnie questioned.

"Not where we're going to be," Lisa replied. "You would have to rely on my teaching again. I'd do my best for you, but there wouldn't be much in the way of treats. I daresay I could take you into Seattle to see the shops once or twice a year."

Minnie shook her head. "I'd like that, but if you don't mind, I'll stay here a while longer at Granite Bay. You see, most of all I'd miss my music lessons, and I'm learning to play really well, I believe."

Lisa returned to the east coast of the island in time to take over the packing from Harriet, who was into her fifth month of pregnancy and felt that the danger of losing this baby was over. Both she and Lisa were looking forward to the move from Quadra Island for reasons of their own. Lisa was thankful to be escaping the cramped quarters of the log house and Harriet was overjoyed to be returning to her homeland. All along she had wanted her baby to be born on United States soil. How else could her son be President one day?

As for Alan, he was jubilant over his new appointment. "Just one more stint in the forests," he told his wife in Lisa's hearing, "and then we'll be free to return to civilisation. I think Seattle should suit us. I looked over property while I was there being interviewed for my new appointment, and the city is growing like a mushroom. Just the place to open our own motion-picture house, wouldn't you say, my love?"

For a moment Harriet was speechless with joy. At the back of her mind there had always been the fear that when the right time came Alan would make the decision to open his cinema back in England. After all, he had not come to the States to settle in the first place, only to gain experience in the cinematographic world and return again, but they had met and been married and she had persuaded him that his future lay on this side of the Atlantic. As a compromise they had gone to Canada where she, loving her own country as she did, felt that at least she was only a railroad journey away from it, and all the time she had sustained the hope that one day she and Alan would live there. Now that dream was to come true.

She threw her arms about his neck in sheer delight, and they kissed rapturously. Lisa, seeking tactfully to leave them on their own, was spotted by Harriet, who slipped from her husband's embrace to hurry after her and pull her back by the wrist.

"Isn't it the greatest news, Lisa?" Harriet laughed in her exuberance. "In Seattle we shall find a rich and handsome husband for you!"

Lisa laughed with her. "I'll keep you to that promise," she joked merrily. Then over Harriet's shoulder she met Alan's eyes and was chilled by the look she saw there. It was almost as if he had been startled into sudden hatred of her through her acceptance of his wife's light-hearted vow.

Eight

"I'm home again! Back in my own country!" Harriet almost ran down the gangway in Seattle's early-morning sunshine to step once more upon her native soil. Alan rushed after her, fearful that she might trip in her haste.

Lisa followed at a more leisurely pace with Leo on a leash. She was still taking in the sight of the city with the deep-water harbour at its very doorstep. The sojourn was to be short, no more than twenty-four hours, which was long enough for Alan to report to the head office of the lumber company that was employing him and afterwards conduct some business of his own. Lisa intended to make the most of the day ahead and see as much as she could of the city, which rose in terraces of parks and boulevards from its busy commercial area to a residential spread with lawns and flower gardens. Even the city's setting was spectacular, bounded as it was by lake and sea, with the distant Mount Rainier dominating the whole Cascade Range.

Harriet was resting in the hotel room when Lisa went out to explore. As she walked along she was soon struck by the number of Scandinavian names that appeared everywhere on shops and stores and the offices of companies. Manson and Foss and Nordstrom. Grothaug and Svensen and Dahl. There was no end to them. She even spotted a drugstore with the name of Hagen on the fascia, reminding her of another she knew by that name.

Not that she needed any reminders of Peter, for even though she kept him locked away in her memories, he came forever between her and any man to whom she might otherwise have responded with liking and perhaps, eventually, with love. It was as if his rejection had gradually blended with the old scars of the past into an impenetrable barrier she had put round herself. Yet within that defence her lips yearned for a man's powerful kisses and her body for male embrace, so that her heart and mind warred with physical desires. The conviction that she would never marry, which she had first held after her rape, had returned in full force and gave her much sadness. It meant that she who loved children would never bear one of her own.

But this day was not to be spoiled with dismal thoughts. Dodging a streetcar and horse-drawn vehicles and one of the noisy automobiles, she crossed Second Avenue to gaze upwards at the new skyscraper of the Alaska Building and was suitably impressed. Afterwards she went to see the State University and sat for a while to gaze at the blue-green sweep of Lake Washington. She also did a little shopping before the day's expedition was over. Some new gloves for next winter in the store called Frederick and Nelson. A box of chocolates in Roger's candy store for Harriet, who had developed a sweet tooth in her pregnancy. And a copy of the Seattle *Times* to discover what local employment was being offered to females. Maybe it was the indirect association of the city with Peter and his homeland that had reinforced the liking she felt for all she had seen of it, but the idea was growing that she might get work as a shop assistant or a cashier with a small apartment of her own when Harriet no longer needed her close companionship. And that time was not far distant. One of the arrangements Alan had made for this day was to take his wife about the city to view possible sites for their forthcoming cinema enterprise. As Lisa drew pencil rings around advertised employment for which she might have applied, she was forming dreams of her own.

They departed with Leo by train from Seattle next morning. The journey was long, for after some hours they changed to a lumber train on its return journey from a delivery of cured planks at a point on the Puget Sound. It was to take them on the final stage of the journey, deep into the forests where the logging had still made little impact on the giant trees that almost shut out the sky.

The train was full of loggers and other lumber workers returning to camp in various stages of drunkenness after much needed respite from their slogging labours, most of them sleeping or lounging on the now empty wagons. Three seats were vacated in the single passenger compartment for Lisa and the Fernleys. Harriet was immediately concerned for one man with a bruised face and bandaged head who lay on the floor, a pillow of a folded coat for his head.

"Poor man," she exclaimed. "Was he in a fight?"

"He was mugged," a logger replied. "It's crazy to go to town looking fresh out of the woods. He hadn't shaved or cut his hair. Muggers lie in wait for lumbermen, knowing they can have a season's wages in their pocket. Don't waste yer pity on him, ma'am. It was his own fault."

Harriet, who never blamed anybody for anything, continued to look sympathetically at the victim. By the time they reached their destination, she herself was suffering a similar exhaustion, due in her case to tiredness and discomfort.

The manager of the sawmill, George Dunn, and his wife, Bertha, a kind-looking woman with a rosy complexion and greying hair, were at the railhead to meet them. Also present were two young women, wives of foremen, both with babies in their arms. Harriet was cheered by the sight. From them she would hear what facilities were available for confinements. Alan had spoken of her returning to Seattle a month before the baby was due to be delivered there, but she would not face that wearisome journey again, not even with Lisa to accompany her.

"Now that you are both here," Bertha Dunn said to her and Lisa, "we women number exactly five."

"Even our babies are boys," said one of the young mothers, whose name was Dolly Underwood. Her companion, who giggled with her at their being so outnumbered on all sides, had been introduced as Mary Senensky.

"We'll be bringing you a hot dinner just as soon as you've had an hour to settle in," Bertha continued, waving aside Harriet's thanks. "The company's store on the site provided the groceries that came on the list you sent. It keeps a good supply of most things from decks of cards and chewing tobacco for the men to specially ordered canned milk for the babies. The men sign chits for what they purchase and their pay is deducted accordingly. We do the same on our husband's accounts."

As George Dunn invited the new arrivals to step into a waiting buggy, they noticed a sign displayed: WIVES WANTED. Alan had seen such signs before and both Harriet and Lisa knew about them, but it was the first time either of the women had seen one for themselves. They exchanged a smiling glance.

"You'll have your fair share of suitors here, Lisa," Harriet whispered behind her hand.

"It's lucky I have you to chaperone me," Lisa whispered back in amusement.

They were driven through the sawmill in order that they should see it and get their bearings. Harriet remained smiling, but in her tiredness she thought her head might split at the grating roar of logs meeting the huge saws, and the screech of the planes seemed even worse. The air was heavy with the smell of new wood mingling with the smoke from the sawdust being burned in cone-shaped containers. There were men everywhere. They yelled above the noise to each other and at the teams of horses newly arrived from the forest with loads. Logs rumbled as men cranked handles to release them on rollers from the wagons, adding to the din. On the stacked planks that looked like rectangular buildings in rows, known as drying sheds, other men ran or climbed, agile as monkeys, going about their energy-consuming work. Harriet was conscious of the stares of those who happened to pause briefly to watch the buggy going by. One man, standing by the crock of drinking water on a bench outside the cookhouse, paused with the dipper halfway to his lips, gaping with astonishment. Harriet acknowledged those who collected their wits in time to give some kind of mannerly greeting. She and Lisa were certainly providing a startling diversion in their straw sailor hats and flowery coloured coats. Oh, the noise of those saws!

It was a relief to Harriet when George drove past the bunkhouses that marked the outskirts of the site, and took them quite a distance along an old skid-road to a house out of earshot of the sawmill. The new home was square and two-storeyed, as were the other houses, glimpsed through the trees, that were provided by the lumber company for prominent employees. It had good-sized rooms and the luxury of a bathhouse, even though the tin bath would have to be filled with jugs by hand. Since the place was furnished throughout, there had been nothing for the Fernleys to provide, except for a cot and other nursery necessities which had been purchased in Seattle and transported with the piano to their destination. Lisa was pleased to find that her bedroom had shelves for her books, a table and a comfortable chair, providing a haven to which she could retreat whenever Alan was at home.

Harriet had been right in her assumption that Lisa would be in great demand, but neither of them had expected the first would-be beau to call that evening before they had finished unpacking. Alan, who answered the door, sent the fellow away. Three more came soon afterwards, wanting to speak with her, and fared no better.

"I told them," he informed Lisa, "that you are my ward. They are to let it be known at the site that my house is forbidden territory and no approach must be made to you without my permission. It's for your own protection. You saw that sign displayed near the railhead."

She raised her eyebrows. Although she knew he needed to be strict from the start with the men on her behalf, she could not help resenting his high-handed attitude. "What if I see someone I would like to get to know while you're away somewhere?" she enquired crisply.

He was aware of her annoyance. It was to be expected, for such was the constant friction between them. His answer came on a sharp note. "Then you'll use your own common sense, I trust. I simply want to ensure that the men know that they'll get the sack on the spot if they attempt any liberties with you or my wife."

In the weeks that followed, when Alan was absent most of the time, nobody broke the rule that he had laid down against calling at the house, but it did not stop those attracted to Lisa from drawing her into conversation whenever they met her on the road or in the store or by the stables where she frequently gave sugar-bits and apples to the work-weary horses, many of them the great shires that had been Peter's particular favourites. Almost without exception the men were powerfully built, whether short or tall, simply by the very nature of the work they were engaged in. It was no trade for a weakling. Accidents were all too frequent as it was.

Although Lisa was careful not to encourage any of those who would have courted her, at least three of the younger men with their good looks, fine physiques, and quick minds, would have had a chance with her if she had felt so inclined. While keeping a distance, she took pleasure in talking with them. It made such welcome change from the endless chatter that went on at the house where Dolly and Mary came daily to visit Harriet and dissect every aspect of motherhood. Much as Lisa loved babies, she found so much intensely domestic conversation increasingly tedious. Alan's home-comings were like a refreshing, if somewhat stormy, breath of fresh air blowing through the house, for he brought news of the outside world and recounted incidents of interest from his journeyings to the lumber camps.

As always when he and Lisa became engrossed in lively and often argumentative discussions, Harriet would listen from the couch where she rested in the advancing stages of her pregnancy, sewing or knitting garments for the baby. She never made any attempt to join in, content that the two people who meant most to her should stimulate each other in such wide-ranging talk.

Another frequent visitor to the house was Bertha Dunn. She was experienced in midwifery and was to deliver Harriet when the time came. Alan was uneasy about this arrangement, wanting a doctor present, but since the nearest one was many miles away, that was not possible. As for travelling back to Seattle, Harriet claimed it would be too much exertion for her now that she was into her eighth month, and he was forced to accept her decision to have the baby in their home. She began to strike off the remaining days on a calender.

Lisa waited on her hand and foot, but persuaded her into the exercise of a daily walk in the autumn air, which was a great effort for her. Leo always accompanied them, except when Alan was home. Then he would follow his master around the sawmill or into the forest when Alan took a gun after game.

It happened that Alan had the dog with him when he was in conversation with George Dunn one morning as they came from the office, strolling past a wagon that was being unloaded. Suddenly there was a sound like a cannon's blast as some chains snapped. Amid shouts of warning a vast log reared up to crash down again in a thunder of noise that shook the ground. Alan and George had sprung clear as had everyone else. Leo, ears flat and head down, streaked away to safety, only to be caught several yards further on by the flailing hooves of a big work-horse snorting and rearing in fright. The dog was sent flying without a sound to thud down by one of the drying sheds. Alan gave a great shout.

"Leo!" He rushed to the dog and saw at once by the gashed head that death from the hoof had been instantaneous. It was an accident that nobody could have foreseen, but that did not lessen the sorrow that wrenched at him as he stooped to gather up the lifeless animal in his arms. Others came running forward to see if any help was needed and then slowed to a halt as they saw it was too late.

"It's going to be tough on your wife," George said sympathetically, clapping him on the shoulder. "Do you want me to do the burying while you go up to the house and tell her?"

Alan's first thought had been of Harriet and the shock it would be. He had bought Leo for her in the first months of their marriage, almost six years ago. He shook his head at the offer that had been made to him. "I'm burying Leo." He would let no one else do that. "But I ask that all here keep word of what has happened to themselves until I can get home."

The men nodded, parting to let him through. Lisa, well wrapped up against the cold November day, halted on her way to the store at the sight of him and the burden he carried. With an exclamation of concern she came darting forward and cried out again, whipping off her shawl to cover the dog with it.

"What happened, Alan?" As he told her she wept, cradling one of the limp paws between her gloved hands. Her voice was husky when she spoke again. "I'll come with you. We'll find a place for Leo in the forest."

"No," he said more gently than he had ever spoken to her before. "Go back to the house and make sure Harriet hears of this from nobody but me."

She set off at a run, but the bad news had travelled faster. A man who had been driving through the sawmill when the accident had happened, overtook Dolly almost at the Fernleys' front door. He shouted out to her what he had seen. To Lisa's dismay she met Harriet rushing along the road without hat or coat, her face ashen, one arm across her swollen figure in support.

Deaf to the pleas of Dolly on the porch imploring her to come back, Harriet called out frantically upon seeing Lisa ahead. "Is it true about Leo?"

Lisa's stricken face gave the silent answer. With a groan of grief that turned to a shuddering gasp of pain, Harriet collapsed into Lisa's arms. Dolly came running to help get her into the house.

Bertha moved in and took charge with Lisa to assist her. For the rest of the day and all through the night Harriet was in excruciating labour. She pulled on the length of sheet that Bertha had tied to the foot of the bed until the pain defeated her and she thrashed about helplessly, her screams harrowing. But shortly after dawn she was safely delivered of a son. His lusty yell brought his father bounding up the stairs in relief combined with anxiety for his wife, but Harriet had come through her ordeal and lay smiling in exhaustion against the rumpled pillows.

She received her first visitors later that day. Dolly came with Mary to exclaim over the new arrival and present her with clothes they had sewn for him. Harriet was more touched by totally unexpected offerings that came to the house in the shape of a wooden boat, a Noah's ark with animals, and a number of other toys made for her by men at the sawmill far from their own wives and families. She thought of the hours spent in the making of the gifts by the poor light of the coal lamps in the bunkhouses.

"My first outing shall be to thank each of these kind men personally," she declared to Alan who had brought the latest offering to her bedside, a rattle with a ball inside it carved out of a single piece of wood.

"I'll escort you myself," he promised, smiling at her.

It was the morning of the third day that she awoke feeling less well. By evening she was bathed in sweat and desperately ill. Alan had word telegraphed down the line for a doctor to come to a dire emergency. Before the high fever from her infected bloodstream took complete hold and she was still lucid, she managed to say what she wanted to Lisa and her husband when each was alone with her. She never knew that the doctor managed to get there by the fifth day after a difficult journey. He saw at once that there was nothing to be done and that had he come sooner it would have been the same. Alan and Lisa took turns at her bedside so that she was never alone. When she died in the early hours of a cold December morning, they were both with her. The baby was just ten days old.

Alan was stunned with grief. Harriet was laid to rest in a plot near the sawmill beside loggers and lumbermen who had suffered fatal accidents, wooden crosses bearing their names. Everybody attended the burial service there, and the great crowd of men stood bareheaded in the first few flakes of snow. One of them, a Pole with a magnificent voice, sang the Twenty-third Psalm. Afterwards the house was a bleak and empty place. Alan never went in or out of it without going first to his son, always picking him up if he was awake and sometimes when he was not, which made it difficult for Lisa to keep him to a routine. But she never made comment. Alan needed comfort in his bereavement, and he could only find it in his son.

When one of the travelling preachers came some weeks later to hold a service at the sawmill, Alan had the baby baptised Harry. Since Harriet herself had made no firm choice, he thought that their child should be named after her.

Lisa devoted herself to Harry, a robust, thriving infant with every sign of being as black-haired as his father when new growth replaced the birthhair on his well-shaped head. He was a handsome baby, and a contented one, giving her almost no trouble. Alan never questioned her care of his son or the running of the house. He left all domestic decisions to her. In their individual grief they were polite to each other and almost formal in their conversation in a way that each found strained and uncomfortable. The lively sparks no longer flew between them. It was as if Harriet's passing had changed them both irrevocably.

There were other changes, too, although at first Lisa was not aware of them. It was only gradually that she realised that Dolly and Mary no longer called at the house as they had done in the past. Since they had always been more friendly with Harriet than with her, she did not give the matter much thought. Bertha was still a regular visitor, eager to take little Harry into her arms and give advice on teething troubles and weaning that were quite unnecessary. Lisa had looked after enough babies in her orphanage days to know how to handle one healthy baby boy. Sometimes Bertha took charge of him for a few hours to give her a break to do other things that demanded her time.

He was six months old when Lisa began to be aware of an ominous shift of attitude towards her among some of the men at the sawmill. There were those who still grinned or whistled their appreciation at the sight of her or tried to exchange a little flirtatious banter, but the less likeable among them made their leers more open and their remarks in her hearing became ribald and offensive. She ignored the unpleasantness as if she were deaf, but it was not hard to guess that these men were putting their own interpretation on her living alone with Alan now that his wife had gone. She had been in the West long enough to know that in pioneering circles women were considered to be either good or bad, and to be suspected of living in sin meant a complete destruction of character.

She understood why Dolly and Mary had stopped calling on her, for in their eyes she was no longer respectable company. She fumed at such stupidity. How did anyone suppose that a widower could have his child cared for without a woman in the house? Moreover, Alan worked longer hours and stayed away for longer periods than he had done when his wife was alive, which should have been a sure indication that his home had lost all attraction for him. At least kind-hearted Bertha had shown no sign of withdrawing her friendship. In any case she was frequently in the house when Alan was there and was able to observe for herself that there was nothing between the two of them, for he was always abstracted and coldly restrained, his personal grief unabated.

For the first time Lisa began to be nervous during Alan's absences. Men had started to hang around the house at times, but as yet nobody had broken his rule about calling there. Then one evening when Alan was away there came a knock at the door. When she opened it she found a man she knew only by sight standing on the doorstep.

"Hi, there, ma'am," he said softly, a look in his eyes that was all too familiar. "I figured you might be lonely and would like to talk a while."

"I'm never lonely," she replied sharply. "Go away. You know better than to break the rules regarding this house."

He rammed his heavy boot in the door as she was about to close it and he leaned an arm against the jamb. "Don't be hasty. You're not scared of me, are you?"

"No, I'm not," she replied icily, "but I want you gone. Get your foot out of this door."

From the parlour, Bertha called out: "Is that my George come for me?"

The man at the door stepped back with a wry grimace. "My mistake. I thought you were on your own." He disappeared into the darkness quickly.

"Who was that?" Bertha inquired as Lisa returned to take up her half of the patchwork quilt they were making together.

"An unwanted caller," Lisa replied uneasily.

Bertha looked thoughtful. "Has it happened before?"

"No, but I've been half expecting something like that to occur. I wouldn't have opened the door if I'd been here on my own."

Bertha paused in her sewing, her needle at rest. "Why don't you leave here, Lisa? This is no life for you, buried in the forest with somebody else's baby to look after night and day. It's different for Dolly and Mary and myself. Our menfolk are here and we want to be with them, but you have no such ties."

Lisa did not look up from her stitching. "I can't leave little Harry. I wouldn't want to anyway."

"I would willingly take over your duties, if that's what is worrying you. With our own children grown and gone from the nest, it would be wonderful for George and me to have a baby in the home again. Alan would be able to see Harry whenever he liked and have a room with us instead of this place, which he wouldn't need any more. He's hardly ever at home these days as it is."

"No." Lisa shook her head firmly. "You mean well, I know, but it's out of the question."

"Tell me why."

Lisa looked up for the first time. "I love Harry as if he were my own. More than that, when Harriet was dying she entrusted him to my care. I intend to look after him until such time as Alan tells me to leave or some other circumstance arises over which I have no control. Even then, I'll continue to do whatever lies in my power for the child."

Bertha's expression crumpled into sadness. "Oh my! It's not right for such a burden to be laid on young shoulders."

"I don't look on it in that light. And I'm twenty years old. I know what I'm doing. There's no need to worry about me, Bertha. I've lots to be thankful for."

However, the next morning Lisa called in the sawmill's old handyman to put extra locks on the doors and windows. She also took one of Alan's double-barrelled shotguns down from its rack on the wall and left it readily at hand in case of an emergency, thankful that he had taught her how to use one as a precautionary measure during her early days at Quadra Island. At night she kept the gun by the bedhead.

There were incidents. She ignored knocking at the door that came in the dark hours. The rapping on the window panes while she held her breath behind the drawn blinds was even more alarming. At times a concertina or a fiddle or a steel guitar was played a great deal nearer than the bunkhouses, making her wonder how many men had left their card-playing or exchanging of yarns to wander along outside with the musicians among them and lounge about within range of her. By day it was no better. When she went to the store bold approaches were made to her. More than once she tried not to hear the lewd invitations shouted down to her by men on the drying sheds, their guffaws following her.

Then the night came when she woke with a start, knowing that someone was trying to get into the house. In the darkness she sprang out of bed and snatched up the gun. She cocked it in readiness and on bare feet crept to the head of the stairs, a pale figure in her white nightgown, her fair hair swirling, her heart pounding against her ribs. The intruder was forcing the front door with a silent determination that would brook no failure. He must have snapped the original locks and was putting a shoulder to the door against the padlocked chain that still held it. But not for long. Any second the wood would splinter and give way. Quickly she decided that the safest place for defence was on the stairs at the place she was standing. With a sudden crash the door burst open and the intruder half fell into the house.

"Stand still!" she cried out, aiming the gun at him. "I'll shoot if you move a step!"

"Lisa! What's going on here?" It was Alan.

She swayed against the banisters, lowering the gun, and her voice shook. "I thought you were an attacker."

"What!" He lit a lamp and stood looking up at her. "When I used my key in the door and it still didn't open, I supposed that the recent rain had swollen the wood and wedged it. Now it appears you've had extra locks put on whilst I was away." His expression hardened. "Who's been frightening you? Tell me the bastard's name." He sounded more than ready to mete out rough justice to the culprit without further delay.

She gave a weary shake of the head. "Nobody I could really pin-point. Things have been getting unpleasant generally and I was afraid. I was attacked once when I was fourteen. On the train coming West another man tried to have his way with me. This time I was going to use the gun to defend myself."

Her knees seemed to buckle, causing her to sink down onto the stairs with her head bowed forward. He hastened up the flight to take the gun from her and break it into its safety position before setting it aside. Then he sat down by her on the stairs and produced from his back pocket a hip-flask which he unscrewed. Tilting her chin upwards, he put it to her lips.

"Take a sip," he urged. "That's right. Try one more."

She coughed over the cognac, but it helped. "I'm all right now." She pushed the flask aside, although as yet she lacked the strength to move. It made her uneasy to realise that in a vulnerable moment she had blurted out what she would otherwise never have mentioned to him or to anybody else again in her lifetime. But such was her present state of mind after weeks of tension, that she felt there was nothing she could hold back from him now if questioned. It would be best to get safely back to bed as quickly as possible.

"Explain this unpleasantness you mentioned," he insisted before she could bestir herself. "Who caused it? How did it come about?"

"Everybody except Bertha thinks we're lovers. That's why some of the men have decided I must be easy game." She faced him squarely. "There. Now you know. And if we sit here talking any longer, Harry will wake up. I'm surprised he hasn't done so already."

"Then let's go into the kitchen and talk there, Lisa. I'll make some coffee."

As she reached her bedroom door she heard the clatter of the stove-lid being levered up for the coffee-pot. Without haste she found her slippers, put on a cotton wrapper and took time over choosing a piece of blue ribbon to tie back her hair. The fragrance of the coffee greeted her descent again. He had set cups and saucers ready on the kitchen table. When she sat down he picked up the pot and poured the steaming coffee out. As she added cream to hers, he pulled out a chair to take his place opposite her. She thought he looked tired and older. Grief had scarred him deeply.

"I've been selfish," he said, resting his arms on the table. "I've been too deep in my own sorrow to think how it has been for you alone here most of the time. I know all about the promise you gave Harriet about my son. She told me. But I speak on her behalf when I say you are released from that vow. You must be free to go where you like and do what you like. I'll make other arrangements for Harry. Do you think Bertha would look after him?"

"I know she would, but you're overlooking one thing and forgetting another. First of all, I made my promise to Harriet and not to anyone taking on the authority to speak for her. Secondly, I chose to stay for as long as you will allow me to. In any case, you can't send me away yet, because until I'm of age you are still officially my guardian."

He regarded her steadily. "Does Harry mean that much to you?"

"He does."

"You must realise that there will always be gossip."

"I accept that."

He stirred his coffee absently, for he had taken no sugar or cream, but he watched the swirling liquid for a while before he looked up again to hold her gaze. "Would you marry me, Lisa?"

She was too astonished to speak at first. "For Harry's sake, you mean?"

"Unless there's someone else in your life?"

"Not anymore." Only she knew that a bitter-sweet ache still lingered on, but that bore no significance in the present discussion. "In fact, I had made up my mind never to marry."

"You're too young by far to have made that decision already, although after what you told me on the stairs about your past ordeals I can understand the reason."

Her direct look compelled an honest answer. "Do you like me, Alan?"

"I like you. How do you feel about me?"

"I've come to like you," she was being as straightforward as she had expected him to be with her, "although I didn't at first."

"I admit to all my faults."

"So do I to mine."

His eyes searched hers. "You do realise that I want you to be my wife, don't you? Not just a mother to Harry."

She spoke with equal frankness. "My one disappointment about not marrying was that it meant I should never have children of my own. Now that can be amended at some time in the future."

"Yes. Naturally."

"Then I accept your offer of marriage."

"I'll do everything I can for you."

"I'm sure you will, and I'm ready to do my share in helping you get your cinema established. I've never been afraid of work."

"I've seen that for myself. I think we should marry soon. We'll move from this place at the same time. There's a bigger site owned by the company only sixty miles south of Seattle. I was offered a chance to go there only recently, and now it will give us a fresh start. It's a sizeable settlement with a hotel and quite a number of houses, all of which have grown up around the sawmill."

She gave a nod of approval. "How long will it take to arrange this move?"

"Two or three weeks. In the meantime I'll contact the travelling preacher who baptised Harry. I met him again only a few days ago. We'll arrange the marriage and our departure on the same day."

"That's a good idea. I think we've settled everything now." She stood up and he rose to his feet at the same time. "Good night, Alan."

"Good night, Lisa."

She hesitated briefly in case he should wish to kiss her, but he remained where he was. She thought it was as well. There had been nothing romantic in the agreement they had made. It would have been quite appropriate to have shaken hands. Yet as she went from the kitchen she was convinced they would make a good marriage. At least it was based on truth and trust and understanding. There were no secrets between Alan and her.

Everything was packed and ready when their wedding day dawned. While their possessions were being stowed aboard the lumber train, the preacher married them in the early morning sunshine in the parlour of the Dunns' home. Bertha and George were the only witnesses. Lisa had a new dress made from a length of rose silk given to her as a gift by Bertha, who had done most of the sewing for her. Fashion's decree of a wand-slender outline with a softly draped bosom suited her admirably, and her retrimmed sailor hat and white gloves completed her outfit.

"You may kiss the bride," the preacher said as the ceremony ended.

Lisa turned her face obediently towards Alan. Nobody present suspected it, but it was their first kiss. His lips, warm and firm, met hers briefly. Then she was being embraced exuberantly by Bertha while George was shaking the bridegroom's hand in congratulation. There was no time for a celebratory feast. Lisa picked up Harry from the sofa where he lay and they all left the house. She stood with Alan at the window of the passenger compartment of the heavily loaded lumber train as it pulled away from the sawmill, and they waved goodbye until the Dunns could be seen no longer.

That evening they alighted at the station of a small town where they had to stay overnight. Side by side they walked down the main street until they came to a hotel. Alan did not ask at the reception desk if there was a bridal suite, for which Lisa was thankful. Instead they took a family suite with a large brass bedstead and a small adjoining room with accommodation for children. Lisa bathed Harry, fed him, and put him to bed in a crib there. Although he was a contented baby and slept well, she took the precaution of asking one of the hotel maids to let her know if he should awake and cry. Then she went downstairs to find Alan, who had passed the time taking a look around the town.

There were potted palms and gilt-framed mirrors in the old-fashioned dining room. Alan had ordered champagne and Lisa tasted it for the first time.

"It's delicious," she said appreciatively.

He did not warn her about its potency, although he made sure that she drank only enough to lessen any inhibitions she might be harbouring about their sleeping together. Both of them did justice to the excellent dinner and by the time they reached the coffee she was merely gently talkative and smiling in a rosy tranquility of mind. Somehow there had been little talk between them over the past eight months since tragedy had struck, and now it seemed they might be regaining their ability to converse together on most subjects. Then, with a suddenness that caught her unawares, it had become time for bed. Panic sobered her, dispelling the golden haze of the champagne as together they ascended the staircase that curved up from the lobby.

She went immediately to see that all was well with the baby. She tidied only a light cover over him for the night was warm. Then she undressed and put on her nightgown in his narrow room, having previously left there all she would need. She took twice as long as she normally did to brush her hair, wanting to postpone the moment when she must re-enter the bedroom. How had she managed to forget for two hours over dinner downstairs that irrevocably waiting brass bed?

Eventually, as she had dreaded, he came in search of her. She was standing by the crib, her fingers clenched over the top rail as she tried to find the courage that had been hers when she had accepted his marriage proposal. At that time the wedding night had been safely distant.

"It's getting late," he said quietly.

She gave a slight nod, still making no move. It was not the first time she had seen him in a nightshirt, for living under the same roof at Quadra Island, and again at the sawmill site, there had been occasions when they had met by chance in their night attire, his dressing-gown usually flowing and untied. Now she saw he had bought a new nightshirt for the occasion. Its pristine whiteness had sharp creases from its folds and the points of the unfastened collar stood up like that of a Regency buck's, quite flattering to his dark looks, although he had merely forgotten to smooth them down into place. He held out a hand to her.

As she put hers into his, her wedding ring gleaming, he drew her at once out of the baby's room and closed the door silently. Still leading her, he went across to hold back the sheet at one side of the bed and she took her place there. A single lamp was still alight in the room and he extinguished it. As he passed by the foot of the bed she saw him in silhouette against the moonlit window, pulling the nightshirt over his head to toss it aside. Warm and naked, he clambered into the bed beside her.

Propping an elbow on the pillow, he leaned over her, bringing his face close, his whisper soft. "Liking each other is a beginning, Lisa. It is friendship, which in itself is a form of love. I know we can build on that friendship, and then maybe the day will come when you find that you feel more for me than you do now." He cupped a hand gently against the side of her face. "I want you and I'm going to make love to you. Tonight I'm banishing whatever nightmares you have from the past. I promise that you'll never again be haunted by them."

His mouth came down on hers in a deep, throbbing kiss. Her involuntary gasp was silenced, his embrace gathering her close. There began for her an initiation into sexual pleasure that made her realise how little knowledge she had gained from her one romantic encounter. At that time modesty and a certain innocence had combined with shameful fear to create a barrier between her and the man who would have loved her. Now there were no such barriers. The heart with its subtle refinements had no voice. The early abusement of her body by a brutal stranger was of no consequence to Alan, apart from his determination to rid her of its shadow. The present and the future were his sole concern. Not what had gone before.

His love-making commenced with enormous tenderness. At first no more than the gentlest fondling accompanied by a soft kissing of her eyes, her ears and the length of her throat until gradually she was lulled and reassured into a state of blissful relaxation. She could not be sure when he removed her nightgown from her. All she knew was that somehow it had been up around her neck and armpits almost from the start, and it was a relief to be free of its hampering folds. Her silky nakedness slid against his as he drew her amorously still further down into the bed.

He became more purposeful. All her long pent-up sensuality was released as if from a dam, enveloping them both. Her flesh quivered from his touch and there seemed to be no limit to the ways he had of causing her intense pleasure, sometimes almost too exquisite to be borne. When he granted her respite, he cradled his head on her smooth stomach between her hipbones and murmured of her beauty, which continued to stir her erotically, and she stroked the back of his neck with trembling fingertips. Then his ardent love-making would begin again and once more she surrendered voluptuously to whatever new discoveries he wished to make, her abandonment complete.

He moved at last to take possession of her. As he passed into her, she gloried in his strength and power. There was no pain, no fear. Only utter abandonment to the rising towards final fulfilment. When it came in an explosion of passion he held her hard as she arched convulsively, sharing his ecstasy.

Some time in the early hours of the morning the baby awakened her. She sat up drowsily, scooped back the long flow of her hair and went to his crib. She soothed him and after a few minutes he was quiet again. She returned to the bedroom. Alan lay fast asleep, one arm stretched out where it had been lying across her. She knelt on the bed, looking down at his sleeping face in the moonlight. Understanding had come to her as to why there had been such hostile excitement between them from their first meeting. Against their wishes each had been violently attracted to the other. She had taken refuge in animosity and he in anger at the trick fate had played on him. Even though it had taken nothing away from his relationship with Harriet, it must have been torment for him, physically and mentally, to have another woman he desired living permanently under his own roof. When Harriet had spoken of finding a husband for her in Seattle, it had been abhorrence at the thought of another man making her his own that she had mistaken for hatred directed towards herself. When Harriet had gone, their particular conflict had been erased for them, the reason overshadowed by the shared grief of bereavement.

She lay down again, lifting his arm gently to slide under it. Tonight she had learned something else about the man who had become her husband. He had not voiced it but she knew it. He loved her. Maybe he had loved her from the moment when they had looked upon each other's faces in the rain-washed glow of a lantern light. It made her yearn to feel love in her heart for him, but life was not as simple as that. At least he had brought fondness to her liking for him. She would cherish the hope that out of that fondness love would come.

Nine

Their new home at the sawmill settlement lay south of Seattle. They had been there almost two years when Minnie wrote to ask Lisa if she might come and live with her and Alan. The Jacksons were moving back East to the province of Ontario and the girl had no wish to return to a part of Canada where she had known only unhappiness. Lisa was baking when Alan brought her the reply to her invitation to Minnie that she should come without delay. Dusting the flour from her hands, she tore the letter open eagerly.

"Minnie will arrive at Seattle by the Vancouver steamship on the fifteenth of June," she informed him, glancing up from the letter. "That's in two weeks' time. Shall you be able to meet her?"

He thought for a moment or two and then nodded. "I have to see the Manson's Engineering Company about some equipment for one of the log-booming grounds along the Sound. I'll combine business with the pleasure of collecting Minnie that day."

"Thank you." She heaved a contented sigh. "It's three years since I said goodbye to her at Quadra Island. She is sixteen now. I'm sure she'll be a great help in looking after Harry. I never knew a more lively and active child than he!"

Alan grinned. He was proud of his son, but the first to admit that Harry was a handful to control, being as strong-willed as he was good-natured and affectionate. "Who's taking charge of him this evening?"

"I'm taking him as usual to Mrs. Saanio. He's always happy there."

It had become Lisa's custom to act as cashier and sell the tickets when Alan gave one of his motion-picture shows at the local hotel, The Rainier, which was a large wooden building painted a bright terra cotta with white outside galleries. Its long saloon was widely patronised by lumbermen, and its spacious hall, which was used for parties, weddings, and political meetings, provided ample room for screen entertainment. The movie shows had proved so popular that everyone at the sawmill site and those inhabitants of the settlement where the hotel was located, expected a performance each evening as a matter of course whenever Alan happened to be at home. The hotel hall had become as near to being a regular cinema as it could be. Whenever movie distributors' agents were in the Seattle district, they travelled out to the sawmill to call on him with their lists of reels and advisory information.

It was easy to see that with time a whole new town would rise up out of the settlement, which was referred to by the local people as Dekova's Place, the name of the old clearing where someone had once eked out a living. Before long that name would be abbreviated and maybe changed in spelling until one day it would be difficult to find anybody able to remember how it had originated. People of assorted trades and professions were gradually moving into the area, many of them new immigrants of nationalities as varied as those of the families already long established in houses at the sawmill site. Several years previously the lumber company had built a schoolhouse for the children of their employees. Now it was absorbing newcomers from the settlement and the need for another one was growing.

Lisa sometimes wondered if Alan would not do better by remaining with the lumber company, who wanted to extend his contract indefinitely, while building up a cinema proper at Dekova's Place until it became a full-time project. He had certainly made no firm decisions about his future in Seattle, in spite of having a number of useful irons in the fire. Recently he had mentioned that certain motion-picture companies were leaving New York to relocate in California, which made that area of interest to him. He was certainly restless and unsettled.

For herself, she was willing to go anywhere with him, glad that she was able to give him support and encouragement and affection. He had spoken of his love for her not long after they had come to this house. It had been a sweet and memorable night, for they had lain together in such immeasurable tenderness that both believed conception must have occurred. During that deeply shared happiness he had spoken the most beautiful words in any language.

"I love you, Lisa."

"I know," she had whispered, blissfully enervated by their love-making, and enfolded her arms about his neck. Sometimes she wondered whether heart-love for him would have come to her if their hopes had been fulfilled. There was no way of knowing. At least she was content in their relationship. Whether he was equally at ease she could not tell. She thought it strange that a man and woman could share the utmost physical intimacies and still not be able to see into each other's minds.

She took Harry, who was dressed for bed in sleeping-suit and dressing-gown, to Mrs. Saanio in good time. The Saanios were originally from Finland and their seventeen year old son, Risto, who was presently employed at the hotel, had been born soon after they had arrived in their new land. Three years later Mrs. Saanio had given birth to the first of ten daughters, who had arrived annually in succession. The older girls clustered about their mother as she picked Harry up and kissed him maternally as she always did. Her English was not good, and she invariably spoke Finnish to him, which he appeared to comprehend without the least difficulty, being used to her. But the girls were his favourite companions and he was allowed to choose which one should read him a story.

Lisa left the house. She always had an easy mind about leaving Harry with the Saanios, although she was careful not to take advantage of their neighbourliness. It was her policy to collect him again as soon as she had seen the last latecomer into the performance. It meant that she rarely saw any of the films, but this evening was the exception that was always made whenever Alan had a new batch of his photographs to show as lantern slides. She was always eager to view his work and the subject matter this time was to be the local community, for he liked to have a theme and this would make a contrast to the slides of the natural beauty of the forests, logging scenes, and wild animals and birds.

It was no great distance to the hotel and she liked to walk. The lumber company allowed Alan the use of an automobile, which remained parked by the house when he was away in the forests. He had taught her to drive and she did use the car from time to time, but a few hours previously he had transported his cinematograph apparatus in it and she had told him not to drive back to pick her up. Once Minnie was installed everything would be much easier with regard to leaving Harry in the evening hours. With the girl at home to look after him, Lisa anticipated being free to come and go with Alan on these occasions. Moreover, she planned to become his pianist, taking over from the present one, who had once been a teacher of the pianoforte, as the woman chose always to refer to it, and made no secret of despising motion pictures as an aberration of the true theatre. The result was that her playing never supported the reels to a full extent.

People were already lining up for admittance by the side entrance of the hotel when Lisa entered the building by way of the kitchen and reached the lobby where she sold tickets. Risto Saanio came from the cinema hall, wiping his hands on the seat of his trousers, for he had just delivered the water-soaked blanket kept in readiness by the projector in case of fire during a performance. He was a tall youth, spare of frame and virile in appearance, with a jaunty air about him that matched his cheerful handsomeness. His features were thin and chiselled, his eyes light brown and full of humour, his curly hair much the same colour.

"Good evening, Mrs. Fernley," he greeted her, whipping a chair into place for her at the table that served as the pay-box. "There's going to be a big crowd this evening, so the benches have been pushed closer together and there's more standing room."

Lisa, who had looked through the door to wave to Alan and let him know she was there, answered Risto as she took the chair he still held ready for her. "Shall you get a chance to see anything of the show?"

She knew him to be avidly interested in movies. He was knowledgeable about all the actors and actresses, able to list their motion pictures and the companies for whom they worked, not only those in the United States but the British and continental ones as well. He never lost a chance to talk to Alan about the cinema in general and always tried to be on hand at the end of the performance to help wind back the films and stack the reels. He was an amiable and talented young man with a good singing voice which almost brought the house down whenever he sang a song appropriate to a scene in a movie. As for dancing, he was a shining light when the local Finns gathered together for a wedding or a baptism and performed the dances from the old country. Only his father took no interest in his ability, being a stern, obdurate man who could not forgive his only son for not following his footsteps into the lumber business. The Saanio men had worked in the forests of Finland for generations past, and it grieved him that his strong and healthy son should break with an honoured tradition to be nothing more or less than a lackey. The fact that he himself patronised the saloon to an excess on Saturday nights was beside the point. Let other men serve him his liquor, but not his son. Mrs. Saanio dreaded the times when her husband was in his cups, for then the constant tension that existed between his son and him erupted into terrible rages on his part. So far he had never struck Risto, but sometimes it had only been at her intervention by putting herself between them. Lisa thought that it would be better if Risto moved out into a room of his own somewhere, but filial duty in that respect made him remain under the family roof.

"I've seen the show already, Mrs. Fernley," he announced in reply to Lisa's question. "I was off duty this afternoon when Mr. Fernley ran the movies through to check them, and I timed the slide-showing for him with a stop-watch." He sounded pleased with his achievement.

"Was it a good show?" She placed her cashbox on the table beside the roll of pink tickets. There was a different colour for each performance to keep out those who tried to get double value for their money.

"One of the best," he decreed. "Would you like me to get you a cup of coffee before we open the doors?"

She glanced at the clock. "No, thank you. There isn't time. If there's going to be a rush, I think we might as well let the customers start coming in."

He shot back the bolts and from that moment forth a constant stream of people poured through. Tickets and money exchanged hands at lightning speed. Risto kept some sort of order and made sure nobody sidled into the hall without paying. Soon all the seats were taken and there was standing room only, but still the patrons came. By the time she was able to close the cashbox and Risto had placed a "House Full" notice outside, Alan had shown a couple of one-reel comedies and had begun on the lantern slides. She slipped into a place at the back of the hall to stand beside the hotel proprietress, whose name was Mae Remotti.

"Have I missed many of the slides?" Lisa inquired in a whisper. Mae had been one of her first friends at the site, an agreeable, buxom widow who ran the hotel on her own and kept order in her saloon, which was not an easy task. But she liked lumbermen and knew their ways. Her late husband had been one of them before he was crushed to death by that enemy of all men in the forests, the hated knobbed tree, which was always cut down by chain saw and abandoned. She treated the men individually as homesick boys, scallywags, tellers of good yarns, lovers, or old friends in need of a hand-out, according to circumstances. She charged fair prices for her drinks, not taking advantage of owning the only saloon for miles around. The wooden menus at the table offered nourishing, well-cooked food, from big bowls of chicken soup at four cents to gefilte fish at seven cents. Portions were always ample, with chunks of home-baked bread on the side. She had snatched a respite from the saloon to watch the lantern slides, hoping that a brawl at the bar would not compel her to leave before they were over. In a low voice she gave her answer to Lisa.

"Only half a dozen. Mostly of the schoolteacher and her pupils. Real cute."

As the slides proceeded, Lisa was filled anew with admiration for Alan's eye for composition and his ability to capture the variations of light and shade. The audience was quick to applaud in appreciation. Often a loud buzz of chatter arose and there were always bursts of laughter at the amusing slides. Mae, enjoying the show as much as everybody else, had her attention suddenly distracted by hearing Lisa's sharp intake of breath.

"Are you sick, Lisa?" she asked with some anxiety. Even in the half-light thrown down by the projected image she could see that Lisa was stiff with shock, her fingers pressed into the side of her face as she stared fixedly at the screen. Following her gaze, the proprietress saw only a pleasing scene of several children running to meet a horse-dealer leading a team of shires into the sawmill. Then the picture disappeared in a second of darkness to be replaced by the last slide of the evening, which showed the same man again in close-up, laughing as he lifted a third child up to join the two others already seated on a horse's back. Mae recognised him. He was one of the Scandinavians, a Norwegian if she remembered correctly. He always had a meal and a drink in the saloon whenever he was in the vicinity. What was his name? Hagen. That was it. Peter Hagen.

Beside her the young woman uttered a low moan akin to pain as the image vanished and thunderous applause broke out again; a moment later she had dashed from the room. Mae followed after in concern. She found Lisa outside the hotel, leaning against the wall with her face hidden from the light of the S-necked lamp above the door.

"Tell me what's wrong," Mae urged sympathetically. Many men and women, drunk and sober, had poured their troubles out to her over the years. Her compassion for her fellow man was boundless, and it was her hope that she had never failed anyone in real despair.

"Nothing's wrong," came the choked answer. "I felt faint. That's all."

"Come back inside. There'll be nobody at the ladies' tables in the saloon at this hour. They'll all be watching the show. I'll give you a dram to clear your head."

"No. That's kind of you, but I'm all right now." Lisa turned to face her. She was pale but composed. "Stupid of me, wasn't it? I'll go home now. Good night, Mae."

In spite of her protestations, Lisa was in a daze as she collected Harry from the Saanio home. He was sleeping soundly and did not wake as she put him into his own little bed. Her feet seemed to be dragging as she went downstairs to rattle the firebox of the stove in the kitchen and put on the kettle. She had never lost the English habit of making a cup of tea in a crisis, but when it was made she sat with her arms resting before her on the kitchen table and left it untasted. To think that Peter had been within yards of her on the site of this very sawmill and she had not known. He had breathed the same air and walked the same ground and she had been totally unaware.

Common sense told her it was as well. It would have been a calamity to have met him again. Just seeing the lantern slides of him had been poignant enough. There was no telling how she might have reacted if they had come face to face. Or would it have been such a traumatic experience? His feelings for her had been wiped out long since by that quarrel on Toronto Island. His eyes would have held only disinterest, perhaps even a complete lack of recognition. That would have been good for her because it would have put completely in proportion what had been nothing more after all than a youthful bout of first love.

On this sensible thought she threw away the tea that had turned cold and made herself a fresh pot. This she drank, recovering herself and deciding firmly to resist the temptation to ask Alan when he had taken the photographs of the children with the horses. As far as she could judge by their outdoor clothing it was probably only about a month ago. Since it was highly unlikely that another team of new horses would be needed at the site for a long time to come, she could put her mind at rest about any chance of Peter coming back in the near future. There was every chance that she and Alan would be established in Seattle before he returned, if ever, to the sawmill again.

She was in bed when Alan came home. For the first time in their marriage she feigned sleep, not wanting to be drawn into talk that night. He moved about quietly in the bedroom in order not to disturb her. When he lay down beside her, putting an arm about her as he always did, she barely stopped herself from crying out in anguish that he was not the man whom she still loved.

As the days went past, Lisa busied herself getting ready for Minnie's arrival. Alan was away in the forests somewhere, giving her plenty of time to redecorate a room for Minnie while managing to keep Harry's fingers out of the paint. She hung the new drapes she had sewn and finally made up the bed with the patchwork quilt with the Blazing Star pattern she had begun before her marriage and recently finished. She liked to be kept busy, but more and more the overwhelming domesticity that prevailed during Alan's absences was becoming increasingly tedious, if not irksome. Little Harry, whose dark eyes and hair made his resemblance to his father quite remarkable, was bright and intelligent and affectionate, a continuous source of joy to her; she thought of him entirely as her own child, devoting most of her time to him, but she had come to need the outlet of the cinema evenings and the performance arrangements entrusted to her. Admittedly, when Alan was away, there was always a certain amount of business correspondence connected with renting the reels, but it was not every day that there were letters for her to write. A call at the house by a film-distributing agent was always a welcome diversion, for she had become authoritative in dealing with them. Those who had not met her before promptly imagined they could push any dud movies on to her, simply because she was a woman, and it caused them considerable surprise when they discovered their mistake. They never tried their tricks a second time.

Alan came home on the eve of Minnie's arrival. "I must leave to catch the late evening train for Seattle right after dinner," he told Lisa. "I have a great deal of business there to get through in the morning before I meet the steamship."

Lisa went out of the house with him when the hour came for him to depart. He wound the starting handle of his automobile and they kissed before he took his place behind the wheel and switched on the head-lamps.

"I almost forgot," he said on the point of driving away. "I'll have to be off to the forests again the day after tomorrow, for six or seven weeks. That means cancelling the three evening shows I intended to put on at the end of the week. Will you see that the usual postponement notices are displayed? 'Bye, Lisa."

He had not waited for her answer, knowing she was familiar with the process. They had had to have these notices printed some while ago. Cancellations always caused disappointment, but everybody understood that his work for the lumber company came before all else.

It was her full intention to carry out the task. When morning came she began stacking the cancellation notices into a basket and was interrupted briefly by the Saanio daughters. They had come to ask if they might take Harry on a picnic, which meant keeping him for the rest of the day as they had done on previous occasions. With their round Finnish faces and sweet smiles, they were already as maternal as their mother towards younger children and were destined to be the bearers of large families themselves when they grew up. She contributed some cake for the picnic, and the girls promised to bring him home before his bedtime.

After seeing off the little procession, Harry beaming with delight at his friends, she went back to finish getting the notices ready. Her task was just completed when a knock came at the front door. She had been half expecting that a movie distributor's agent might call that day, and a list of the films she wished to order lay on the parlour table. Briskly she went to open the door. The man standing there was Peter. He swept off his hat and the sunshine went leaping into his fair hair.

"How are you, Lisa?"

For a few suspended moments the sight of him seemed to fill her whole being. His height and breadth and his well-remembered smile eliminated all else. The greatest impact of all came from his fjord-blue eyes holding that tender, penetrating look that had once been there all the time before the painful quarrel had dashed it away.

"Peter!" She could only say his name. Maybe it was enough. Her voice had made mellifluous song of it on the overwhelming gush of love from the depths of her heart.

"It's been a long time," he said, not taking his eyes from hers. "I searched half of Canada for you after returning to Toronto a week after our parting to find you gone."

"I never knew." Again an involuntary inflexion revealed her emotions all too nakedly.

"That's what I assumed, when no reply ever came to the letter I left at Sherbourne Street." He crossed the threshold, for she had drawn back in silent invitation that he should enter, holding the door still wider. "I was sure that however much I deserved it, you would never have ignored the request I had penned."

She had closed the door and taken his hat to hang it on a peg. They faced each other there, in the white-walled hallway of the quiet house. Outside, the everyday din of the sawmill seemed remote and far away. The years that had passed might have been as many minutes. There was no strangeness between them.

"What was that request?" she asked almost inaudibly.

"I wanted your forgiveness."

Her long-lashed hazel eyes gleamed sadly in the paleness of her face. "You always had it."

His voice was low and heavy with regret. "It was the greatest mistake of my life not to have let that train leave Toronto without me."

"I waited in case you came back to look for me."

His face tightened painfully. "If only I'd known."

She clasped her hands together, leading the way through to the parlour. "How did you discover I was here?"

"Business kept me at Dekova's Place overnight. I stayed at the hotel. This morning when I was paying my bill, Mrs. Remotti mentioned seeing me with my horses on the lantern slides. Almost in the next breath she asked if I knew an Englishwoman by the name of Lisa Fernley. Although the surname was not the same, I was certain it would be you."

"Then you know I'm married."

"Yes."

"Still you came?" She sat down on the sofa and he took a seat beside her.

"I had to see you. Nothing could have kept me away. God knows how many miles I've travelled, or how many questions I've asked while looking for you. It's only a couple of months since I came back from Canada again. I never imagined I'd find you in the States."

At her request he outlined the route of his long search for her. When she realised they had both been in Calgary at the same time, she exclaimed with surprise. "I was working there then. Where did you stay?" She gave a nod when he told her, knowing the place well, for she had walked past it many times. "To think we might have met nearby, outside the Imperial Bank or by Doll's Jewellery Store, or any of the emporia in that street. I went that way almost every day." Her fingers laced themselves together restlessly. "So near and yet so far."

"I put inserts in the local newspapers wherever I went."

She gave a regretful shake of her head. "I rarely saw a newspaper. I couldn't afford to buy them and where I worked nobody was interested in reading."

"What happened to make you leave Toronto as you did?"

She told him everything as it had occurred. When it came to her marriage to Alan she made no secret of how it had come about for reasons of companionship and protection. "Alan is good to me," she concluded. "I could not wish for a better husband, and I think of his child as mine."

He leaned forward from the waist with some abruptness. "Do you love him?"

"You have no right to question me about my feelings." Her face was half turned away from him as if she were afraid of what he might read there.

"I have every right, because I love you." His passionate declaration sent her rising hastily to her feet, still turned from him.

He stood up and moved close to her. "Lisa. Listen to me. I have to know."

She closed her eyes almost with despair as he took her by the shoulder and gently brought her around to him again. To say what she wanted to say would release a situation that must be kept at bay at all costs. But when she did raise her eyes again to look up into his face all was said between them without a word being spoken.

Spontaneously he reached for her and she fell against him with a soft cry of home-coming. Their kissing was wild, adoring, and insatiable. His crushing embrace absorbed her into him and all else was obliterated except the miracle of his mouth on hers. She felt split asunder by the wonder and marvel of his kisses and clung to him frantically, only wanting their passionate contact to last forever. When eventually he did draw back to gaze at her again, he continued to hold her pressed against him, his hands spread across her back, strong and caressing.

"I'm never letting you go now that I've found you again," he said with such worship in his expression that she was dazzled, still held in thrall by the spell of their reunion. "You're in my blood. You have been since that day in Liverpool. I love you more than ever."

"I love you, too."

They kissed again. She felt as if she was slipping down into a well of desire for him from which there was no escape now or ever, all the restraints of their past meetings lost to her. She had waited for him without knowing she waited. She had continued to love him more than she had ever realised. Her heart had kept watch for his return while she had made herself believe that it could never be.

"Leave this house with me now," he urged. "Just as you are. Bring nothing with you. I want to get you away from here."

She almost said yes. The affirmative reply trembled on her tongue and how she did not utter it was a mystery to her. But his passing mention of the house had been a lever back to reality. He saw and felt the change that came over her. She leaned back against his supporting hands and pressed her own onto his arms to bring some small distance between his body and hers.

"I can't," she whispered, with a catch in her throat.

He thought he understood. "Where is Alan Fernley now? I know he's away because Mrs. Remotti told me you were here on your own at the present time. I'll go and see him first if you wish. I didn't intend to snatch you away without some confrontation with the man. As you say, he's been good to you and for that reason alone I respect him. I'm even grateful to him for taking care of you. God knows what would have happened otherwise."

She regarded him tenderly. "I never thought you could be so changed."

He compressed his lips together wryly. "Losing you taught me many things. I was bigoted and jealous in those days. I've learned wisdom if nothing else, my dearest love."

"Compassion, too?"

"I like to think I have."

She placed her hands lightly on the sides of his face and spoke imploringly: "Then show me compassion by not trying to force me into any hasty decisions."

"I was patient all the time I was searching for you, but now that I've found you again my patience has run out completely."

"Then I beg you to make a special effort to bide your time a while longer. I have others to think about besides myself. Alan is coming home from Seattle today with Minnie, a former Home girl like myself, and she is looking forward to living here. I couldn't leave within days or weeks of her arrival. She has suffered too many disruptions in her life. Then there is little Harry. I could never give up my right to care for him in any way that Alan would allow, and how would you feel if he came to stay with me for weeks or months at a time?"

"Anything you wish is agreeable to me." He covered her hands with his own to draw them down from his face and implant a kiss into both of her palms. "I like children. You know that. I'll enjoy teaching him to ski and fish and climb and handle a boat."

She smiled, a docile prisoner in his clasp. "Thus speaks the true Norseman of his favourite pursuits."

He smiled at her. "Those pursuits will make a man of the boy here in the States as in my homeland." His eyes grew serious again in his love for her. "I want you to bear my sons, Lisa. I want to love you as my wife until the end of our days."

She gave a long, blissful sigh. Her head eased into rest against his shoulder and he enfolded her in a quiet embrace. She was too moved for further speech, needing to let all he had said sink wonderfully into her and to contemplate life at his side with no more partings to tear either of them to shreds. He kissed the top of her head, almost in reassurance that he was going to make all her hopes and dreams come true. She felt safe and protected and secure within the curve of his arms, able to withstand any forces that might rage against her. When she raised her face to his again, they kissed lovingly with a soft exploration of lips until such an onslaught of passion for each other assailed them that it was only the anchor of being in Alan's home that kept her from surrender to him. She broke from his arms and moved away breathlessly, a long strand of her hair disarranged and lying across her shoulder.

"Not here," she beseeched, shaking her head as if he might argue with her.

"I agree." He was not insensitive to their surroundings and fully comprehended how it was for her.

"In fact, not until I'm free," she insisted vehemently. "I won't deceive Alan."

He had always known her to be a woman of conscience. "Then tell me when I shall speak to him. Tonight?"

"No." She was adamant. "I'm the one to explain matters to him and ask for a divorce."

"I should be with you." He was anxious for her. "We must see him together."

Again she shook her head determinedly. "He'll not become violent, if that's what you're thinking. You see, he loves me." Her voice wavered and she stood almost helplessly, her arms limp at her sides. When Peter moved forward to offer comfort, she withdrew from him before he could reach her. "Don't hold me anymore. Not today. I lose my head when I'm close to you and I have to think carefully. I'll have no chance to talk to Alan this evening with Minnie only just arrived, and he's leaving again early in the morning. I'll have to wait until he comes home again."

"When will that be?"

She shrugged in her uncertainty. "Six or seven weeks."

"Are you saying we mustn't meet during that time?"

She hugged her arms as if suddenly chilled. Now that they had found each other again she did not know how to endure six minutes or six days without him. Six weeks stretched ahead interminably. "Shall you be coming back to the sawmill before then?"

"More than that. There's something you don't know yet. I've been needing a depot not far from Seattle and within easy reach of the lumber camps. That's why I stayed overnight at the hotel. I've rented stables in the settlement and fixed everything with the owner of the property only yesterday. I'll be moving a new shipment of horses in there before long."

A warm wave of relief swept over her. He would be near. She would see him. Times of parting would only be short. "What would you have done about the stables if I had agreed to go away with you today?" she queried.

He looked amused that she should imagine they would have presented any obstacle. "I'd have soon found some other place. Something nearer Tacoma, perhaps. Who can tell? That doesn't have to be considered now. I'll be organised nearer the time you're ready to leave with me."

She closed her eyes briefly in blissful anticipation. "It's hard to believe I'm not dreaming. Oh, there's so much I want to hear about your travels and how you started horse-dealing on your own. Why don't we go for a walk and you can tell me everything on the way?" She felt a great need to be out of the house, wanting to be released from its fetters for a little while. Fetters? She had never thought of her home before in that light. Somehow it emphasised how greatly everything had changed for her since she had opened the door to Peter and had known how it was to have love in her heart again.

They followed a path well used by local people that took a semi-circular route through forested land to reach the settlement. It took a little longer than walking along the road, but it was more pleasant and they were in no hurry, only happy to be together. She asked about his brother Jon.

"He's in a lumber camp not far away. Yes, he's still in this country. His son is eight years old now and he's never seen him. It wouldn't do for me."

"Why doesn't he send to Norway for his wife and child?"

"Because it is still his intention to return to the farm there one day. It's greed that keeps him here. He keeps saying he will have one more season before he goes home, but when that season ends he signs on for another. At least he saves what he earns and transfers it regularly to a bank in Norway. Well, most of it anyway. He keeps back some for a binge once in a while."

"Do you see him occasionally?"

"I met him in Seattle only recently. He was wearing a good suit of clothes, but he was still bearded from the forest with his hair down to his shoulders and already drunk. I sobered him up and took him to a barber's where other loggers were getting trimmed. The floor, gouged over the years by those spiked boots that some of them always wear, was inches thick in hair-clippings. Then my brother found when he came to pay the barber that a poke of golden dollars had been picked from his pocket before meeting me and he was broke. I lent him sufficient to have a good time and get back to camp afterwards. I might as well have saved my money. Can you guess what happened?"

She smiled at his twinkling glance. "I've no idea."

"Half an hour later I was having a whisky in Joe's Saloon. It is always crowded with lumbermen and is reputed to be the longest bar in the West. The doors suddenly burst open and in reeled my brother, drunker than ever and shouting: 'Everybody have a drink on me!' "

She tilted her head back and laughed with him. They were holding hands as they always had done when walking side by side. The path was dusty underfoot, for the weather had been consistently hot and sunny for quite a while. When he kissed her before they left the seclusion of the trees, the dust motes hung in the sunshine about them and the air was fragrant with the forest scents of leaf and bark.

She took her hand from his as they emerged into Dekova's Place. Gossip flourished as it always did in close communities and for Alan's sake she wished to give no cause for it. She knew the farrier from whom Peter was renting the stables, which were located behind the smithy. The three of them chatted together until Peter went to check on the property where some feed for the horses had been delivered earlier that day. A loft above the stables would be his sleeping quarters whenever he had to stay there and she resisted the temptation to go and view it.

They lunched together at the hotel in the section of the saloon reserved for ladies with escorts or family parties. Risto Saanio waited on them, quick and efficient. Mae came to see that everything served was to their liking.

"My hunch was right then," she commented, only able to take a guess at what the reunion might mean to them from what she had observed of Lisa's reaction to the lantern slides and then the Norwegian's fierce excitement upon hearing the young woman's name. "I figured you two must be acquainted."

"It was kind of you to put us in touch with each other again," Lisa said evenly.

Mae eyed her curiously. She was kind but not wise. The unspoken words hung in the air. "How long since you two last saw each other?" she inquired casually.

"Nearly five years," Peter replied.

"Five years!" Mae almost gaped. That long a time and they could still look at each other as if their eyes were made of velvet, no matter how they might try to disguise it. If there wasn't some kind of lasting love between them, then her name wasn't Mae Remotti. Maybe she had interfered unwisely. Alan Fernley was a man she liked and admired too much to want to cause him personal trouble. If he had had a wandering eye she would have directed it towards herself, for he had that look about him of being good in bed, which was instant attraction for her, but he never cast a glance beyond his beautiful wife and she couldn't blame him for that. Yet had Lisa's beauty ever bloomed as much as on this day when she sat opposite a man from out of the past? Mae did not think she had ever seen her looking more radiant.

"Try a slice of the cherry pie," she advised them as Risto cleared plates away. "It's fresh-baked."

But they only wanted coffee. And each other. Mae could read that thought as she busied herself looking after other customers, her covert attention drawn time and time again to the couple talking quietly together, believing it wasn't noticeable that they were holding hands. Dear God! What had she started? There was enough misery in this world without stirring up any more. Why hadn't she kept to the good sense of the old adage about letting sleeping dogs lie?

Peter came to the cash desk to settle for the meal. "Thank you, Mae," he said seriously. She knew he wasn't referring to the well-cooked food or the service or even for the pennies and nickels she was handing him in change.

"You're welcome," she replied, wishing she could give warning that he should go away and stay away before anything went seriously wrong.

As he and Lisa left the building she crossed to the window and watched them say goodbye. The ache of it reached her and she pressed a beringed hand against her bosom as if the pain echoed there. They did not touch or kiss, only gazed at each other as they spoke some soft words of farewell. Then Lisa turned quickly to hurry, without looking back, along the road that led to the habitations around the sawmill. He, as if determined not to make their parting conspicuous, set off in the opposite direction to go striding out of sight.

Late that night, the bleep of the horn on Alan's automobile announced his return with Minnie. Lisa flew out of the house as the girl alighted. They hugged each other, exclaiming excitedly until Minnie drew back, straightening her hat, which had been knocked askew.

"Hey! I wanted to look my best when you saw me again. I made Mr. Fernley stop along the road to let me look in my mirror and tidy my hair. I wear it up now. Can you see?"

"Only enough out here in the darkness to tell me you've really grown up. Come into the house where there's some light." Lisa tucked the girl's arm in hers and together they went indoors while Alan unstrapped the trunk on the luggage rack at the rear of the automobile. Minnie, breaking free, whirled around to face her and strike a pose reminiscent of a mannequin in a fashion magazine.

"Well, Lisa?" Eagerness and trepidation. "What do you think?"

Ever the desperate need for reassurance. That, at least, had not changed. Otherwise three years had wrought a remarkable difference. Minnie was still herself in many ways, but she had grown taller with a slight and yet lovely figure which made her simple, home-made clothes appear to be much more stylish than they really were. Her glossy dark hair, of which she was justly proud, was dressed similarly to Lisa's own with a middle parting and drawn back to a knot at the back of the head, since pompadour fashions were no longer the mode. Her features, always good without a commonplace prettiness, had taken on a beguiling piquancy through which her personality shone with a diamond brightness. When she reached the age of twenty, and some of her gaucheness had evaporated, she would be breathtaking.

"You've grown into a lovely-looking girl!" Lisa pronounced with perfect honesty.

"Have I really?"

Lisa moved forward with a chuckle to take her by the arm again. "Don't fish for more compliments. In any case, you don't want them from me really. We'll leave that to the boys you will be getting to know around here. Now I'll show you to your room."

Minnie was pleased when she saw it and admired everything from the bouquet of fresh flowers in a vase on the chest of drawers to the rainbow colours of the patchwork quilt. Alan brought up the baggage, which consisted of a small tin trunk, and set it down on the floor.

"It weighs a ton," he joked. "Did you bring half the rocks of Granite Bay with you?"

"I've collected quite a lot of things in three years and I didn't want to leave anything behind." Minnie sparkled at him coquettishly. "Anyway, the weight of that trunk is nothing to someone as strong as you."

He gave her a sideways, smiling glance without rising to the bait and went downstairs again. Lisa, observing her, decided that Minnie had learned a great deal in three years. "How was Evangeline Jackson when you left her?" Lisa was wondering how much of the girl's new attitude was due to the companionship of the Jacksons' precocious daughter.

Minnie, removing her hat to put it away on the closet shelf, made a face. "We were scarcely speaking at the end. I was blamed for everything, needless to say."

"Blamed for what?"

Minnie's gaze shifted. "You mean Mrs. Jackson hasn't written to you?"

"Yes, I've had at least three or four letters about their going back East and over your travel arrangements and so forth. What else was there?"

Fluffing up her flattened hair with her fingers, Minnie gave a sigh. "Trust Mrs. Jackson to make a martyr of herself to the end. She's too meek and kind for her own good. That's why she could never keep a teaching post before she came to Granite Bay. Evangeline told me. Discipline went to pieces in a schoolhouse when Mrs. Jackson moved in. There are some teachers who invite persecution and Mrs. Jackson is one of them."

"Yet she taught you well, and you have excelled at the piano, according to reports that we have received from her."

"A class of two hard-working pupils in her own home was a different case altogether. I was determined to catch up with all the schooling I had lost through no fault of yours, Lisa, and Evangeline's pride wouldn't allow me to get the better marks. Evangeline always had to be the first with everything and everybody. She had the advantage of me academically, being naturally bright, whereas I had to struggle with my lessons. Then gradually I began to pass her in her best subjects, and she couldn't hold a candle to me at the piano. She grew to hate me for it—and for other things."

"What other things?"

Minnie moved restlessly. "Do we have to talk about it now?"

"No, of course not. You must be tired from the journey and hungry, too."

"I'm not hungry. Mr. Fernley and I ate an enormous dinner at a grand place in Seattle before we caught the train." Minnie's mood had lifted again to one of exuberance. "If there had been time he would have taken me to one of the theatres. *Romeo and Juliet* was on at the Lyric, being performed by a touring stock company. Wouldn't that be marvellous to see? Mr. Fernley has promised that I shall go to live theatre at the first opportunity. In the meanwhile I'm to be his new pianist at his motion-picture shows." Hastily she made amendment. "That's on the understanding that my piano-playing proves to be as good in his opinion as it was in Mrs. Jackson's. He seems to think I'll learn to cue myself into the screen action in no time at all."

Lisa was thoroughly taken aback, seeing her own plans in that direction would be set awry unless she kept a firm hold on the situation. She had taken it for granted that Alan understood that she would wish to become the pianist. Now it appeared that he had not. "You and Alan have tried to arrange a lot between you in a remarkably short time."

She hoped she did not sound disgruntled. Apparently she did not, for Minnie's beaming face had not changed expression. "I suppose we have," she agreed cheerfully. Having crossed to her tin trunk, she knelt down to unlock it. "To be honest, I dreaded his meeting me in Seattle. I've never forgotten how grim he was that night we first arrived at Quadra Island. I always avoided him whenever he came to Granite Bay. Now I've discovered he's nice when one gets to know him." The raised lid had revealed neatly packed clothes which she proceeded to lift out. "Mrs. Twidle used to say he was one of the best of men and I'm afraid I never believed her."

"How is Agnes? She wrote that she was going to miss you."

"I'll miss her as well. I loved going to her house. There was always a warm welcome." She took out of the trunk a package wrapped in tissue paper and sat back on her heels to hand it up to Lisa. "She sent you this. It's a belated wedding present, because she didn't want to risk sending it in the mail."

"I'll take it downstairs to Alan and open it with him." Lisa paused in the doorway. "Come down as soon as you've freshened up. On a warm night like this I'm sure you can do with a cool drink of my home-made lemonade."

"Yes, I am thirsty. When am I going to see Harry? He's asleep, I suppose."

"You can take a peep at him before you come down. The nursery is opposite this room."

"I promise not to wake him."

In the kitchen Alan had poured himself a cold beer from the ice-box. He took a swig from his glass as he followed Lisa through to the parlour. "What have you there?"

"A wedding gift from the Twidles." She put it down on the table and read the card that was with it. "Agnes says it's something she has long treasured, as it is from her childhood home in Toronto. She could think of nothing better to send with her and Henry's good wishes for our future together."

Carefully she unwrapped the tissue paper. Revealed was a Dresden bon-bon dish with lattice-work, the characteristic dark blue and rich ornamentation of the fine porcelain enhanced by exquisitely painted flowers. The sight of it struck such a poignant chord in her that tears sprang into her eyes.

"What's the matter?" Alan put down his beer and took hold of her arm anxiously.

"It's beautiful." She made no attempt to wipe away the tears running down her face. "Too beautiful. It reminds me of a plate I longed to possess throughout my orphanage childhood. Before everything began."

"Before what began?" He was watching her attentively.

"Leaving England to come to a new land. The start of a new life. Everything." She picked up the dish and held it reverently, tears still flowing as if they could not be stemmed.

"I'm sure it wasn't Agnes's intention to make you homesick."

"She never knew about the plate. I haven't even thought about it myself for a long, long time. And I'm not homesick in that sense. I suppose my reaction is due mainly to the surprise that we should suddenly own such a glorious piece of porcelain."

That was only part of it. There was another reason that she could not divulge. She had had the sensation of time playing tricks with her. In the past the plate she had coveted had never been hers and the man she had wanted had been similarly denied her. Now she had the porcelain dish, which far surpassed the plate, almost like an omen, and Peter was waiting on a final stretch of patience to make her his own.

"Where do you intend to display the dish?"

Alan's practical query helped to restore her self-control. She took the gift across to a corner cupboard and moved a few ornaments to give it a shelf to itself. Minnie entered the room while she was engaged in this task. Leaving the girl to admire it with Alan, she dried her cheeks as she went to fetch a jug of lemonade, some glasses, and an English plum-cake she had baked upon first hearing that Minnie would be coming, wanting it to mature richly. Returning with the tray, she found they had gone from the parlour out onto the porch.

Alan, who had been pointing out the direction of the sawmill and other landmarks to Minnie, turned to take the tray from Lisa as she came through the screen door. Minnie settled herself in the rocking-chair, her head against the bright cushions, and was completely relaxed. When refreshments had been passed round, Lisa took the spare wicker chair, while Alan sat on the porch steps. The planes of their faces were highlighted by the soft lampglow from the doorway. Conversation was mainly between the two friends, Lisa wanting to hear the latest news of the Twidles and Granite Bay. Minnie obliged, steering away from any mention of the Jacksons whenever possible and in her turn wanting to know about the people who lived in the neighbourhood and where, and how often, dances and other social events were held. It was clear that she had come desperately starved for fun and entertainment from the quiet environs in which she had spent the past four adolescent years under the staid supervision of the Jacksons.

"I had an unexpected visitor today," Lisa said when an opening presented itself, a little amazed that she could sound quite calm. "Do you remember the Norwegian emigrant, Peter Hagen, whom we met at Liverpool, Minnie? He brought you back to me after you had dashed off in the embarkation shed."

"I remember being caught and brought back to you, but I can't recall what he looked like."

Lisa did not expect otherwise, since Minnie had long been gone from Toronto before she and Peter had met again. Moreover, she had never considered making a confidante of the child Minnie on her adult feelings for him. "He's a horse-dealer these days. Doing well, I think. He heard my name from somebody and came to see if I was one and the same English girl whom he had once helped with a bunch of runaway children."

"Who gave the fellow your name?" Alan inquired lazily from where he lounged, a shoulder against the green painted porch pillar by which he sat, his fingers curled about the replenished beer glass resting on the step at his side.

"Mae Remotti." Lisa held her breath on the tense expectation of further questioning, but it was not forthcoming.

"It's strange how chance meetings can occur," he commented reflectively. "It's happened to me a couple of times quite recently."

"Who were they?" Minnie's tone was flirtatiously provocative. "Old flames?"

He grinned across at her. "No such luck," he gave back. "One was a fellow engineer I knew in Winnipeg, and the other a fellow passenger from the four-berth cabin I shared on the ship across the Atlantic to New York."

"Four-berth!" Minnie gave an exaggerated groan of envy. "What luxury! Lisa and the rest of us were packed like sardines all the way to Halifax. What was New York like when you landed there?"

Lisa sat back in her chair, feeling completely drained by what she had achieved and relieved as the talk flowed safely past her. She had mentioned Peter. It was the first step and she had taken it. By the time Alan was home again, Minnie would have adjusted to her new surroundings and the situation should be clearer. Then she would face him with what she had to tell and with what she had to ask of him.

Later, as she prepared for bed, she realised that the existence of Peter was the only secret in her life that she had ever kept from Alan. At the time of their marriage, Peter had been a bitter-sweet and private memory that had no bearing on anyone's life but her own. Now all that had changed. For the first time ever she lacked the strength and the will to struggle against the course that was sweeping her along. And she knew why. She had surrendered entirely to love.

Alan left early in the morning. Minnie slept late, which was to be expected. Her first action of the day was to make friends with Harry, who liked her at once and took everything out of his toy-box to pile into her arms and all about her as she knelt on the floor beside him. He followed her around, talking to her after she had put the toys aside and rolled up her sleeves to wash the kitchen floor, take a broom to the porch, and complete a number of other household chores. There was no idleness in her. She was as capable and efficient and as energetic towards work as she had always been. With no man present for distraction, her coquettishness and heightened self-awareness of her own female charm remained below the surface.

"I won't get up late tomorrow morning," she assured Lisa, who had had a busy morning herself at the laundry tub. They had both changed into fresh cotton dresses and were seated on the porch, gently wielding heart-shaped fans of dried palm for the hot weather continued unabated. Harry was having a mid-day nap upstairs.

"You deserve a rest after all the travelling." Lisa had her eyes closed. Her own mental exhaustion had remained with her from yesterday and her sleep had been fitful.

"At least you know I'm not normally a lie-abed," Minnie stated. "Unfortunately at Granite Bay Mrs. Jackson was always holding up my punctuality for breakfast, and everything else, as an example to Evangeline, who was never on time for anything. No wonder she grew sick and tired of my name."

Lisa's lids flickered open. "I think I should hear now whatever it was you felt unable to disclose when you arrived."

Minnie made a wry grimace. "You're not going to be pleased with me, I warn you. You'll think you've been landed with a wanton on your hands."

"I'll be the judge of that when I've heard you out."

Minnie rose abruptly from the rocking-chair and leaned

against the pillar by which Alan had sat the evening before. She entwined an arm about it with unconscious grace, but drew away sharply almost at once from its sun-baked surface. "Ouch! That's hot. Everything is too hot." She brushed a hand across her brow, her rising state of agitation not inducive to coolness. "Isn't there a lake for swimming anywhere around here?"

"There's a lake shore a few miles away. Alan and I have been to swim there twice when he has been home and we've had the lake to ourselves. Nobody goes there on a working day but at weekends it's a popular place for picnics among those who live around here. Folk who haven't a horse and buggy of their own go in hired wagons."

"How do you and Alan get there?"

"By automobile. It's a rough ride and the last half mile through the trees to the lake has to be on foot."

"Let's go there now! Alan told me that you're a good driver."

Lisa glanced at her locket-watch. It was no chore to drive that distance and it would refresh her to do something positive. "We'll go then. I'll get Harry ready."

"I'll prepare a picnic. We'll talk on the way about the Jacksons."

Lisa gave an amused shake of the head. "I think we must wait until we get to the lake. You'll soon find out why."

The reason was obvious as soon as Minnie took Harry on to her lap in the automobile. He disliked the boredom of that mode of transportation and promptly became fractious. "I want to walk, Mama," he protested vehemently.

"When we get near the lake," Lisa replied soothingly as she drove away from the house.

It took all Minnie's efforts to keep him entertained until they began being tossed about along the rutted forest track once the road had been left behind. This he enjoyed and his good humour was restored. When they left the vehicle he promptly ran ahead of them along the beaten path.

"When shall you tell him you're his stepmother?" Minnie asked.

"I'll not make an issue of it. He'll learn gradually that his father was married before and his own mother died."

"Wouldn't you prefer that he should never know?"

"He has a right to the truth and I'd never wish to deny him that." Lisa could recognise from Minnie's tone of voice that what she was asking was a prelude to something more. "Are these questions linked to what you have to tell me?"

"Yes. Indirectly."

While speaking they had overtaken Harry, who had found some small rocks for them.

Lisa swept him up with a laugh and held him high, breaking into a run to bear him the last few yards until the trees parted and the lake spread out in a sparkling blue entirely rimmed by forest. Harry wriggled to be set down at once and when released he began to play with stones on the shore at the water's edge. Minnie put down the picnic basket she had been carrying and flung herself full length on the grass in the shade. Lisa sat down beside her, keeping an eye on Harry.

"Well?" she prompted.

Minnie gazed skywards, an arm under her head. "The Jacksons are moving back East for Evangeline's sake. Mr. Jackson has gone ahead to start work for a new firm in Ottawa and get a house there. His wife and daughter are to make the journey in two stages. They'll stop somewhere along the line in Alberta and find a place where Evangeline can have her illegitimate baby. Then Mrs. Jackson will pretend it is hers when they arrive in Ottawa and nobody will ever be any the wiser."

There was a pause before Lisa spoke. "What was your rôle in all this?"

"I was an equal partner with Evangeline in the escapades that led to her getting in the family way. We met two young loggers working at the boom outlet in the bay. They would never have been allowed to call at the house and we began to meet them secretly."

"Where was that?"

"In the forest behind the house. They worked during the day, but they would come across to our side of the bay at night. Evangeline and I used to climb out of our bedroom window once her parents had gone to bed." She sat up and tore angrily at a blade of grass. "Before you start censuring me, I tell you it's impossible to describe how boring it was in that household. Mr. Jackson was so strict and his wife so strait-laced. I hadn't noticed the monotony of everything when I was younger, because I found it wonderful to be in a real home, but gradually I didn't know how to endure the rules and restrictions. Evangeline kept up a constant battle with her parents and her temper displays were devastating, made all the worse when Mrs. Jackson held me up once again as an example of good behaviour."

"I have a certain sympathy with Evangeline there."

"Oh, I agree. I suppose it was a natural culmination of everything that, when she and I did break loose, it should be with reckless abandon. You see, we found the loggers, Don and Billy, so much fun to be with. There were jokes and laughter and horse-play and games that maybe we shouldn't have played. Unlike Evangeline, I never touched the liquor they brought with them. Not because I was being goody-goody but because I knew I mustn't lose my head. I've heard enough in my life about what it's like for girls who have landed themselves with a bun in the oven."

If the whole discourse had been less serious, Lisa might have smiled at the old English euphemism that she had not heard since leaving her homeland. "You showed good sense there," she endorsed quietly.

"Billy didn't think so. He became steadily more sulky about not getting his way with me. One night he flew in a rage about it and blackened my eye. At the same time Evangeline, having realised by now she was well and truly in the family way, was screaming at Don for declaring bluntly that he was not the marrying kind. In the midst of the quarrelling, Mr. Jackson arrived unheard with a lantern and shotgun to discover all four of us. The boys fled and we never saw them again. They were gone from the site with their gear when Mr. Jackson went in search of them next day."

"What happened then?"

"Evangeline denounced me as having persuaded her into all of it against her better judgement. I said nothing. All I wanted was to get away from there. Reservations about your Alan's attitude towards me had to be overcome, something that had always daunted thoughts of rejoining you, or else I was going to find myself homeless. That's when I wrote to you."

"I'm glad you're here," Lisa said sincerely.

Minnie leaned forward and hugged her. "This is the third time you've rescued me. Twice from Mrs. Grant's clutches and now from being turned out by the Jacksons with nowhere to go. I hope that one day I'll be able to do something as a small return for all you've done for me. Will you remember that?"

Lisa merely smiled at the well meant offer. She thought how good it was to have Minnie's company again.

The rest of the afternoon at the lakeside passed pleasantly. They both swam, splashing about in the shallow water where it was warm, with Harry, naked as a cherub, between them. He slept in Minnie's arms all the way home.

Two days later Lisa went to pick up her shopping basket and found that it still contained the undelivered notices that should have cancelled the motion picture show at the hotel that same evening. They had completely slipped her mind, firstly through the trauma of her reunion with Peter and afterwards when Minnie had arrived to occupy her time and neighbours had offered them hospitality in welcome to the newcomer.

It was too late to distribute the notices now. There was only one course of action. She knew how to load the reels and run the projector. The show should go on as programmed. Minnie could take her place as ticket-seller and the custom of Harry being delivered into Mrs. Saanio's charge should go unchanged.

Minnie was overjoyed to be of assistance with the movie shows sooner than she had anticipated. "What fun! Do I get to see anything of the programme? I've never seen a motion picture."

"You can remedy that this evening when it seems as if the last latecomer has drifted in. Any drunks have to be barred. You can summon Risto Saanio to get rid of them by a special emergency bell if he's not there. He's the young man who has always been so helpful to Alan and to me on these cinema evenings. The proprietress knows it's good for business in the saloon and the restaurant to have such crowds of people coming to the movie shows, which is why we have an arrangement with her for Risto to be free of his other duties when we need him."

Lisa transported the cinematograph apparatus by automobile to the hotel that afternoon. It was Alan's policy always to leave it under lock and key except in his own home. Risto was surprised to find her in charge as he came down the hotel steps to unload the heavy projector in its carrying box. When she explained that she had overlooked the distribution of the cancellation notices, he congratulated her on taking on the show. As he set up the projector, a task to which he was well accustomed, the pianist arrived to watch the run-through of the reels and adjust her music accordingly. Risto, who was free of his duties elsewhere, lounged back in one of the chairs with his long legs stretched out before him and watched the whole programme through. One reel had not been rewound before delivery by the distributors and appeared backwards and upside down when projected, giving Lisa and him some spontaneous amusement. The pianist, ill-tempered as usual, merely banged her fingers away from the keys and tapped her foot irritably until the reel was put to rights.

In the early evening Minnie arrived at the hotel, having handed Harry safely into Mrs. Saanio's care. Risto, setting the ticket-table into place, straightened up and stared at her as Lisa made the introductions.

"Glad to know you," he said, bowing his head in the Finnish manner to which he had been brought up. He wanted to go on staring at her. Her willowy figure and clear-formed face made her appear fragile and forceful at the same time. He was intrigued and showed it.

She, in her turn, was almost struck dumb by his unfamiliar courtliness, which was at odds with his brash young appearance. Nobody had ever bowed to her in her life before. Neither could she remember ever seeing such smiling eyes as his. The very depths seemed to twinkle at her.

"I'm pleased to meet you, too."

"Is Mrs. Fernley your sister?" he asked her.

She exchanged a quick smile with Lisa who was setting out a roll of green tickets. "We've always been asked that and we feel like sisters, but there's no blood tie between us. I hear that you keep order if anyone gets objectionable, Mr. Saanio."

"Call me Risto. Yes, I'm the hotel's right-hand man."

"Cinema assistant as well?"

He grinned at her. "That's linked to my hotel work more than you might think. The motion picture shows give most of the male patrons a powerful thirst, and they crowd the saloon afterwards where I join the other barmen in serving them. We expect to be extra busy there tonight. That's why I won't be able to walk you home."

She arched her eyebrows. "What makes you think I'll need an escort? I'll be riding with Lisa in the automobile."

"That's okay then. We'll make another arrangement. I have a couple of hours to myself every afternoon. I'll call for you tomorrow at two o'clock." He turned his attention inquiringly towards Lisa. "If that's permissible, Mrs. Fernley?"

"Hey!" Minnie exclaimed, setting her hands on her hips. "Hold your horses! Maybe I don't want you to walk me anywhere."

He saw she was having difficulty in keeping at bay the smile playing at the corners of her rosy mouth. "Then we'll sit and talk somewhere. We have to get to know each other some way."

She had a gurgling laugh and could no longer restrain it. The merry banter between them would have lasted longer if Lisa had not called the situation to order by getting Minnie to sit down at the ticket-table to have everything explained to her.

The movie show that evening maintained its usual standard. Fortunately there was no hitch or misloading of reels, nothing to reveal to the appreciative patrons that it was the first time Alan Fernley's wife had managed a show on her own. As the audience departed she faced with confidence the next two evenings for which the programme was booked. Soon she and Minnie were alone in the room, the only sound the rewinding of the reel, which was done by hand. To her surprise, the girl made no move to come forward to assist, but remained leaning against the wall where she had previously joined those obliged to take standing room, her gaze still directed on the blank screen as if she were transfixed.

"I've never seen anything more wonderful than when William Humphreys took Julia Swayne Gordon into his arms," she breathed, her eyes starry. "Such passion! Then later when he rejected her, how her tears flowed. Oh, those clothes she wore, and the jewels in her hair. It must be the greatest thrill in the world to be a movie star."

There flashed through Lisa's mind what Alan had told her of the lives of movie people whom he had met in New York. There had been harassing by rival companies, film cameras shot to pieces by hired gunmen, and exhausting hours of filmed acting in broiling sunshine on flat roof tops to capture maximum light. Perhaps everyone would fare better in the exodus to California. She had read in one of the movie distributors' news-sheets that a valley of cultivated fruit orchards named Hollywood was being used with the landowner's permission for the taking of some film sequences. It sounded idyllic.

"I should think in the right location film acting would be enjoyable," she agreed.

Minnie bestirred herself and came across, her eyes still dream-laden. "I've played Portia and Juliet and Lady Macbeth. Mrs. Jackson would read the other parts while Evangeline and I were a cast of two to recite our lines. Evangeline always acted with such verve and quite outshone me." Her voice grew more ruminative. "Yet last Christmas when we gave a performance for a few people I saw Mrs. Twidle wipe her eyes when I expired as Juliet. Wasn't that strange?"

Mae Remotti entered the room just then. "Congratulations, Lisa," she said with satisfaction, advancing with the click of heels and a shimmer of dark blue satin. "I hear the show was a big success. Alan will be proud of you. You could put on a programme every night of the week if you wished."

"Three evenings in a row will prove to be plenty, I'm sure."

Mae wagged a well-manicured finger admonishingly. "Don't make any hasty decisions. These motion-picture evenings mean extra dollars and cents to me as they do to you. In business nobody throws away a chance to make more money. I know the equipment is heavy for you to handle on your own, but that's no problem. Risto can collect and deliver it again for you every day in one of the hotel wagons. What do you say?"

"Go on, Lisa," Minnie urged eagerly. "Remember you have me to help you."

Lisa's thoughtful expression showed that she was beginning to mull over the possibility more seriously. "I have to think of Mrs. Saanio. She can't be expected to take care of Harry six evenings out of seven, but she might allow Tuula, her eldest girl, to sleep at my house each night to be with him. I'm sure the girl would welcome some pocket money."

"That's settled then," Mae declared quickly.

"Not quite," Lisa countered. "I'll extend the present programme to six evenings on a trial run and see if the attendances keep up."

"They will," Mae replied confidently.

She was right. There was no lessening of numbers in the audiences. On the contrary, when Friday and Saturday night came a "House Full" notice had to be placed outside half an hour before the show was due to commence. The only crisis arose with the pianist's temperamental refusal to play each evening for a whole week. She gave notice and walked out minutes before the show was due to begin. Mae dealt with it by allowing Risto to leave the bar and run the reels while Lisa took the vacated seat at the piano. He became established as the projectionist, his skill at mending broken film at lightning speed appreciated by the audience, who always began to stamp their feet when there was a breakdown. With Tuula Saanio sleeping at the house overnight in charge of Harry, all Lisa's immediate problems were solved.

Minnie gave up driving home with Lisa in the automobile when the evenings ended. Instead she chose to sit beside Risto on the wagon when he followed with the cinematograph equipment stowed aboard. Their friendship was advancing steadily and each enjoyed the other's company. He eventually took a chance and stopped the horse and wagon to put his arms about her in an attempt at a kiss, but she gave him such a shove in the chest that he was almost unbalanced from the driving seat.

"Okay!" he exclaimed good-humouredly. "I'll wait until you beg me to kiss you!"

She giggled as he knew she would. What was good between them was their ability to laugh at most things together. He felt she had had little laughter in her life and suddenly everything was fun for her. It was as if she were blossoming before his eyes, all shades of the past cast away. It never occurred to him that she was falling in love with him as he was with her.

Lisa began to organise her daily routine on different lines. The distributor's agent, whom she had been expecting on the day of Peter's reappearance into her life, arrived most opportunely when her decision to continue the film shows had been made. He arranged that certain movies she required urgently should be rushed to her and listed her requirements for the next eight weeks. She could not look beyond that span for personal reasons, not knowing what might have happened or where she would be when that time had elapsed.

It was for this reason that Lisa began to instruct Minnie on how to accompany on the piano whatever was being enacted on the screen. If she had not been going away she would not have surrendered the piano to anyone else, but she had no choice. The girl was quick and alert, which was important, and her musical talent vigorous and enthusiastic, only needing guidance to moderate for gently romantic and quieter scenes. Lisa's instruction took place during special morning showings of reels run by Risto.

"It's rush-about music for comedies," Lisa explained, "and some of the French light operas provide just the thing. When there are lulls in the film story some neutral music is in order. Rousing overtures for cowboys and Indians, heavy opera for dramatic scenes, something sweet and tender for love and one or two set pieces for scenes of pathos."

Minnie did well for a first attempt. As the sessions progressed and she snatched every free minute for practice, she became steadily more proficient until Lisa felt that eventually Minnie would be able to take over from her when she herself had gone away with Peter. She was determined not to leave Alan bereft of consideration and had decided to appoint a respectable middle-aged widow in the settlement to keep house for him in addition to caring for Harry until he could stay with her at frequent intervals. She found it heart-breaking to think of being apart from the child, and clung to the hope that with time Alan would find it convenient for Harry to be with her for longer and longer periods. The presence of the housekeeper would provide chaperonage for Minnie and preclude the kind of talk that indirectly had precipitated her own marriage.

Risto took great interest in Minnie's practising at the piano. "When are you to play for a show?" he asked her.

She shrugged. "I don't know. I'd like to be given a trial run but maybe Lisa thinks I'm not ready yet. At least she can be sure that I could step in if an emergency with Harry or some other unexpected crisis should keep her away."

It would have suited Minnie to have been the full-time pianist, simply because if the first "House Full" notice was not displayed before the commencement of the show she never managed to see the earlier reels, and she had become a film addict. She and Risto discussed the main movies at length, both of them seeing each one enough times to observe backgrounds, spot faults, and note acting tricks and mannerisms. The snatches of dialogue flashed onto the screen to clarify the plots became so familiar to them after the five days' viewing that they could repeat whole lengths to each other, speaking the individual rôles with dramatic gestures and exaggerated eye-rolling and much hilarity. Quotes from the current movie of the week would pepper their normal conversation, creating private jokes between them, so that when the words appeared on the screen she, standing by him at the projector, which had become her usual place, would sometimes become so convulsed with giggles that he was infected by her mirth and had difficulty in concentrating on the task in hand.

By chance they were alone one evening in the hall before the show started. Almost automatically they dropped into the dialogue of the current movie until they realised simultaneously that it was the lead up to the scene of passionate embrace. They trailed off the words that were not their own and fell silent, looking at each other. There was no light-hearted foolishness in them now. Only a shared sense of wonder illumined their faces as they drew together. She felt him trembling as he put his strong, young arms about her. They sank into a kiss, she responding to the eager passion of his mouth, and when they drew apart at the sound of voices approaching in the lobby outside, they gazed at each other with intensity. Each knew that the kiss had been a turning point in their relationship. Henceforth, nothing would be as easy and uncomplicated as it had been previously. They were in love.

It was when Lisa was playing some introductory music for a performance during the fourth week of her independent enterprise that she knew Peter was one of those taking their seats. How she knew it was impossible to say. There was no tingling down her spine, no sensation of being stared at, only an intimate knowledge throughout her whole body that he was close at hand. Searching her memory, she tried to recall if she had experienced a similar awareness, without realising its source, when they had both been in Calgary or when he had visited the sawmill unbeknown to her. She could well have mistaken it for the bouts of restlessness that had ever come upon her when sometimes her thoughts had drifted to him.

She did not look round, but continued to play herself into the programme with a few dramatic chords as the opening reel projected its flickering image on the screen. In the interval before the main motion picture, she did turn her head, it being her custom to acknowledge with a smile and a nod those people she knew who had caught her attention. And there he was, seated no more than a few feet from her, and as their gaze locked across the short distance between them she felt herself drawn deep into the love she saw in his eyes.

When the show was over and the patrons were departing, he came to her as she was stacking her sheets of music together. "How are you?" he asked her.

She cradled the music against her with an arm. "I'm fine. And you?"

"I've missed you."

"Oh, my love," she breathed. Then she glanced about her, for the hall was far from empty yet. "We can't talk here."

"Later then. I'll wait for you."

She shook her head despairingly. "I must drive home straight away. Minnie would ask questions if I deviated from my routine at this late hour of the night."

"Let me at least ride home with you and I'll walk back."

She could not refuse him that one small favour. "Wait for me by the automobile. It's parked by the trees at the side of the hotel stables. I'll be about half an hour."

He nodded and departed. She went to pull the curtains across the screen, which remained as a semi-permanent fixture on the wall, and afterwards helped Risto and Minnie with the rewinding of the films and the stacking of the reels. When everything was done, Risto hurried out to fetch the horse and wagon and bring it to the side entrance to facilitate the loading up of the equipment. Lisa waited, as she always did, until everything was in its place and Minnie had taken up her seat beside Risto. Normally she overtook them on the road. Tonight she would not.

As the wagon rolled away she shot home the bolts of the door, checked that all the lights in the hall had been extinguished, and then set off through the kitchen, her cashbox with the evening takings under her arm. Those still working there bade her good night as she left the stifling heat and cooking aromas to emerge into the warm air of the night, which seemed almost cool by comparison.

She had gone more than a few steps when she heard someone coming behind her. Thinking that Peter must have been strolling about while waiting for her, she swung around expectantly in time to glimpse a brutish-looking man leaping for her. Her sudden turning saved her from the unseen attack that would have been made upon her, and gave her a second to scream before he landed a savage punch in her breast and snatched the cashbox from her. She fell sprawling and screamed again. Footsteps clattered from the kitchen as people ran out to see what was amiss. The cook reached her first.

"Mrs. Fernley! Are you hurt?"

She sat up with his supporting arm about her shoulders. Pain filled her breast and she felt nauseous with it, but she chose to shake her head. "I'm all right. Somebody stole my cashbox."

"Don't you worry," he said. "I guess that guy ain't going no place with it."

There was certainly a lot of noise and shouting to be heard. Those in the saloon had poured out to join the crowd gathering somewhere out of her range of vision. Somebody else gave a helping hand as the chef assisted her to her feet. Then Mae was there, taking over and having her brought through to the private parlour. The door was shut and she was able to lie down on the velvet couch. Mae peered closely at her.

"No damage to your face, thank God. But you're white as paper and in pain, too, I can see. Where's the injury?" When told, she used colourful language to describe what she would do in return to the thief if the opportunity for revenge could be hers. "As for you, Lisa," she continued, "a cold compress on your bruises and you'll spend the night here. As soon as Risto returns with the wagon, he can go back and tell Minnie where you are and why. That will give him a double portion of spooning with her at the gate."

In spite of the pain she was in, Lisa smiled faintly. "You've noticed how they feel about each other, too, have you?"

Mae, handing her a drink of water in a glass, for she had refused anything stronger, raised an eyebrow and directed a clear look at her. "I know love when I see it. Sometimes it causes a whole lot of trouble that should never be."

Lisa returned the glass and closed her eyes wearily. "Don't preach, Mae. And don't let your conscience trouble you about bringing Peter and me together again."

"I must have been crazy."

"We would have met sooner or later. He had already rented some local stables."

"So I've heard since, but at least the responsibility wouldn't have been mine in the first place."

Lisa frowned anxiously, raising herself up from the cushions. "I wonder where he is. He'll be worried when he hears I've been robbed."

"Hears about it?" Mae chuckled. "He caught the thief. He

heard you scream and by the time he reached the yard others were going to your assistance, so he gave chase. The cashbox is intact and in future you'll leave it in the hotel safe overnight and pay the takings into the bank from here in the mornings. Peter is waiting to see you, but your bruises need attention first and you can receive him afterwards."

Wearing one of Mae's less flamboyant silk robes over a voluminous nightgown of satin and lace, Lisa was installed in the hotel's best bedroom when Peter came to see her. She exclaimed at the sight of his torn suit and cut mouth.

"You're hurt!" She hurried to him.

"No, I'm not. The thief was just desperate to get away and I was equally determined that he shouldn't. The result was a punch-up." He took her hands into his, his knuckles bandaged. "I can't do justice to kissing you on the lips at the moment," he added regretfully, giving her a light kiss on the cheek. Seeing that she was suffering some reaction to the shock she had received, which had not been helped by the sudden sight of his damaged appearance, he led her across to a couch where they sat down.

"It didn't matter about the wretched cashbox," she said huskily. "Suppose that man had had a knife or a gun?"

"Maybe he did. I don't know. I didn't let him get the chance to use either and that's what counts. In any case, I didn't know he had robbed you at the time. All I knew was that he had attacked you, and for that I wanted to kill him."

Her cheeks became hollow and her lips quivered uncontrollably. "I'm scared that we love each other too much."

"That's nothing to be scared about." He drew her to rest against him, her head against his shoulder. "We just have to sort out our lives as soon as we possibly can. Have you heard from Alan?"

"No, I haven't. When he's far away in the logging camps it isn't often I get word from him. It does happen occasionally that someone, such as a travelling preacher, might be coming this way and will bring a letter, but that's rare. Why do you ask?"

"I brought a new team of horses to the stables today and tomorrow I start moving them to one of the logging camps. I reckon it will take me four days to get them there. It may happen that I'll meet Alan somewhere and, in spite of what you say, I want to speak to him and get everything into the open."

"No! I must be the one to tell him. Please!" She hugged an arm about his neck in her desperate plea.

"I find the waiting hell."

Her upturned face was filled with anguish. "You think I'm being cruel to you, but I long to be with you for a few hours away from every spying eye and wagging tongue."

He spoke softly. "I know somewhere."

She shook her head despondently. "Impossible. Perhaps you don't realise what a close community this is. For a married woman to be sighted with another man in her husband's absence gives rise to talk immediately. It's only thanks to Mae's discretion that nobody knows you're with me now. I will not let Alan hear gossip before he hears the truth from me."

"You were seen publicly with me last time."

"Oh, once was harmless, but we couldn't repeat it. In any case, Alan wasn't away in the forests then."

"He was in Seattle that day."

"That's not the same. It's the long absences of menfolk that make wives fretful. That's when they're watched by other women, and woe betide those that slip from the straight and narrow path. They are ostracised at once. I know myself to be watched as closely as any logger's wife whenever Alan is away for weeks at a time. For his sake I'll take no risk."

"You're the only woman who drives an automobile in this district, aren't you?"

"Yes. I am."

"Then you're free to go where you like and no one can follow you."

"On some terrain a horse and buggy is faster."

He smiled and took a map from his pocket which he spread out between them. "You know this road?" he asked her, pointing to the one along which she had driven Minnie and Harry to the lake.

She bent her head forward. "Yes. Is that the route you're taking tomorrow?"

He nodded and traced a trail around the lake that led on past it in an easterly direction until his fingertip came to a spot marked in ink. "That's a log cabin hidden amongst the trees. It belongs to a friend of mine. He's away for some weeks, but when he knew I was to be in the area he offered me the use of it if I needed to rest the horses or sleep overnight. It's a long walk from where you would have to leave the automobile, but there wouldn't be a spying neighbour for many miles. Will you meet me there?"

She hesitated only briefly before shaking her head, her face torn by the decision she felt compelled to make. "I've only a limited amount of will when I'm with you, my love. It would be all too easily swept away in such sublime isolation, and I must remember that Alan still has the right to stand between us."

"I'll be at the cabin for two days."

There came a hasty knocking at the door and Mae's voice called to them. He went to admit her and she entered at once. "You can leave now," she said to him. "There's no one around at the moment. I'm protecting Lisa's good name if it kills me."

He grinned at her. "You're a good friend, Mae."

She threw up her hands in a gesture of impatience with her own foolishness and waited while he kissed Lisa once more on the cheek. Then together Mae and Peter went from the room. Left alone, Lisa looked again at the map, drawing it onto her lap from where it had been left open on the couch beside her. The inked markings of the cabin's location seemed to leap out at her. Although she ripped the map across several times in quick succession, she knew in her heart that she would be able to find her way there by day or night for as long as she lived.

Ten

When morning came Lisa was free of the aftermath of shock although her bruise matched the amount of pain it had caused her. She had bathed, dressed and breakfasted by eight o'clock when Minnie arrived in great anxiety. The girl had left Harry with Tuula Saanio and brought Lisa a bunch of flowers which she accepted gratefully.

"They're lovely, but I don't deserve them. See how well I am today."

"I wanted to come back last night, but Risto said Mae was in charge and putting you to bed and I was not to worry." She gave a gulp. "But I did worry." With a gush of tears she threw her arms about Lisa. "I remembered how it was on the train to Calgary."

"Hush. It was nothing like that. Don't upset yourself, Minnie dear. Dry your eyes. That's better. Have you eaten? No, I thought not. I'll order some breakfast for you."

Minnie was in luck. Risto served the food, soon convulsing her with giggles as he behaved like a comedy waiter in a movie, pretending to stumble and almost drop the tray. Afterwards he danced about as if he had burned his fingers on the coffee-pot. Fortunately they were in Mae's own parlour or else his antics would have brought forth a furious reprimand.

"That boy!" Mae shook her head between exasperation and

amusement as she handed Lisa the cashbox that she had taken from the safe, where it was to be placed every night in future. "He should be on the stage, not waiting at table. Oh, my! Look at him now! He's juggling with the bread rolls." She slapped her hands together sharply and stamped her foot. "Risto! Stop!"

He caught the rolls deftly and tossed them back into the basket, which he bore out of the room with gliding steps as if on skates. Lisa and Minnie both burst out laughing afresh, but Mae's patience had ebbed. She made to follow him out to the kitchen but Minnie quickly blocked her way.

"Don't be cross with him, Mrs. Remotti," she pleaded, her eyes dancing. "That's the best breakfast I've had for a long time."

Mae chucked her head in sustained exasperation, although she took notice of the girl's appeal and let him be. "He's seen too many movies, that's his trouble," she declared.

"It's too late now," Minnie answered merrily. "He's like me. We're both movie-struck."

Minnie went with Lisa to pay the cashbox money into the bank after they had left the hotel. Lisa had decided it should be a daily event instead of the twice-weekly procedure it had been before. Everyone they met had heard of the attack on her, women stopping in the hope of gaining more details, the men raising their hats and expressing the hope that she had recovered from her ordeal. If she had had any thoughts of meeting Peter as he had wished, however innocently, this particular morning would have eliminated them. People in a small community seemed to gather news of everybody's business in a matter of seconds, almost as if they drew it in from the air itself. She looked across at the rented stables as she and Minnie went past and saw the place was locked up. Peter had departed early with his horses for the forest. She followed him in her thoughts.

She tried not to think of him too much as day after day went by. It was Alan on whom she wished to concentrate, deciding how best to present her situation. He had always been fair to her and she could not believe he would stand in her way when she requested her freedom. As for loving her, he had never repeated those words since the night he had first told her.

Perhaps the lack of a reciprocal reply on her part had confirmed for him that it could never be otherwise for her, and he had reconciled himself to that fact. It would make everything easier for them both if that should prove to be the case. She became gradually more hopeful that all would go well. At times when she glanced at the calendar on the wall, she noted in her mind's eye Peter's progress through the forest, and his return journey. When it drew near the day when he would arrive at the cabin she began to suffer for the disappointment that would be his when she failed to appear, for he had made it clear that it was his hope that she would reconsider and be there. She tried to find some consolation in the resolve that she would make up for every lost moment they had both endured when at last they were together in true belonging.

A sense of desolation became acute in the morning when, after a disturbed night of looking after Harry, who was cutting a new tooth, she awoke to the certainty that Peter would have installed himself in the cabin. He would be watching for her in vain as one hour and then another went by. Downstairs, when Tuula Saanio left to go home to breakfast as she always did after staying the night, Lisa forgot to thank her for looking after Harry, a courtesy that normally was natural to her. Then she was unnecessarily brusque with Minnie for some minor carelessness and afterwards was sharp with Harry over something equally unimportant. Already highly irritable from his inflamed gum, he became twice as difficult and obstreperous.

Lisa knew no relief when Minnie bore him out of the house to divert him with a walk and playtime. She sank down in a chair and put her head in her hands, trying to blame her tiredness on a poor night's sleep and for the screaming tension of her nerves, but knowing that it came from an entirely different cause.

It seemed like the last straw when Minnie came rushing back into the house an hour later, making the screen door bang and shaking the house. "Guess who's here!" the girl cried, whirling into the parlour where Lisa was trying to divert her thoughts with some letter-writing. "Alan is home! Harry and I met him leading his horse into the sawmill stables. I've run ahead to let you know."

Lisa sat for a few moments with the pen motionless in her hand. It seemed almost more than she could bear that Alan should return today of all days. She made some acknowledgement to Minnie for bringing the news, put the pen back in the ink-stand, and rose to check her appearance automatically in a mirror before going out onto the porch to meet him.

He approached the house holding Harry in the curve of an arm and carrying his saddle-bags in his free hand. At the sight of Lisa in her cool green cotton dress, framed by the pillars of the porch, he increased his pace.

"Are you all right? I've just heard at the sawmill about the mugging that took place." He sprang up the porch steps and dropped the saddle-bags with a thump on the boards to put his arm about her shoulders and kiss her soundly, Harry wriggling in between them.

"I've suffered no ill effects," she answered. "I've almost forgotten about it. I had to make a statement in court and the man has been imprisoned. There were plenty of witnesses to his attempt to get away with the cashbox and how he was floored by a well-aimed fist."

"I'm thankful to hear it. But what's all this about you being outside the hotel with the cashbox anyway? I hear you've been running the motion-picture shows in my absence."

She faced him fully. "I have done so. Do you mind?"

He grinned at her fondly. "Mind? I'm proud of you. Let's go into the house, and while I bath and change out of these clothes you can tell me all about it. Later I want to talk to you about something important."

Previously they had always made love immediately upon his home-comings, but with Minnie in the house that would not be possible. Lisa was thankful. She did not want to be touched. Not by Alan. Not today. Not tomorrow. Never again.

She sat on a chair, relating almost everything as he soaped his strongly muscled body and washed away the dust of travelling. After explaining how she had forgotten to deliver the cancellation notices in the acceptance of all the hospitality that had greeted Minnie's arrival, she went on to tell of the success of the first evening that had led to Mae Remotti's suggestion that the performances should continue nightly. Somehow she managed to keep Peter's name out of the entire discourse, even when Alan questioned her further about the attack on her. She was afraid that if she mentioned him her eyes, her voice and her whole expression would give away her feelings, and the time to tell Alan was not quite yet. In any case, he had said he had something of importance to discuss with her. The least she could do was to hear how she might advise him in whatever the matter should prove to be.

It would be difficult to say whether Minnie or Harry was the more pleased to have Alan home again. The child would not leave him, bringing toys and wanting to play ball and climbing onto his father's knee until excitement made him fractious again and there were more tears that Lisa had to dry and console. Minnie, who had begun her overwhelming attentions by boiling shaving water for Alan and heating what had been needed for his bath, ran to fetch his pipe and tobacco jar after he had eaten. Then she sat by him to talk incessantly about the movies and how Lisa had taught her to cue in to the screen action on the piano, and much more about all that had happened in his absence. Lisa left them together on the porch, taking Harry up to his room where she sat on the bed with him in her arms until he fell into a much needed daytime nap. She was in need of quietness herself, and the moments were precious to her as she sat in solitude with the sleeping child.

She had no idea how much time had elapsed when Alan came in search of her. She put a finger to her lips, laid Harry carefully onto the bed and then left the room. Alan took her by the hand to draw her into their bedroom where he shut the door. She stiffened defensively, supposing he had only one purpose in mind, but his first words dispelled that fear.

"I have to talk to you and there's no chance anywhere else in this house. Is Minnie always so ebullient?"

A smile passed across Lisa's lips. "When she's happy. And she's happy that you're home again."

"She's been asking me how soon I propose to open a cinema in Seattle. It appears she has a beau whom she wants me to employ as a full-time projectionist."

"That's the Saanio boy. They're in love with each other. What did you say to her?" Lisa had drifted over to stand with her hand resting on the nearer of the twin posts at the foot of the bed. Alan crossed leisurely to the window where he raised the blind that kept the room cool throughout the heat of the day. Sunshine burst through the lace curtains to flood the room with a searing brightness. He remained with his back to her, looking out of the window.

"I told Minnie it would not be possible," he answered.

"Why?" She was puzzled. "If he's willing to move to Seattle you couldn't employ anyone better. He's been an invaluable help to me and there's virtually nothing he doesn't know about film projection and how to maintain the apparatus."

"I've changed my mind about Seattle as a place of residence for us. It's time now to put my ideas for launching a cinema into action. I've no intention of allowing my contract with the lumber company to be renewed in spite of pressure from their top sources. I'm looking farther afield now."

"Have you decided it shall be in California, then? That shouldn't present any problem either." At all costs, when her own plans were put into action, she wanted Minnie to continue to be happy. She was convinced that the girl would not miss her so much if Risto was near. It was important for Harry that a contented atmosphere be maintained. As for the housekeeper she had earmarked, everything would go well there because the woman had been born in San Francisco and would be pleased to be returning to California. His next words took her completely by surprise.

"We're not going to California. Our cinema is not to be there." He turned and stood silhouetted against the bright window. "I've decided we shall return to England. London is the place. I'm taking you home, Lisa. Home to England."

Her hand tightened about the bedpost, the pressure she was exerting turning her finger-nails white. She stared back at him in shock. "I don't understand."

"I feel a great need to go back to my roots. They're your roots, too. England is where we both belong. It was no choice of yours that you were taken from your native land in the first place."

Her throat was tight with apprehension. It was dawning on her that all unwittingly he was making it impossible for her to voice her own cherished plans for a future with Peter. "I thought you liked living in this part of the world."

"I do. But it was for Harriet's sake that I put this country before my own in a choice of habitation."

"Your son is American born!" The words burst from her.

"We can raise him to love the land of his birth and the land of our birth. He will be doubly blessed."

"You've been away from England for a long time. Things may not be as you anticipate in opening a motion-picture house there."

"I've been in communication with British business contacts. Cinemas are mushrooming there as they are here. I want to be in at the beginning with what I have to offer the movie-going public."

She swallowed deeply. "Think the matter over again, I beg you. Why not try your luck with a cinema in Dekova's Place or Seattle or Los Angeles or anywhere in the States? On that success you could branch out in England later."

"I've had plenty of time to consider every detail of this move as I've travelled on my own between the lumber camps. It's been in my mind for a long time. You must have noticed how I've shelved several options that have come my way. More and more I've become convinced that it would be advantageous in every respect to make London my centre."

"Why couldn't you have forewarned me?" she cried out.

"I did talk to you about it months ago. You seemed to favour the idea."

Her head dropped in a weary nod. "That was last year. A lot has happened since then. I haven't given it another thought since. You were considering California after that."

"I had to weigh everything up. Now I've made the decision for the well-being of you and Harry and myself. It's the right one. I know it."

"When do you plan to return to England?"

"I daresay we could get a passage from New York within three weeks."

"So soon!" She was stricken. "That only leaves a matter of nine or ten days before leaving here."

"It's putting pressure on you, I know, but you'll have Minnie to help you pack. I feel the sooner we depart after my contract expires at the end of the week the better it will be."

"What about Minnie? I can't leave her homeless."

"Of course not. I fully realise you feel responsible for her and naturally she comes with us."

"What does she have to say about going back to England?"

"I haven't told her yet. I wanted to talk it over with you first."

She was outraged. "You haven't talked over anything! You've given me an ultimatum."

His eyes narrowed curiously at her. "That's an odd expression to use. You speak as if I've threatened you somehow. When you said you would marry me, I told you I would do everything I could for you, and that means loving and caring for you throughout my whole life."

She had not wanted him to speak of love, but unashamedly she used it in a desperate attempt to sway him. "You would have stayed in the States for Harriet's sake." Her voice rose in a frenzy of appeal. "Why not do the same for me?"

He came and took her by the shoulders with gentleness. "If it was in your best interests, I would remain. But the situation is entirely different. Harriet was American and I simply kept a promise that one day I would bring her back to live in her own country. You are as English as I am. There is nothing to keep either of us here."

She wanted to scream out that there was everything to keep her in this alien land. Scream and scream and beat her fists against his chest in fury that he should be instrumental in this trick of fate that was reversing all her hopes and smashing her dreams. Only one plea was left to her. She knew it to be doomed and yet she had to utter it in all its futility.

"Let me stay on here and keep Harry with me."

He misunderstood her reason. "Until I'm established, I suppose. No, darling, I need you with me. As for Harry, I don't want to miss another day of his childhood. I've had to be away from both of you far too often. There'll be no more separations." He drew her, tense and unwilling, closer to him. "It's natural that you should have misgivings about going back to England. Most of your years there were spent in a dismal orphanage. Things will be different when you're with me. To date, I've had little chance to give you the good things of life, but those days will come."

She found herself beyond speech, her distress too great, her despair too overwhelming. He had made up his mind where his future lay and there was no turning him from it. Whatever she said or did, Alan would be taking his son to England with him. She knew that once he had learned of Peter he would not be vengeful, but however willing he might be to share the boy's time with her, the sheer distance factor of the span of the Atlantic Ocean would keep her from ever seeing the child again. If she was lucky, she might just see Harry when he was grown to manhood. In the meantime she would be deprived of all the years that she felt belonged as much to her as to his father. The original bond created by a dying woman had been overtaken and surpassed by her own devotion to the child. On an agonised moan she pulled herself from Alan to grip the bedpost with both hands as if for support and press her forehead to it. Again she moaned involuntarily.

He half reached for her as if to draw her to him again for comfort, but the tenseness of her whole frame was a warning in itself and he let his hands fall to his sides. His tone was compassionate and caring. "You need a change of air and scene more than you realise. You've been working hard with the cinema and running the house and looking after Harry and coping with Minnie. I'll drive down to the hotel soon and organise everything for the movie show this evening. You give it a miss this time and take a good rest."

She raised her distraught face and looked over her shoulder at him, forcing herself to speak of more mundane matters. "What about the musical accompaniment?"

"Minnie can play the piano. It will be experience for her."

"She's quite good. You'll be pleased."

He reached out and stroked her hair. "Do you want to tell Minnie the news of our going to England, or shall I?"

"I will," she replied in a choked tone. "But not until tomorrow. I must be composed myself. It's going to upset her dreadfully to be parted from Risto." She gave a start as a sound came from the neighbouring room, her own troubles momentarily forgotten. "There's Harry. He's woken up. I'll go to him."

He restrained her gently when she would have moved towards the door. "You are having a few hours to yourself. Remember?" Taking her face between his hands, he tilted her lips to meet his. His mouth was strong and loving, her own soft and unresponsive. She supposed he blamed her present distress for the absence of a swift return to his kisses, never suspecting that so much more was involved. She withdrew from him as quickly as was possible. He paused in the doorway. "Everything will go well as long as we're together, I know it."

The door closed and she was left alone. Wearily she passed a hand across her forehead. She could hear Alan talking to his son, and then the child's merriment when borne downstairs in his arms. Minnie's voice greeted them in the hall before the three of them moved outside the house for a game of ball. Not long afterwards it became apparent from the increased noise that Tuula had arrived and was being drawn into the play. The carefree sounds did little to ease Lisa's anguish as she paced the floor, trying to think of some solution to the dilemma that faced her. If only there was a way to solve that ocean-wide distance of separation! Then gradually, and at first almost imperceptibly, a faint glimmer of hope began to dawn.

She went quickly to the window as the sound of the automobile starting up alerted her, and was in time to see Alan driving off on his own to the hotel. It was not yet midafternoon, but he would be checking the apparatus after his absence, running reels through and being generally busy and fully occupied until the show was over and the packing done. That meant the automobile would be parked in its customary place at the side of the hotel stables. It would not be missed if she took it for three or four hours.

On this conclusion she became purposeful in her movements. She stripped off her clothes, bathed her face in the cool water she had poured from the ewer into the rose-rimmed basin, and refreshed herself completely. In a complete change of undergarments and wearing her coolest dress of cream sprigged muslin, her hair brushed and repinned into its knot, she skewered a lacy straw hat on with a hat-pin and hastened downstairs. Harry, having lemonade and cake with the two girls in the shade of a tree, spotted that she was dressed for an outing and ran to her.

"I'll come, Mama!"

She stooped down and gave him a hug. "Not this time, Harry, dear. I'm going visiting."

He did not like visiting. It meant best clothes and sitting still. He was easily persuaded to run back to the girls. Minnie called to her: "Shall you be back before I leave extra early for the movie show?" Happy pride filled her voice. "I'm playing, you know."

"You'll be a success, I'm sure. No, I'll not be back, but Tuula can take charge."

Tuula nodded her fair braided head. "We'll be just fine, Mrs. Fernley."

Minnie, wishing to ask something out of Tuula's hearing, rose to her feet and came across to walk a few steps at Lisa's side. "Will you speak to Alan about Risto for me? I don't think he took me seriously when I said that Risto wants to work for him when he gets his Seattle cinema."

"He took you seriously," Lisa replied, "but the cinema isn't going to be in Seattle."

"Then where is it to be? Risto won't mind its location. He doesn't want to spend the rest of his life in Dekova's Place."

"I can't stop to talk now, Minnie."

The girl frowned, peering closer at her. "There's something wrong, isn't there? What is it? How can I help?"

"I've a problem to work out, that's all. Don't worry. I'll explain everything to you tomorrow."

Lisa hastened away. She walked quickly along the dusty road into the settlement and soon arrived at the hotel. She went to the automobile, wound the starting handle vigorously, and, when the engine throbbed into life, climbed in behind the wheel and drove away. The stable-hand waved to her and she waved back. The sight of her driving the vehicle had become a familiar one. Nobody but Alan would think to question her presence in it at that hour of the afternoon, although it would be registered by every woman sighting her from store or house or in the street that Alan Fernley's wife was driving out of Dekova's Place to some destination as yet unknown to them. To a farm to buy eggs? To the railroad depot? To visit a neighbour with a new baby? The possibilities were endless. Lisa felt satisfaction in the knowledge that on this occasion none would discover whither she was bound or whom she was shortly to meet.

She had known in the first instant of Alan's disclosure of the return to England that she could never bring herself to leave Harry. Even if her maternal feelings had not been as strong as they were, she could not have abandoned him. Her own experience of growing up motherless had taught her the sadness of that situation, and she had seen too many children bereft of loving care to let Harry go from her into the all-powerful control of an English nanny, not all of whom were filled with the milk of human kindness. Alan would be a good father, but Harry would need her as much. She had two alternatives to put to Peter. One was that he should also move to England where they could marry after the divorce and have Harry to stay with them for lengthy periods as she had originally hoped; the other possibility would be so hard on both of them that she hoped she would not have to voice it.

The forest closed about her as she drove along. The only person she saw was an old logger, long since retired from camp life, who sat on a boulder at the side of the road cutting off a quid of chewing tobacco from a tin. He lived in a shack in the forest and made wooden buckets and spoons and other domestic items for sale in the settlement. She was one of his customers.

"Good afternoon, Mr. Mcpherson," she greeted him. It was highly unlikely that any word of his sighting of her would drift elsewhere. He was a close-mouthed individual who preferred his own company and took no interest in other people's affairs.

"Hi, ma'am," he replied dourly, glancing askance at the automobile. He did not consider anything but a horse suitable for transport. Not that he owned one. God had given him two good feet and he used them.

She reached the deserted spot where all vehicles, horse-drawn or otherwise, had to be left for reasons of terrain, and continued on foot. It was much cooler by the lake, where a breeze of increasing strength passed across the expanse of cerulean blue water and rustled away fiercely through the tree-tops. She took off her hat as she walked along and swung it in her hand, following the trail that kept close to the lakeside, the old hoof-prints of passing horses hard-baked into the ground. As she progressed, her pace increased and if anything she was stimulated and not tired by the exercise. It was as if she was being borne along by love and when at last she broke away from the lake to go deeper amongst the trees again, she began to run. She ran until she came to the great rocks and boulders that hid the cabin from anyone passing along the trail. Then she stopped, for Peter was sitting high on one of them where he had been watching for her.

"You're here!"

He clambered down swiftly, lightly clad in dungaree trousers and a blue cotton shirt open at his sun-browned throat. She rushed forward again and reached him as he jumped the last stretch and landed in front of her. Then she was in his arms and they were lost in a madness of kissing as he sought her mouth again and again. He hurried her, still locked in kisses, between the rocks into the clearing where the cabin stood. When it seemed to him that she would have halted, even drawn back from the threshold in spite of being held fast in his embrace, he simply swept her up in his arms, kicked open the door and bore her into the shadowed interior where he set her on her feet.

She gasped when her mouth was freed, her hands flying to her hair in a vain attempt to stop it swirling down about her shoulders as he released it from its pins. Then she clutched at the front of her dress, but with his unique skill that she remembered from the past, he appeared to have loosened the buttons at the back of it with a single sweep of his hand, so that it was already slipping from her shoulders. A tug and it was around her ankles, her waist petticoat with it. She stood there in her chemise and lace-trimmed bloomers and white stockings with pink ribbon garters.

"No, no, no!" She thrust out her hands in a vain attempt to keep him at bay. He merely caught her by the wrists and pulled her close to recapture her mouth with his own until her will melted. She was floating in love. There was no other explanation for finding herself seated on the side of the bed while he knelt to roll down her stockings, not with haste now, but with care as if to reveal her legs was an unveiling. Somehow she managed to find her voice.

"I came to talk." Her voice sounded weak and shaky to her own ears.

"Of love." It was a statement made categorically by him on her behalf. Her left foot was free of its stocking and he raised it to kiss her toes.

"Of love and going away," she ventured.

"Our going away." Again a statement.

"No." She felt as if her heart was in her throat. He was kissing her right toes now and her whole foot was quivering. Her fingers dug into the bedclothes on either side of where she was sitting, and again the sensual waves passed through her as she struggled to utter what she had to say. "Alan is returning to England. I have to go with him. I can't let little Harry be taken from me."

Her words seemed to hang in the air almost as if taking shape and becoming tangible. Their effect on him was terrible to see. White-faced and appalled he became motionless, a kneeling statue with his lips still bent over her foot cupped in his hand. Outside the hot summer wind whirled with gathering strength in the tree-tops and around the cabin. Abruptly his head jerked up, fury and pain and disbelief in his eyes. He exclaimed harshly: "You came here to tell me that!"

"It's an unexpected complication, but it's not insoluble," she cried in a rush.

He returned her feet to the floor and sat back on his heels, still staring at her. "What do you have in mind?" he questioned bitterly, setting his hands across his thighs with elbows jutting. "Am I to accompany you to England and become an English gentleman? Am I to leave the freedom I have found to scrape a living in a land where my knowledge and experience would be superfluous? Nobody knows more about horses than the English. Do you think Alan would let his son come to a back-street tenement or a stable-hand's quarters? I think not. So what is your solution to this new turn of events?"

She sat numb. Without realising it, he had closed irretrievably the one loophole that she had felt remained open to them. He had not seriously believed that she expected him to surrender the new life in a new land that he had made for himself. What he had said had been an outlet for anger and disappointment that once again some barrier had arisen between them, something that he saw as being solely of her creation this time. How could she have considered even briefly that she had any right to crush his pride in his present achievements, the success he was making of his chosen trade, and even his whole individuality by persuading him to go to England where most likely conditions for him would be just as he had predicted. She was only thankful that she had not voiced it. It left her with the alternative suggestion that she had hoped would never be needed.

Her soft whisper came brokenly. "I'm asking you to wait a while longer for me to be free to share your life."

He rose slowly to his feet and stood looking down at her. "How long?" His tone was hard and uncompromising.

She tried to answer him but tears were springing to her eyes and constricting her vocal cords. All that came from her was a sudden deep cry of desolation as she dropped her face into her hands, head bowed and her knees drawn up with her feet on tiptoe as if huddling into a private misery that he could not share. Her noisy sobbing was beyond any control. She, who tried always to dispense with the uselessness of tears, was now unable to hold back a gushing flow. With her gleaming fair hair hanging loose and in her half-clad state, she looked unprotected and vulnerable, making him feel he had never loved her more. He gave a groan of despair that she should suffer and sat down on the bed beside her to draw her close.

"Don't cry, Lisa!" he appealed urgently, kissing her brow and temple and whatever part of her face was not hidden by her hands. "I'm not angry with you. I'm just mad at every damn thing that's contriving to keep us apart. How long do you want me to wait? Three months while you sort things out in England? Or is it six months that's needed for a divorce over there? Don't say a year. I wouldn't know how to get through another year without you."

She took her hands away from her face and flung her arms about his neck, pressing her tear-wet cheek against his. Her sob-choked words tumbled forth. "More than a year. Long enough for my child to grow to an age when he could cross the ocean from England to visit me. Wherever we were living in the States I could go to New York to meet him from the ship and see him off again."

He broke her limpet-hold about him and shook her by the shoulders as he glared furiously at her. "Are you asking me to wait another six or seven years for you?"

"I'll not stay with Alan during that time," she assured him frantically. "My marriage to him will be ended." Her eyes were so aswim with tears that she could barely focus and she took his face between her violently trembling hands. "I'll work and save somehow to see you at least once or twice until we can be together for always."

"I'm through with waiting! I want you now! You're letting another woman's child keep us apart. What of *our* children? Are they never to be born?"

She shrank into herself again, doubling forward distractedly. "Try to understand, I beg you."

He sprang to his feet and began to pace back and forth, running his fingers through his hair. "I can't bring myself to believe you would do this to us. We were given a second chance to be together and you are prepared to throw it away."

"No! That's not how it is!" She thrust herself up from the side of the bed and took a step towards him. "I'm twenty-two and you are twenty-six. We're young. We'll still be in our prime when I can come to you. You mustn't speak as if decades are going to divide us!"

He half turned to make some maddened reply and his glance chanced to take in the window. His whole expression changed from one of frustration and rage to sheer dismay. *"Herre Gud!"* he exclaimed forcibly in his own tongue. Then he threw himself forward to pull the door open and rushed outside.

She saw the billowing smoke without grasping immediately in her state of distress what it portended. It came to her in the next instant when she comprehended the meaning of the ominous crackling in the distance which the stout walls of the cabin and their own tempestuous discourse had kept at bay.

"A forest fire!" she exclaimed in alarm as he came darting back in again.

"Gather up all the blankets," he instructed, grabbing a small axe from the shelf of tools to thrust it through his belt. "Move fast! I'll fetch my horse. We must get out of here and to the lake at once!"

She tossed on her dress, not taking any precious time to fasten its back buttons, and thrust her bare feet into her shoes. Then she ripped the blankets from the bed and two heavy Indian ones of rich pattern ornamenting the walls. Last of all she snatched up her petticoat and stockings from the floor where they lay, adding them to the roughly folded bundle of blankets that filled her arms. In her haste she forgot she had accidentally dropped her hat onto the grass when Peter had picked her up in his arms on her arrival. With her range of vision hampered by the large bundle she carried, she stepped on the straw crown and crushed it as she ran to meet him coming around the corner of the cabin, leading his frightened horse by the bridle. It was wide-eyed and snorting, tossing its head at the billowing smoke and the unmistakable stench of the wind-borne fire filling the air. Peter needed all his strength to keep the animal in check.

"Keep close to me," he told her, hastening his charge between the boulders in the direction of the trail.

She obeyed, running in the wake of the horse and him. The blankets were heavier than she could have imagined possible, the weight seeming to threaten her arms in their sockets, but there was no chance for Peter to give her aid, for the horse was struggling to get its head and bolt. Behind them the fire was getting closer. It was as if the iron door of a giant furnace had been swung wide to release its roar and scorching power upon them. The sweat ran from every pore of her body with exertion and heat; the shoulders of her unfastened dress had slipped to cut painfully across the top of her arms; but she did not dare stop to adjust them.

The lake came in sight amid the foliage ahead. Peter, reaching the water's edge ahead of her, splashed into it with the horse and gave it a mighty whack on its rump that sent it leaping forward into the deeper water where it began to swim away. He waded back swiftly to where she stood stunned with horror at the sight of the blazing trees that bordered the lake to the east and to the west, and had completely cut off the track that she had taken earlier. Behind her, to the north, the fire was leaping forward to join up in a dreadful semicircle of flame. Only the south shore of the lake was as yet untouched.

"Will the fire reach the sawmill and the settlement?" she cried out in terror.

"No. The wind's blowing in the opposite direction." He did not pull her into the water as she had expected, but rushed past her to push amongst the undergrowth where he began to haul forth a rowboat. She dropped the blankets to give him a helping hand. They were both coughing from the smoke.

"Does this boat belong to the cabin?" she asked breathlessly, her lungs hurting.

"Yes. Thank God we were in time to reach it ahead of the flames."

As it slid into the water, he lifted her into it, picked up the blankets and tossed them in after her. One of her stockings was lost in the process, gliding away on the ripples. He took the oars and set them in the rollocks and pulled strongly away from the shore. At his instruction she spread a blanket in the bottom of the boat for some comfort and pulled another over her as protection; the folded petticoat made a little pillow for her head. All around them the water spat and hissed as sparks and burning debris plummeted down from the flaring tree-tops swaying in the wind.

He was making for the south end of the lake, hoping that it would escape the fire, but before he was a third of the distance he rested for a few moments on his oars and then pulled them in.

"It's no use," he said, "we'll have to see the fire through from this boat."

She raised her head and saw that the spread of lake shore where not so long ago she and Minnie and Harry had shared a picnic, was being devoured by the flames, the terrible circle of fire almost complete. The thankful thought flew through her mind that neither Alan nor Minnie would suppose her to be in the forest fire when her absence was discovered, and would be spared anxiety about her. She must hope that they would imagine her to have taken refuge with whomever they might deduce she was visiting.

There was a swish of air above the boat. She screamed out as she saw a blazing branch descending. It landed with a crash that rocked the boat in a firework display of thousands of vivid sparks. She screamed again as the sting of pain from some of them seared her cheek and she heard the frizzling sound of her hair burning.

Peter moved so fast that the branch was knocked out of the boat with barely a scorch mark, and his bare hands extinguished the flicker in her hair almost before she knew it. Taking the axe from his belt, he knocked out the thwart on which he had been seated for the rowing and tossed it overboard. His next move was to spread the blanket on which she had been curled up further along the boat, making more space for them both to lie full length. While she took advantage of the space he had made for her, he dipped the Indian blankets in turn into the lake, wringing out the excess water which was a strenuous task that made the muscles ride in his arms. Skilfully he spread them right across the boat as protective covers. He had to lie on his back beside her to tug the second one into place. They were encased in humid, dusk-like shadow and they turned on their sides to face each other, sharing her little makeshift pillow.

"We're drifting towards the middle of the lake," he told her reassuringly. "We'll be safe."

"How long before the fire burns itself out or is brought under control?" she questioned anxiously. "Hours and hours? A day and a night?"

"I hope so," he whispered, moving his lips onto hers and beginning to caress her breasts with a delicious gentleness that was almost unbearable to her. The errant shoulders of her still unfastened dress were drawn down again, and his kisses, slow and subtle and warm with love, passed with it, bringing all her long yearning for him into full flood. She could no more have held back than she could have halted the flames consuming the forest. It was to her as if she had been snatched from death into this haven with the man she loved, a small capsule of time having been specially created for the two of them with all else shut out by the monstrous fire that had lost its power to terrify her.

They undressed each other with tender exploration, she becoming as familiar with his body as he with hers. Their ardent kisses and trailing fingertips and sweet fondling punctuated their love-whispers with sighs of pleasure. Blissful tears trickled from the corners of her eyes when he enfolded her thighs to press a kiss against her that held all the homage of an adoring man for his woman's ultimate perfection. Quite simultaneously, a kind of wildness entered into their passion as if there was the fear that all they meant to each other could never be assuaged, but when the moment of their belonging came she saw in his eyes, as he saw in hers, a look of pure unbridled joy that nothing had ever surpassed this time in the whole of their lives. He thrust deeper into her and wave after wave of ecstasy broke over her, drawing her still further with him into the realms of lasting love.

Night fell but there was no darkness except for the wind-blown pall of smoke; the sky was filled with a red-gold glow as if a sunset had been permanently ensnared, and the lake all around them held the same liquid colour. They slept wrapped in each other's arms, legs entwined, and then stirred to make love again, sometimes gently, at others with overwhelming passion, but always with some new caress, or touch, or movement to extend their growing experience of shared joys and pleasures that were entirely their own. The pattern of these secret happinesses continued throughout the ensuing hours. Neither had ever felt more loved.

Not long after dawn they became aware of a curious stillness. He folded back the blankets overhead and they raised themselves up to look out. The rising sun shone warm and beatifically upon their shoulders. The wind had dropped completely. The air was almost hushed, although the aroma of charred wood was still all pervading. The smoke was rising straight upwards from smouldering clumps and from the small pockets of flickering fire still in possession of the split stumps of fallen trees, which lay at angles everywhere like a scattered profusion of giant charcoal matches. She gazed around as if scarcely able to believe that this encircling scene of destruction had once been that of a beautiful forest. Peter's horse stood forlornly on a sandy spit where doubtless the first retreat of the flames had begun some hours before.

"We have to wait awhile yet," Peter said, drawing her down again. He possessed her for the last time in the boat that was now sun-filled, their limbs agleam in the radiance, her tumbled hair full of golden lights. The bitter-sweetness of their fading idyll gave a wondrous intensity to the final union of his flesh with hers. They remained in soft kissing, his lips on her mouth, her throat and her eyes, before reluctantly they drew apart, her arms loosening a loving hold about him.

Afterwards they bathed in the lake, since the boat had drifted into shallow water, and he cleared a space amid the charred debris that floated there. They returned to the boat to dress. She put on her one surviving stocking. He fastened the buttons down the back of her dress, kissing her spine between each one as if he would have turned the clock back if it had been possible. She could not pin up her hair, for the pins lay somewhere amid the ashes of a burnt-out cabin, but she tidied it as best she could. Lastly she tied it back with a piece of cord that Peter found for her among some fishing tackle in the bow.

They sat holding hands in the boat. She was quiet and preoccupied. Questions and explanations lay ahead of her when it was safe to go ashore. Not for a moment did she expect to find herself pregnant as a result of their mutual passion, for although they had made love with complete freedom and abandonment she had come to the conclusion long ago, over the many months of her marriage, that she was barren. Neither rape nor her husband's love-making had brought her to fruition. She saw it as another of fate's quirks that was beyond explanation. Slowly she turned her head to face Peter and spoke emotionally.

"You do realise that if Alan will have me back after this night with you, that I must go, don't you?"

"Then nothing has changed?" His face became agonized and yet curiously he was not surprised. Somehow he had known how it would be.

"Nothing, except that we have memories to cherish until we are together again."

"If you leave me, you'll never come back." He saw she was about to make some vehement protest and he shook his head quickly. "You will mean to, I know that. But if the child has the slightest need of you he will always come first. Since you think of him as your own, that's not unnatural, because you love with conscience, Lisa, my sweet. That's the way you are and how you'll always be. You see, we must accept that the boy may ail, or suffer an accident, or simply continue to look to you for maternal love and support. Whatever the reason, you'll not feel free of your duties until he is as near fully grown as makes no difference."

"You are saying I must make a choice once and for all. There can be no compromise." Her voice faltered on the clarification.

"I have a life to live, and it would grind me to dust if I was forced to wait year after year and then you never came." He spoke determinedly. "I could wait for a definite date of reunion, but that's all. Give me that date."

She was very pale, her eyes full of pain. "You know I can't."

He twisted his mouth bleakly. "You could if you wished, but you realise only too well that what I have foretold is true."

"I'll love you always!" The words tore from her heart.

"I'll never stop loving you, but I can't live in limbo. I must be with you or without you."

She looked as if she might die. "Am I never to see you again?"

"The decision is yours."

She turned her gaze away from the starkness of his expression, unable to bear what she was doing to him and yet powerless to retract, for he had spoken the truth and there was no querying the facts. She started violently when the sombre silence between them was suddenly broken by a male voice hailing them across the water from the south shore.

"Hi, folks! You okay?"

Neither she nor Peter had noticed the newcomer's approach through the charred fern and verdue as he dodged among the trees propped at curious angles. She recognised him instantly as Mcpherson, the old lumberman she had driven past the previous day. He had come to a halt with arms akimbo, his jaws moving rhythmically on the tobacco he chewed as Peter answered him.

"Yes! I'll row the boat over. Is the terrain safe?"

"The ground is still smoulderin' in places. Do you have boots? No? I brung a spare pair with me hopin' I'd find Mrs. Fernley safe and sound where you are right now. You can wear 'em and she can ride the horse."

He turned to plod on along the water's edge, the spare boots tied by string over his shoulder, to reach the horse, which whinnied and tossed its head nervously. He caught the bridle and dived about in one of his capacious pockets to find something edible, which the horse accepted greedily when he held it out. There was nuzzling for more as he clapped the horse's neck and spoke calm words of reassurance.

Peter set the oars in the rollocks and rowed the boat to the south shore, the bow knocking aside branches and other floating deadwood. As it beached, he sprang out and turned to lift her onto land. As he held her close to his body for no more than a matter of seconds, they looked deep into each other's eyes and all their shared feelings were mirrored there.

"Here's the boots." Mcpherson had come up to them, leading the horse, and he chucked the caulked and spiked footwear of the logging trade that he had once followed onto the ground at Peter's feet. He turned to Lisa. "I'm sure glad to find you safe, ma'am. That fire came up like a match to tinder. It's lucky the wind kept in the direction that it did. The sawmill and the settlement escaped completely."

"What of your home, Mr. Mcpherson?" she asked.

He spat a stream of tobacco juice before replying. "By-passed, ma'am. They used to call me Lucky Mack in my loggin' days. Some sparks ignited the roof, but I was keepin' it damp with buckets of water and no damage was done that can't be repaired."

"It was kind of you to come looking for me. How did you know I'd been trapped by the fire?"

"An hour ago I sighted your burnt-out automobile. Come on. We'd best be goin'. I reckon there'll be search parties out for you any place near the water. That's always the hope folks follow when someone is missin' after a fire." He stooped to make a step for her with his linked hands and she mounted the horse, pulling up her skirt to sit astride its bare back, for Peter had had no time to saddle up in their flight from the fire. Quickly she clutched at the mane for a fast hold, for she did not know how to ride. It was still her hope that Alan and Minnie had been spared anxieties about her.

Progress was slow. Whole areas of smouldering earth had to be avoided and there was the constant danger of collapsing trees. The tobacco juice that Mcpherson emitted from the side of his mouth at fairly regular intervals occasionally caused the ground to hiss. The whole time smoky dust and thick ash flew up all around them, getting in their eyes and settling on their skin and clothes. Her muslin dress became dark-streaked and small pieces of falling twigs caught in her hair. They eventually came to the road and there at the side she saw the twisted mass of metal that had been her transport to the lake.

Gradually evidence of the fire thinned out to scorched bark and singed foliage. Finally greenery took over with a sweet coolness and fresher air. Peter called a halt to remove the uncomfortable caulk boots, which had been two sizes too small for him, and put on his own shoes. Mcpherson took the boots from him and prepared to take his leave, but Peter stayed him with a question.

"Do you know a trail to get Mrs. Fernley back to her own home without going through Dekova's Place?"

Mcpherson's face did not change its expression although he shifted the quid in his mouth. He knew full well what lay behind those words. If the couple had met by chance in the forest and found a mutual shelter in the boat, it would have come out naturally in the conversation. But that had not happened and the way in which they looked at each other would have told any simpleton that they were lovers. "I reckon I do."

"Then would you take her there? That is, if she has not changed her mind about coming with me." Peter gazed up into Lisa's eyes and she gazed down into his in a final sharing of love. Hers became brilliant with tears, but slowly she shook her head. As she reached out a hand to him he enfolded it in both of his own.

"Goodbye, Peter."

"Farewell, Lisa." He kissed her fingers and then released them.

Mcpherson guided the horse around and in through the trees away from the road. She tried to keep herself from looking back, but finally she could no longer resist and turned for one last glimpse of him. But he had gone, unable to endure the sight of her passing out of his life.

It was a long and roundabout route that they followed. Neither she nor Mcpherson spoke, she too choked for idle conversation, he silent because he preferred it. Eventually they came onto the path that ran between the sawmill and the settlement.

"I'll get down here, Mr. Mcpherson," she said, "and walk the rest of the way."

He helped her dismount. "What about the horse?"

"Would you return it to the stables behind the farrier's? Mr. Hagen will be there."

"Okay."

"Thank you again."

He continued to regard her as phlegmatically as if he had done no more than sell her one of his kitchen buckets. "You're welcome, ma'am."

It did not take her long to reach the row of whitewashed houses at the edge of the sawmill. To her dismay she saw neighbours gathered at the gate of her house and she darted back quickly into the shelter of the bushes by the path, unable to face their inquisitive stares and questions at the present time. Almost blindly she stumbled back the way she had come for some distance before leaving the path to lean back against a tree out of sight of anyone who might pass by. In her mind's eye she followed the progress of Mcpherson with the horse. By now he would be handing it back to Peter. When it was rested and fed and resaddled, Peter would ride it out of Dekova's Place and away to take up the threads of his life again as if their reunion had never been. Yet they had loved each other too much and too long ever to be free of memory, no matter how many years went by.

Such was her stunned and unhappy state that when the sound of a horse approaching from the settlement reached her ears she thought, on a flash of hope, that Peter was taking a detour by way of the sawmill to catch sight of her once more. Swiftly she ran out onto the path and saw it was Alan in the saddle of his own horse, his face and clothes as smudged with ashes and black dust as her own, his expression haggard and wrenched by despair.

"Alan!"

He stared at her almost in disbelief. Then he gave a great shout and flung himself from the saddle to snatch her into his arms, crushing her to him with such force that she was breathless and could not speak. To her sorrow she realised he had thought her lost in the fire and it was as if she had come back from the dead.

When he drew back from her it was to shake his head as if the miracle of her being safe and sound was still beyond his comprehension. "When I was unable to trace you at any farm or more distant neighbour, I began to fear you had been caught by the fire along one of the isolated skid-roads before reaching your destination." The strain of all he had been through continued to give his face a taut, stretched look, his eyes showing that he had had no sleep for twenty-four hours. "I've been with the search parties. I was returning home to see if any word had been left there."

"I drove to the lake."

"So far?" He was surprised.

"That's where I left the automobile and it's a burned wreck now. I survived in a boat on the water. Mr. Mcpherson found me and brought me back on a horse. There's more to tell. Much more. But I want to get home first, only the neighbours are outside there."

"Everybody has been anxious about you. Don't worry. I'll keep them at bay."

With his arm around her and leading the horse, he brought her from the path. Risto, sighting them going past, ran out of his parents' house to oblige Alan by taking the horse to lead it to the sawmill stables.

"Great to see you safe, Mrs. Fernley," he said to her.

She managed a smile. Alan gave Risto instructions that the sawmill whistle should be sounded in a long, single blast to let the search parties know that Lisa had been found—seven blasts being the signal for disaster. Then he hurried her along, staving off with a hand held up the women who came running from all directions.

"If you please, ladies. My wife has had a narrow escape from the fire and I'd be grateful if you'd let me get her home to rest."

Minnie, sighting Lisa's return from an upper window, came flying down the staircase as the front door opened. "Lisa! There's a burn on your cheek! Your hair is singed! Oh, oh, oh!"

Later, when Lisa was alone in the bedroom, she looked in the mirror at her reflection and studied the line of the burn which had been treated with some salve. The burn was not severe and would heal quckly, but with her fair skin it was almost certain that a faint discoloration would always remain there and she would need a little paint and powder to hide it. Only she would ever know what had preceded it, for Alan had drawn his own conclusions about her disappearance and had asked for no explanations. He had simply assumed that, upset about his news of a return to England, she had made the excuse of visiting to Minnie in order to have some time to herself in the open air. He actually said that he quite understood how she would have wanted to escape the house to think things out and come to terms with the change in their lives that leaving the States would mean to them. After all, Minnie had quoted to him her remark of having a problem to sort out.

She felt no shame in failing to contradict his conclusions. Since she and Peter had parted forever, she saw no reason to condemn Alan to unnecessary misery and jealousy by a heartless confession that would do no good at all. If circumstances had demanded it, she would not have shirked the issue, but she had been spared that by Alan himself. He would not lose by it. She had made her choice. After the respite that would be allowed her for the shock of the fire, she would continue to be the wife and partner he had always expected her to be. That was her debt and she would settle it.

Turning from the mirror, her carapace of calm resolution cracked without warning. "Peter!" she screamed out on an agonised note, throwing herself across the bed.

Afterwards she believed it to have been the moment when Peter had ridden out of Dekova's Place, never to return. The stables were up for rent again the next day. There were no means of checking the hour of his departure, but the conviction remained. Certainly she never again gave way to a similar lapse. Work was her antidote for not letting love thoughts take hold. She packed china and bed-linen into trunks and boxes, threw out unnecessary items that had been hoarded without purpose, and made sure that none of Harry's favourite toys would be overlooked when the day came to close and lock the lids.

Minnie also occupied her attention. The girl was pining already at the prospect of being parted from Risto, who was similarly downcast. They were making promises to write, and Alan had taken photographs of them for each to exchange with the other as a keepsake. There had been no more movie shows since the night of the forest fire, which had coincided within a matter of days with the last of the film bookings she had made. At the time she had expected Alan to make his own arrangements, never realising that all would be at an end. With no cinematograph duties to perform, Risto saw less of Minnie, being kept busy in the saloon or waiting at table. This reduction of their time together, coming when every minute counted, was an additional hardship for them. More than once Lisa came across them kissing and cuddling and whispering together and she was full of compassion for them. Minnie became a little more distrait with every passing day, but when the eve of departure finally arrived she spent it alone with Risto, who had managed to get the time off from the hotel. She was pale and courageous when she re-entered the house. Lisa regarded her sympathetically.

"What time are we to be up in the morning?" the girl asked tremulously.

Alan answered her. "Early, I'm afraid. We catch the train at eight o'clock."

Lisa went across to her. "I'll give you a call at six."

Minnie nodded and flung her arms about Lisa to hug her emotionally. Then she tore away up to her room, her head bowed in weeping. Her door slammed and the locking of it showed that she wished to be quite alone after the poignant parting that had taken place that evening.

Lisa was up at dawn and Alan came down soon afterwards. At six o'clock, with breakfast on the table, she went upstairs to tap on Minnie's door. "Time to get up," she called. There was no reply. She tapped harder and there was still no response. Then she tried the handle and the door swung open. The bed had not been slept in and the valise, previously packed in readiness for the long transcontinental train journey from Seattle to New York, was gone. On the chest of drawers an envelope stood propped against a candlestick. Lisa picked it up and saw it was addressed to her. She read it through. Slowly she went downstairs to break the news to Alan.

"Minnie and Risto have eloped," she said quietly, sitting down and handing him the letter.

His reaction was as she had expected. "Good God! I must go after her. She's too young to know her own mind! We'll postpone everything."

"No." Lisa spoke firmly. "What does her age matter if she's truly in love as I believe her to be. Risto will look after her."

"But she says they're going to California to try their luck in the movies!"

"They're both talented. I think they stand a good chance of getting work."

He frowned at her incredulously. "Are you prepared to leave here today without lifting a finger to bring her back?"

"Yes." She stood up. "I'll waken Harry now. We mustn't miss that train into Seattle."

As she went upstairs again, she recalled that she had been only seventeen when she and Peter had fallen in love. Not for anything in the world would she attempt to separate Minnie from Risto. In her heart she wished them joy.

Eleven

Three months later Peter received an urgent telegram from his brother to meet him at an appointed hour. The place selected was the lobby of a Seattle hotel that faced the giant totem pole in Pioneer Square. Contrary to Peter's expectations, Jon arrived sober, clean-shaven and well clad in new clothes. He wore, somewhat surprisingly, a dashing hard-topped hat, which Lisa in her English way would have called a bowler. Peter almost sighed aloud as yet again she slipped unbidden into his thoughts when he least expected it. At times of low spirits, an almost permanent condition since she had made her terrible decision to end everything with him, he doubted that he would ever be free of her. Neither drink nor other female company had had any effect. In the past, when she had haunted him, there had always been a grain of hope. Now there was none. He considered it ironic that it should be he himself and not his brother who was somewhat the worse for drink at this hotel meeting.

"How are you, Jon?" he asked.

"Never better." Jon set down a spanking new suitcase to remove a glove of good quality leather to shake his hand firmly. "It's not so with our father, I'm sorry to say. I've heard from Ingrid that he's dying. I'm leaving for Norway on the eastbound train to New York in two hours' time. I'm going home."

The news of his parent's imminent demise hit Peter hard. At

the time of his emigration he and his father had accepted that their farewells to each other were final. But now that the hour had come, his inner grief was as acute as if those words of goodbye had never been spoken. Already in a state of deep depression, the look of strain on his taut features became more acute as Jon filled in the details for him.

"Shall you be in time to see Father?" he probed.

"There's just a chance, I'd say." Jon did not appear unduly concerned either way. He took a large gold watch from his pocket to check the time. It appeared he had spared no expense in rigging himself out for his home-coming. "Let's eat. Here at the hotel if you like. At the same time you can think up whatever messages you'd like me to give those back home."

Peter, sobered completely by the prospect of bereavement, felt clearer in the head than he had been for quite a while. "There'll be no messages. I've a mind to see Father once more myself. I'll travel with you and stay for a couple of weeks in the old country."

Jon stared at him. "But we may arrive home too late."

"Then I'll still be able to pay my last respects. I'll meet you at the train."

He left Jon without further delay and went to call on a fellow dealer who was willing enough to handle his next shipment of horses, for the quality he dealt in was well known in the trade. Prices were soon settled and arrangements made. His own riding horse was also to be entrusted to the dealer's care.

"What if you don't come back?" the man asked as he and Peter came out of the office where they had conducted their dealings. "Accidents happen, y'know."

Peter regarded him cynically, able to follow his line of thought. "Not to me. That shipment line is mine by contract and unless I decide otherwise, it remains mine. Understand?"

The dealer shrugged and grinned slyly. "You can't blame a fellow for having an eye to extra business. Good luck on your trip."

In the last quarter of an hour before getting to the station, Peter bought a silk shawl for his sister-in-law and a train set for her son, Erik. The cardboard box for the latter was cumbersome, but it fitted into his wooden travelling box, which he shouldered as easily as he had done when he had left home first.

It was a strange feeling to be on vacation as the train rattled eastwards. He doubted if he would ever have seen Norway again if it had not been for his brother bearing the news of their father at that particular phase of his life. Normally nobody could afford the time or the expense to travel such great distances, and Lisa's dream of herself and then her stepson travelling to and fro across the Atlantic would have been laughable if the circumstances had not been so tragic. On the thought of her he passed a hand across his forehead as if he could brush her physically from his memory.

There was no difficulty in getting a berth on the same ship as Jon when they reached New York. It was a Norwegian merchantman bound for Bergen. Quarters were simple and quite cramped, but in comparison with the steerage quarters of the previous voyage that they had both made in turn, it was like a luxury liner. They found it satisfactory to be served huge platefuls of *lapskaus* and *fiskepudding* and *kjöttballer* such as they had not tasted since leaving their homeland.

Peter was not prepared for the sense of exultation that filled him at the sight of Norway's grandeur once again. The Rockies paled into insignificance beside these rugged snow-covered mountains, threaded with frozen waterfalls that dipped into fjords as deep as the peaks were high. On board the coastal steamer carrying him and his brother on the final stage of their journey from Bergen to Molde, he stayed at the rails, defying the bitter winter weather, to gaze shorewards for hours at vistas of incomparable beauty that he had taken for granted in his callow youth.

As it was Christmas time, every fishing vessel had a Christmas tree tied to its mast, as did the coastal steamer. When Peter and Jon stepped ashore at Molde, the windows of the houses and shops twinkled with festive lights in a warm welcome. Jon had sent a telegram from Bergen, the first indication that Ingrid would have had that the husband she had not seen for nearly a decade had returned at last.

On the quayside Jon was recognised immediately by a

neighbouring farmer who had come to collect a crate of goods from the coastal steamer. "It's Jon Hagen, isn't it?" he exclaimed heartily, shaking Jon's hand vigorously. "Home from America, are you? And Peter! It's been a long time. Wait until I've loaded my goods and I'll drive you home to the farm."

"What news of our father?" Peter inquired at once.

"Still holding on to life when I left the valley this morning."

It seemed as if they were to be in time after all. Darkness was gathering in as the town was left behind them and they were swept along by sleigh into the silent countryside, their driver plying Jon with questions that were answered with a good deal of bragging. Peter said nothing. When they came level with the farmhouse, they alighted and thanked the farmer who drove off into the darkness.

The sleigh-bells had been heard inside the house. The door opened, letting a stream of golden light fall across the two brothers as they approached the steps leaving footprints in the snow behind them. Ingrid stood silhouetted in the doorway. She had put on weight and looked older and more severe. Peter stood aside to let Jon precede him. There was no emotional greeting between husband and wife. They shook hands formally like strangers. It was Peter who put his arms about her and hugged her, she responding almost with relief. As she drew back, both men realised she was dressed entirely in black.

"You've come too late," she said sadly. "Your father died a few hours ago."

The funeral took place a week later. The snowy road was spread with juniper all the way to the octagonal wooden church at the edge of the fjord, and a long procession of mourners followed the coffin. Jon and Ingrid walked with their son between them. Erik was stricken with grief for his late grandfather, who had filled with love and kindness the gap left by the stranger now home from America. He did not like the intruder with the boastful tales who made out that everything was so much better over there. Why had his father come home in that case? He and his mother had managed the farm between them to date and they could have gone on doing it alone. Uncle Peter made no such boasts. Just talked normally about everything, his talk all the more interesting for being frank and unbiased. He thought his mother preferred Uncle Peter to Papa. There was a softer look in her eyes whenever she spoke to him.

After the funeral, Peter's remaining days at the farm drew quickly towards a close. He made final skiing expeditions to places in the valley with which he had become reacquainted. He had forty-eight hours left before his departure when he returned to the farmhouse at noon one day to be told by Ingrid that he had a visitor waiting to see him.

"I don't know her," Ingrid said as he stuck his skis in the snow and stooped to remove his boots before entering the house. "But I know *of* her. Her name is Astrid Dahl. Her father is a widower and a drunkard. They live in Molde near the quayside."

Peter went into the parlour with its white wooden walls and the tapestries that his great-grandmother had woven. The visitor was studying one of them and turned at the sound of the door opening. Her likeness to Lisa washed over him and ebbed again. There was really no true resemblance beyond a delicate articulation of features and eyes large and expressive and full of soft lights. Her hair beneath the fur hat was fair but curly, whereas Lisa's was silky straight. It struck him that Astrid had dressed with care for this call on him. She had loosened her coat as a concession to the heat from the crackling stove, and the blouse she wore with her ankle-length skirt of dark serge was crisp with starched white frills that formed a flattering collar.

"I'm Peter Hagen, Fröken Dahl," he said to her. "You wished to see me?"

At his invitation she sat down and he took a chair opposite her. "I'll come straight to the point," she said. "I'm here on my father's behalf to put a business proposition to you."

He supposed it would be a matter of selling something, probably a locally made product, in the States upon his return there, which was not in his line at all, and decided to make that clear immediately. "I'm a horse-dealer, that's my trade. I specialise in supplying teams of work-horses where they are most needed."

She nodded. "I know. That's why I've come to you. I'm giving you the chance to buy my father's hackney carriage business, which would simply be a natural follow-up to what you have been doing in America. I don't want our horses to fall into the hands of someone who would dispose of them in order to use the premises for other purposes."

He raised his eyebrows and released a breath, surprised at all she had said. "I regret having to disappoint you, but I'm sailing back to Bergen the day after tomorrow to take ship back to the States. You must be confusing me with my brother. He is the one who has come home to stay."

"No, I'm not. I know Jon is the farmer and you're the youngest in the Hagen family. I made sure of all the facts before paying this call. You're not married. You have no one dependent upon you. And you're rich."

He burst out laughing, throwing back his head. "You're wrong on the last point. I've yet to make my fortune."

She had flushed angrily, seeming to imagine that she and not the conclusion she had drawn was the object of his mirth. "You must be rich. Nobody comes home from America unless he has made a lot of money. It's financially impossible otherwise, unless they are people like your brother who have saved the fare out of their first year's wages and never touched it afterwards. I had it on good authority that when you emigrated from Norway it was to be forever. Therefore it stands to reason that you have made money."

He became serious, seeing she was upset. "I came home in the hope of seeing my father once more before he died. Nothing else would have brought me. It is because I'm a bachelor and my own master, with no responsibilities towards anyone else, that I was able to leave everything to make the journey. No employer would have allowed me the great length of time it takes for the round trip. But I'm not wealthy. Far from it. Neither have I come home to stay. There is nothing further from my mind."

"But why go back?" she retorted. "Surely you must know by now that there is no country in the world like ours. We have a new freedom since you left. Danish and Swedish domination has gone forever. King Haakon was voted overwhelmingly to the throne by a national referendum. We have a sweet liberty that none shall ever take from us again."

Her vehemence intrigued him. Again he was reminded of Lisa in this girl's determination to hold on to a purpose, which in her case was to make him the purchaser of her father's business. In his opinion, she had the character and the forcefulness to run it herself. He voiced the observation.

"Do you think I don't want to?" she cried, springing to her feet and pacing up and down, almost wringing her hands in frustration. "I could make the business successful. More and more the grand private yachts and the cruising ships call in at Molde. Once, when the Kaiser and his party came ashore, I took our prettiest horse and wagonette down to the quayside for hire, and afterwards drove two gentlemen and their ladies to the best views. If I'd had a fleet of wagonettes I'd have made as much money as if I'd been to America!"

"We're back to finances again," he remarked easily. "I think it would be best if we dropped the subject. I'm afraid you're wasting your time." He stood up from his chair to show that the interview was at an end.

She flung out her hands to him. "Can't you see what I'm offering you? The business is a bargain! You could build it up as I would have done if my father's debts hadn't dragged us down and down."

"And the nature of those debts?"

She drew her lower lip under her teeth and frowned unhappily. "My father likes to drink. It's as simple as that. When I was a child it was a prosperous little business, but after my mother died he simply gave way completely to his predilection for alcohol. I'm afraid that these days we owe money everywhere. He has borrowed on everything we own. All his promises and his attempts to keep sober have come to naught. Now the bank is to foreclose. Unless I can find a purchaser willing to pay a price to get us out of our financial difficulties we shall be left penniless and without a roof over our heads."

He was deeply dismayed. It had not been his intention to draw painful domestic details out of her. He had thought to show by her own answer that the business had foundered on its own and was not the bargain she had purported it to be. He recalled too late that Ingrid had mentioned the father was an alcoholic, and realised that he might have guessed there was some connection.

"What price are you asking?" he heard himself say.

She raised eyes so ashine with sudden hope that he was further dismayed, feeling that he was being caught in a whirlpool. The price she gave was one he could have managed with a loan if he had been looking for investment in a business, which he was not.

"Come with me now and see the premises," she urged, refastening the buttons of her coat as if he had already agreed to accompany her. When he shook his head and raised his hand in a gesture to emphasise the futility of her request, she pretended not to notice, seemingly absorbed in pulling on her gloves. "I have the sleigh outside. I will drive you back again afterwards. Don't feel you have to decide at once either way. I do want you to see the horses. If you love horses as I do you will appreciate the drive into town for that alone."

Maybe if she had not displayed an affection for horses that was similar to his own, he would not have found himself putting on an overcoat to face the winter weather with her. Perhaps if she had not continued to remind him of Lisa in a will-o'-the-wisp way he would have bluntly refused the whole preposterous proposition she had put to him. Whatever the reason, he went to take a seat in the sleigh beside her, she talking all the time as if even now she feared that if she paused for breath he might utter too soon the dreaded negative answer that would bring her own existence to destruction.

It was a marvellous ride. The bells on the sleigh jingled merrily and all around them the snow lay soft and sparkling over tree and roof and mountain slope. When they came within sight of the town, with the fjord lying like molten silver beyond, she drew the horse to a halt, its breath and theirs hanging mistily in the cold air.

"Look!" she said, pointing across the wide fjord to the panorama of eighty-seven peaks of the Romsdal Mountains on the far side. "Where else in the world could you wake to such a view each morning? You've come home to Norway, Peter Hagen."

He smothered a grin at her exuberance and her persuasiveness. They drove on into town and came to the premises she was offering for sale which were located close to the quayside and faced the fjord. There was a three-storeyed house in need of paint and repair, and the stables and a coach-house on the side were in a similar state of neglect. Nevertheless, it was a prime site and he could see at once why she had feared the premises' being purchased for some other line of business to the cost of her horses' well-being.

"I know the house is large," she said quickly as if to forestall any comment, "but my father and I could have the ground floor and you could have the rest. In lieu of rent I'd be willing to keep house and bookkeep and drive a wagonette when needed. My father would help tend the horses and look after the garden."

She seemed to have thought of everything. He followed her into the stables. There were four horses, including the one in the sleigh-shafts, and all were the Westland breed—small, sturdy animals of the characteristic cream colour, with a clearly defined black streak running through the pale manes and tails. Gentle-eyed, patient, hard workers and sure-footed as any goat on mountain slopes, they had been dear to his heart since childhood. He clapped their necks and gave them the apples that Astrid had taken from a box on the shelf to hand to him on the way in.

"They're fine animals," he commented, "and in good condition."

"I've made sure they've never gone without anything they have needed," she answered quietly.

He glanced at her out of the corner of his eye. She was stroking the head of one of the horses, unaware of being observed, and her whole face reflected her affection for them all. He was certain that although she had kept the horses in good bran and mash, she herself had known what it was to go hungry.

He wandered on into the coach-house and examined the vehicles there. Half a dozen ancient wagonettes and a carriole that would have been more at home in a museum, were all there was to be seen, except for something under an enormous dust-sheet. He lifted a corner and then gasped, pulling the sheet away. It was a comparatively new automobile, its gleaming black paintwork badly damaged where it must have suffered a collision on the right side, the mudguard and running-board badly twisted, the front wheel at a curious angle.

Behind him Astrid heaved a heavy sigh. "That was our last effort to put the business back on its feet. It was my idea that we should start a motorised taxi service, and I practically went down on my knees to the bank manager for a final loan. Then, in spite of my father's resolution to turn over a new leaf, he smashed it up while drunk."

"You should have driven it yourself."

"I wanted to, but he wouldn't allow me to learn. Not that I haven't learnt more or less how to handle it simply by observation."

"Why haven't you had it repaired?"

"Nobody will give us credit any more."

He walked around the automobile, keenly interested. Horses were his first love, but the day was coming when mechanisation would take over completely. He had seen increasing signs in the lumber camps. Although to date his horse trade had not suffered, simply because of the good name he had made for himself as an honest dealer, he had faced the fact that before long he would have to consider an alternative means of livelihood.

"When does the bank intend to foreclose?" he asked.

"The day after tomorrow."

He was taking a look at the engine which seemed to have escaped damage, and he raised his head to meet her eyes. "That's the day I leave here."

She held herself completely still, tense and anxious, and she mouthed more than spoke her reply. "But you're not going, are you?"

There was some grease on his fingers from the engine and he reached for a piece of rag from a nearby bench to wipe them clean. As he did so, he stood straight-backed and regarded her steadily. "No, Astrid. I don't believe I am."

Later, when everything was settled and the property and

business were his, he mulled over the extraordinary change to his life's plans that had come about in such a comparatively short while. He intended to make a success of his future, the surge of ambition taking over once again. Already he had ideas springing to mind how profits could be gained and innovations made. As for Astrid, he had realized almost from the start that in her he had found a woman with the forceful spirit and sexual magnetism to match his memories of Lisa. Perhaps with time she might even obliterate them. If she did, he would love her for it.

In London, Lisa's antidote to memories was work. At first it had been both strange and familiar to be back in her own country. The streets had seemed too narrow and the buildings too close, giving her an almost claustrophobic sensation after the open spaces in which she had lived for such a long while. Nevertheless, the beauty of England had pulled at her heart, moving her to tears on the train from Southampton to London as she had viewed the clustered villages and the hills and woods of gentle watercolour hues, the gardens glowing with late summer flowers. Then she had experienced a full sense of homecoming.

They were met at Waterloo Station by Alan's only close relative, his cousin Sylvia, who welcomed Lisa like a sister. She gave parties to introduce them to many of her friends, not wanting Lisa to feel lonely, and after three weeks put her house at their disposal, as previously arranged, while she herself departed for India to rejoin her army-major husband there. Before leaving, she found a capable young nursemaid, Maudie Harris, to take charge of Harry when Lisa was otherwise engaged. Lisa liked the girl, as did Harry, which gave her an easy mind about giving most of her time and all her assistance to Alan, who had located a building suitable for conversion into a cinema not long after their arrival back in England.

It was an old music hall that had waned in popularity and had been closed down for a number of years. After a surveyor had pronounced it sound in structure, Alan had consulted his bank and the necessary funds were forthcoming. While he dealt with the architects and builders and suppliers of cinematographic equipment, Lisa handled the paper work, met British film distributors and renters, visited studios to see the making of future offerings and selected colours and fabrics for the refurbishing of the building. One of the great points in its favour, as far as she and Alan were concerned, was the fact that it was located in an area that encompassed a complete cross-section of the community. He was as keen as she was that they should be able to offer good entertainment as much to those who could only afford a few pence as to people able to pay much higher prices. Factories and slum dwellings, good shops and middle-class homes, art galleries and museums and elegant residences were all to be found within a radius of the building. Although its location was several miles from the theatre world of the West End, Alan never doubted that the day would come when a larger, grander version of the first Fernley cinema would open there.

"This is a stepping-stone," he had said to Lisa on the day the purchase of the property was completed. "There will be several more before we can open in Leicester Square or thereabouts, but we're on the way now."

She was pleased when he gave her a free choice in the naming of their cinema and decided it should be known as The Fernley. It was a good name with which to begin a whole chain of cinemas and made a refreshing change from all the Electric Palaces, Picture Palaces, Picturedromes, Theatres Elite and the innumerable Majestics and Empires. Set in illuminated bulbs above the glass-canopied steps of the entrance, the letters made an eye-catching spread across the arched facia that could be sighted from all directions in the traffic-congested streets. The patrons would pass under these lights through opened glass doors into a vestibule where the pay-box was situated, before passing on into the foyer. There was a wide staircase branched to the Grand Circle and the Balcony above it. This area was thickly carpeted and everywhere the walls were gilded and ornamented. Lisa had chosen the rose-tinted chandeliers with special care. The aim of cinema proprietors of any forethought and business acumen was to give patrons an exotic setting to waft them from the mundane into the fantasy world that awaited them.

Sometimes, when Lisa watched Alan checking on the progress of the building's conversion, she could tell by his absorbed expression that he had come into his own at last. He would have been a truly happy man if it were not for the fact that in their personal life things were not as they should be. Although to him she blamed her lack of response on tiredness or whatever reason seemed plausible at the time, her excuses were lame ones and at times she despaired of herself. It was natural that as a result tension between them was acute on occasions. Sometimes they quarrelled fiercely over a trifling matter that neither really cared about, simply as an outlet. More than once there was such burning anger in his eyes that she was reminded of the time long ago on Quadra Island when Harriet had vowed to find her a husband in Seattle. She longed for his sake to tear down the barrier that she had set against him, but the truth was that although she was reconciled to a life without Peter, she had not yet readjusted to her marriage bed. She felt nothing and wanted to feel nothing. Work had become her fulfilment.

As the conversion of the building neared completion, Lisa appointed the female staff. With so much unemployment everywhere, women came from far afield to apply for vacancies, forming such a long queue outside the cinema in the bitter February weather that some passers-by thought the place had already opened and a performance was due to commence. Lisa interviewed each applicant and regretted she did not have more work to offer, but Alan was too heavily committed to the bank to allow more than the minimum amount of staff for the time being. Her choice of a cashier for the pay-box proved to be particularly fortuitous. The woman, Ethel Morris, was married to a retired boxer, Billy, who had similarly applied to Alan to be commissionaire and, whenever it should prove necessary, the chucker-out. After Lisa and Alan had talked together, they offered the couple the chance to be caretakers in the living accommodation incorporated into the property. The additional position was accepted without hesitation.

All that remained was for Alan to take on two projectionists, both with diplomas issued by the British Bioscope Company to endorse that they were fully qualified electrical bioscope operators, and a fireman, whose duty was to keep the fire buckets filled, check that the emergency exits were always ready to open, and generally keep an eye on the safety of the property. According to a new law, film was no longer allowed to drop down freely into a container from the projector to be rewound after the programme, but had to pass from one closed cannister into another. Alan had these fitted to his projectors, which were run by belts attached to a small engine, which eliminated the handcranking that had previously been necessary.

The days before the opening of The Fernley were dwindling down on the morning Lisa arrived with a letter, coming at a run through the vestibule into the foyer in search of Alan, who had gone earlier to the premises. She found him in his office.

"I've heard from Minnie!" she exclaimed excitedly to him. "She took your cousin Sylvia's address with her after all, hoping that her letters would be forwarded on to us even if we were no longer staying there. She and Risto are married and they're both working for one of the film companies in Los Angeles."

"Acting?" Alan asked with interest.

"Yes. Isn't it wonderful news." She perched on the edge of his desk to read it to him, her sheath skirt having the fashionable tango split in the front that showed her silk-stockinged legs halfway to her knees.

It was the happiest letter that Minnie had ever written. Upon their arrival in Los Angeles they had gone, more by luck than judgement, to an old barn that had been taken over as a studio only that day by a motion-picture company newly arrived from New York. Goods and equipment were still being unloaded. Such was the rivalry between companies that no time could be wasted and the cameras had already been set up outside and filming was about to start. Minnie and Risto and some other hopeful applicants were signed on at once; they were handed costumes from a wardrobe trunk and their first day's work began. In a restaurant scene, supposedly set in a Paris cellar, the two of them were diners and had to toast each other with wineglasses while gripping the check cloth under the table to prevent its flapping about in the breeze and giving away the fact that it was all being filmed in the Californian sunshine. Since then they had played a variety of crowd parts, for one-reel movies were made in a week.

Now there was a sudden move towards the longer feature film, and Risto was to be a gladiator, and she a slave-girl, in a four-reeler that was going into production. Minnie felt the tenure of their steady work was due in part to their having been at the studio from the first day, for most people, from cameramen to directors, appeared to think they had come with the company in the exodus from New York and treated them now as experienced players. Whatever the reason, she and Risto in very minor rôles as characters of Ancient Rome were, nevertheless, to have their own farewell scene in the new movie. They would be in the background, echoing on another plane the more dramatic parting between the leading actor and actress, but their acting ability was being called upon and they intended to do their best. She added that for professional purposes she was being known as Minnie Shaw, explaining that as she and Lisa had always been taken for sisters it had been a natural choice to take her dearest friend's maiden name. She closed the letter with loving greetings and implored forgiveness for any upset she had caused by running away with her darling Risto, but it had been the only solution to not being separated forever.

"Good luck to them," Alan said sincerely. "It seems as if we'll be seeing them on our screen here before long."

"Maybe one day they'll appear on lobby cards like these on the desk." Lisa leaned her weight on one hand to peer over at the sepia-tinted images of scenes from the opening night's film, which had been sent with other advertising material from the distributor. These cards were set up on decorative easels in the vestibule to give patrons a foretaste of the pleasures to come and tempt the hesitant into buying a ticket. She helped Alan make a selection before taking a seat at her own desk to deal with some business correspondence awaiting her attention.

Before the day ended, she wrote a long reply to Minnie's letter and enclosed a photograph of Harry that had been taken on his fourth birthday. She had previously sent one to Agnes

Twidle. By a strange coincidence, Agnes herself had survived a forest fire at Granite Bay about the same time as Lisa had escaped. Agnes also had taken to a row-boat and was on her own throughout the ordeal, for Henry had been away at the time. Miraculously their house and orchard had escaped completely, although the flames had passed close by.

All this news was included in the letter to Minnie as well as everything of interest about the new cinema. As Lisa sealed the envelope she glanced across at the 1912 calendar on the office desk and noted that only ten days remained before the March date of the opening night. For the first time she realised that it was in its way an anniversary, for it was exactly nine years since she had run away from the orphanage in a vain attempt to avoid being shipped to Canada, a doomed escapade that had changed the whole course of her life.

The Fernley's opening night arrived. Queues began to form long before the programme was due to begin. Tremendous interest had been aroused through publicity in the local press about the three-reel feature film, which was *A Tale of Two Cities* and would run for the amazing length of three quarters of an hour. It was to have a supporting programme of a two-reel cowboy movie and three one-reel comedies; a gazette of topical news, which included the visit of the King and Queen to the Earls Court Exhibition; and a screen magazine reel of forthcoming attractions.

Alan, as manager and proprietor, was in white tie and tails, and Lisa, who was to play the piano alone in the orchestra pit, had a new evening dress to wear. It was a silver-beaded tunic of pink chiffon over white, combining the softly draped bosom with the straight and slender silhouette. A final touch was a silk rose tucked into the coils of her hair at the back of her neck.

"You look beautiful," Alan said to her in the last moments of waiting before the doors were opened to the public.

Her smile twinkled at him. "You look handsome yourself, Mr. Fernley."

He chuckled, putting his arms about her. "Then kiss me, Mrs. Fernley."

She rested her hands against his shoulders and looked at him with a fond seriousness. "Good luck with the Fernley Cinema, Alan. May it bring you all the success you deserve."

"It's our venture, darling. Not mine alone. None of it would mean anything to me without you." His embrace tightened about her and they kissed.

As they drew apart, he turned to signal with a nod to Billy to open the doors. Billy, smartly uniformed in dark blue with brass buttons in his rôle as commissionaire, his Boer War ribbons on his chest, saluted and went forward with long strides to release the bolts. Lisa sped away to take her seat at the piano below the screen, a green-shaded light giving her a spot of illumination for the sheet music. There was a special score for the feature film, since some of the bigger movie-makers were now selecting their own accompanying music which was delivered with the reels.

From beyond the doors into the auditorium there came a rumble of hurrying feet. She struck up a medley of popular tunes as the first patrons streamed in to take their seats. There were exclamations at the plush-covered seats and the concealed lighting that gave a glow to the plaster ornamentation of flower-garlands. Unlike most cinemas, the cheap seats at the front were not plain wooden benches but leather-covered editions of those in the rest of the rows. The appreciative remarks reached Lisa clearly where she sat a few feet from the poorer patrons.

Then the curtain across the screen within its procenium arch parted. A projected slide showed the kindly bearded face of King George V, and Lisa played the national anthem, which befitted the importance of the occasion. Everybody sang as they stood in the rows and as the last notes died away seats were resumed. A more utilitarian slide requested that ladies remove their hats to facilitate the view of others. When the rustling of hands sliding out hat-pins and removing fashionably large head-gear had subdued, the programme commenced.

As Lisa played she felt she could easily have been back at Mae Remotti's hotel in Dekova's Place, for the reactions of the audience to the movies on the screen were exactly the same. They laughed uproariously at the comedies, cheered the cowboys and growled or hissed at the villains. When a film jammed in the projector's gate and broke during a comedy reel, their groans in unison were followed not long after by a stamping of feet from the stalls to the Grand Circle and the Balcony as patience became stretched at the time the projectionists were taking to repair it. A cheer greeted the flickering return of the first frames to the screen, and after that there were no more hitches. Women brought handkerchieves out of their purses and wiped their eyes, some stifling sobs, when Sydney Carton mounted the steps of the guillotine in the final scene of *A Tale of Two Cities.* Lisa played the last dramatic chords and the performance was over. Just as in Mae Remotti's, a few patrons took time to come to Lisa and say how much they had enjoyed her accompaniment.

"It was real nice," one woman said, still wiping red eyes, her wide smile showing how much she had enjoyed the programme.

"Thank you. I hope you'll all come again."

They declared in turn that they would and bade her good night. Lisa stacked her music together and put it ready for the matinée the next day. From now on there would be non-stop performances from six o'clock nightly for six days of the week and the same number of matinées.

Alan took her out to a champagne supper before they went home. Both were convinced that they had a sure-fire winner in The Fernley and it was cause for a special celebration.

By the end of the year the financial returns had exceeded their most hopeful expectations. They hired a three-piece orchestra for the evening performance, and Lisa continued to play at the matinées. With a complete change of programme in the middle of the week, many patrons came twice in order not to miss anything. Some women came three times to one movie if the hero caught their fancy. Friday and Saturday nights were occasions for family outings when a husband brought his wife and all their offspring. With cinema fever getting a grip on the whole country, as it was elsewhere in the world, many a man was being drawn away from his favourite pub, and the womenfolk were thankful for it.

The movie in which Minnie and Risto had their farewell

scene reached the screen of The Fernley early in 1913. Both Lisa and Alan thought they did well. Although she did not write often, Minnie did keep them informed of her own and Risto's progress. They were continuing to get small parts that were only a degree ahead of crowd parts, but everything was promising.

Not long after this film was shown, Alan managed to acquire a property adjoining the cinema building. It was incorporated into the main structure, providing them with a large apartment on the upper floor, which meant they could leave Sylvia's home and have a place of their own at last. At ground level they opened a cinema café that served afternoon teas and light suppers which soon proved to be an additional and highly profitable attraction. It was Lisa's ideas that tea dances be introduced and the evening orchestra further engaged for this afternoon diversion. Once again it was a move of great success and the dancing space was filled every afternoon with those enjoying the tango, the fox-trot, the one-step and the two-step as well as a variety of other popular dances from the Bunny Hug to the Turkey Trot.

The Fernley had been opened eighteen months when an incident occurred that caused Lisa some upset. Billy had found two barefoot slum children hiding in the balcony while he was checking that no property had been left behind after an evening's performance. They had waited outside and slipped in when patrons were leaving, their intention being to conceal themselves there to see the programme free of charge when the cinema opened next day. He had turned them out unceremoniously and was taken aback next day when Lisa, upon hearing his report, angrily demanded to know why he had not taken their names and addresses.

"I didn't think you'd want to put the police on to them, ma'am," he said with a frown.

She shook her head vigorously. "Of course not. I would have wanted you to make sure that they had a home to go to, and that they were not just being turned back into the streets. You should have telephoned me, Billy. I'd have come at once. Please remember that if anything similar should occur again."

As the days went by she could not dismiss those unknown children from her mind. Then an idea came to her which she thought out in every detail before voicing the proposition to Alan.

"I'd like to put on a Saturday-morning movie show especially for children, pricing the stall at a half-penny and a penny while retaining normal prices for children accompanied by adults in the Grand Circle and Balcony. Well? Do you have any objection?"

"None at all," he replied, smiling at her. Trust Lisa to think of children at all times. Her devotion to Harry never failed to move him. However busy her day, she always spent some hours with the child, teaching him the alphabet, reading to him, playing games in the house or garden and taking him for walks in the park. Although Alan never failed to wish that his wife would spare some of her devotion for him, he did not begrudge it to his son and he loved them both dearly, his passion for Lisa unabated. Recently they seemed to have quarrelled less, their shared enthusiasm for the picture-house a kind of buffer between them, but that did not reach beyond their bedroom door and there their problems remained. He believed that if she could have conceived his child all differences between them would eventually have faded away. It seemed a cruel trick of fate that she, with her strong maternal instincts, should be denied true motherhood.

"In Leeds there's a renter of movies suitable for children," she told him. "Instead of writing for lists, I'll go there myself on the train. It will give me a chance to see the old orphanage and visit Mrs. Bradlaw if she's still superintendent there."

When Lisa alighted at Leeds station, she almost seemed to see the ghostly images of herself and the rest of the orphanage party that had once huddled there under the eagle eye of the evil Miss Drayton. Never would she have believed then that one day she would be on the same spot again looking every inch a lady in an elegant heliotrope coat with mother-of-pearl buttons and an enormously large hat trimmed with pale green plumes.

She completed her business first with the movie-renter,

whose offices were decorated, as these places always were, with posters of the movies they had on offer, mostly in garish colourings. Upon leaving there, she walked to the orphanage, covering the ground she had traversed countless times when she had lived in the city. She found the large building to be virtually unchanged and rang the polished brass doorbell for admission. A young girl in the standard grey uniform opened the door to her, and she asked if Mrs. Bradlaw was there.

"Yes, madam. What name shall I say?"

"Mrs. Bradlaw knew me as Lisa Shaw."

As the girl went to the study door to tap and enter, Lisa saw that the red-gold porcelain plate she had always admired was still in its place on the shelf. Its trick of catching the light had not been dimmed by time and she recalled how it had inspired her to think that the colour of love must be blazing sun-gold. The hue of passion. She had never thought to glimpse its full magnificence in a forest fire.

"Please come this way, madam."

The orphanage girl was showing her into the study as if she would not have known the way. She entered and there was a slightly older-looking Mrs. Bradlaw with much greyer hair than before coming from behind the desk to greet her.

"What a delightful surprise, Lisa! How are you?"

"I'm well and married to an Englishman, which is why I'm back in England, and I have a stepson of whom I'm immensely proud. And you, Mrs. Bradlaw?"

"I'm still fighting for more enlightened attitudes towards my girls. Do sit down. Take the wing-chair with the cushion."

Lisa raised her eyebrows smiling. "That was always reserved for guests of importance as I remember."

"You fill that rôle today."

As they seated themselves, Lisa asked the question that was uppermost in her mind. "Did you ever receive the letter I wrote you about the Herbert Drayton Memorial Society?"

"Indeed I did! I put the authorities on to the matter straightaway. Did you never hear the outcome?"

"I never received a reply from you. Later I realised that it might have been withheld from me by Miss Drayton's assistant, Miss Lapthorne."

"For your own safety, I refrained from acknowledging your letter until much later, when that wretched Emily Drayton was receiving her just deserts. By then there was no trace of you and my letter was returned."

"Please tell me what happened," Lisa implored.

The whole account was then forthcoming. Mrs. Bradlaw, her worst suspicions confirmed by Lisa's letter, had contacted her Member of Parliament, who instigated an inquiry into the society and forbade the shipment by the woman of any more children. But by then Emily Drayton had taken fright and she retreated to the States where she lay low for a couple of years beyond the jurisdiction of the Canadian authorities, who had been alerted by their English counterparts as to what had been going on. Then Emily, imagining that everything had been forgotten, and unaware that she was a marked woman in Canada, returned to her home in Toronto. The police were keeping a look-out for her return and promptly arrested her to charge her with fraud and procuring. When the house was searched, the remains of her assistant were found in the basement. For a time it seemed that the charge of murder might be levelled against Emily Drayton, but a pathologist's findings cleared her.

"Poor Miss Lapthorne," Lisa said sadly, remembering the pathetic, dithering creature who had held Emily in such high esteem and must have been heart-broken at being left behind.

"You knew the woman well?"

"Yes, I did. What was the result of Emily's trial?"

"She went to prison for five years. I believe the case was reported in the Canadian newspapers very fully. How strange you never read any report of it."

"By that time I was on Quadra Island, which was far away from everything. A delivery of newspapers was few and far between there."

"You must have had a difficult and adventurous time. I'll ring for tea. I should like to hear whatever news you can give me about the other girls in the party that went with you from here, and how you yourself met your husband and came home to England again."

Over tea, Lisa told her as much as she knew about those in the orphanage party who had been scattered from the centre in Sherbourne Street. Mrs. Bradlaw shut her eyes for a moment in distress at hearing of the fate of poor little Amy and of what Minnie had been through before meeting Lisa again. She shook her head wearily, but not with surprise, upon hearing that Rosie had ended up in a Calgary brothel.

"She is still there as far as I know," Lisa said. "I hear from Teresa from time to time. She is happily married, with two sons, and has moved with her husband to Victoria in British Columbia."

Before leaving, Lisa asked to see the orphanage, and she spoke to many of the children. She would have liked to take them all home with her and spent so much time with the little ones that if she had stayed another minute she would have missed her train back to London. Her generous donation to the orphanage funds was to be spent on a special treat for all the children.

It was not long before the first of the special movies she had ordered were delivered to The Fernley and the Saturday-morning shows became a regular part of the cinema's organisation. These shows soon became a nightmare to the usherettes posted in the stalls, for they hated the boisterous behaviour, the ear-splitting whistling, the banging of seats and the fights that broke out between the boys. A delegation of usherettes finally came to see Lisa in the office, one of them limping through having tripped suddenly over an urchin's boot which had been deliberately stuck out into the aisle.

"We are requesting unanimously that you cancel these Saturday-morning shows for all our sakes, Mrs. Fernley," the girl chosen to be spokesman for the rest said to her in fervent appeal. "The din at times is enough to make our heads split. You have heard it when you've played the piano in place of the relief pianist and you know we're not exaggerating."

"I can't cancel them." Lisa's tone was firm. "The shows are

profitable for one thing. The better-paid seats are nearly always full, and that covers the reduction on the front rows and the stalls downstairs."

"Then put up the price of the cheaper seats! That would keep out the worst of the ragamuffins."

Lisa shook her head adamantly. "I don't want to keep them out. Some of the poorest slum children in the district come to these performances. It's the only chance they get to hear music and appreciate good acting and glimpse a world beyond their own terrible living conditions. I've seen those barefoot children collecting up bottles to take to the nearest shop that gives a farthing back on those returned. That's the only way they can get into a picture house and often it's a long search in rain and bad weather to raise the money for admission. That's why when some of the little ones come mistakenly with the bottles themselves to Mrs. Morris in the pay-box, she always accepts them. She knows my instructions are that no child be turned away."

"They piddle on the floor!" a young usherette burst out in fastidious outrage.

"I know that happens," Lisa replied evenly. "When I've been at the piano I've seen it trickling past me from under the curtain around the orchestra pit. That's why I had the curtain raised an inch. The little ones can't control their bladders in the excitement of seeing the cowboy fights and the comedy chases. But the floor isn't carpeted in the stalls and the cleaners use disinfectant when they scrub there with plenty of suds immediately after the Saturday-morning shows."

"Then you're expecting us to carry on as before?" The usherette sounded close to tears.

"No. I'll arrange longer intervals to give the children more time to go to the toilet facilities, and I'll give prizes of complimentary tickets to older children who keep themselves and the younger ones in order during the performances."

The new arrangements took effect. The Saturday-morning shows became more orderly, and Lisa had the satisfaction of knowing that many deserving children were able to attend more regularly through the complimentary tickets.

A few more months went by and a 1914 calendar appeared

on Alan's office wall. Recently, Mack Sennett comedies had begun to delight cinema audiences and played to packed houses at The Fernley. Risto, with his flair for comedy, had moved to the Sennett studios at Glendale in California, but his interest had swung more to being behind the camera than in front of it, and his original ideas for visual gags had drawn him into the production side. Minnie, putting Risto's career before her own, had moved with him from their first studios, where she would have preferred to stay. Lisa could understand and sympathise when she saw Minnie being subjected to custard pies in the face, falling over in puddles when the Keystone cops raced past and being the centre-point of many mad rescues. Minnie made it clear in her letters that she had almost had enough of it and had written that D. W. Griffiths, the director whom everybody was talking about, was taking on a cast for a feature epic to be called *The Birth of a Nation,* and she was hoping for a part.

Minnie's luck was in. She secured a good part as a Southern belle. Her news, over which Lisa would normally have rejoiced greatly, lost much of its impact since it was received on the June morning when the newspapers at the Fernleys' breakfast table blazed headlines on the assassination of Archduke Franz Ferdinand of Austria and his wife at Sarajevo by Serb terrorists. Lisa, who kept abreast of world politics through all she read and her discussions with Alan, did not need the sight of his grave expression as he studied the report to know that a Balkan crisis could have serious consequences if other nations chose to involve themselves.

This development occurred a few days before the first holiday she and Alan had ever had together. He had almost decided on the site of a second cinema, and they both felt it would be good to get away from London for a rest before a new wave of work and activity hit them. By the time they set off in their automobile for Brighton with Harry and Maudie, it had become known that Serbia and Austria were mobilising, and Russia, Germany, and France were following suit. Great Britain had taken on the rôle of peacemaker.

Their hotel at Brighton faced the sea. On the golden sands and under a July sky of brightest blue, the rattling of sabres seemed very far away. They swam and went on the Pier and built sand-castles with Harry, who was bouncing with energy and whose skin turned a honey-brown as the days went by. In the evenings after dinner when he slept and Maudie was left in charge, Alan and Lisa strolled arm in arm along the promenade under the stars and in the glow of fairy lights strung between the lamp-posts.

"We must come on holiday more often," Alan said to her one night as they wandered back to the hotel after listening to a concert by a regimental brass band in the open air. "It suits you."

She smiled back at him, looping both hands in his crooked arm. Her hair had a soft aura from the fairy lights and her pale dress of georgette crêpe was wafting against her form in the balmy breeze. "I never knew days away from routine could be such fun. Apart from the weekends we have with friends sometimes, it's the first real holiday I've ever had."

He gave a mock groan, adopting the pose of hand to head used by screen villains brought to remorse. "What a brute I am to have made you work so hard."

She laughed, giving him a playful little punch. "You know I didn't mean that. It must seem curious that Harry, who is six and a half, and I, who am twenty-six, should both be enjoying our first vacation."

"There'll be many more from now on," he assured her. "We'll make a point of having more time out of London."

"Maybe when the second Fernley cinema is a success, we might think of getting a house in the country where we could spend some time."

"You'd like that, would you?" he asked with a chuckle.

She raised her eyebrows in puzzled amusement. "What's funny? Tell me the joke."

"We already have a country house."

"What!" Her exclamation was so shrill in her astonishment that other strollers along the promenade glanced in her direction. She clapped a hand over her errant mouth and continued in a giggling whisper. "You mean it, don't you? What is it? An old barn? A ruin somewhere?"

"No. Surely you remember I told you long ago that my grandparents left me their home when they died shortly before I went to the States?"

"Yes. But I suppose at the time I imagined you had sold it. I know it was the maturing of some bonds they left you that enabled us to invest in a cinema of the size and scale of The Fernley, which we couldn't have done otherwise. Where is the house?"

"Near the village of Twyford in Berkshire. It's not all that far from London but too much of a distance from the cinema to travel daily. In any case, we can't afford to live there yet, not with a second cinema in the offing, which is going to stretch our bank balance until it's launched. By keeping the house shut up and unoccupied I don't have to pay rates on the place. There's a village woman, once housekeeper to my grandparents, who has a key to clean it up sometimes and light fires to keep out the damp."

"Could we go and see it?" she asked eagerly.

"Yes, of course. We'll drive out there one Sunday soon."

"I'll take a picnic. Harry would love that."

That night when he made love to her it was better between them than it had been for a long time. He began to hope that things were on the mend at last.

In the morning the alarming news had broken of Austria's declaration of war against Serbia. "As long as Germany and the other Great Powers keep out," Alan said to Lisa as they crossed the street to reach the promenade and the beach, Maudie and Harry running ahead, "there is a chance of keeping the conflict confined."

That was not to happen. On the first and second days of August, Germany in support of Austria declared war against Russia and France respectively. Forty-eight hours later, when the Fernleys were fishing from the Pier, Alan giving Harry his first lesson in handling a rod and line, there came cheering and shouting in the distance along the promenade.

"What's all that about, Mr. Fernley?" Maudie questioned, shading her eyes with her raised forearm to gaze shorewards, a tin of worms for the fishing-hooks in her charge.

"I'll go and find out." Alan exchanged a deep glance of shared foreboding with Lisa as he handed the rod to her and joined others streaming off to investigate. As Lisa began to roll in the fishing-line, a knot of icy dread lay heavy in the pit of her stomach. When Harry made a protest at what she was doing, she answered him firmly.

"I'm afraid there'll be no more fishing this time, Harry dear. I believe when your papa comes to tell us what he has learned, he'll be wanting us to return to London with him right away."

Something in her voice quietened any further protest from the child, who could tell she was upset. He began to help her in her task as best he could, while Maudie, suddenly equally subdued as if she and his Mama shared a secret sorrow between them, began to tip the worms over the rails into the sea.

When Alan returned, he found Lisa waiting hand in hand with his son, her straw hat-brim and the ruffles of her polka-dotted dress flapping a little in the freshening wind, the ribbons of Harry's sailor hat aflutter. They, with Maudie behind them, formed a little tableau of calm and composure that was in refreshing contrast to the terrible excitement of the milling throngs that he had just witnessed on the promenade.

"Germany has violated the neutrality of our staunch ally. German forces have invaded Belgium. It is war, Lisa. Our beloved country is at war."

She flung herself into his arms. They stood wrapped in close embrace while all around them other people reacted in their individual ways to the spreading news. Some wept and others cheered or stood in stunned disbelief. An enterprising Pier stallholder had whipped out a tray of Union Jacks and proceeded to sell them to a rapidly forming queue, creating a bright flutter in all directions. Harry, bewildered by all that was happening around him, moved to grab hold of his stepmother's skirt and his sense of security was immediately restored. He hoped his father would buy him one of the Union Jacks that everyone was beginning to wave. He wanted to be part of that brave show of red, white, and blue.

Twelve

Lisa noticed that the first thing Alan did upon their return to London was to file away all the papers on the proposed second cinema. It was being shelved for the duration of the war. Although many people seemed to be of the opinion that the fighting would all be over by Christmas, he did not share that optimistic view. Before the first week was out, one of the projectionists, who was in the Territorials, was called up and Alan had to engage a replacement. Billy Morris, eager to change his commissionaire's uniform for that of his old regiment, went to volunteer, but he bore the tell-tale scars of debilitating wounds suffered in the Boer War and he was turned down as unfit for service. His bitter disappointment was matched by his wife's relief at not having to go through constant anxiety for his safety all over again.

The Fernley continued to play to packed houses. Its comfort had always won over patrons from the more barren cinema-halls in the vicinity, and Lisa maintained a high standard of booked films. Khaki and navy blue uniforms began to appear liberally in the audience as more and more men were called up from the reserve or volunteered for service with the forces. Marching troops and horses and wagons bound for the boat-trains became a familiar sight, and bystanders cheered them on their way. Recruiting posters began to appear on hoardings and buildings and on the sides of the red London buses. Before the first month of the war was out, the Germans had occupied Brussels and taken several important stragetic positions, and the battle of Mons had been fought. There were casualty lists in the newspapers.

On the first Sunday in September, Alan drove Lisa into Berkshire to pay the promised visit to his late grandparents' old home. As it happened, Harry had developed a cold, and Lisa had thought it best that he should stay at home. It would also give Alan the chance to talk to her without interruption when the moment was right for him, and she had planned things to say in her turn that should put his mind at rest about the future. In Brighton there had been a brief lull in the tension that always lay below the surface of their lives, but once the holiday was over everything had been the same as before. Away from London she was hoping that they might recapture that harmony of companionship for a few hours, and as the drive progressed she knew her hopes were to be fulfilled. The gentle green countryside, the woods, the quiet villages, and the hedgerows full of wild flowers were like balm after the hectic war atmosphere of the city. A glorious feeling of relaxation swept over her and she could tell that Alan was similarly affected.

Maple House stood in two acres of land. She loved it at first sight in spite of its shuttered look and neglected lawns and garden. There were plenty of fine old trees that had given the house its name, and an orchard with a stream that ran alongside. It had been built about 1820 and, although large, it was quite unpretentious, a rectangular limestone block enhanced by graceful windows and a semicircular porch. She was out of the automobile almost before it had stopped and ran to try to peer in through a crack of the inner shutters, but everything was tightly shut.

"We'll live here one day, won't we?" she asked eagerly as they stood in the porch, he selecting the right key from the bunch he held in his hand. "We could put up a swing for Harry in the orchard and he would have all this wonderful space in which to run about."

Alan's glance was amused. "You haven't seen the inside of the house yet. It's old-fashioned."

"That won't bother me."

As the door swung open she skipped over the threshold ahead of him into the hall. While she stood looking about her, he went into the drawing-room and opened the inner shutters to let in the autumnal light. All the furniture was covered in dust-sheets, and faded patches on the walls showed where pictures had hung. She followed him into the room to lift the corners of the sheets and exclaim at the fine old rosewood and walnut furniture. He told her that the pictures, mostly oil-paintings and watercolours, were stored in crates somewhere in the basement, as were the china and silverware. When she had fully examined the room, she stood with her hands clasped, taking a deep breath of the dust-moted air as if it held all the fragrance of a flower garden.

"This is a real home." Her eyes were shining. "I can tell. It has roots. I could make them my roots since I have none of my own. Let's see the rest."

They explored from the basement kitchen to the attics. As they went through the bedrooms, she played a game of allotting one to Harry and another to their own use, and selecting guest-rooms. She exclaimed with admiration over the bathroom with its rose-patterned Victorian bath in a mahogany surround. When they were downstairs again and she had looked into every nook and cranny, they went out through the rear door to the stables. There he unlocked a pair of double-doors and flung them wide to reveal an early type of horseless carriage residing inside. She gave a hoot of delighted laughter and scrambled up into the high seat behind the steering wheel.

"Did your grandfather actually drive this?" She pressed the bulb of the horn and the blast of noise would have done credit to a fog-bound ship.

"Yes." Alan leaned an arm on the door and set a foot on the running-board as he looked up at her. "As a small boy I had my first experience of a drive in this vehicle. We wore dust-goggles and driving coats. My grandmother had one made to fit me. I'm sure my interest in engineering stems from the days when my grandfather used to tinker about with the engine whenever it broke down, which was quite frequent, needless to say."

She sat back in the seat and looked wistfully through the open doors at the old house. "Is it really beyond our pockets to live here? Not all the time, of course, but maybe we could drive down after the last show on Saturday nights and return to London on Monday mornings."

"Would it mean so much to you?"

She shut her eyes on a blissful sigh before meeting his gaze again. "I never realised it until I was in the house today, but I've been a rolling stone all my life. I confess to you now that the greatest hardship I have ever known was to leave the States to come back to England. There were special reasons that contributed to it being such a yoke to bear, but one factor was that, apart from all else, I had begun to feel that I belonged to the West. Do you know, I was the only one in the orphanage party who did not weep when she saw the vastness of the prairies. I had a lot to plot and think about at the time, but somehow it was as if I had a sense of destiny that enabled me to adapt to the changes taking place. I knew happiness at Quadra Island, and again at the sawmills in the States. For a while I even thought it would be good if you opened a proper cinema at Dekova's Place instead of moving to Seattle or anywhere else. I was settling down. I was beginning to feel that I belonged, and for a rootless orphan that meant more than any words can describe. Naturally that was before—" Her voice trailed off and she looked ahead again, her gaze abstracted, her fingertips trailing absently along the wheel.

"Before what?"

She shrugged as if shaking off thoughts she wanted to keep at bay. "Before you made your decision to return to England, of course," she said briskly.

For a few moments he had believed her to be on the brink of opening her heart and telling him what had created those barriers between them that had become seemingly impossible to break down. He knew she had never loved him, but she did care for him in her own way, perhaps more than she knew.

"There are means by which this house could be opened up for

you and Harry to make a home here," he said, the omission of himself deliberate.

He saw her face blanch and her hands slip from the wheel into her lap. "You've volunteered for service, haven't you?"

He nodded. "The Royal Engineers is to be my regiment."

"I've known you would go from that moment on the Pier at Brighton when you said we were at war. When is it to be?"

"I'll be called to an Officers' Training Corps camp in about ten days."

"So soon!" She pressed her fingers into her white cheeks. "This house must have cast a spell on me. I'd forgotten the war! I'd forgotten everything. What must you think of me? I went blithering on about coming here at weekends when the whole purpose of leaving Harry behind, as far as I was concerned, was for us to talk about our being separated by your going away. I was sure you would tell me today."

He opened the door of the vehicle to take the leather-upholstered seat beside her. "Since we came back from Brighton, just about four weeks ago, I've been putting everything in order and tying up business ends here and there. A capable manager can take charge of The Fernley without finding anything overlooked in files or records. I've been interviewing men with previous experience of cinema management all the week."

She was aghast. "I don't want anyone else there! I'll run the cinema in your absence. I know all the ropes. I can handle everything."

"What about this house? Now that a second Fernley cinema has to wait until the war is over, there's some spare cash to put the place to rights for you."

"The house can wait until you're home again. Oh no, Alan! The responsibility of The Fernley must be mine alone."

"It would mean doing my work as well as your own. You'd never have any free time."

"I wouldn't want any when you're away. I was prepared to tell you all this today. I never thought you'd consider letting anyone else take over from me."

He began to smile. "I haven't. You shall be in charge. I've been looking for a reliable assistant manager, not someone to take away your authority. It was only your enthusiasm for my grandparents' old home that made me wonder if you'd prefer to wait in the countryside for my return from the war."

She shook her head quickly. "The waiting would seem twice as long if I had nothing to do."

"I've short-listed three suitable applicants. Would you like to be at the final interviews tomorrow?"

"Yes, I would." She reached out a hand and cupped his face. "I pray this war will be over soon," she declared fervently.

"It will be once I get to France," he joked drily.

She managed a little chuckle, but there was only sadness in her.

Before leaving the house they picnicked in the orchard, sitting on a plaid motoring rug spread out on the grass. While Alan refastened shutters and relocked doors, Lisa picked rosy-red apples from the low branches and filled an old basket they found in the stables to take the harvest home with them. When they drove away, he drew up outside in the road to get out and padlock the gates. She looked back over her shoulder to register a last glimpse of the house through the trees. She hoped that the next time she saw it Alan would be safely back from the war and that her sense of belonging to the place would still be there. This quiet corner of England could not be less like the sweeping west of North America, but she loved both areas with equal attachment, and neither could ever replace the other in her affections.

At first Lisa did not have any preference for the three applicants who were interviewed the next day. All seemed to be agreeable men and well qualified to fill the post. Her choice finally settled on Reginald Hardy, who was slightly older than Alan. Tall and thin with a longish nose and kindly eyes, he was smart in appearance and well-spoken. She thought his only fault might be that he would want to shoulder too much, and she had no intention of letting control of The Fernley slide out of her hands.

Mr. Hardy began work the next day, Alan introducing him to the cinema's own particular routine. The newcomer was well acquainted with everything and everybody when the day came for Alan to leave. It was a departure without fuss, as was wanted, his farewells at the cinema having taken place the night before. He hugged and kissed his son, who was then led away by Maudie, leaving him alone with Lisa.

"I hope to see you in about six weeks," he said to her. "In any case, I'm sure to get embarkation leave before I'm sent to France. We'll have some time together yet, my darling."

They exchanged a long kiss. Then he took up his suitcase and hurried down the stairs from the apartment to the taxi waiting at the kerb. She watched the taxi out of sight from the window.

His expectation of leave came to naught. The demands of the war meant the least possible delay in getting highly qualified men of his calibre to the Front, particularly as the Germans had taken many inland Belgian towns and it was essential to keep them from reaching the Channel ports. Six weeks later he telephoned Lisa to meet him at Victoria Station the following day at noon when he would be on a troop boat-train to take ship at Folkstone. She allowed plenty of time to get there, but the congestion of traffic and two long hold-ups due to a recruiting rally delayed her until she feared she would miss him altogether. Plunking the fare into the taxi-driver's hand, she turned to speed into the station, dodging in and out of the milling throng of passengers, military and civilian, to reach the platform. With the exception of the sergeants in charge, the soldiers were all aboard the train and many whistled and called out to her as she ran along, managing to avoid collision with other people there to see off sons, fathers and brothers. Then, ahead of her, she suddenly sighted Alan anxiously watching out for her. His expression and hers changed to one of mutual joy that she was in time. As she rushed into his arms the troops in the nearby carriages roared their approbation at their officer's good fortune in securing an enviable kissing session with such a pretty woman.

"It was the traffic," she explained, still breathless from her running as they drew apart, his arms still about her.

"I guessed that, but I was sure you'd get here somehow."

"How are you?" Her eyes searched his face solicitously.

He grinned at her. "In the pink, as the soldiers say."

"Harry has sent you a picture he painted." She took it from her purse and he slipped it into his pocket to look at later, unable to spare one of these last moments for anything but the sight of her lovely face.

"Thank him for me," he said fondly. "Tell him I'll put it up on display wherever I am, be it tent or trench."

"He asks about you all the time."

There was the slightest pause. "Don't let the boy forget me."

She understood the significance of those words and her heart contracted with fear for his safety in all the dangers that lay ahead. For a moment she almost answered with forced light-heartedness that the boy would have no chance since Alan would soon be home again for good, but this was a time for promises and not for any pretence, however well intentioned. "He'll never forget you. I'll see to that."

He nodded satisfied. All along the train, doors were slamming as those in charge went aboard to rejoin their comrades. One of Alan's fellow officers was leaning out of a carriage close by, keeping the door open for him to make a last minute dash. Time was running out. As the guard blew his whistle sharply and waved his green flag, Alan gave her a passionate kiss of farewell.

Suddenly she found she could not let him go without saying the words to him that she had never said and which she knew he had always longed to hear from her above all else. "I do love you, Alan."

His face became transfigured. She could never have believed that a man about to face the most horrific confrontation conceived by the human mind could have looked so happy. From the train his companions were shouting to him to come aboard, the wheels taking their first turn. He pressed his loving mouth to hers once more and then tore himself from her to leap into the carriage. The door slammed after him and he leaned from the open window as she ran alongside.

"I'll get leave soon," he called exuberantly to her. "Those of us who surrendered our embarkation leave in view of the emergency are to be the first on the list for Blighty in a few weeks time!"

"I'll be waiting!"

The gathering speed of the train outdistanced her, its smoke wreathing back over the platform. She came to a standstill and waved until she could see him no more. It had been the truth when she had said she loved him. It was a very different love from the consuming, everlasting passion she felt for Peter, but it was in no way demeaned by that comparison. She knew she would remember that joyous look on her husband's face until the end of her days.

She retraced her steps at a much slower pace amid others leaving the platform, feeling thoroughly inadequate at being unable to assist in some way the efforts of Alan and those with him in the struggle in which they would soon be engaged. As she was about to go from the platform, she noticed a band of busy women, some of them wearing Red Cross arm-bands, emptying tea-urns and stacking thick china cups on long trestle tables to be washed up in bowls of steaming water. They had supplied refreshments and cigarettes free of charge to the troops that had departed with the train. Swiftly she approached a dignified-looking woman in Red Cross uniform who appeared to be in charge.

"Do you want any more helpers? I'm eager to be of some use in the war effort."

"What welcome words!" The woman smiled at her. "We need all the help we can get for every kind of duty. Are you a member of the Voluntary Aid Detachment of the Red Cross?"

"No, I'm not. But I'd like to join."

"Splendid! I'll give you an enrollment form now."

Lisa read it through in the taxi during her return to the cinema. She found she could not be a fully fledged V.A.D., as those of the Red Cross Voluntary Aid Detachment were known, until she had attended first aid lectures and passed qualifying examinations. Upon arriving at The Fernley she went straight to Mr. Hardy to arrange that he be left entirely in charge for a couple of hours every evening while she attended a course of lectures in a church hall not far away.

As soon as her training was completed successfully, she went to a special outfitter in Golden Square to buy her Red Cross uniform. She felt honoured to wear it and had her photograph taken in it at head and shoulder level to send to Alan. He wrote back that he had never seen a more beautiful nurse, and he was keeping the photograph in its leather folder in his left-hand pocket over his heart.

All his letters were love-letters. At times the tenderness of the phrases he used moved her intensely, particularly as she knew that these poignant outpourings were often written in the dank misery of a dug-out in the mud-filled trenches while shells whistled overhead and bombs burst open the earth. After the extraordinary and unofficial truce at Christmas when soldiers on both sides had come out of their trenches to meet in No Man's Land and exchange festive greetings, the war continued with unabated ferocity.

She saw the aftermath of those battles, some of which were won and some lost, when she was on reception duty at Waterloo Station where trains brought in the wounded from the hospital ships that docked at Southampton. On the first occasion, she stood numbed by the sight of the train disgorging countless stretcher cases and soldiers with bandaged heads and eyes and arms in slings. Some were missing a limb and were helped along by medical orderlies or hobbled gamely alone on their crutches. While she was standing as if transfixed, one of the soldiers on crutches slipped and fell heavily. She rushed to him while the busy orderlies, seeing she was in V.A.D. uniform with the Red Cross on her apron front, left him to her care for the time being. He was lying on his back, his crutches scattered, and was looking up at the grimy glass roof high above him.

"Are you all right?" she cried anxiously, dropping to her knees to lean over him. The tears of compassion were spilling from her eyes. He was about forty years old and there was a pinned-up trouser-leg over the stump of his thigh. At the sound of her voice his gaze shifted to her face, his own ashen from the pain that had seared through his whole body from the fall, and he managed a lopsided grin.

"Clumsy, ain't I? Don't cry, nurse. I could do with a smile from your pretty face. There ain't been much smiling lately where I've come from."

It taught her a lesson. She never again gave way to her emotions. The wounded wanted encouragement and not pity. They received it from her with every train she met. She also arranged that men in hospital blue be admitted free to the Fernley movie shows.

Sometimes recruiting sergeants came to the cinema and addressed the audience from the stage, while in the foyer a table was set up for men to enlist on the spot. There was always a queue of those wanting to sign their names, stirred equally by the patriotic newsreels and the sergeants' accounts of enemy atrocities against Belgian women and children.

It was after one of these recruiting visits that Lisa found Mr. Hardy sitting in the deserted foyer with his elbows propped on his knees and his head in his hands. "What is the matter?" she exclaimed anxiously. "Are you ill?"

"No, Mrs. Fernley." He dropped his hands and straightened up at once, his reassuring smile not matching the disquiet in his eyes. "It's been a long day. A spot of tiredness, that's all."

"Would you like some time off?" She sat down beside him. She had come to know him quite well during the months they had worked together. Contrary to her original uncertainty about him, he had never once tried to usurp her position, but had given her loyal and energetic support which had enabled her to carry out her V.A.D. duties and spend extra time with Harry when he needed her, such as when the boy had succumbed to measles and been quite ill for a while.

"You are most considerate, but I really don't need a holiday," he replied. "In fact, I'm bored when I'm not working. A break would do me no good at all."

She thought loneliness was half his trouble. He lived in lodgings and what relatives he had were somewhere in the North of Scotland. It was becoming more difficult every day for a man in civilian life to find a girl-friend, for many women no longer liked to be seen with a male partner not in uniform.

"Well, think about it, anyway," she advised. "It can always be arranged."

Not only had Alan's hopes of an early leave come to nothing, but the first months of the year went by with no sign of his coming home. Sometimes she wondered if he was engaged in special work that made it difficult to release him, but naturally there was no hint in his letters that this might be the case. From information gathered from officers she met and from what she read in the newspapers, the Royal Engineers were spread thinly throughout the British Expeditionary Forces, but in concentrated and highly efficient groups that bridged rivers and carried out other such tasks. The Royal Engineers figured strongly in the casualty lists and there was no telling what courageous risks they had taken to bring their names into those tragic columns.

Minnie, following events closely from the newspapers in the States, wrote with concern about the Zeppelin raids on the English east coast, fearful of Lisa's and Harry's safety if they should reach London. But those huge airborne monsters were subject to the whims of the wind and weather and nobody took the threat very seriously. Then on the last night of May, a Zeppelin, escaping anti-aircraft fire, dropped bombs on London, resulting in casualties. The recruiting sergeant gained still more volunteers as a result.

At the end of June, Lisa received word that Alan was coming home on leave. She was at once filled with happiness at the prospect of seeing him safe and sound while, at the same time, she experienced trepidation as to how it would be between them after this long span of separation. After everything he had been through in the fighting, he might have expectations of her after her declaration of love that would be impossible for her to meet, however willing. She truly cared for him, but what she felt was not new and in the past it had not overcome the barriers that were part of their lives. Why should things be any different now?

With a week before his home-coming in which to make plans, she sent Harry and Maudie to friends at a seaside resort on the south coast, well out of range of any raids. Alan should have some time with Harry, but not before he and she had had a few days together on their own. Then she set other arrangements into motion very speedily and everything was ready when she drove their automobile to Victoria Station to meet him. There were other women waiting for their menfolk, and it was easy to see that they had put on their best outfits, as she had done, for the occasion. She doubted if any one of them was assailed by the nervousness that she was experiencing. It was like being a bride again.

The train came into sight, grey smoke puffing from the locomotive. The women surged forward along the platform in their excitement, but she stayed near the ticket-gate, her heart palpitating madly. Carriage doors were opening, passengers alighting, and reunions taking place. And there he was. The army captain with the thin, haggard face and war-wearied eyes.

In her hours of duty as a V.A.D. she had seen many returning men with the look about them of having gazed into hell, and she had prepared herself for a change in his appearance. Nevertheless, it came as a great shock to her that he should bear the marks of ordeal to such a degree. She held out her arms, his image spangled through the tears she would not release, and he caught her to him with a deep moan of love. The clean, sweet bouquet of her made him dizzy. It was as if all his lonely dreams of her had taken on a reality beyond his immediate comprehension.

"Now I'm going to drive you home," she said to him as they left the station.

He threw his belongings into the back of the automobile and took the seat beside her. The sight of London was disturbing to him. Reminders of the death and destruction he had left recently were all around him. He saw it in the posters of Kitchener's face and pointing finger demanding voluntary service. It was there in the uniforms passing by on the pavements and crossing the streets. He heard it in the pipes of a Highland regiment on its way to a boat-train. He had hoped to unwind and forget for two whole weeks that elsewhere men had gone mad and nothing would ever be the same again. Although he shared everyone's opinion of the Kaiser and the German generals, he felt no hatred towards the enemy in the fighting lines and he was not alone in that. There was a curious and terrible comradeship in knowing that beyond the barbed wire of No Man's Land the Germans were sharing the same appalling conditions of trench mud and rats and lice and, until the onset of better weather, sometimes icy water up to the waist. He had known rage against them and fury fit to split his brain, such as when they used poison gas at Ypres, but hate was not there. Maybe everything would have been easier to bear if it had been.

He became aware that Lisa was not taking the route he had expected to follow. "Which way are you going?" he asked her. He remembered her writing in a letter that the first trainload of wounded from France had had to face the further endurance of being in ambulances deliberately detoured by cheering London crowds, who had misguidedly wished to express their feelings. He, although completely unscathed, had no more wish than those poor wounded would have had that the drive should be longer than was absolutely necessary. Not that the apartment could provide him with the healing quietude he greatly needed, for its being adjacent to the cinema would mean instant involvement.

"I told you," she said calmly, looking ahead, "I'm taking you home. Really home. We're on our way to Berkshire."

He raised his eyebrows in surprise. "Have you opened Maple House then?"

"Only for the duration of your leave and just the rooms we'll be using. Your village caretaker organised an army of helpers at short notice to scrub and polish there."

He spoke on a silent laugh of pleasure and sheer relief. "Marvellous!"

"We'll have the place entirely to ourselves for a week. Then Maudie will arrive with Harry. He's looking forward to seeing you so much."

"What have I done to deserve you, Lisa?" There was a kind of wonder in his voice as he leaned across to kiss her on the neck. His romantic tribute was observed with interest by passengers in a bus driving alongside. He saw only her.

They broke their journey to dine at an old coaching inn, and then drove on to Maple House. It was dark when they arrived, but Lisa had arranged that lamps should be lighted at an earlier hour so that the windows gave a glow that reached out to them as they drew up outside. The dusty atmosphere had been completely banished from the house, which smelt of beeswax and freshly laundered curtains and the scent from the vases of many-hued garden flowers that had been placed everywhere. In the hallway they turned to each other.

"Welcome home, Alan," she said softly.

He drew her to him in silent embrace, momentarily beyond words. Somewhere in the trees outside a nightingale was singing.

They went upstairs together. There was white, hand-embroidered linen from another age on the wide mahogany bed and the lamps were pink silk with beaded fringes. The windows stood open to the moonlight and the stars. For his sake she let nothing intrude on that night. No thoughts of past or future came to her. It was her gift of reconciliation and renewal to the man she had married, the time-honoured tribute of a woman to the returned soldier in a spate of war, and the night was entirely his. On his part, he led her to a release of ecstasy that she had long believed she would never know again. It brought them to a state of such enormous tenderness for each other that the night surpassed even the special one that had brought them close for transient moments not long after their marriage. This time all barriers were down.

The week passed all too quickly. They walked in the countryside, lazed in the sunshine and the shade, and prepared simple meals together. Their love-making was rich and rewarding. Afterwards there was always a sweet contentment.

When Harry arrived, the pattern of their time together changed a great deal, but was no less pleasurable. Maudie took over the domestic arrangements leaving the three of them together. They played games of cricket and croquet, dammed the stream for a boating-pool, explored the nearby woods and went for picnics. Lisa and Harry shared the swing and the seesaw that Alan had set up, and every day the sun shone and the nights were still and balmy. Finally it was time to leave. The shutting up of the house was to be left to the village caretaker, who would come in as soon as they had gone. This enabled them to drive away leaving windows and doors open as if they were about to return shortly. It made everything a little easier for them, although the moment of departure was poignant enough.

They drove to the London apartment. Alan, refreshed and rested physically and mentally by the country sojourn, went immediately into the cinema to greet the staff and discuss certain business matters with Mr. Hardy. Lisa had mentioned the assistant manager's bouts of depression, for increasingly the man was low in spirits for days at a time, but in answer to Alan's tactful questioning he announced himself well satisfied with his recent raise in salary and had no complaints about the long hours he worked. It left Alan with no more idea than Lisa as to what the man's trouble might be.

That evening Alan took Lisa to the theatre. They saw a lively musical show and afterwards had supper at the Savoy. Their last night together, which was as ardent and passionate as the rest had been, had its own special moments unique to times of parting. He would not let her accompany him to the station this time. To bid her farewell in the company of others would be more than he could bear.

"Come back soon," she implored, locked in his embrace.

"Nothing shall keep me away for as long as before," he promised her. They kissed and he went from her. And she was engulfed by the wave of emptiness that swept in on her as the door closed behind him.

By the middle of the following month, Lisa was wondering what could be amiss with her. At times the smoke of somebody's cigarette, or even a pleasant aroma from a coffee-shop could make her feel quite nauseous. Another two weeks went by before a sudden bout of morning sickness confirmed what she had stopped hoping for long since. Weak and trembling from the onslaught, she gasped with sheer joy, pressing the flat of her hands to her stomach through the thin silk of her nightgown. She was pregnant at last.

As soon as the doctor had added medical confirmation, she wrote the news to Alan. According to dates, the baby had been conceived during the first week of his leave, perhaps even on that night of supreme tenderness between them. She would always cling to the belief that it was that night. Her feelings for Alan entered a new phase. It was her hope that he would get back to be with her when the baby was born. He echoed that hope in the letter he wrote upon receiving the good news. In subsequent correspondence they settled on names for a son or a daughter. She wanted the choice to be his.

In September another Zeppelin got through to London. The casualties were not as high as those suffered in the constant raids on Grimsby and other places on the east coast, but the shock effect of a second raid on the heart of England was considerable. Lisa had no idea that it was to be instrumental in bringing about a change in the organisation of The Fernley. The only forewarning came when she returned one afternoon after fetching Harry from the day-school he was attending, always seizing any chance to be with him. Leaving him in Maudie's care in the apartment, she went through the connecting door into the cinema to be met by the girl who sold chocolates in the intervals.

"I told Mr. Hardy I must have fresh supplies before the matinée," she reported indignantly, "and he went out without giving them to me."

"Gone out? That's not possible. Mr. Hardy is always on the premises when I'm absent and vice-versa."

"Well, he's not here. One of the usherettes saw him in his hat and coat."

Lisa was most annoyed. Mr. Hardy's behaviour had reached its limits this time. She would have to speak severely to him upon his return. "I'll get the chocolates for you," she said. "Follow me."

Lisa went into Mr. Hardy's office where the stores were kept in a side-room. She took what was needed from a cupboard and gave it to the girl, who hurried away into the auditorium. Lisa relocked the cupboard and was returning through the office when she noticed something on his desk that made her stop in her tracks. It was a white feather. Symbol of cowardice. She reached out slowly to pick it up and found that more than one lay there. Spreading them out on the blotter she saw that there were seven in all. Now she understood what had caused the sensitive man such fits of depression from time to time. The door opened and she looked up, the feathers still spread out before her. Mr. Hardy had come into the office, his pale face tautening at the evidence she had discovered.

"I've joined up, Mrs. Fernley. I'm sorry to leave you single-handed but I can't take any more insults to my patriotism and my integrity."

"Who gave you these feathers?"

"Mostly women patrons after a performance was over. The last straw came today on the bus to work when a woman handed me one for everybody to see just as she was about to alight, shouting out that any man prepared to let Zeppelins bomb London without fighting back deserved hanging."

"Why didn't you tell me what was happening? I've realised that something was wrong."

"I couldn't bring myself to tell you of my humiliation."

She sighed deeply. He could not be leaving her at a worse time. "Are you going into the Army?"

"Yes. They want me right away. I report this evening."

She left him to finish off such clerical work as he had in hand. When he was ready to leave he shook hands with everybody on the staff and came to her for the most important words of farewell. "It's been a privilege to work for you, Mrs. Fernley. May I ask to be considered for my old job here again when this war is over?"

"Yes, indeed. Good luck and a safe return."

When he had gone she went into her office and sat down to take stock of her situation. There was nothing to stop her running the cinema entirely on her own as she had wanted to do originally when she learned that Alan would be going to war, except that now she was pregnant and must have a deputy she could trust to leave in charge when the time came for her confinement. Fortunately there was someone of her own sex on the premises who had had office experience before taking over the pay-box. Moreover, she liked the idea of having a woman assistant, for it meant the two of them would be carrying on an enterprise normally shouldered by men. The war was bringing women to the fore, after centuries of domestic enslavement, to handle machinery, the wheels of transport, and administrative positions of authority previously supposed to be entirely beyond their ken. It was exciting to be part of that evolvement.

The discovery that she was pregnant had made Lisa look to the future with renewed energy, and she was resolved not to let the war create a stalemate of the Fernley enterprise, particularly since its present rôle was of vital importance in giving people the relaxation they needed in these difficult times. Alan had had to shelve his expansion plans for the duration of hostilities, but there was no reason why she should not give the matter her attention.

"Would you like to be my assistant manageress?" she asked Billy's wife after explaining the work to her in detail.

"Yes, I would." Ethel Morris's eyes gleamed with satisfaction in her round red-cheeked face that was framed by greying hair. "And I suggest that Miss Unwin, the usherette, take my place as cashier. She's a good, honest young woman."

Not only did Ethel Morris prove to be as efficient in her new post as she had been in the pay-box, but having borne children herself she was considerate and helpful towards Lisa in her pregnancy. They worked well together.

It was a source of disquiet to Lisa, among all else of concern, that in spite of having drawn close to Alan in a way that once she could never have believed possible, memories of Peter still slipped at unguarded moments into her heart and into her mind. It always happened whenever she read in the newspapers that yet another neutral Norwegian merchantship had been sunk by German submarines, for any vessel carrying on normal trade in supplies to Britain had to run the gauntlet of enemy torpedoes. Then she would picture again the West Coast of the United States and wonder where Peter was now, knowing how this abuse of his old country's shipping, and the loss of the seamen's lives, would anger and distress him.

Sometimes at night when frustrated yearnings assailed her, she would sigh with despair that it was Peter whom she thought about and not her husband. There were even occasions when he came into her dreams, and always they were of the beginning of their relationship in those far-off Toronto days. She could interpret the meaning as a subconscious desire to turn the clock back for a second chance, and she railed against herself for it. Vain regrets about the past were useless, and it was what she did with the present and the future that was vitally important. Her pregnancy was her all-consuming joy. As it advanced, so did her new plans that she was putting steadily into action.

The war swept on ferociously. In France one evening in early April, Alan returned mud-caked with his Sappers from tunnelling under No Man's Land to lay mines before an attack and found some delayed mail awaiting him. He read in Lisa's neat hand that she had been safely delivered of a daughter, Catherine, who was strong and healthy and quite beautiful. They were both doing well.

His leave to England was long overdue. Twice it had been cancelled when an urgent need for highly skilled engineers had outweighed all else. It was almost a year since he had seen Lisa and then, when his allotted leave did come, the dates were put forward by two weeks and he knew the reason for that, too. A great battle was in the offing. He could not be spared when it started and was wanted back in time to take over special duties.

He had no chance to let Lisa know he was arriving sooner than expected. Arriving at the cinema during an evening performance, he was greeted warmly by Billy, who shook his hand heartily.

"Good to see you again, Mr. Fernley. No, your wife isn't here. She's at the new place this evening."

"What new place?"

Billy looked uncomfortable. "Didn't you know, sir? She's opened a second Fernley cinema. Not as posh as this one, but it's comfortable and there's a full house every night."

Lisa had finished playing the piano for the last performance of the evening at the new Fernley cinema when Alan arrived. She did not see him at first, for she was collecting up some posies of flowers that patrons had brought her from their gardens. People who attended a cinema regularly, particularly the women, often showed their appreciation of the pianist's accomplishment with modest offerings. It had happened to her at Dekova's Place and again at the first Fernley as it was happening here. As she turned with the flowers in her arms, she saw Alan standing in the aisle of the deserted auditorium.

She gasped involuntarily, clutching the blossoms closer to her. This was not what she had intended. Not wanting to cause him any unnecessary anxiety while at the Front, she had decided to break the news to him upon his return on leave and let him see for himself how everything was working out. That he should have discovered her harmless deception for himself boded ill. It could bring about a rift in what was so newly healed.

"This is quite a surprise." His gaunt, tired face gave no indication of how angry he might be and his wearied voice was expressionless. "For both of us."

"I agree." It was not in her nature to make excuses for what she had done.

"How did you manage financially to get this place going?" He gazed around from where he stood. It had been a large meeting hall as far as he could judge. Plush seats had replaced the original seating and this costly outlay had been offset by Lisa's inexpensive and imaginative decor of coral-painted walls shading upwards to a midnight blue ceiling studded with appliqued silver stars. She had put the right emphasis on comfort and created atmosphere on a shoe-string. He could make a guess that she had equipped the projection-room with the spare projectors made by him and that had been kept in The Fernley store-rooms. She was practical and economical, and he had every confidence that she had thought out this expansion of the business most carefully. From outside the building he had approved the busy location and noted from the posters and the lobby cards that she was booking Chaplin of the comedies and William S. Hart of the Westerns and Pearl White of the serials, all guaranteed to draw the public. Lisa knew what she was doing. It was a consoling thought that whatever happened to him, she would have the strength and stamina to carry on with life and bring up his children in the way he would have wished. She returned his gaze as she gave him an answer to his query.

"The first Fernley enterprise was well able to share some of its profits," she explained tensely. "The bank-manager loaned me the rest. I convinced him that this area was in dire need of a cinema and I was the one to run it."

"What about a licence?"

"I talked the local council into giving me one in my own name."

Amusement began to twinkle in his eyes. "There can't be many women granted that privilege."

"I believe there's less than half a dozen in the whole country. You and I are really partners now."

He came and took her by the shoulders. "We always were as far as I was concerned."

She uttered a cry of relief, dropping the flowers to throw her arms about his neck and gave back his kiss rapturously. When they reached home, she led him into the nursery and picked up their fair-haired daughter to place her in his arms. Catherine awakened and looked at him with eyes that matched his own.

As it happened, the reels of a new Douglas Fairbanks movie were being run through next morning before the first showing at a matinée the following day, and Minnie had a big part in it. Lisa and Alan watched it alone together in the auditorium. Minnie had developed a piquant beauty that enhanced her considerable acting ability. It was obvious she had been well directed and her talent fostered by those who had recognised the potential in her. More than that, she seemed to have the kind of face the camera loved, for it dwelt lingeringly on her every change of expression as she went through the whole gamut of emotions from joy to heartbreak. At times her lustrous, expressive eyes seemed to fill the screen. Lisa, forgetting momentarily that this actress wringing the heart-strings was once the waif she had mothered when she herself had been only a girl, blinked away some tears as the movie ended.

"She's superb," Alan pronounced.

"The press call her another Mary Pickford. It's wonderful for her, isn't it? By her letters, she's quite unchanged by her growing success."

"I'd thank Risto for that. From what I remember of him, I'd say he was keeping her feet firmly on the ground."

"Yes, that's true. I know I had no doubts about his looking

after her when they eloped. The insecurity she had suffered in her childhood had left its scars. He was the anchor that she needed."

After the showing they left for the house in the country, taking the children with them. Harry had adapted better than expected to the arrival of a sister, which made everything easier for Lisa. The time at Maple House passed by much as before in quiet, contented days with no mention of the war, and newspapers kept temporarily away. When the moment came for parting, it had never been harder for Alan to leave Lisa, for he knew what lay ahead on his return to France.

A week later, on the first of July, he was in the great attack on the Somme. Later he received the Military Cross for his extreme bravery in action, but was never to speak of what he had done, for to him it had simply been his duty as he saw it. He was slightly wounded in the process, but was patched up at a field dressing station and was not considered a serious enough case to be included in the list of over 57,000 British casualties, including 20,000 dead, incurred in that single day. The slaughter he witnessed at the Somme left a mark deeper than anything else he had been through previously. He was grave in demeanour and greatly changed when he went on leave eight months later. He wept over the beauty of his wife's body as if he had never seen her naked before, and in her arms found succour and release from nightmares.

When the United States entered the war, there was cheering in the streets of London. Lisa found a Stars and Stripes flag that she had brought back from Seattle with her, and she hung it from the window of the apartment. Her thoughts went, as they did so often, to Peter's possible whereabouts in that vast land, and to Minnie, who was now playing leading rôles in her own right. Her lovely, elfin face gazed glamorously from the lobby cards and her name was now more familiar to movie-goers than ever before. She did not write as frequently these days as she had done, being in great demand in the life she led, but her letters showed that she was still the same at heart.

Lisa was leaving the apartment one morning to go to the other cinema when she opened the street door to see a telegraph boy getting off his bicycle at the kerb. He came towards her with a yellow War Office telegram in his hand.

"Mrs. Fernley?" he asked quietly.

"Yes," she replied huskily, her heart giving a great thump of fear. She took the telegram from him and drew back inside, her hands trembling so much that she could hardly open it. With regret the War Office informed her that her husband had been severely wounded in action.

Her V.A.D. uniform entitled her to be present at Waterloo Station when he was brought back to London after spending some time in a French hospital. A bullet had entered his right shoulder-blade, brushed past the spine, and broken some ribs before coming to rest between the heart and the base of the right lung. The operation had been successful, but paralysis of the legs was a result of spinal involvement. The hope was that it was a temporary condition that would right itself with time. As the stretcher cases were borne from the train, Lisa moved among them, giving cigarettes and lighting them for those able to celebrate a return home with a smoke, and all the time her eyes searched for Alan. He saw her from his stretcher before she saw him and called out to her. She rushed across to bend her head and kiss him. "You're home!"

"How are the children? How are you?"

Holding his hand, she walked alongside the stretcher answering his questions. He gave her no chance to ask him how he might be, and she respected his wishes not to be reminded verbally at this moment of reunion about his weakened state. She went with him to the ambulance, but had to leave him there, for he was being taken to a military hospital in Cambridge.

The following Sunday she drove there with the children. Alan was pushed in a wheelchair by a nurse out into the sunny grounds where Lisa awaited him with Harry and Catherine. At first his daughter was shy, having no recollection of this stranger with the rug over his knees, but gradually he won her over and she sat happily with him. Lisa showed him a newspaper cutting that Minnie had sent her.

"Look," she said. "There's Minnie setting off on a nation-wide tour to promote Liberty Bonds with Charlie Chaplin and Douglas Fairbanks and Mary Pickford. She writes that Risto will miss her because they've never been apart for more than a few days at any time. We have one of her films showing at both cinemas at the moment. It's called *The Lost Heart.*"

"Is she good in it?"

"Better than ever, I think."

In a New York hotel suite, Minnie had dashed to the dressing-table mirror and was dabbing her nose with a powder puff. "Quick!" she called to her maid. "Get my new white satin négligée! The one with the swansdown trimming."

There had been a telephone call from the lobby desk to say that her husband had arrived and was on his way up. She had not seen Risto since the Liberty Bond tour had started weeks ago, and when he had let her know he would meet her in New York, she had been too excited to sleep. She adored him more than ever for taking the long journey all the way from California to be with her for a short vacation. They would make love as soon as he came through the door and afterwards they would go out on the town to celebrate. Then they would come back to the suite and make love, and make love, and make love all over again. She sighed in delicious anticipation, giving a touch of expensive French scent to her cleavage and behind her ears.

As the négligée was held out for her, she slipped her arms into it, drawing it forward over her shoulders and her pretty lace-trimmed silk underwear. Then she hastened to the full-length cheval-glass to regard her reflection anxiously. Did she look her best? Six years of marriage had not dimmed in the least her passion for Risto, or his for her, their faithfulness to each other unsullied and unassailed. She often pitied the men who pursued her, their hopes doomed from the start.

"Is there anything more, ma'am?" her maid asked her.

She shook her head. "After you've let my husband in you may go." It would be fun to make a grand entrance from the bedroom with her swansdown and satin trailing about her. Knowing Risto, he would probably throw himself back from his feet in one of those comedy falls in exaggerated appreciation or enact something equally crazy. There was always laughter with Risto. Laughter and love. Mostly love.

The doorbell rang. The maid went from the bedroom to answer it, organdie apron strings drifting, her feet making no sound on the deep pile of the carpet. At highly charged moments, Minnie sometimes felt quite detached from her surroundings, able to marvel that she, an abandoned waif from a Leeds orphanage, should have come to such luxury and success along a previously unseen path. And she knew she was only on the first rungs of the ladder of fame. One day she would reach the very top.

There was Risto's voice! Her heart was beating wildly. A word or two from the maid and then the door of the suite closed. They were on their own. She swept through the bedroom doorway uttering a verbal fanfare.

"Tra-la-la!" Then her voice failed her and trailed away to an agonised whimper at the sight of him standing there in army uniform, his expression serious. "Oh, dear God! What have you done?"

"Minnie, honey. I didn't know how to tell you. To let you know I was in training camp would have ruined the tour for you."

She had slumped back against the door-jamb as if her legs were losing the strength to support her. "They've cut your hair," she said dully as if that were all she could absorb for the moment.

He tossed his hat on to a chair and somewhat self-consciously he ran a hand over the short crop. "That's the style the Army favours."

"I hate it." Her voice took on power and she straightened up, clenching her fists. "I hate that uniform! I hate you!"

He frowned in distress, seeing that things were to be even worse than he had feared. "You don't mean that. Ever since Britain went to war you've been wanting the States to go in on the side of the Allies. You've talked of little else at times. You must have realised that when it did happen I would serve my country. I couldn't stand aside."

She seemed to be following her own line of thought. "I would have left the tour if I'd known you had joined up. I could have been near the camp. We could have had time together that you have thrown away." Suddenly she screamed out hysterically in anguish and hurled herself at him with beating fists. "You bastard!"

It took all his strength to subdue her. She was like a wildcat and they struggled until they fell to the floor together. Then she lay sobbing forlornly, a forearm across her eyes, the tears rolling down into the carpet. He spoke soothingly to her.

"The war can't last long now. Who knows? It may be over before I set foot in France."

Her voice was choked. "When do you sail?"

"We have seven days and seven nights together, honey. Let's make sweet memories out of them." He took hold of her wrist and drew her arm gently away from her face. She glanced up at him with a melting look of love in a frame of lashes aglitter with the still rolling tears.

"Let's begin then, Risto darling," she whispered tremulously, her lips soft and moist. "I've missed you so much."

He threw off his uniform and it fell everywhere. When he buried his mouth and his heart and his flesh in her on the discarded négligée and the soft carpet, her response was ecstatic. Later he scooped her up in his arms and carried her through to the bed. Apart from their having the champagne dinner in the suite instead of going out, everything was as she had anticipated and they revelled in each other. Both were of the opinion that no man and woman had ever been more perfectly matched than they. Their loving shut out the whole world for the time that was left to them.

When the troopship sailed out of New York Harbor, bands played on the quayside and flags waved. Risto watched from the rails until Minnie's courageously smiling face became a pale blur and finally dissolved into the mass of the crowd seeing the ship on its way. Their last moments had been intruded upon by a photographer who had recognised her, and his flashlight had attracted the attention of other people around them. Some had even pushed between them for her autograph. At least no outsider had been able to intrude on the farewell of love they had conveyed in their eyes to each other. That had been theirs alone.

Now he had to look ahead to the job that had to be done. For him it was to be behind an army newsreel camera on the battlefields. He was to film tragedy instead of comedy, courage instead of slapstick, and the landing of shells instead of custard pies.

The skyline was drawing away. As the Statue of Liberty slid past the troopship, Risto was not alone in saluting her. After all, that statue symbolised the reason for his going to war. He wondered how long it would be before he saw the torch of liberty again. Soon there was nothing visible on the horizon; the country of his birth gone beyond the ocean's rim and the woman he loved with it.

Alan was nine weeks in hospital before the full use of his legs returned to him. After that he was given two months' sick leave and Lisa fetched him home to the apartment. He began to do some work in the office and she did not discourage him, seeing that he needed to occupy his mind and his time.

She was in her own office at the other cinema one afternoon when there came a knock on the door. Writing at her desk, she answered automatically, without looking up: "Come in."

Somebody entered. "Hi, Lisa. Remember me?"

She sat back in her chair and stared with astonished recognition at the young, good-looking Yankee soldier standing there. "Risto!" she exclaimed in delighted disbelief. "I can't believe it! How wonderful to see you." She sprang up to come around her desk where they hugged each other in greeting. "I had no idea you were in the Army or that you were in Europe, but then the last time I heard from Minnie was when she was setting off on a fund-raising tour."

"That's when I volunteered for the Army. She didn't know about it until I met her in New York on my embarkation leave. I guess I should have forewarned her, but parting was going to be hell whichever way I did it. Looking back now, I don't know how either of us survived saying goodbye."

"Oh, poor dear Minnie. Where is she now?"

"Back in Hollywood making a new motion picture. Richard Barthelmess is tipped as her leading man. I told her I'd get to London to see you as soon as I could."

"You're most welcome now that you're here. You will stay with us, won't you?"

"I'd be glad to. Your husband has invited me already. He told me where to find you when I went to the other movie house first."

She heaved a sigh of pleasure. "It does me good to hear an American voice again. I always wish I could hear Minnie's voice when she's on the screen. Alan says that one day sound will be linked to film."

"Do you miss the States, Lisa?"

She leaned back against the desk and looked down at her hands, absently twisting one of her rings. "I miss it. I miss the people I knew there. But it was right for Alan and me to leave when we did. If we hadn't, he would have come away to the war in August 1914, and I wouldn't have been here when he needed me. Sometimes things work out for the best, although we don't realise it at the time."

"I hope you'll come and visit us in California when this war is over."

"I'd love to do that."

"That's a date then!"

Risto spent the whole of his furlough with Alan and Lisa. She took time off to show him the sights of London and secured seats for the best musical shows. He bought far too much candy for Harry and Catherine, who found him good company. He was often on his knees helping Harry lay out his train set or mending a particular doll for Catherine, a favourite of hers with a tendency to lose its arms from their sockets. There was lots of motion-picture talk between Alan and him, and when there were reminiscences of the old days at Dekova's Place, many private memories were stirred poignantly for Lisa. On Risto's last night in London she and Alan gave a party for him and some of his buddies, who were also in town. She made sure that she invited enough pretty girls of her acquaintance to go around, and there was dancing until the early hours of the morning.

Lisa, Alan, and the children all went to see him off at Victoria Station. He shook hands with Alan and Harry and kissed Lisa and Catherine. "I've had a swell time. You folks have been wonderful to me."

"Come back whenever you can," Alan said, and Lisa endorsed the invitation with a smiling nod.

"I will. Thanks again! Goodbye!"

The train bore him smiling and waving away from them. They were never to see him again. He was killed some months later in Lorraine and the news came in a letter written by one of his comrades who had been at the party. Lisa gave way to a terrible grief. It was as if something had snapped in her. She wept for the waste of a talented life and for Minnie deprived of the love of a lifetime. By now Alan had been invalided out of the Army as a result of his wounds, and so was able to be with her at a time when she was greatly in need of his presence and comfort.

It was probably due to her run-down state that she, normally so resilient, fell victim to the influenza that had begun to sweep Europe and America like a scourge. With the Germans in full retreat and the war nearing its end, the epidemic took a further terrible toll of lives. In a large hotel across the street from the cinema, coffins were carried out by night in order not to distress the other guests. In the apartment, Lisa lay delirious and had to be nursed night and day. The harassed doctor became increasingly grave when he visited her. He did what little he could before hurrying off to his other patients, many of them dying before he could get there.

Alan sat constantly at Lisa's bedside and held her hands in her calmer moments, but mostly she tossed about restlessly, her dilated eyes not seeing him, her mind in the throes of fever. She was bathed constantly with cool water to try to reduce her temperature, but nothing appeared to aid her. It seemed as if he was to lose her, and vainly he tried to will some of his own strength into her.

Then one morning she was very quiet and still. The nurse gave Alan a reassuring smile. "She's sleeping, Mr. Fernley. The worst is over. She's going to pull through." Then, seeing him cover his eyes with his hands, she withdrew from the bedroom tactfully, realising he would wish to be alone with his wife in his thankfulness.

There was a murmur from the bed. He leaned forward quickly to catch what was said. "What did you say, darling?"

"Those bells. Why are the bells ringing?"

"The war is over. An armistice has been signed."

She whispered again. He smiled at her simple request, rising from the chair to go to the door and call Harry to tell him what his stepmother wanted. The boy nodded seriously, and when he came back into the bedroom he brought a Union Jack to her bedside.

"Here you are, Mama," he said, putting it into her hand. "It's the flag you wanted to wave."

"Thank you," she sighed. "Oh, thank you."

Outside all the bells of London continued their jubilant chimes.

Thirteen

Lisa watched her children grow. And she saw Alan go from strength to strength in the cinema sphere. It was due in no small part to her having had the foresight to acquire the second cinema and to invest shortly afterwards in a couple of plots of land in two other areas that had been going at a low price. Had she not made these purchases at the right time, enabling Alan to start building as business continued to flourish, he would have had to wait several more years to acquire anything similar. Her former assistant, Reginald Hardy, had returned from the war minus his left arm, and Lisa kept her promise by seeing he was duly installed as manager in the original Fernley cinema. Maudie had married a sailor, but as he was in the regular Navy and would continue to be at sea, she was glad to stay on as nursemaid to Catherine, though Harry, long since independent of her, was now in boarding school.

Seven-piece orchestras now accompanied the movies. Vocalists were hired to synchronise their voices to any singing taking place soundlessly on the screen, such as Risto had done occasionally in Mae Remotti's hall. Sometimes the enthusiastic applause merited a rerun of that particular section of reel as an encore. Lisa supervised the booking of films as she had always done, and the Fernley cinemas could be counted on by patrons for a good programme and full money's worth. Lisa always included a serial, those with Pearl White still being extremely popular. There was always a regretful shout of "Oh!" from the audiences when the words TO BE CONTINUED left the heroine clinging to a cliff top or tied to a railway track or in some other dire predicament.

Although Mary Pickford was everybody's sweetheart, Minnie began to emerge as a star in her own right. It seemed to Lisa that the loss of Risto had given a new and poignant quality to her acting, her expressive face reflecting light and shade as subtly as when wind-blown clouds let sunshine come and go. Her visage dominated posters and lobby cards, bringing in the patrons to see her star with such leading men as Gilbert and Barrymore and Navarro.

For a long time after Risto's death, Minnie did not reply to any of Lisa's letters. When at last she did begin to write again all the exuberance had gone from them. They were never the same again. It was disquieting to Lisa when gradually Minnie's name began to appear in the gossip columns. When she married a film producer, Lisa had hopes that her friend was finding some happiness again, but before the year was out they were divorced.

Lisa always made sure of booking an exceptional movie for the opening night of a Fernley cinema. It was her hard bargaining that had enabled Alan to open his first specially built cinema with *The Four Horsemen of the Apocalypse.* She had previously noticed a striking-looking actor named Rudolph Valentino in minor rôles, and was sure that his first important movie was destined to be a big success. It exceeded even her estimation. Return bookings of it had to be made immediately and there followed the extraordinary phenomena of hundreds of women of all ages everywhere queueing for any cinema showing Valentino films. They moaned and sighed and wept and cried out when he danced the tango with a sensuality that almost made the screen burn. When he appeared in *The Sheik* and the rest of his romantic rôles, the sexual excitement he created seemed to permeate the very air of the cinema and affected the most staid matrons. After his death, many women came to see his movies in black with mourning veils. They sobbed openly, and once

Lisa had to attend to a woman who had thrown herself prostrate on the floor by the screen.

It was a great day for Lisa when a Fernley cinema opened in Leeds. She arranged that the children of the orphanage should attend a special matinée and afterwards a tea with a gift beside each plate in the cinema's tearooms. Mrs. Bradlaw, who stubbornly refused to retire as principal, was Lisa's special guest at the opening performance.

It was while Lisa was in Leeds engaged in sharing Alan's work that she and Mrs. Bradlaw evolved a fund-raising plan to rehouse the children of the orphanage, for the bleak, damp building belonged to a past era that had vanished with the workhouse and was no place for a new, post-war generation. For quite a time now Lisa had had groups of the children for summer holidays in the country air at Maple House which she and Alan had established as their permanent home. With faster motor cars and better roads, communication was far easier, although they still kept an apartment in London to give them the proximity essential to much of their work.

It was shortly after the opening in Leeds that Lisa had her hair bobbed. Although Alan did not care for it at first, he had to admit that the short style suited her and eventually he became accustomed to it. She liked the sensation of freedom it gave her, for it echoed the new clothes that were so easy to wear. Her hips were slim enough to take the dropped waistline that rested there, her slender legs shapely enough to be enhanced by the short skirts. Although she was in her mid-thirties, she looked like a girl in the head-hugging hats and wrap-around coats. Frequently at parties she was approached by much younger men, who thought she was unattached, and had no idea that Alan Fernley was her husband.

She and Alan had come home from one such party to their apartment to find Harry waiting for them. He was seventeen and, in their absence, had arrived home from school at the end of term. They welcomed him and Lisa made the usual maternal inquiries as to whether he had eaten and how he thought his exams had gone.

"I want to talk to you both," he said very seriously.

Lisa sat down at once to listen, the chiffon points of her skirt floating into place. She thought father and son made a handsome pair, Alan in his dinner jacket, Harry casually dressed after changing from the dark suit made compulsory wear by his somewhat grand public school.

"Go ahead," Alan said, lighting a cigar. Neither his wife nor his son smoked and it was only the fragrant aroma of his cigar that drifted across the room.

"I want to join the Fernley circuit of cinemas," Harry stated on an unnecessary fierce note of determination as if immediately refusing to brook any opposition. "I know it's been your wish that I should go on to university and all the rest of it, but that's not for me. I was practically raised in a cinema and that's where my interest lies."

He stood there, broad-shouldered and tall and healthy with the black curly hair, good features and strong chin that he had inherited from his father. In his sunny disposition he was more like the mother whom he had never known and there was a look of her across his dark eyes. Lisa viewed him with pride. He had always been to her as her own flesh and blood. If she had regrets about other actions in her life, she had never once had second thoughts about the rightness of having kept her promise to Harriet. Although she had not looked for compensation, it had been there in his loving regard for her, the solid relationship they shared, and in all the joy she had had in his childhood.

Alan was less than pleased by the announcement that had been made. It was his natural wish that his son should enter the family business, but he had wanted the lad to broaden his horizons educationally before going into a career that had no set hours on the executive side and often meant a long working day that excluded much relaxation.

"You've thought it out carefully, have you?" he demanded.

"Yes, sir. I'd like to start as assistant to Reginald Hardy. I can learn about the organisation of a small cinema from him before I move ahead to manage one of the bigger places on my own."

"That's what you've planned, have you?" Alan said sharply. "I can tell you now that it won't be like that at all. You'll start at the bottom and you'll work your way up. There'll be no favours from your mother or from me. Neither shall there be from anybody else because you happen to have the surname of Fernley. Understand?"

"Whatever you say." Harry did not look in the least dismayed. It was enough that his father had virtually agreed that he should follow the career he wanted without further delay.

"Very well. You shall start next Monday at The Fernley in Kilburn as a cleaner." Alan ignored Lisa's involuntary, half-protesting gasp. "How does that suit you?"

Harry's eyes twinkled and he grinned widely. "I've had plenty of experience in polishing the brass handles of the entrance doors." It was true. As a boy he had often given a helping hand to Billy Morris who had kept the handles as bright as the buttons on his commissionaire's uniform. "I think I should do well in my first appointment."

Alan's severe expression relaxed into an answering grin and he shook hands with his son. "Then welcome into the Fernley circuit, Harry. Let's see how quickly you're able to earn promotion."

Lisa was happy that everything had been resolved with such amiability. She had no idea then how thankful she was to be a year later that Harry had made his decision to join the business at that particular time, for when she was prevented from giving Alan her constant support his son was able to take her place.

It happened that she and Alan were in Edinburgh for the signing of a contract for the latest site of a new Fernley cinema when there was a telephone call from Harry to their hotel on Princes Street. By then he had served a span as cleaner and usher, spent two months in a pay-box and was presently in a projection-room. Alan took the call and Lisa was able to tell immediately by the change in his voice and expression that something was terribly wrong.

"How badly hurt is she? Which hospital? Your mother and I will be on the next train south. Goodbye, Harry." He replaced the receiver and turned to face Lisa, his expression grave.

She thought her heart had stopped. "Is it Catherine?"

He nodded, taking her hands into his. "She's been in an accident. She was knocked off her bicycle by a motorbike skidding on the wet road. Her injuries are bad, but she's alive and the surgeons are fighting for her. Harry rang from the hospital."

The train journey south was the longest Lisa had ever known. In spite of the landscape rushing past the windows, it seemed to her that the wheels were scarcely moving. At King's Cross they took a taxi straight to the hospital where Harry met them. Maudie, who had been cycling with Catherine on her way home from school and had gone with her in the ambulance, broke down and sobbed when she saw Lisa.

"Don't blame yourself, Maudie," Lisa urged, still in a state of shock herself. "It was an accident nobody could have foreseen. We must be brave for Catherine's sake."

Maudie sank down once again on a seat in the corridor while Lisa and Alan went with Harry to the surgeon who had asked to see them as soon as they arrived.

"Your daughter has come through the operation as well as could be expected," he told them, "but it is only fair to warn you that the next few days will be critical. She is still unconscious, but you may see her and sit with her. Please be prepared. You will find her barely recognisable, although some of the bruising is superficial."

A nurse showed them into the room with its pale green half-tiled walls and white bed. Lisa pressed a shaking hand over her mouth to stifle a cry and Alan supported her with an arm as they looked down at their child lying there in bandages. Swelling and bruising to the face eliminated any resemblance to the pretty, carefree eleven-year-old to whom they had waved good-bye only a few days before. Lisa sank down into a chair at the bedside, torn with love and anguish, her face stark and dry-eyed.

"I'll bring your old doll to you, darling," she whispered tremulously, "and Teddy. You'll be pleased to see them when you wake."

They brought her childhood toys, which Catherine still treasured, and a favourite little basket of chocolate fishes covered in silver paper that had come from Paris and which she had admired too much ever to eat. All the time her life was hanging in the balance and she did not know they were there, although they kept tireless vigil night and day. On the morning she finally opened her eyes and recognised them, they were both gaunt with exhaustion and worry, but everything was forgotten in their rejoicing that she had pulled through and would be well again.

"When shall I be going home?" was the first sentence she spoke with any strength, but it was some weeks later before she was able to leave the hospital. Then Lisa took her home to Maple House to recuperate and regain her health completely.

Catherine's convalescence was a lengthy one, and it was natural that before long Alan began to draw his son into the place that Lisa had vacated temporarily in the business. Gradually a good partnership formed between father and son despite frequent clashes. Harry was brash and raw at times in handling matters, but he was learning fast on the executive side, and often presented ideas that Alan respected and incorporated into the publicity and other aspects of the enterprise. The two of them became accustomed to Lisa's being at Maple House with Catherine. As the months went by it was accepted, almost without discussion, that she would not be returning to work, particularly since the doctor had advised that Catherine attend a local school in the good country air instead of returning to her previous one in London. About the same time Maudie's husband came out of the Navy and went to work in a Portsmouth pub where Maudie joined him. Her going made it all the more necessary that Lisa should make no move that would disrupt Catherine's existence further and hinder her returning confidence in herself.

With a cook, two housemaids, a kitchen maid, and a gardener, there was nothing for Lisa to do domestically. If it had not been for the campaign of fund-raising for the orphanage, to which she was able to rededicate herself with fervour as soon as Catherine started school again, she would have found the days immeasurably long. She had never been without work in her life before and idleness was totally unnatural to her. At least Alan managed to get home to Maple House several nights a week and always at weekends. Harry she saw less, for he led his own life and either stayed in town, which he did most of the time, having taken his own apartment, or brought a party of friends home for the weekend.

Then the carpets were rolled back for dancing to the gramophone and there was tennis on the house's two courts in summer, and expeditions to local football matches in winter, with chestnuts toasted by the fire afterwards. Noisy sportscars in primary colours were their sole means of transport. Harry had a different girl-friend every time, although there was a certain similarity about them, for each one smoked cigarettes in long holders, had nails painted red by the newly invented polish that had been introduced on the market, jingled with bangles and beads, and executed the Charleston with a vigour that invariably revealed the rolled tops of their pale silk stockings and a gleam of thigh.

Alan continued to discuss the cinema business with Lisa as he had always done, but more and more her connection with it lapsed to become almost entirely social. As before, she went to film parties with him and gala nights and many other occasions. An event of supreme importance was the showing of the first talkie. She heard Al Jolson speak from the screen and gasped with everybody else, although in her case, knowing the cinema world as she did, it was more the portent than the wonder of it. Not long after that, talkies came thick and fast. Silent films were still shown but many of the most important feature movies were reissued with dubbed sound, and she heard the roar and thunder of the chariot race in *Ben-Hur,* which had been silent when it was first shown at the opening of one of the Fernley cinemas in the North.

It was Lisa's suggestion that Harry be given a trip to the United States as a twenty-first birthday present. "It's time he saw the country where he was born and his mother before him. I know he has long wanted to visit California and see the studios there."

"I'd like that myself," Alan commented. "Before we came back to England I had thought of our going to live in Los Angeles. Remember?"

She remembered. With her mind and her heart she remembered many things. "When Risto invited us to visit I was sure we would take up that invitation before too long. It would still hold with Minnie. She would love to see us. We really must go one day. In the meantime, what about Harry's coming-of-age gift?"

"Yes, of course we'll give him the trip. Minnie will arrange an entrée for him to the motion picture studios, I'm sure."

Harry's trip to the States coincided with the Wall Street crash. The troubles and confusion of the land in which he had first drawn breath merely drew him closer to it, for he felt curiously at home from the moment he stepped ashore. He spent some time in and around New York before travelling on to California where Minnie had invited him to stay. He wrote home that her house in Beverly Hills was a marble palace with a huge swimming pool in which her monogram was inlaid with gold. As for Minnie, she was even more beautiful than her screen image had led him to expect. She had taken him round the studios where he had met Jean Harlow on the set of *Hell's Angels* and spent hours with technicians and cameramen at their work, which was of particular interest to him. He had been invited with Minnie to a party at Pickfair, where the glamorous gathering had consisted almost entirely of famous faces, and Minnie herself entertained on a lavish scale. It was obvious to those at home that Harry had been made most welcome by her and that she was doing all she could to give him a memorable vacation.

Harry was never to forget the time with her. She widened his experience considerably and rewardingly during the whole of his sojourn in California. Minnie herself, lonely in spite of her exotic surroundings, many acquaintances and public adulation, was deeply touched by this link with her youth and with Lisa, who had protected her throughout many of those traumatic years.

Lisa continued to strive for the rebuilding of the orphanage. Mrs. Bradlaw, feeling her age at last, finally surrendered the post of principal, but then only because her successor, whose name was Mrs. Frampton, was a woman of her own calibre and of like mind. Lisa found in Mrs. Frampton a fighter as strong as Mrs. Bradlaw for the rights of children, and the three of them worked in complete harmony towards the goal of a new orphanage.

One of Lisa's major fund-raising events was a film charity evening at a Fernley cinema. Several well-known movie actors and actresses from British studios attended to help raise money. The occasion coincided with Catherine's fifteenth birthday and she wore her first real evening dress. She had suffered no lasting facial scars from the accident and was growing into womanhood with a clear ivory skin, thick-lashed dark eyes, and fair hair that had deepened to a rich, golden shade. At the buffet supper after the performance, she talked without shyness to various people of her aim to join her father and brother in the cinema business as soon as she was sixteen and could leave school.

"I'll take a secretarial course to prepare myself for the office work. Eventually I hope to organise bookings and shoulder responsibilities as my mother did in the first Fernley cinemas."

Listeners glanced in surprise towards Lisa at this information. They had either never heard, or had forgotten, that once she had been a kingpin of the enterprise. Neither was it known generally that a recent reduction in the price of the cheaper seats throughout the circuit had been at her instigation. Times were bad for many people. There were hunger marches and much unemployment, and after seeing the depressed workless hanging about the streets in Leeds, which she visited frequently to consult Mrs. Bradlaw and others on the fund committee, as well as in other places, Lisa had faced Alan and Harry with her demand. Prices were to be accommodated in order that people out of work could spend a few hours in the warmth and comfort of a cinema, which would be lacking in their own homes, and forget their troubles for a while through the enjoyment offered on the screen. Just as she had once bent the rules for the benefit of slum children, she wanted consideration given to adults in similar distressed circumstances. The new ruling went through. It gave her great satisfaction for more reasons than one. It appeared she could still make her mark on the Fernley circuit when the need arose.

In the summer of 1932 Catherine obtained her school certificate and left the school she had attended since recovery from her accident to go to a secretarial establishment. It was a two-year course. She completed it at a time when her father was moving into the greatest venture of his life. Lisa had been the first to hear the special news that he had to tell.

"I've put in a bid for a prestigious site in the West End. We have Fernley cinemas all over the country and a great number in London itself, but I've been waiting for exactly the right location where we can stand side by side with our rivals in Leicester Square. This is to be the Fernley cinema that will surpass all others elsewhere!"

"I'm so glad," she exclaimed happily, linking her hands behind his neck and kissing him. "It's been a dream of yours for a long time. Now it is to come true!"

It pleased her to see the enthusiastic support that he received from Harry, who flung himself into the enterprise to the exclusion of all else, except perhaps some time with his current girl-friend, whoever she happened to be. For months he and Alan had consultations with bankers and investors, architects, contractors, designers, artists and electricians. Even when they were away from the business premises, they continued to talk on the same topics with each other.

Lisa watched from the sidelines. The days when she had selected colours and fabrics for decor and furnishings had long since gone. As the project advanced, Alan spent more and more time in London, sometimes working over the weekends with Harry. When she did arrange a dinner or cocktail party, Alan invariably telephoned to ask her to make his excuses, as he could not get away, and there had not been a house party since before the project started. Also, Harry's friends were less frenetic than they had been previously, most of them having settled down to marriage. After his visit to the States, it had been noticeable to Lisa that his girl-friends became in her opinion far more suitable as prospective daughters-in-law than previously, but as yet he had not singled out one in particular. Catherine, upon the completion of her course, moved into the London apartment with her father, and Maple House became quieter than ever before.

Fortunately Lisa had much to keep her busy, for her fund-raising campaign for the orphanage finally came to fruition. An elderly neighbour, who had attended all the local functions she had held to raise money, died and left a handsome bequest in her will to the charity. Without delay, they were able to construct a large and well-built mansion in beautiful grounds where the children could live in family groups with a housemother, a principle laid down by Dr. Barnado, who had always been Mrs. Bradlaw's guiding light. Lisa was invited to perform the opening ceremony. Since it had become her policy to invest in good clothes, she wore a Schiaparelli coat of blue wool against the cold weather, its length mid-calf, its buttons a hallmark of the designer in the shape of circus horses, which she thought would be as amusing to the children as the fashion world claimed them to be unto itself. With the principal and staff grouped with the local dignitaries beside Mrs. Bradlaw, who in her eighties was still as upright and determined as she had always been, and the children gathered in a big semicircle, Lisa put the key in the entrance door to unlock it. It swung wide to cheers and applause. She turned to receive a bouquet of pink carnations from one of the younger orphans, who wore a cheerful red plaid outfit. No more institutional grey or threadbare castoffs, but bright serviceable clothes that would enable them to blend into school life and social activities without being set apart from others by their attire. Lisa held out her hand to Mrs. Bradlaw, who had also received a bouquet.

"You shall be the first to enter, Mrs. Bradlaw."

"No, my dear. You represent every one of the children who never knew the benefits with which this generation is to be blessed. It is right and proper that the privilege should be yours."

So Lisa stepped first over the threshold and took with her memories of Amy and Minnie and Rosie and Teresa and many more, seeing them as clearly in her mind's eye as if she were fourteen again.

Upon her return to Maple House, Lisa cleared up some correspondence during the next few days. Then she packed a suitcase and drove to London, deciding to stay a week or two in the apartment in order to do some shopping and see the progress that had been made on the new Fernley cinema. She also wanted to be with Alan. She felt she had neglected him during the past hectic months. Previously they had always been in close contact over everything, even though in the business she had become a background figure, and recently they had virtually seemed strangers to each other, each being involved in their individual projects that had kept them apart more than ever. It was almost as if Alan and Harry and Catherine had drawn away from her into their own dedicated little group and she had been left outside and practically forgotten. Yet this feeling was dispelled by Catherine's warm welcome when she arrived. Alan was not at home.

They exchanged news while Lisa unpacked her suitcase, as Catherine folded garments away and hung up dresses. Then they returned to the spacious drawing-room and sat on the window-seat with a view of the park. This apartment was far larger by many rooms than the one adjacent to the first Fernley cinema, and was luxuriously appointed. Its Art Deco style and furniture provided a rich and exciting geometric setting in sharp contrast to the mellow atmosphere of Maple House.

"It's ages since you last came to London, Mother. The new cinema is almost finished now. Another few weeks and it will be ready for its grand opening."

"I'm looking forward to seeing it. There's been no chance before now. I've spent most of the past months travelling to Leeds and back. Now my time is my own again."

"We've missed you. Why don't you move here and be with us? You could keep Maple House for weekends and holidays as you used to before I had that accident."

Lisa shook her head, smiling. "I'm happiest in the countryside these days. It's fun to come to London of a while, but the city is not for me anymore. I'm hoping that when the new cinema is launched, your father and I can pick up our lives together again."

"Maybe you shouldn't wait until then."

Lisa shot a direct look at her, alerted by a faint note of unhappiness in her daughter's voice. "Why do you say that?"

Catherine avoided her eyes, seemingly engrossed in tracing with a fingertip the sunray pattern on the cushion of the window-seat. "Although Daddy is busy, I can tell he's lonely without you."

"You are here."

"That's not the same. I'm out a lot in the evenings with friends. I wouldn't blame him if sometimes at a day's end he couldn't face returning to a deserted apartment on his own."

"I see." Lisa sat motionless. She felt sick and hollow inside. There could be few wives who received warnings of another woman from their own daughters. It appeared she had neglected Alan far more than she had realised. "In that case I mustn't be selfish about living at Maple House. Your father means more to me than anything else. I'll have some more of my clothes and other things sent here and I'll stay all the time he needs me."

Thankfulness suffused Catherine's face. "He'll always need you! I know."

Alan certainly appeared more than glad to see his wife when he came home. That night his love-making was as ardent as it had ever been and she began to hope she had arrived in London in time to avert a serious rift in their marriage.

In the morning she went with Alan to the West End while Catherine took the Underground to the head office of the circuit where she was working. When they came to the new cinema, Lisa was astonished by its size. She had seen the plans, viewed the building in its earlier stages, and thought she had gained a fairly clear picture of how it would be, but this shining marble-faced edifice was like a treasure house out of the Arabian Nights, designed psychologically to give an atmosphere of ultimate escapism.

Alan showed her through it with pride. From the ticket hall with the gold-star light fittings and panels with mirrored mouldings, they went through to the lofty foyer decorated in rich and cleverly muted shades of crimson and purple and still more gold. Side by side they went up the thickly carpeted staircase with the gilded railings and on this upper level were the opulent Moorish bars, the restaurant with a draped silken ceiling and doors resembling those in a harem, and the tearoom like an exotic garden.

Alan opened the double doors into the Grand Circle for her. She stared in amazement at the colossal size of the auditorium, which would be filled with music by a large electric organ designed to rise up into sight before a performance and during intervals, and descend again afterwards. The vast screen above it, framed by a theatrical proscenium arch of spangled red and gold, was faced on either side by what appeared to be the terrace of a Moorish village, set amid exotic plants enhanced by hidden coloured lights. This theme was carried right around the walls with exotic Moorish grilles that disguised the ventilation and more balconies and foliage and false archways that hinted at mysterious depths beyond. The domed dark blue ceilings was set with twinkling stars and more hidden illumination, released by a prearranged signal with Harry and changing from moonlit blues through the pinks of dawn to the golden glow of sunshine and the orange hues of sunset, and back again.

"It's fantastic," she declared with a perfect turn of phrase. "I congratulate you, Alan. In its own way it's curiously beautiful, too. What movie is to open it?" She was certain he would choose as a first showing something glamorously suited to these stunning surroundings. A movie with Marlene Dietrich perhaps. Or Mae West. Or Joan Crawford. On the male side it might be Gable or Cooper or Colman.

"The best way to answer that is to show you the lobby cards. I asked Catherine to bring them by taxi if they had arrived on her desk by this morning. Let's go downstairs to the managerial office and see if she's there."

Lisa looked amused. "I can tell you're planning a surprise for me. Am I allowed to guess whose film it might be?"

He grinned at her. "You may guess if you like, but I'm giving nothing away."

She laughed, linking her hands about the crook of his arm. She was convinced that Minnie's latest movie had been selected. That made her extremely happy. Moreover, with everything so right between Alan and her this day, as it had been last night, she began to wonder if she had misread Catherine's meaning. Maybe her daughter's only concern had been simply for her father's loneliness.

When they drew near the office the door was ajar and they could hear Harry talking to someone. Thinking it must be Catherine, Lisa darted ahead, exclaiming as she entered: "Show me Minnie's lobby cards!"

She caught her breath on her utterance. It was not her daughter who stood there in a loosely fitting Garbo coat with an upstanding collar, but a tall, attractive-looking woman of about thirty, her eyes very blue, her hair a luxuriant chestnut. This is she, Lisa thought immediately. How or why she knew was impossible to tell, but she did not have the least doubt that it was this woman's shadow that lay across her marriage. Harry was introducing them.

"This is Miss Davis, who is in charge of the head office, Mother. She has been a right hand to us during these past months."

Lisa acknowledged the introduction. Rita Davis had a pleasing smile, a hint of dimples in her cool cheeks. "I'm sorry if you were expecting Catherine, Mrs. Fernley. She had some work I wanted her to finish, so I brought the lobby cards myself."

Behind Lisa came Alan's voice, casual and even. "Thank you, Miss Davis. That was considerate of you."

"It was a pleasure, sir. Now if you will excuse me, I must be getting back." She left the office, a wisp of expensive French scent lingering after her, her heels high and tapping across the marble floor of the foyer.

Alan went to the desk to take up the top lobby card of the stack that Rita Davis had delivered, and he turned to display it for Lisa. "There, darling. You were right in your guesswork, as you can see."

Only she knew that his words could have held another interpretation for her. She forced herself to focus on Minnie's beautiful face, framed in a swathing of diaphanous veiling asparkle with sequins, gazing at her soulfully from the lobby card above the movie's title: *Love's Glory.* The artwork at the side, a drawing of her in her leading man's arms, combined to emphasise to the cinemagoer that this was a movie of intense passion and drama.

"That's a wonderful choice," she endorsed with feeling, keeping herself in strict control. "Nothing could be more apt than that Minnie should figure in this special venture with us all."

Harry came around the desk to face her, his face jubilant with what he had to tell. "I've more good news for you. Not only will it be the world première of *Love's Glory,* but Minnie herself has promised to come from Hollywood to be here for it!"

She almost broke down. The reunion would mean more to her than either her husband or her stepson could realise. She and Minnie had been through much together in the past and now, when she had this crisis to face in her marriage, there was to be a return to that sustaining friendship. Minnie would be a tower of strength to her.

Lisa drove to Southampton to meet the *Queen Mary.* The liner was docking as she waited on the quayside. Nearby the press had gathered to go on board. Advance publicity had let it be known that Minnie Shaw, once widowed and four times married and divorced, would be arriving that day to appear at a world première of her new movie in two weeks' time. Lisa had been given a special pass to go to Minnie's stateroom, for once the film star had emerged there would be photographs and on-the-spot interviews, giving no chance for two old friends to speak to each other until much later.

"You may go aboard now, ma'am."

The waiting was over. Lisa in her beige Chanel suit, pearls, and a soft felt hat, went up the gangway to be met at the top by Minnie's personal secretary, Blanche Stiller, a hard-faced, crisply business-like woman. She led the way to Minnie's stateroom, opened the door to announce Lisa, and retired. The luxuriously appointed suite was like a flower shop with baskets of roses, carnations and orchids making a riot of colour. In the midst of it all Minnie was rushing forward with arms outstretched.

"I don't believe it, Lisa! You haven't changed a bit!"

"Neither have you!"

They laughed and cried as they kissed each other's cheeks, both talking at once and locked in a hug together. When they drew apart breathlessly, Minnie pushed Lisa down into a chair before darting across to a side table where she took a bottle of champagne out of an ice-bucket and poured out two glasses.

"I always drink champagne at important moments in my life nowadays," she declared merrily, "and in between as well!" She handed a glass to Lisa. Then with a swirl of skirt, she stood back with her head to one side to scrutinise her friend. "I was wrong. There is something about you that's different. I know! It's your hair. You've had it bobbed. It's short." Abruptly she lifted her chin and took a shuddering breath. "Wow! I have a shivery feeling of *déjà vu.* I remarked on Risto's army hair cut when I first saw him in uniform. Is it an omen, do you think?"

Lisa in her turn had been revising her first impression. Minnie was too thin. Far too thin. Her bias-cut dress of jade crêpe de chine, clinging lightly to her frame, revealed only too clearly the slight breasts and sharp hip-bones. And there was a brittleness about her every movement. It spoke of screaming nerves just below the surface, and her face, still extraordinarily beautiful in a gamine way, bore evidence of more sadness than happiness, more strain than ease.

"No, it's not an omen, Minnie. Risto is particularly in our thoughts today. That's what is good about old friendships. The past is always close to the present. Time evaporates. He looked handsome in uniform."

"He did, didn't he?" Minnie said reminiscently as she sat down in the neighbouring chair, her silk stockings gleaming on her long legs. "There's never been anyone else, you know. Oh, I don't count those four slobs I married or the other men I've slept around with, not even the nice ones. I loved Risto. I still love him." She clenched a fist and gave her knee a hard thump. "That bloody war! What it did to women of our generation! It left hundreds of thousands of us as widows and spinsters, and took from us all the children who would have been born." Tears shone in her eyes but she blinked them back, raising her glass to Lisa. "I didn't intend to get gloomy. Here's to us, Lisa! And to sweet memories!"

Lisa drank the toast. "Is there anyone new in your life, Minnie? Someone who might bring you love again?"

"No. I've been hibernating lately in any case. Trying to get away from telephones and people and studios and the press."

"Why? Haven't you been well?"

Minnie turned aside the question as if it had not been spoken. "More champagne? My glass is empty." She leaped up from her chair to refill it, her talk coming rapidly. "How's Alan? Is he still as handsome a devil as he was? I remember fancying him when I first came from Quadra. That was before I'd seen Risto. After that I never wanted anyone else. Speaking of Quadra reminds me of Agnes and Henry Twidle. Do you still hear from them?"

"Regularly. Not all that long ago Agnes had a visit from her mother and sister. Unfortunately, upon stepping ashore at Granite Bay, her mother exclaimed: 'What a God-forsaken place!' Much as Mrs. Grant did when we first arrived there. Henry turned on his heel and didn't speak to his mother-in-law for the whole of her vacation with them, and Agnes says he had vowed that he never will again."

"Oh dear. That's hard on Agnes and she's such a lovely person. Never a word of complaint throughout the rigours of those winters and little outside communication."

"The West of that continent has been built on the courage of women like Agnes."

"Tell me now about Catherine. Is she lucky enough to have grown up looking like you? People must think you're her sister. You're six years older than I and yet you would be taken for the younger of us. What's the secret? Your good marriage? I suppose Alan is still at your feet as he always was." She prattled on, giving no time for answers, almost as if a tightly wound up spring inside her had been released and suddenly there was no controlling it. "You're a lucky woman to have a man like that in love with you. And you only married him for Harry's sake, didn't you?"

Lisa was sharply taken aback. "Whatever led you to that conclusion?"

Minnie flapped a hand elegantly, her diamond rings flashing fire. "I knew you too well not to be able to see for myself that you weren't in love with him. There was someone else. It was that Norwegian, wasn't it? The one we first met in the embarkation hall at Liverpool and who turned up in Dekova's Place to rescue you when you were mugged with the cashbox."

"He didn't rescue me. He made a citizen's arrest on my attacker after knocking him to the ground."

"But he rescued you in that forest fire, didn't he?"

Lisa felt the colour surge into her cheeks. "You're probing too deeply, Minnie. That was a long time ago."

"You weren't alone in the boat on the lake. He was with you for about thirty-six hours altogether, wasn't it?" She was on her third glass of champagne and as she took another mouthful of it she wagged a finger to acknowledge that she was recalling how it had all happened. "I remember how you looked when you set off from home that day. Desperate and in love and more than a little scared. Admit it! You were lovers, weren't you?"

Drawing in her breath, Lisa released it with a long sigh. "Yes, we were. I thought that secret was mine alone."

"Your eyes are giving you away. You still feel about him the way I feel about Risto. We both lost by different paths the one man in our lives who meant most to us."

Further reticence was pointless on that subject. "It's strange how our lives have run parallel, isn't it?" Lisa spoke in a quiet, ruminative tone, her thoughts turning inward. "Just as if we had been blood sisters. I rarely think of Peter these days. But I haven't forgotten him or the time we had together in Toronto and Dekova's Place."

There came a knock on the stateroom door and Blanche Stiller entered briskly. "Are you ready, Miss Shaw? The press have been on board for some time now."

"Don't harass me!" Minnie scowled, moving from her chair only to refill her glass again.

"We'll miss the train to London if you don't get finished with the press soon."

Minnie eyed her vindictively over the rim. "You'll miss it. That's what you mean. You know it was arranged ahead that I should leave Southampton by automobile with Mrs. Fernley for her country house. If the train goes, you can cool your heels on the railway station for the rest of the day for all I care."

"You're drinking too much again!" Blanche Stiller retaliated on a spiteful note.

"Mind your own damn business!"

"I'll fetch your coat." Before she could reach the wardrobe, Minnie halted her with a shrieked order. "You leave it where it is!"

"But Miss Shaw—"

"Shut up and get out!"

The woman flounced out in a temper, muttering to herself. Lisa, who had been watching her friend closely, made a request quietly. "May I face the newspapermen with you when you're ready, Minnie? I'd find it interesting."

Minnie shot her a frantic, sideways glance, the muscles of her mouth pulling down convulsively. "You know, don't you?" she said in a voice harsh with dry sobs.

"I can see that something is wrong."

"I think I'm losing my mind." Abruptly Minnie sprang to her feet and wrung her hands agitatedly. "I'm terrified of everything these days. Life! Death! People! Every damn thing. Coming to see you has kept me from going over the past few months. I kept telling myself I'd be okay when I was with you again. You'd put things right. Like you used to. I wouldn't have had the nerve to defy Blanche just now if you hadn't been with me."

Lisa felt as if the ground had been cut from under her. She had been anticipating support in her own troubles from Minnie and instead she was being called upon once more to supply the strength and to be the support of another. "I'll do whatever I can."

"You don't think me stupid?" It was almost a childish cry of appeal.

"Have I ever?" To Lisa it was as if the clock had turned back. She saw in Minnie's face something of the paralysing hysteria that had been there after the attack in the boxcar on the prairies. Minnie was as much in need today of comfort and reassurance as she had been then; the danger of mental breakdown had to be averted. "The sooner we get away from this liner, the sooner we can talk. Let's get the press over with and then the time is ours."

Minnie nodded. Used to being waited on, she stood while Lisa fetched her sumptuous silver fox coat and then slipped her arms into it. She was trembling violently. Almost automatically she put on the large black hat with the upturned brim and dashing sweep of feathers. A further application of scarlet lipstick and then she was ready in appearance, if not in spirit, to meet the press. She hung back as Lisa opened the door for her and clutched the soft fur collar up around her neck protectively and not against the mild spring weather that would await her on deck, but in an unconscious gesture of defence.

"It will only take a little while," Lisa said encouragingly, "and then we'll be away from here."

Minnie jerked herself forward as if pulled by a string. At the door she paused and looked almost wildly at Lisa. "Wouldn't it be grand if my old Ma could 'ave been on the quayside today?"

Lisa stared at her. Minnie had lapsed into the rough English accents of her childhood, but whether by chance or design it was impossible to say. "Shall you try to find her when you're in England?"

Minnie's face, which changed expression as constantly off the screen as it did on, grew sad. "She's dead," she said, resuming her normal speech. "I was sent a copy of her death certificate by someone engaged in tracing missing relatives. I've come to England twenty years too late to see her again."

Urged on by Lisa's gentle but persistent pressure on her arm, she went obediently in the direction of the First Class deck where the press awaited her, only slowing down when the doors to that section of the ship came into view. Her whole body began to stiffen as if preparing for retreat. Quickly Lisa gave her a cheerful push as if she were indeed a child again.

"Go to it, Minnie! We made mincemeat of Emily Drayton and Mrs. Grant. The press is nothing compared to them!"

Lisa did not know whether she had done the right thing or not, but her impromptu therapy had results. Minnie burst into slightly too hectic giggles at the absurdity of the comparison, and then walked through the door a steward had rushed to open as if she were going on to a film set, her dazzling smile switched on like an electric light bulb, her chin swept high, and her furs flung open seductively. There came a barrage of camera flashes.

Minnie performed for the press as she had done countless times before, posing and smiling and turning this way and that. When they found a high seat for her she sat on it obligingly, pulling her skirt a little higher at their shouted request and allowing them to take cheesecake shots of her splendid legs. To Lisa she looked like a beautiful automaton. Blanche Stiller, hovering nearby, watched the film star piercingly for the first warning signs of an indulgement in too much champagne being accelerated by the cold sea-wind blowing across Southampton Water. Fortunately there seemed to be no sign of such a disaster and Minnie was giving the interviewers what was expected of her.

"Yes, it's swell to be in England for the world première of my latest motion picture . . . No, I have no new marriage plans . . . Who? Oh, he and I were just good friends . . . Naturally I shall consider any offers to make a movie here . . . Sure, a rôle on the London stage would be a challenge and I'd welcome it . . . How should I know if Frenchmen make the best lovers? I've never been married to one!"

It was all there. The stock answers and the stemming of anything likely to lead to a harming of the public image of the goddess dedicated solely to her career and her belief in the honourable estate of marriage. The fact that she had been photographed at night-spots and premières and Hollywood parties with countless different men merely added to her glamorous image. To her less worldly women fans it appeared as if she was worshipped on a pedestal for her beauty and inaccessibility. The more sophisticated usually envied her wide selection of handsome lovers, many of whom were screen heroes themselves.

Blanche Stiller came up to Lisa and muttered in her ear. "Hear how Miss Shaw's voice is rising in pitch? She's getting near the end of her tether. I'd like to fetch her away now, but she's in a mood to do the opposite of anything I suggest. I daren't risk a scene. You're her friend. Would you try?"

Lisa pushed her way through the press to Minnie's side. "Time to go," she said without ado.

There was no protest from Minnie, only from the press. She gave the newspaper men and women a final smile and wave like departing royalty and left the deck at Lisa's side. Then preceded by the photographers, who jammed the gangway to get pictures of her coming ashore, she gained the quayside, waved again to cheering fans pressed against the barriers and minutes later was being driven by Lisa away from the docks and through Southampton. Her hat was flung on the back seat and she raked her fingers through her hair.

"Thank God we're out of that!"

"Do those sessions take place wherever you go?" Lisa asked.

Minnie gave a nod. She was very pale. "Sometimes I'm afraid I'll scream in their faces. I feel it rising in my throat. It's as if I were trapped in a cage by pressures draining my true being away and leaving only my outward shell, which goes on walking, and talking, and giving toothpaste smiles that have no reality. Thanks for coming to the rescue. That bitch, Blanche, should have done it. Sometimes I think she gets a sadistic pleasure in watching me suffer these ordeals."

"You're misjudging her. I'd say she simply doesn't understand the extent of the torment they cause you."

Minnie was staring through the windscreen in astonishment. "I'd forgotten the streets were so narrow over here. Have they shrunk since I was a child?"

Lisa smiled. "No. That's the way they always were."

"So different from the States." Minnie shook her head in continued surprise over it. Then, as they left the city behind, she exclaimed at the beauty of the undulating landscape spreading out all around them. "Do you remember that I'd never seen a cow in a meadow until that day when we were on the train to Liverpool? All I'd ever known had been the slums and gutters of Leeds until the orphanage took me in. How is old Mother Bradlaw these days?"

They talked as they drove along. Lisa thought her companion was becoming more relaxed, but she had put away within herself any thought of sharing with Minnie the burden of Alan's unfaithfulness, which lay heavily upon her. She must hide away her own confusion and unhappiness. Minnie must never suspect that she was at a loss to know how to handle her own life when her friend was looking wholly to her for aid on what was obviously the brink of a nervous breakdown.

Minnie was charmed with Maple House. The lawns were like velvet and the flower-beds bright with crocuses and early daffodils. Japonica was opening pink buds against its sunny walls and hardy camellias were coming into bloom along the north side of the house. As they went into the entrance hall, she cried out at the sight of a red and gold porcelain plate displayed in a niche.

"I know that plate! I've seen it before. It used to be at the orphanage."

"Mrs. Bradlaw gave it to me when the institutional building was closed down. She remembered I once almost broke my neck trying to get hold of it and she thought it would be a special souvenir to remind me of those days. She didn't know how special," Lisa added, more to herself than to Minnie who had discarded her furs and was already on a tour of exploration. Lisa handed her own coat and hat to the maid who had come into the hall and went after her friend, who was full of appreciation of the finely proportioned rooms, and the rich glow of antique rosewood and walnut.

"What a perfect house! And such a peaceful one. The world seems far away."

"I'm glad you like it. I felt at home here from the first moment. Let me take you to your room now. The cabin trunks that you sent ahead arrived about three weeks ago, and they have been unpacked for you."

Minnie linked arms with Lisa as they went towards the curved staircase. "I have a breath-taking gown for the première. Adrian designed it. He designs all my movie clothes now. I wouldn't let anyone else do them." They were halfway up the stairs and she paused, listening intently. "How quiet it is. No police sirens. No traffic. No screaming fans. Only the birds singing. I always wanted to see Maple House after you first wrote about it."

"That's why I thought you'd prefer to come here instead of to our London apartment. Alan will be joining us this evening and tomorrow Harry and Catherine will arrive to complete the family gathering with you."

When they reached the guest-room that was to be hers for her sojourn, Minnie cried out at the sight of the patchwork quilt covering the bed. It was the Blazing Star quilt that Lisa had sewn some years ago in another land. As if in a trance, Minnie went to spread the flat of her hands caressingly over the unfaded colours.

"This was in my room at Dekova's Place!"

"That's right. Oh, whatever is the matter?" Lisa hurried forward anxiously as Minnie dropped down to her knees at the side of the bed and pulled the coverlet into folds against her suddenly crumpled face, her eyes closed tight on some inner shaft of pain.

"Risto and I made love under this quilt many times."

Lisa sat down with a sigh on the bed, her hands in her lap. "I never suspected that."

"It happened sometimes when you were away from the house. Then there were nights when he'd climb up by that tree outside my window when you were asleep."

"We are certainly letting out the secrets since we met today." Lisa's lips held a sad little smile.

Minnie moved forward on her knees to put her head on Lisa's lap, still clutching the quilt like a child with a comforter. "I wish we could go back to those days. The only true happiness I've ever known was with him. After he was killed my life fell to pieces. I went quite crazy for a while. I've been a little crazy ever since. Now it's getting worse and I'm scared."

Lisa stroked Minnie's head maternally. Her friend's hair was coppery-gold these days with the rigid waves and the curls at the side of the face and nape of the neck that were so stylish. Yet it was as if it were the lank-haired orphan child she had protected who was huddled against her once again. "Have you consulted doctors?"

"I'm not on drugs, if that's what you're thinking. Not that I haven't tried most things, and I'm not an alcoholic, although sometimes it helps to drink champagne. It gives me a lift and

I'm inclined to take more than I should. Otherwise I never touch anything these days. I went through a spate of hard drinking and had the sense to see in time that I was ruining my looks and my work. And don't mention psychiatrists. I've wasted hours on their couches and I've often thought they should have been on them instead of me." She uttered a wry and mirthless laugh.

"What do you think is the cause of your depression?"

"I can answer that in a nutshell. I've worked and played too hard for a long time, but I can't find a way out. I feel constantly bruised and wounded. It's as if the bullets that killed Risto ricocheted and struck me in passing. He died and I'm living. But at times it's as if I'm more dead than he."

Lisa recalled how she had once said to Alan that Risto was Minnie's anchor. With his going she had lost the one stabilising factor that had been more necessary to her in movie circles than it would have been if she had followed a more conventional path in life. Yet there must have been something out of the ordinary to have triggered off a deterioration over the recent weeks. Perhaps another love affair that had gone disastrously wrong. Lisa was aware of something in Minnie's behaviour pattern that stirred a chord in her memory and recollection came disturbingly to her. "Are you sure you're physically well, Minnie?"

"I've had a check-up recently and there's nothing wrong with my body. I tell you it's my mind. If it snaps, I'll be lost forever. Oh, help me, Lisa! For God's sake, help me." She began to wail in what was an outflowing from an abyss of despair and it was terrible to witness such primitive distress.

"I'll help you," Lisa vowed vehemently, "but we'll have to talk much more when you feel up to it. There's no rush. We have all the time we need."

When the sobbing eventually subsided through Minnie's sheer exhaustion, Lisa helped her on to the bed, removed her shoes and pulled the quilt over her. By the time she had pulled the curtains across the windows, Minnie appeared to be sleeping.

With slow steps and feeling quite drained, Lisa went downstairs again. In the hall she leaned a hand against the wall and held her brow with the other while she came to terms with the situation that had arisen. Minnie needed rest and quiet. That meant the plan to return to London with Alan after the weekend would have to be shelved. She and Minnie must stay on at Maple House indefinitely. Once more Alan would be left virtually on his own in the apartment. And in all the last-minute hustle before the première, Rita Davis would be constantly at his side. Her arms would be waiting to offer respite by night from the tumult of the day. For Harry's sake she had lost Peter. Was it to be for Minnie's sake that she was to lose Alan?

He arrived home at six o'clock that evening. She saw him from the window as he came from leaving his Bentley in the old stables that had been converted into garages. His years suited him; a brindling of grey at his temples and a physique kept sparse and trim by exercise. In his well-cut suit and with his groomed appearance, he looked what he was, a highly successful businessman with an intelligent approach to everything that came his way. Catching sight of her through the glass, he exchanged a smile as he passed the window to enter the house. She went to meet him.

"Well? How's the famous film star?" he inquired jovially after giving her a kiss.

"Not well, I'm afraid."

"I'm sorry to hear that. Was she seasick?"

"It's more serious than that."

In the drawing-room over a drink, she told him of the state that Minnie was in. He was concerned and shook his head over what he had heard. "Poor kid," he said sympathetically, picturing Minnie for the moment as the gauche young girl she had been when he had last seen her and not by her screen image. "What are you going to do? Call in Sarah Baker? She's your doctor and your personal friend. I think she would be particularly understanding."

"I'll consult her to make sure I'll be doing whatever is right for Minnie, and arrange that they meet. But at the present time Minnie is set against seeing any more doctors professionally. She seems to think I'm the only one to see her through this emotional crisis. In some ways she reminds me of Harriet when I first came to Quadra Island."

It was a long time since either of them had mentioned Harriet to each other. She saw a raw look come into his eyes as doubtless it came into her own, both of them aware that, as once Harriet had unwittingly stood between him and his love for her, now there was somebody else taken through his own free choice. "Why do you think that?" He drained his whisky glass to break his gaze with hers.

"I'm not sure. There's the same tension and the same restlessness." She had almost said remorse and had amended her words in time. Alan had never known of Harriet's second miscarriage, brought on through foolhardiness, and the fact that she was gone did not release the sharing of a confidence not for his ears, even though it had lost its significance long ago.

"What about the première? Will she be fit to attend it?"

"I hope so, and I know she has every intention of making an appearance, but in the meantime she must relax completely. At least here at Maple House I can keep people away. So far only Blanche Stiller knows her whereabouts and I want it to stay that way."

"Then you and Minnie won't be coming back to London with me on Monday morning?"

"No. I don't suppose I'll see you again until the evening of the West End opening. Unless you can manage to get home next weekend?"

"There won't be a chance. I'll be far too busy."

To Lisa it was as if Rita Davis was there in the shadows of the room, smiling her cool smile, poised and confident and ruthless, patiently biding her time. Yet her name had never been raised in any conversation that Lisa had had with Alan. Not even in reference to his work, when it would have been normal for either of them to have mentioned her, particularly since she was training Catherine in the specialised work at the head office from whence Alan ruled his cinema empire.

They shared a silence which on Alan's part was tantamount to an admission of his infidelity, and on Lisa's revealed that she instinctively knew the truth, for she had always been interested in their closest employees and could have been expected to ask about Rita Davis whose appointment he had never spoken of to her. Neither was able to bring the subject into the open. Although danger to their marriage had appeared to recede while she had been with him in London, she sensed a resurgence of it in his adamant insistence that he would be unable to come home to Maple House the following weekend.

Upstairs, Minnie had been disturbed from her rest by the sound of Alan's Bentley being driven past on the gravelled drive. She felt refreshed by her sleep and it was good to wake up to the knowledge of Lisa's maternal protection under which she had sheltered so often in the past. An hour later, bathed and changed into a midnight blue gown with barbaric gold embroidery on its epaulets, she came out of her room to meet Alan on the landing similarly changed for the evening into his dinner jacket and on his way downstairs. They greeted each other warmly, she kissing him on the lips.

"Isn't it exciting that we should all be together again," she exclaimed, linking her arm in his as they went downstairs to the drawing-room. "I've been looking forward to it for months. Ever since Harry wrote on your behalf to ask me if I'd come to England for the West End première. You are looking as handsome as ever. I remember how you used to come home from the forests in a passion-rousing aroma of timber and sweat and saddle-leather." She leaned against him on tiptoe to sniff appreciatively at his newly shaven chin. "Now it's expensive shaving lotion and Havana cigars. Equally male and basic. Mmm! Delicious!"

He laughed and she with him. She might have been the same brash girl flirting with him when she came from Quadra Island, instead of a woman whose signature and handprints were immortalised in the cement of the forecourt of Grauman's Chinese Theatre on Hollywood Boulevard. When Lisa, in a rose silk Cocteau print, joined them soon afterwards, Minnie was still talking non-stop and as effusively as she had done earlier in the day. She continued in the same vein throughout the whole evening.

When Alan and Lisa were in their room getting ready for bed, he was thoughtful as he pulled off his black bow tie and removed the gold links from his cuffs. "I can't see Minnie being well enough for the première. She's on the borderline of a breakdown, as you say. Sometimes she spoke as if the three of us were back in the house at Dekova's Place. It became more marked as the evening wore on." He sighed. "Wore on, indeed. She never used to prattle away at that speed, did she?"

"No. She's a sick woman."

He looked across to where Lisa sat in her coffee satin camiknickers on the dressing table stool, rolling down her silk stockings in turn. "You eased Harriet out of her moods of depression. You'd probably do better on your own with Minnie without calling in medical advice."

She straightened up to meet his eyes. One ribbon shoulder strap had slipped down over her arm revealing the swell of her breast. "I'm not as confident about handling problems as I used to be. I feel a little lost myself at the present time."

"Oh?" He did not take up the opportunity she had given him to broach the subject uppermost in her mind as it surely was in his.

In the guest-room, Minnie lay on top of the bedclothes and naked under the quilt that she had drawn up to her chin. She trembled under its patchwork warmth. It was as if she waited for Risto to take her with him down into the rainbow-hued depths of love.

Fourteen

When the day of the première of *Love's Glory* arrived, Minnie was much improved by her two weeks at Maple House. She was calmer and quieter and more content. She and Lisa had taken long walks in the countryside, spent hours talking together, and been undisturbed by visitors with the exception of Blanche Stiller who, in London, was bearing the brunt of the telephone calls, frantic transatlantic cables from the studio, and the general hubbub of the press that preceded such an event as a new cinema opening with a motion picture rumoured to be Minnie's best yet.

The week before, Blanche had driven to Maple House. "When the hell is she going to make an appearance?" she had demanded of Lisa, who had kept her from Minnie in person and on the phone. "Everybody thinks she is putting on a Garbo act and it won't do. That's never been her image. Hers is friendly, gamine, pert, beautiful—a combination of innocence and worldliness. Never, never a glamorous recluse wanting to be alone."

"She's still not well."

"Don't say that!" Blanche held her head and paced up and down. "I don't want to hear it! She is not sick in bed and she's walking about and breathing. That makes her fully able to show herself at the opening ceremony of the new Fernley. Her producer will murder me if I don't get her there! The studios employ me, you know. I'll be kicked out for incompetence and black-listed!"

"We'll see how Minnie is when it comes to the time."

"Let me talk to her!"

"That's out of the question."

"You're holding her against her will!" Blanche shouted wildly. "I'll secure a writ of habeas corpus!"

"Don't talk nonsense. Good morning, Miss Stiller."

Blanche Stiller had returned several times and each time the woman departed in a fury. Lisa always stood at the door to watch her drive off after once finding that she had gone prowling around the house to look in at the windows in the hope of finding Minnie on her own. And she was the last person Minnie wished to see at the present time.

"Keep her away, Lisa," she had implored. "She can pressure me into doing whatever the studios demand in the way of publicity and I don't want to face strangers yet."

During their talks together Minnie had admitted that it was as Lisa, remembering Harriet, had suspected. She had suffered a miscarriage. Sarah Baker, Lisa's doctor and friend, with whom Minnie had struck up a friendship, corroborated that many women went through such periods of depression after a miscarriage, and she was keeping an eye on her. Lisa still felt that Minnie had not revealed everything. Perhaps whatever she was still keeping to herself was the very key that would bring her back to normality.

After a final discussion with Alan over the telephone, Lisa put it to Minnie that she was not expected to attend the première on their behalf. Minnie showed intense relief. It had obviously been hanging over her like a dark cloud.

"Are you sure Alan doesn't mind?" she queried anxiously.

"He wants to see you well again as we all do. You've made such good progress that Sarah Baker agrees with me that it might undo all the good that has been done for your nerves if you return too soon to motion picture circles."

"But you'll go to the première, won't you?" Minnie was insistent. "It's the greatest moment in Alan's career and you must be with him."

"I hoped you'd say that. Sarah has offered to come and stay the night here, because with the party afterwards we won't get back to Maple House until the following day."

"I don't need a doctor in attendance. The servants will look after me."

"Sarah won't be here in her capacity as a doctor, only as a friend, and she'll be company for you."

Minnie smiled appreciatively. "It's kind of her. I'll be glad for her to be with me."

Lisa left for London in the afternoon of the great day, travelling by train. She would be driven back by Alan. Catherine awaited her at the apartment in a state of high excitement. She had laid Lisa's new Fortuny evening gown on the bed in readiness. She herself would be wearing white satin with a halter neckline and completely bare back.

"Daddy wants us to get to the cinema early to avoid the crush," she explained.

Lisa went to the hairdresser and returned in good time. Her gown was of finely pleated lilac silk with an attached waist-length overblouse that wafted against her figure as only a Fortuny garment could, feather-light and gleaming over breasts and hips by the skill of marvellous cutting and construction. With diamond earrings and a corsage of orchids Alan had ordered for her, she swung on her cape of creamy fox fur and looked, according to her daughter, more fabulous than any film star. Smiling, she held out her hand to Catherine.

"Let's go then! Tonight's the night!"

As they set off in a taxi for the West End, a fast car was speeding towards London from Maple House. When Sarah Baker left her own car in the drive and was admitted by a maid, she was astonished to hear that Minnie had gone to the première after all.

"But I thought it had been decided that she wouldn't go!"

"I think the plans were changed at the last minute," the maid replied. "An American lady came to collect Miss Shaw and take her straight to the cinema."

"How very odd. Was no message left for me?"

"No, Doctor."

Sarah Baker returned to her car with the overnight case she would no longer need. She was puzzled but unperturbed except as to how Minnie would react to the sudden excitement after the peaceful days at Maple House. That worried her. It was not the first time Minnie had put her career before her health. As a doctor, Sarah had heard a little more in confidence than had been divulged to Lisa. Still concerned, she made a snap decision when she reached the gates of the house and, instead of turning the car into a homewards direction, she swung southwards to reach the London road.

Coloured searchlights fanned the London sky from the roof of the new Fernley cinema. The frontage blazed with Minnie's name and the title of the film. Enormous crowds had gathered outside to see the stars arrive and in the hope that Minnie Shaw might appear. The press had played up the *will she?—won't she?* angle at Blanche Stiller's instigation. The polished limousines drew up one after another outside the red-carpeted entrance to allow the famous and other less well-known personages of the film world to alight. The foyer thronged with men in white tie and tails, the women in exquisite clothes and jewels, Schiaparelli's shocking pink much in evidence with those who followed closely the dictates of Paris. Lisa stood out in her Fortuny gown at Alan's side. Rita Davis was stunning in black velvet.

It took a long time to get everybody out of the foyer and into the auditorium. There were always the publicity-seekers lingering to have a few more photographs taken by the press cameras there. Harry, at his most charming, managed at last to usher the last of these up the gilded staircase to the Grand Circle when the attendants' attempts had been repeatedly ignored.

Lisa and Catherine sat with the British film stars and other important people in the flower-bedecked front row of the Grand Circle. The organ descended with its last melodious chords, vanishing from sight as the lights lowered throughout the auditorium. The buzz of chatter subsided as the looped silk curtains parted and the screen music announced spectacularly that *Love's Glory* had begun.

It had been tipped as a smash hit, and before the movie of love, loyalty, and desertion was half-way through, the whole audience realised that Minnie was destined to be nominated for every award available for her performance. It was in the last few minutes before its close when an attendant delivered a verbal message from Alan to Lisa who was sitting on an aisle seat, for he had wanted her to join him quickly at the movie's end.

"Mr. Fernley wants you to go to the foyer now. It's urgent."

Lisa slipped from her seat and went out of the auditorium. Hurrying down the stairway she was astonished and concerned to see Sarah talking anxiously with Alan and Harry. All three turned as she approached.

"Have you seen Minnie?" Alan asked at once. "Sarah says she's here. It sounds as if Blanche fetched her away after you had left."

"Then there is only one place she'll be at this moment," Lisa exclaimed. "Blanche will push her onto the stage when the movie ends!"

As they ran along the maze of barren concrete passageways leading to the rear of the auditorium, they met Rita Davis running towards them, her expression jubilant. "Minnie Shaw is here, Alan!" she cried, any pretence at formality forgotten in her excitement. "I was coming to tell you. I've just guided her and her studio representative to the stage steps!"

Nobody answered her. She drew back against the wall in bewilderment as, with grim expressions, they rushed past, and then followed after them. From the auditorium a thunderclap of applause greeted the film's end, and it swelled into a standing ovation. Alan, in the lead, burst through the door into the anteroom from which wooden steps rose to the stage. Blanche was half-way up the flight and she swung around in triumph.

"Too late! She's on!"

Her voice was almost drowned by a roar of approbation within the auditorium. Lisa darted up the steps to reach the side of the stage where she was hidden from the view of the audience by velvet curtains hanging from the proscenium arch. Alan and Harry joined her. Minnie had gone a third of the distance across the wide stage and had come to a standstill. She was a vision in a silver lamé gown that hugged her slender body and burst into spangled tulle from her hips, her only jewellery a pair of sparkling pendant earrings. Her back being towards those in the wings and her head too slightly turned for them to see more than the curve of her cheek, her expression was hidden from them, but the rigidity with which she stood filled Lisa with alarm.

"I must get to the steps on the other side where she can see me." Lisa grabbed up her skirt to facilitate her swift descent of the steps. She charged through another door into a passage that was parallel with the back of the screen. When she reached the far side and was again at stage level, she could see that Minnie was scanning the audience with an extraordinary searching look that was blended of shock and disbelief. To the audience it merely emphasised a modest incredulity that her movie should have been such a success. The ovation increased in volume as she gave them an almost childish wave. Her lips moved. By a trick of acoustics against the screen, Lisa could hear what those in the auditorium could not. It came on the high trembling note that presages hysteria.

"Where are you, Ma? The ship's goin', Ma! Don't let 'em take me away!"

"Minnie! I'm here!" Lisa's voice reached the stage by the same echoing vibration.

Minnie's head jerked about like that of a puppet. At the sight of Lisa standing with her arms outstretched to her, her expression broke after a few suspenseful seconds into joyful recognition and tears. The audience, imagining she was welcoming the arrival of some esteemed representative from her studios, which would have been customary, brought forth a renewed wave of applause. Lisa swept forward to embrace Minnie and hold her violently shaking frame in support.

"It's all right now, Minnie," she said through a wide smile to sustain the audience's belief that this was all arranged. "We're together as we always were."

Alan, coming swiftly from the opposite side at a signal glance from Lisa, took up Minnie's trembling hand and kissed it as if solely in gallant homage for her remarkable performance on the screen. Comparatively few in the auditorium had known Lisa's identity, but everybody recognised Alan Fernley as the entrepreneur whose magnificent cinema had opened with what was undoubtedly the motion picture of the year, and the clapping continued unabated. Minnie stood there between her two friends, each of them holding one of her hands hard and reassuringly, and she dipped her head at last into a stage bow to acknowledge the applause.

It was enough. Harry released the silken curtains by an emergency switch and brought them rippling down to hide her from the audience's sight. He was just in time. Alan caught Minnie as she collapsed and Sarah came running to give whatever medical aid was necessary.

In the ensuing minutes after Minnie had been carried down the steps to the anteroom, Rita seized the first chance she could to have a word with Alan. "What did I do wrong?" she asked anxiously.

He smiled at her. "Nothing, as it happened."

"That's a relief. I was worried." She returned his smile thankfully. The brief exchange did not go unnoticed by Lisa.

During the quiet weeks that followed at Maple House, Minnie made a full recovery. A few days after the première she had told Lisa of the abortion she had had. Lisa was less surprised by the information than might have been expected, having long since drawn her own conclusions.

"Why didn't you tell me before?"

"I know your opinion on the subject. You could never condone what I have done."

"Why did you do it?"

"I'd never wanted a child by any man other than Risto. It was the first time I was careless enough to allow myself to become pregnant and I feared for my career and my reputation. Moviegoers are narrow-minded about the morals of people like me. We can't make mistakes. We have to live up to the images that the studios have created, at least in our public if not in our private lives. So I went ahead with the abortion."

"And you have regretted it ever since."

Minnie's desolate expression was an endorsement in itself. "I never realised the psychological effect it would have on me. It's not just guilt, but the realisation that I threw away my chance to have someone of my own to love again."

"My poor Minnie." Lisa regarded her compassionately. "I always wanted more children. After Catherine was born I was sure there would be others. Now there never will be."

"Women still have children at your age." It strengthened Minnie to take on the rôle of comforter.

"It's not that. I think my marriage is almost over."

"I don't believe it!"

"There's another woman."

"Are you sure?"

Lisa sighed on a nod. "Perhaps it's poetic justice if we think back to a forest fire."

"No! That's not the attitude to take. You gave up everything for Alan."

"That's not strictly true. Alan and I have had a rich and rewarding relationship. I can only suppose he has always felt there has been more love on his side than there ever was on mine. Maybe Rita Davis can offer a perfect balance."

Contrary to Lisa's expectations, Alan came to Maple House for most weekends during the time that Minnie took to make her recovery. With the new Fernley cinema launched to success, he obviously felt able to allow himself some leisure time. There were absences, which Lisa marked to herself with pain, but as the weather grew warmer and the days longer he sometimes drove home to stay overnight during the week as he used to do. Lisa might have felt more hopeful if Catherine had not renewed a campaign of pressure to get her to return to the London apartment.

"I can't return all the time Minnie needs to stay at Maple House," Lisa pointed out.

"Well, when is she going back to the States? I love her, as we all do, but she's disrupted your life long enough."

Lisa uttered a soft, affectionate laugh. "Minnie has always disrupted my life whenever she and I have been together."

Catherine showed no sign of amusement, her face remaining deeply serious. "It's time to put yourself first for once. Bring Minnie with you to the apartment if you must, but come soon."

"Sarah Baker wants Minnie to have a holiday before there's a move like that and she seems to think I need one, too. A cruise has been recommended."

"Oh? Where? The Mediterranean?"

"No. Minnie would be recognised on a big cruise ship and she'd get no peace from autograph seekers and the rest. She and I are going to take a voyage by local steamer up the coast of Norway to see the fjords and the midnight sun."

It had been Sarah's suggestion. She had done the round trip herself the previous summer from Bergen to the North Cape and declared it to have been a holiday beyond compare. Mostly the steamers on the route went about their own business. Mail and cargo were collected and delivered en route at main ports of call as well as at many tiny villages hidden away amid scenic splendour, and all the way local people embarked and disembarked as those in other lands might use a bus service. As a concession to passengers wishing to make a vacation of what was an everyday voyage to other people, there were a few simple and spotless cabins for their accommodation.

Minnie had seized on the proposal enthusiastically. "That's a swell idea, Sarah! Lisa and I can laze on deck in the sun and sight-see when we wish. My movies are shown in Norway, but I doubt if anybody will know or care who I am in the daily bustle on a steamer." Then she shot a glance at Lisa that was blended of sympathy and encouragement. "Surely you would like to see Norway? We both knew someone who emigrated from there to the States a long time ago."

"I think I should like that." Lisa was smarting that day from Alan's cancellation by telephone of his coming home at the weekend, and suddenly she felt there would be balm to all the hurt in seeing something of the Scandinavian country that Peter had left behind. She remembered the name of the town nearest to his family farm. It was Molde. When she looked at the brochure of the route that Sarah had brought to the house, she saw that Molde was one of the ports of call. "Yes, we'll go to Norway, Minnie. I'll arrange bookings right away."

They travelled by train to Newcastle-upon-Tyne and took ship there to cross the North Sea. In the morning they awoke to see the rocky coastline of Norway sliding past the portholes. Later that day they sailed up the Bergen fjord while seagulls wheeled overhead and the ancient maritime city lay against the slopes of seven mountains, its buildings soft-hued with roofs and spires of russet, grey, and copper-green. This was the home of the composer Edvard Grieg. This was the theatrical centre known to Ibsen. This was the harbour from which Peter Hagen and thousands of emigrants like him had sailed over many decades for the New World. Lisa, standing with Minnie in readiness to go ashore, felt herself picking up threads of love with Peter from the past as if the years between had never been.

They spent two days in Bergen visiting the old churches and the mediaeval houses on the Hanseatic quay, having a guided tour of Grieg's green and white wooden house in the picturesque setting of Troldhaugen, and taking the funicular railway to a mountain look-out to admire the spectacular view. By chance one of Minnie's movies was being shown at the largest cinema, and although now and again a head would turn as somebody gave her a second glance, she was not pestered once by any invasion of her privacy. She and Lisa openly ate prawns from a paper cone in the fish market without fear of photographers flashing cameras. They also bought cartons of ripe cherries sold by farm children who had come into town, enjoyed exotic brandy-cured smoked salmon at the Grand Hotel, and indulged in slices of delicious cream cake almost every time they sat down at an open air café table to drink a cup of coffee and rest their wearied feet from all the walking their sightseeing had involved. They were both having a marvellous time and the holiday had barely begun.

Lisa sent picture postcards of Bergen to Catherine and Harry but nothing to Alan. It had not been her intention to omit him, but it was almost as though the accumulated distress over Rita Davis had finally caught up with her and brought about a complete change in her attitude. She simply did not want to pen his name or write to him. Just as Minnie was already benefitting from the change of air, which Sarah had insisted would be the final healing touch, so she was revelling in a freedom from the constant worry that Alan had invoked. In Peter's homeland she had become herself again, strong and independent. Let Alan have another woman for the time being if that was what he wished. Whether, when the holiday was over, she would end their marriage and relegate him forever to Rita Davis, remained to be seen. The choice would be hers entirely. In the meantime she was her own mistress again and it was exhilarating.

They boarded the S.S. *Vesteraalen* in the evening hours for the coastal voyage north that would take them far beyond the Arctic Circle. They sailed at ten o'clock, as the persistent daylight of the northern summer defied the night hours, and went to sleep with the sound of the gentle waves being sliced through by the steamer's bow.

Lisa was up first and joined soon after by Minnie in the dining saloon. They breakfasted and watched the ever changing views of the wildly undulating rocky coast through the table window. When the North Sea swell gave way to the Norwegian Sea, they were in west fjord country where the mountains reached new heights and waterfalls cascaded in thundering torrents or in spray as delicate as bridal veils. Wild flowers grew in abundance on the lush lower slopes from which came the distant clank of cowbells. By noon they were in the port of Alesund and they went ashore for an hour while some cargo was unloaded and replaced by more goods. The town was built on three islands, and every turn of the street presented a phalanx of moored boats of the herring-fishing fleet. A rich and salty atmosphere prevailed.

Lisa used her box camera to take a snap of Minnie against a great rock covered with nesting seabirds in the centre of the town, and afterwards bought some more postcards in a corner shop on the way back to the steamer. As they set sail again, Lisa was gripped by a special excitement. The next port of call was Molde, the town that held Peter's birthplace within its vicinity.

When she stepped ashore there she would be a short distance from the family farm to which his brother must surely have returned some years ago if everything had gone according to plan. Would there be time to drive out and see it? Not to call on anybody living there, but just to view it. Or was that wise? In her regained mood of independence she felt suddenly divested of past and present involvements. It would be better to remain that way without tempting providence.

Minnie noticed that Lisa became increasingly quiet and withdrawn as the afternoon wore on. The steamer sailed deeper and deeper into the great Molde fjord, leaving a trail of ripples in its wake across the sun-diamond water. Six miles wide in places, the fjord was flanked on either side by mountain scenery of a grandeur almost beyond belief. Yet Lisa made no attempt to use her camera. It remained lying in the deck-chair, while she stood with one arm resting on the rails and her other hand in the pocket of her white jacket, the hem of her yellow dress fluttering gently about her calves. She was watching for Molde to come into view. Suddenly she gave a delighted gasp and swung around to where Minnie was sitting.

"There it is! The fragrance! It's coming on the breeze."

Minnie rose to her feet and went to face ahead at Lisa's side. She caught the scent. It was sweet and heavy, coming in faint little gusts. "What is it?"

"The Molde rose! Peter told me about it once. It's a dark red rose that grows nowhere else in the world. That's how Molde has become known as the Town of Roses. He said that in summer its perfume reached out to incoming ships." Lisa inhaled it blissfully with her eyes shut. When she opened them again the town itself was coming into sight in rising tiers on the south-facing slopes of the fjord, its houses and hotels painted in pastel shades of pink and white and grey and green, its solitary church spire shining in the sun. As the steamer headed for the quayside, it became easy to pick out the Molde rose growing in gardens and in flower-beds bordering the streets and clustered about the church where beeches and limes and chestnut trees provided gentle shade from the late afternoon sun, still high and brilliant in a cloudless sky. A smart crimson touring car with the top down was waiting to take any travellers from the ship off on a local sight-seeing trip while the steamer lay alongside. Lisa and Minnie had already decided to take advantage of this facility as they went down the gangway.

The driver, a middle-aged man in a chauffeur's cap, greeted them as they approached and held the door of the vehicle wide for them.

"Good afternoon, ladies. Welcome to Molde."

"Thank you," Lisa replied. "What a beautiful town it is."

"We think so." He closed the door when they had settled themselves on the rear seat and took his place at the wheel. His commentary as they drove along was conversational and not irksome, his English faultless. "On your left is the Alexandra Hotel, named, as so many hotels are in Norway, after a member of your Royal family. Our own Queen Maud being an English lady unites us closely to Great Britain. We have more visitors from your country than anywhere else, although recently with Germany making a financial recovery under Herr Hitler we have had many Germans coming here this summer. I've never seen people use cameras more, and such costly ones! They don't only take pictures of the scenery, but they include railway stations and electric power plants and every inlet and harbour. It strikes me as odd sometimes. Almost as if there was a sinister purpose behind all that photograph-taking."

Lisa had found mention of the German Chancellor a jarring note in an otherwise beautiful day. There had been disquieting reports of what was going on in that country under his government. In an English newspaper she had purchased in Bergen, there had been further distressing accounts of Jewish children having stones and tin cans thrown at them by their fellow schoolmates. The driver was still on the subject of cameras.

"I hope you ladies have a camera with you, because the view from Varden where I'm taking you is something that everyone wants to record, whether they are Norwegian, English, German or from anywhere else in the world."

It was Minnie who answered him. "Yes, we do have a camera," she said, for Lisa appeared to have lost herself in contemplation of the bright little town with its small shops and clean streets where flower-filled baskets hung from lamp-posts, complementing the riot of roses elsewhere, and more blossoms tumbled in abundance from the sides of every window-box. Soon the town was left below them as the car took a winding route up the mountain side through thick forests of fir and pine to the place the driver had mentioned. The view had not been exaggerated and was a positive feast for the eyes. Before them stretched the wide blue fjord, a few islets set like jewels upon the surface, and beyond lay the whole vista of the snow-capped range of the Romsdal Mountains, almost a hundred peaks to count. Their escort named some of them while Lisa used her camera, clicking away until she had to load a new roll of film. She sat down on a wooden seat to do it, accidently dropping the camera's leather carrying-case. The driver picked it up and held it, watching her at her task.

"Do you happen to know where the Hagen farm lies?" she inquired tentatively, her attention on the camera in her lap.

"Yes, I do." He immediately supposed her to have verbal greetings from overseas for the Hagen family. Norwegian-Americans frequently delegated friends and acquaintances on vacation to the homeland to carry messages to relatives in the vicinity. "Is it Jon Hagen you wished to find? Or Peter? The other brothers don't live around here anymore."

Her head jerked up and she stared at him, her pupils dilating. "Did you say Peter? But he lives in the States!"

The man shook his head. "He came home years ago for his father's funeral, bought a transport business, and never went back. He's my employer. He has commercial interests in Bergen and Oslo in addition to those here in Molde, and he's a director of a local bank. Not long before his wife died he had a fine house built on the slopes just above the town. He has done well. A successful man in every way."

Lisa's heart was thumping against her ribs. "Has he children?"

"Twin sons. Clever, hard-working boys like their father. They spend their summer school vacations working on their uncle's farm. That's where they are now."

"And where would Mr. Peter Hagen be at the present time? In Molde?"

"No. He's in Oslo on business for a few days."

"Would he be back here when the steamer calls in on the return voyage south again?" She appeared intent on strapping the camera into the case that the driver had handed to her while they had been speaking. Out of the corner of her eye she could see that Minnie was watching her, observing that her frame was too taut, her fingers a little too precise in their movements.

"We can stop at the office on the way back to the boat and I'll inquire for you, madam."

"Thank you. I'd like to leave a note for him."

Minnie spoke warningly. "There's no time for that, Lisa. We don't want to miss the sailing."

The driver hastened to reassure her. "I won't let that happen, madam. You'll catch the boat with time to spare."

As they drove into town again, Minnie attempted to dissuade Lisa from trying to arrange contact. She was convinced that she must protect Lisa from what would be a most heart-aching and traumatic ordeal. The past could not be revived. It was lost to Lisa as it was to her.

"Leave well enough alone, I implore you. You've no idea what it would do to you to see Peter again. He's been married. Probably he hasn't thought about you for years. You could put him under an embarrassing obligation by letting him know when you'll be back in Molde."

"This is something I have to do."

Minnie sighed heavily, able to tell by the set of Lisa's profile that no amount of argument was going to sway her from the action she was taking. Although Minnie was irritated by her friend's stubbornness, she was glad to see that Lisa had somehow rallied on this holiday to become again the person she had always been. There had been a lapse. At the time of their reunion aboard the *Queen Mary,* Minnie had not noticed any change in her old friend except the new coiffure, but since she had pulled out of her depression helped by Lisa's selfless encouragement, she had seen that there were other changes which had not been apparent before. It was as if Alan's infidelity had been the one blow too heavy for Lisa to sustain on her own behalf. She could still fight for others, but not for herself, prepared to let life wash over her instead of attacking whatever should come with a courageous vigour as she had done in the past. This resolve to see Peter was a striking out against ennui and personal frustration. Minnie felt like cheering and weeping at the same time.

The driver drew up outside a well-designed office building. He escorted Lisa inside and they were met by Peter's secretary, who spoke excellent English. She informed Lisa that Peter would be returning to Molde the day after tomorrow, and put a pen and ink and paper before her on the desk to write a note to him. When it was written, Lisa sealed it in an envelope and handed it over. She was assured that he would receive it immediately upon his return.

On board again she watched Molde slip away as the steamer headed out again from the fjord. It would be an early-morning call for the vessel when it touched there on the return trip. Would she see Peter waiting on the quayside?

For the next nine days the holiday with Minnie continued as if Lisa's thoughts were not forever flying southwards to Molde and Peter's return there. The grandeur of the scenery did not ebb. One range of mountains gave way to another as the steamer followed the course of the Gulf Stream, the fjords changing from sapphire through to emerald, each town and village port of call offering individual sights of interest and of charm. Minnie bought a troll carved out of wood and Lisa some hand embroidery. Far north, at Tromso, they began to glimpse Laps in costumes of scarlet and blue, tending herds of grazing reindeer. Finally they came to the edge of Europe at North Cape. There they stood with other passengers at the ship's rails, bathed in a golden glow, their shadows stretched out across the deck behind them, and saw the orb of the sun descend to brush against the sea's horizon at midnight and, without more ado, rise still in its entirety into the sky again to continue unbroken the summer of everlasting light.

From that point the steamer made its turnaround port of call and started southwards again. Lisa was counting the days. Their last visit ashore before reaching Molde once more was to view the cathedral at Trondheim. When Lisa went to bed that night she asked the stewardess to give a knock on her door at five o'clock. But she was awake before it came, already showered and dressed and up on deck to see the re-entering of the Molde fjord. Towards seven o'clock in the warm morning air the steamer drew towards the quayside. Peter was waiting there, a big blond man with a sun-bronzed face and clad in a light summer suit. She felt her love surging out to him. He was holding a bouquet of Molde's crimson roses.

They waved to each other simultaneously. He had a grin of pure pleasure spread across his face, and she was palpitating with joy that this moment had come. As the steamer slowed steadily alongside the quay, he kept pace with the place where she stood, calling up to her.

"How are you, Lisa? It was the greatest surprise of my life to find your letter waiting for me!"

"I'm fine!" she called down to him. "Minnie and I have had a marvellous time since we arrived in Norway. You look well."

It was a light, inconsequential exchange such as old friends anywhere might voice upon meeting after a long absence from each other. As the gangway went into place, she hastened to be the first to disembark. As she stepped ashore they faced each other fully. As had happened once before, it could have been yesterday that they had parted. Their eyes held searchingly. Hers were always brighter in colour at times of high emotion. He remembered that well as he observed the green and gold flecks in her irises that were aglow today. Neither he nor she made any move towards a kiss of reunion. It was too soon and too public a place for however it might be when their lips met again.

"Hello, Lisa," he was saying.

"Hello, Peter."

She took the bouquet he handed to her and raised it to inhale the fragrance deeply. "The roses are as beautiful as you once described to me."

"It's taken longer than I originally supposed it would for me to have this chance to give some to you."

"I have them now."

"It's wonderful to see you again."

"This is a happy day for me."

"For both of us." Taking her hand into his as he had always done, he indicated a nearby parking place. "My car is over there."

"I see it's American," she remarked as they went towards it.

He chuckled, opening the car door for her. "A far cry from the transport I used in the States. My sons like to hear tales of the West as we knew it."

"How old are they?"

He went round to the front of the car and answered as he slid in beside her. "Fourteen."

"I was sorry to hear that you lost your wife," she said compassionately.

"It was a hard blow to take. The boys miss her as I do. She was a fine woman."

As he began to turn the car out of the parking spot, Minnie, who had just awakened, came rushing up on deck. The rough haste with which she had thrown on her négligée was apparent in the number of feathers loosened from its mariboux trimming and floating about her in the sunlight. She waved frantically to catch Lisa's attention.

"Wait! Lisa!"

Lisa, catching the sound of her name, turned her head to look out of the open car window. "Yes, Minnie?" she called, shading her eyes against the brilliance of the sun on the sparkling water.

"Be back in good time! Don't miss the sailing!"

To Minnie's chagrin no promise was forthcoming. Lisa's expression was calm, smiling, and enigmatic as the car swept her away. Minnie was left fuming to herself for having overslept. She had intended to be up to accompany Lisa throughout this hazardous reunion. The look on her friend's face had increased her fears as to what the outcome of it would be. Had Lisa made up her mind already to stay behind when the steamer sailed? And, if she had, for how long? Or forever?

Peter drove Lisa up to his home, which was situated just above the town. They talked the whole way, she telling him about Harry and Catherine and Minnie. Alan was mentioned in connection with the war and the cinemas. Peter, in his turn, told her how it had come about that he had not gone back to the States as he had intended.

"What about since then?"

"I've been twice. Both were business trips. I'll be going again before long."

"You don't come via Liverpool any more?" She was joking a little.

He shot her a twinkling glance. "No, it's the Norwegian line from Oslo to New York for me these days."

They reached the house and drew up in the driveway. Built in clean, advanced lines, it was in harmony with its isolated setting of forested slopes and its frontage was almost entirely fashioned from glass to command an unbroken vista of the fjord and the Romsdal Mountains. Indoors everything was of white pine with contemporary tapestries of geometrical design in rich hues, the furniture upholstered in pale hide. A Munch painting held a place of honour. Yet it was a far humbler piece of craftsmanship that caught her attention. In a corner of the room was Peter's travelling box, its colours worn by time, its battered corners bearing witness to its passage in steerage quarters, its tossing about in horse-drawn wagons over rough terrain, and its transportation in rattling trains over thousands of miles of the American continent.

"It's your box!" she exclaimed, going to kneel down by it. "You brought it home!" Then so many memories came flooding over her that she put a hand over her eyes, fighting against breaking down. He came and dropped to one knee beside her, but when he would have looked into her face she turned her lowered head away.

"I'm remembering," she said in a cracked voice. "That's all."

"I've never forgotten."

He took her by the shoulders and drew her with him to her feet again. She dropped her hand to her side and he waited, still holding her at a little distance from him until she was ready to raise her bowed head and meet his eyes. Everything they had felt for each other in the past was still there, changed in context perhaps, weathered by endurance, mellowed by other powerful relationships, but the unique bitter-sweetness of their special love remained for each to see.

He whispered her name. Slowly his arms went about her and the strong pressure of his hands on her back brought her to him. As his mouth descended to take hers, she uttered a little cry, throwing her arms in abandonment around his neck and meeting his kiss with an unleashed ardour of her own. They were locked together. Their kiss went on and on, neither wishing or wanting or able to assuage the force of love in a single embrace.

The steamer was preparing to sail. In agitation Minnie paced the quayside, intending to delay by any means she could muster the raising of the gangway. Again and again she looked at her diamond-and-platinum watch. The loading of cargo had been completed. The bags of mail had been delivered and taken aboard. A couple of late-coming passengers had arrived in a taxi, but still there was no sign of Lisa. Already Minnie was wondering how to face Alan and admit to him that she had let his wife go off alone with the one man able to persuade her that he and she had been given another chance to renew their lives together.

"Please go aboard now, madam. We are ready to sail."

Minnie looked in panic at the young steamship officer in his white-topped peaked cap who had spoken to her. She brought all her melting charm into play. "Mrs. Fernley hasn't returned yet. You can't sail without her."

"I regret we cannot delay for any reason. Our schedule is strictly timed. If you please, madam." He made a courteous but firm gesture towards the gangway. Not even for a request from Minnie Shaw, whose beautiful face he knew well from the screen, could the coastal steamer be delayed by as much as a minute.

Deliberately Minnie dawdled on the gangway, stopping to look back over her shoulder in the direction from which Lisa should come, but without result. The officer followed her, a hand on each of the rails as if he half-expected her to dart down again. Then suddenly she saw the flash of sun on Peter's car as it came into view.

"Mrs. Fernley is here!" she exclaimed breathlessly.

Peter had sprung out of the car and he cupped Lisa's elbow to escort her to the ship. Behind them the window-boxes of the Alexander Hotel held an abundance of scarlet, white, and blue flowers. Lisa herself was carrying the bunch of Molde roses that Peter had given her earlier. When they reached the gangway she drew one of the rosebuds from the bouquet and tucked it into his buttonhole, each of them gazing at each other. Then she turned and hurried up the gangway, the impatient officer springing up after her and signalling that all were safely aboard. The gangway was hauled away. Hawsers were released for'ard and aft. Azure water churned as the steamer edged out from Molde's quay.

Lisa stood watching Peter as the distance between them lengthened inexorably. Spoken and conventional farewells in the hearing of others had been unnecessary. They had made an ending together that had been a final enrichment of all that had been between them. He had wanted her to stay but had understood why it could never be. It was too late.

When the last faint speck on the quayside that was Peter and even the pastel spread of the Town of Roses was lost to sight, she moved from the rails and went to her cabin with her bouquet. Minnie was waiting for her there.

"Are you going to see Peter again?" she demanded anxiously.

"No." Lisa put the roses into a vase that the stewardess had given her.

"Never?"

"That's right."

Minnie gave a wail. "If only I'd known!" She sank down in a chair twisting her hands together. "I've done a terrible thing."

Lisa, having given a last touch to the arrangement of the flowers, regarded her with puzzlement. "What are you talking about?"

"I cabled Alan that you were meeting Peter!"

"Why?" Lisa sat down slowly on the edge of the bunk.

"Because I didn't want to see you go back to Peter and I was convinced that was what you intended to do."

"Yet you've always compared my love for him to yours for Risto. What made you so against my having another chance?" Lisa's eyes sparkled with a rare anger. "Are you admitting to jealousy?"

"Maybe I am! I don't know. But it's more than that. Alan is the one who's loved you more than anybody. It's your own fault that he has allowed himself some diversion that means nothing to him. You've neglected him. You've always put somebody or something before him. He has never come first in your life. I didn't want to see you go from him once and for all without giving him the opportunity to do something about it."

"What are you holding back?" Lisa demanded perceptively. "Are you saying that Alan knew there was more between Peter and me than has ever been spoken of?"

"He's always known. Harriet told him."

"No! She promised to keep it secret!"

"Alan knew that. But when she was dying Harriet became fearful for your future. She implored Alan to remember you were alone in the world, and in a confused and feverish state she spoke of the hardships you had endured. The early loss of your mother and the later loss of a Norwegian emigrant, Peter Hagen, whom you had loved dearly. Then, during my first evening at Dekova's Place, when we were sitting on the porch, you spoke of meeting Peter again. Why do you think he took you back to England when he did? It was to get you away from Peter! Nothing else! He had been going to surprise you with the news that he was purchasing a house in California and his intention was to move there when he left the lumber company, and I was to go with you. He told me much of this when we were all frantic with worry about you in the fire. As soon as I heard he had switched arrangements to go to England, I guessed the reason why."

Lisa put her palms together and laced her fingers with slow deliberation. "You have just confirmed what I have often wondered about. Why didn't you tell me at the time?"

"I was selfish, I suppose. I didn't know what the outcome

would be if the truth came out and I was afraid of anything that might separate Risto and me."

"I can understand that." Lisa's eyes were at their most thoughtful, reflective and absorbed. "My secret dream has always been that one day I should meet Peter again, never supposing that it could happen, and that he would ask me once more to spend the rest of my life with him. Then today, when that dream could have reached total fulfilment, I turned away from it. I love Peter. I'll always love him, but the years have bound me closer to Alan. Maybe that's the strongest kind of love. I don't know. All I do know is that I've had to fight for many things in my life. Now I'm going to fight for Alan. All the time you and I have been voyaging north with this reunion with Peter getting nearer every day, I've been weighing up what my decision would be. Before I even saw Peter again, Alan had won the day."

Minnie was distraught. "Now I've ruined everything for you! I've brought it all out in the open."

"Maybe that's the only way that Alan and I can rid ourselves of the barriers that have always been between us. When did you send the cable?"

"Yesterday. The reply was delivered to me while we were at Molde." Minnie took the crumpled cable from her pocket and held it out to Lisa. "He's on his way to Norway now. He'll be in Bergen when we get there."

Lisa read the cable and then closed her eyes briefly with relief, a smile on her lips as she folded it up again. "It's going to be all right."

"I don't understand."

"Don't you realise what this cable means?" Still smiling, Lisa handed it back to her. "He doesn't want to lose me. He's coming to get me back somehow. No doubt he thinks he did it before and he'll do it again. Only he doesn't know yet that this time there'll be no opposition." Putting her head to one side, she regarded Minnie more seriously. "I remember you said once that you wished the chance would come your way to do something for me in return for whatever I've done for you during our years of friendship. You did it a thousandfold in sending that cable, Minnie. You've eased what might have been a difficult path. You will have brought Alan and me truly together for the first time."

The next day the steamer sailed into its home port of Bergen. Alan was on the quayside, having left for Norway immediately upon receiving Minnie's cable. His dread had been that he would find only Minnie on board, but when he saw his wife with her, the tension in his face did not relax. For all he knew, she might have come to Bergen only to break the news to him that the past had claimed her after all. Yet he would not let her go. No matter what she had resolved, he would not leave this northern land without her.

Minnie's tact in leaving the two of them on their own to sort out all they had to say to each other culminated in her declining Alan's invitation to join Lisa and him on a motoring tour to Sweden and Denmark, travelling home from Copenhagen.

"It's kind of you to suggest including me, but I'll go back on the North Sea ferry as originally planned," she said. "It's a long time since you two have been able to get away on your own, and in any case I have appointments to meet people in London about making a motion picture there before I return to the States."

There was no immediate reconciliation between Lisa and Alan. She had no wish to rush anything and he was assailed by jealousy over what might, or might not, have happened between his wife and her former lover during their brief hour of reunion. Nevertheless, as he drove the hired car through countryside thick with wild flowers out of Norway into Sweden, the strangeness and the rawness of the situation began to ebb, for each had the will to begin again and the love to overcome whatever difficulties remained. Gradually, and not without pain on both sides, everything was talked out between them.

"I've made mistakes," he admitted sadly. "Too many. And I should have realised, knowing you as I do, that whoever is fortunate to be loved by you is loved forever. I must have been crazy to think that Peter Hagen had been swallowed up by the past."

"Is Harriet quite lost to you?" she asked quietly. It was rare for them to speak of his first wife in recent years.

"No. I remember her. I remember loving her. But that part of my life ended in her death. It had to. Memories have to take their rightful place."

She nodded reflectively. "I know that now. Sometimes it takes a long while to work them out, that's all."

He reached out and took her hands into his. In understanding. In friendship. And in love. The path was cleared for their future ahead.

Upon their return home to England they went straight to Maple House. Lisa rang Catherine and then Harry to let them know that she and their father were safely home again. She had expected Alan to make a host of business calls immediately, but instead he suggested they take a stroll around the garden to see how it had fared in her absence.

It was a warm evening and the roses had opened wide to the July sun during the day, a carpet of fallen petals under many of the bushes. Alan's arm was about her waist.

"We'll take vacations more often," he said. "With time, Harry will carry most of the responsibility of the Fernley circuit and I'm training him towards that end. That means eventually you and I can do whatever we want with our lives together."

They had reached the orchard, and she paused, bringing him to a standstill, and looked back at their home. It stood large and mellow in the sunset, the windows catching the rose-gold light. "There's something I'd like to do with the house or, to be more specific, the wing where the orphans used to stay on summer holidays. Now that the orphanage itself is in the countryside, the children will be going to the seaside instead of coming here. What I have in mind for that wing will need your agreement."

"You have it," he said without hesitation. He could tell by her tone that it was something far more important than a spate of redecoration and refurbishing. "What did you have in mind?"

She dived into the pocket of her silk jacket and pulled out a cutting from an English newspaper she had bought abroad which she opened wide. It was a photograph that had taken up the full spread of half a page. She gave him one corner to hold while she held the other, turning it to the late sun's glow, and they studied it with their heads together. It showed the sad, frightened faces of a group of little Jewish children, newly arrived in England from Nazi Germany. Some were orphaned, some sent by parents desperate to get them to safety while there was still time, and all of them in a state of terror at finding themselves in alien surroundings that might prove to be, for all they knew, as terrifying as the conditions of the country they had left behind. In them she saw faces from her own childhood. Amy and Minnie and Cora and Lily and Bridget and many more little children who had been made to suffer through no fault of their own.

"You speak German, don't you?" she said to him. "And I could learn."

He drew her gently to him and held her within his encircling arms. "So you want to begin all over again, do you?"

She nodded seriously. "In more ways than one. For this venture I'd want your help and support the whole way. We'd be partners all over again."

"How soon can we take the first of these children?"

Her eyes reflected the depths of her feelings for him. "I love you, Alan. With all my heart."

He had waited a long time for that full declaration—ever since he had first set eyes on her far away in another land. They kissed lovingly. Then with his arm about her waist again they continued their stroll through the quiet orchard. Already she was looking forward to the sound of children's laughter amid the trees.